**"You need** ███████████████ **nd keep away** ███████████████ **smine** **whispered.**

He bristled. He was probably used to being the protector. "You're supposed to stay with Liam."

"No, I'm supposed to protect Liam and, in the process, also protect you. Right now, there may be a threat out there. I'd suggest you let me go investigate."

Jaw still tight, Colton dropped his hand and gave Jasmine a sharp nod.

She drew her weapon and opened the door enough to slip through. "Lock this behind me. Don't open it unless I give you an all clear."

Colton's dog, Brutus, was on the right side of the house, still barking. When Jasmine rounded the corner, Brutus stood with his back to her, facing the front yard. He'd stopped barking, but deep growls rumbled in his chest, and his body rippled with tension.

A rustle sounded a few yards to the side of them, raising the fine hairs on the back of Jasmine's neck. Every sense shot to full alert with the impending threat of an ambush...

# HER HOLIDAY
# MOUNTAIN MISSION

## CAROL J. POST
## &
## LISA PHILLIPS

Previously published as *Bodyguard for Christmas* and
*Yuletide Suspect*

## LOVE INSPIRED
INSPIRATIONAL ROMANCE

# LOVE INSPIRED®
## INSPIRATIONAL ROMANCE

ISBN-13: 978-1-335-23094-2

Recycling programs for this product may not exist in your area.

Her Holiday Mountain Mission

Copyright © 2020 by Harlequin Books S.A.

Bodyguard for Christmas
First published in 2018. This edition published in 2020.
Copyright © 2018 by Carol J. Post

Yuletide Suspect
First published in 2017. This edition published in 2020.
Copyright © 2017 by Lisa Phillips

This edition published by arrangement with Harlequin Books S.A.

For questions and comments about the quality of this book, please contact us at CustomerService@Harlequin.com.

Love Inspired
22 Adelaide St. West, 40th Floor
Toronto, Ontario M5H 4E3, Canada
www.Harlequin.com

Printed in U.S.A.

# CONTENTS

BODYGUARD FOR CHRISTMAS                    7
Carol J. Post

YULETIDE SUSPECT                         231
Lisa Phillips

**Carol J. Post** writes fun and fast-paced inspirational romantic suspense stories and lives in sunshiny central Florida. She sings and plays the piano for her church and also enjoys sailing, hiking and camping—almost anything outdoors. Her daughters and grandkids live too far away for her liking, so she now pours all that nurturing into taking care of two fat and sassy cats and one highly spoiled dachshund.

### Books by Carol J. Post

### Love Inspired Suspense

*Midnight Shadows*
*Motive for Murder*
*Out for Justice*
*Shattered Haven*
*Hidden Identity*
*Mistletoe Justice*
*Buried Memories*
*Reunited by Danger*
*Fatal Recall*
*Lethal Legacy*
*Bodyguard for Christmas*
*Dangerous Relations*

Visit the Author Profile page
at Harlequin.com for more titles.

# BODYGUARD FOR CHRISTMAS

Carol J. Post

He healeth the broken in heart,
and bindeth up their wounds.
—*Psalms* 147:3

Thank you to all the people who supported me
in writing this series:

My sister Kim, for all the help with research,

My critique partners
Karen Fleming and Sabrina Jarema,

Mom Post for beta/proofreading,

My editor, Dina Davis, and my agent, Nalini Akolekar,

My sweet, supportive family,

And my loving husband, Chris.

# ONE

The wrought iron gate swung inward under a steel-gray sky. Colton Gale eased his Highlander through the opening to climb the road leading into his Atlanta subdivision.

Passing between those large brick columns used to always bring a sense of contentment and warmth. Maybe someday he'd find it again.

"You all right, bro?"

Colton glanced at his twin in the front passenger seat. For someone who lived life flying by the seat of his pants, Cade could be remarkably perceptive.

Colton forced a half smile. "Yeah."

Cade nodded, silent assent to let it drop rather than acceptance or agreement. "Thanks for going with me this morning. Since you've been back in town only a week, I know you've got other things to do."

"No problem."

When their father retired, he'd signed over the antiquities business to both of them. As co-owner, Colton's signature was required for official business, like renewing their line of credit, which they'd done that morning.

But giving his John Hancock when needed was

where his involvement ended. His job as an assistant district attorney kept him plenty busy. Besides, Cade was the one with the art and antiquities degree. He was also an expert schmoozer. Everyone seemed to let down their guard and trust him, whether it was warranted or not.

Colton rounded a gentle curve, where a huge oak spread half-bare limbs over the road, then cast another glance at his brother. Though their looks were identical, he'd never had Cade's charisma.

Now the differences in their personalities were even more pronounced. For Colton, studious and sincere had become almost brooding. Though Cade had tried to pull him into the social scene, Colton wasn't interested. The transition from widowed to single and available didn't happen overnight. Even six months later, putting on a party face required more effort than he was willing to give.

He heaved a sigh. He knew the platitudes. He'd used them himself—*Life is short. No one is guaranteed tomorrow.* Somehow, he'd thought those were for other people. The last thing he'd expected was for tragedy to strike his own perfectly ordered life.

"When we get to your house, I'll have to leave to get to my appointment." Cade's words cut across his thoughts.

Colton nodded. He'd expected as much. The business at the company's bank had taken longer than anticipated. Little Liam would be disappointed. He adored his uncle Cade. Anytime Cade stopped by, Liam always tried to talk him into staying longer.

Well, *talk* was a misnomer. Except for during frequent nightmares, Colton's son hadn't said a word in almost six months. But the silent pleas with those big brown eyes were just about as effective.

Colton rounded a gentle right curve. These were his favorite homesites, with yards that backed up to the stucco wall that surrounded the subdivision, woods beyond.

"Stop." Cade held up a hand. "Pull over."

He hit the brake, following his brother's gaze out the passenger window. A pickup truck was parked in the circle drive in front of the house catty-corner from his. A woman slid a five-gallon bucket from the bed onto the tailgate.

The place had been for sale when he'd left town. Someone had apparently bought it and was doing renovations. From what he'd heard, it had needed it.

Cade put his hand on the door handle. "Have you met your new neighbor? She's pretty hot when she's not covered in drywall dust."

"I thought you had an appointment."

"I do. But I can always make time for a lady, especially when it involves introducing one to my stick-in-the-mud brother."

*Great.* When Colton's life had fallen apart and he'd needed to get away, Cade had been at the end of his apartment lease and happy to house-sit. During his almost five months here, he'd probably checked out every single woman in the neighborhood. "I don't need to be introduced."

"We can at least be gentlemen and help her unload those buckets of paint."

Colton heaved a sigh, killing the engine, then followed his brother up the drive. The woman cast them a glance, then did a double take. "Whoa, you guys must be twins. One of you is Cade."

Cade raised a hand. "That would be me. And this is Colton, the smarter, better-looking one."

Her mouth split into a wide smile, and her dark eyes sparkled below a pixie haircut a shade deeper. He could see why Cade would classify her as "hot."

Cade had a variety of preferences. Colton measured every woman against one. The comparisons weren't intentional. They just happened, like a deeply ingrained habit. The thoughts were pointless, because he wasn't even considering dating, regardless of his meddling brother's efforts.

The woman extended her hand. "Jasmine McNeal. I'm hoping to have this place move-in ready in another two weeks." After a firm handshake, she turned back to the truck and reached for the paint bucket.

Colton stepped forward. "Let us get those for you."

"I can handle them."

Yeah, she probably could. She was short, didn't even reach his shoulders. Jeans and a sweatshirt hid her build, but judging from the way she was handling the paint bucket, she was probably well acquainted with the gym.

But he wasn't the type to watch a woman haul construction supplies, no matter how strong she seemed. While she lowered one bucket to the concrete driveway, he reached into the bed and pulled out the second one.

Cade closed the tailgate. "Sorry to greet and run, but I've got an appointment." He started down the driveway at a half jog, throwing the next words over his shoulder. "I'm borrowing your gate control. I'll put it back in your car before I leave."

Colton followed his new neighbor into the house and

placed the second bucket on the concrete floor next to hers. Everywhere he could see, carpet had been removed. The walls had numerous patches varying from fist-size to more than a foot in diameter.

She followed his gaze. "Pretty bad, huh? The old owners were carrying the mortgage, and when they had to foreclose, the new people got ticked and totally trashed the place. I'm making progress, though. Someone's bringing in a hopper tomorrow and texturing the walls. Then I'll be ready to paint."

She leaned against the doorjamb between the living and dining rooms. "So, are you visiting Cade?"

"The other way around. Cade was house-sitting for me while I've been gone. He's pretty well moved out now."

Over the past week, while Cade had worked on gathering his possessions, Colton had done some clearing out of his own, a task that had hung over him for the past half a year. The first four weeks, he hadn't been able to even think about it. He still wasn't ready, but it was time.

So three boxes occupied his back seat, with several more packed into the rear. He'd planned to drop the clothing by a thrift store and put the jewelry in the safety deposit box at his own bank. He hadn't made it to either place before having to get Cade back home. He'd have to run back out this afternoon.

She walked with him to the door. "Thanks for toting the paint."

"No problem." When he stepped outside, a single beam of late November sunshine had found its way through the clouds blanketing the sky. Across the street, Cade was backing his Corvette through the wrought iron gate at the end of Colton's driveway. What stood a short distance beyond wasn't the most extravagant residence in the neighborhood, but the yard was neatly manicured and the three-bedroom, two-bath home exuded warmth and elegance. Not bad for a former foster kid.

The gate rolled closed, and Cade stopped next to Colton's Highlander to return the control. Although the community was gated, the wrought iron fence that circled his property added an extra layer of protection. So did the rottweiler who regularly circled the half-acre grounds surrounding his home.

Except Brutus wasn't waiting at the fence. A vague sense of unease wove through him as he scanned the yard. In his job as an assistant district attorney, he'd made some enemies and received several threats. Most he hadn't taken seriously. A few he had.

He wished his new neighbor farewell and hurried to his vehicle. At a push of a button, the gate rolled open. Still no dog. The uneasiness intensified.

Colton slid from the Highlander and hurried toward the house. Nothing looked amiss in front.

But where was his dog?

He climbed the porch steps, heart pounding. His three-year-old son and babysitter were inside. He fumbled as he tried to insert the key into the lock. When he finally swung open the door, fear morphed to panic. At the opposite end of the foyer, every drawer in the Bombay chest was open, the contents strewn across the top and overflowing onto the tile floor. On either side, the living room and den were in the same condition.

"Liam!" He ran into the family room. "Meagan!" Where were they?

*Dear God, let them be okay.*

He headed toward the hall. At half past one, Meagan would have already put Liam down for his nap.

Movement snapped his gaze toward the dining room. As Colton ran into the room, a figure disappeared through the back door, little legs bouncing on either side of his waist. Colton's knees went weak, almost buckling under him.

Someone was taking his son.

He tore into the room, shattered glass on the floor barely registering before he burst through the back door. Two figures ran toward the rear fence, knit ski masks covering their heads. At his shout, the man carrying Liam turned, then dropped his burden.

Liam hit the ground and landed in a heap, legs curled under him, face turned to the side. A vise clamped down on Colton's chest. Liam wasn't moving. *Oh, God, please...*

No, if the men had harmed him, they wouldn't be trying to kidnap him.

When he dropped to his knees next to his son, his breath whooshed out. Liam was breathing. His eyes were squeezed shut, and soft whimpers slipped through his parted lips. Colton scooped him up, and little arms went around his neck with a strength that surprised him.

Rapid footsteps approached, and Colton swiveled his head. "Meag—"

But it wasn't Meagan who'd stopped a short distance away, face etched with concern. It was his new neighbor. What was she doing there?

He rose, clutching Liam to his chest. "I have to find my babysitter."

Jasmine shifted her attention to the back of his property, and he followed her gaze. A man dropped from one of the lower limbs of his oak tree to disappear behind the wall. A second shimmied out to follow his accomplice.

Colton squeezed his son more tightly. He'd get a tree trimmer out pronto. That same branch had probably given them a way into the property.

As he turned, a dark shape snagged his gaze. It lay several yards from the oak's trunk, partially obscured by the shrubbery lining the back wall. Brutus. He pressed his lips together. As soon as he found Meagan, he'd check on his dog.

When he looked at Jasmine again, she was already punching numbers into her phone. "I'm calling 911."

"Thanks." He'd let her handle it. He ran back to the house. Next to the door, jagged glass surrounded a large hole in the dining room window. He'd check out the security footage later. Or the cops would. He had a camera in back and one in front.

Once inside, he ran room to room, still holding his son while he shouted Meagan's name. An image rose in his mind—features twisted, hatred shining from eyes so dark they were almost black. One defendant whose threats had sent a chill all the way to his core.

Colton had gotten the man a life sentence. Death would have been better. Drug dealer, gang leader and ruthless killer—men like that didn't rehabilitate. Before being led from the courtroom in shackles, he'd turned to Colton and made his threat, cold fury flowing beneath the surface. *You didn't get a death sentence for me, but you just secured your own.*

Maybe Perez *had* sent someone for him, and taking Liam was his way of drawing Colton out. Or maybe it was someone else, determined to exact the worst kind of vengeance.

When he started down the hall, a cell phone lay on the floor. Meagan's phone. His chest clenched. Eighteen years old, her whole life ahead of her.

*Oh, God, please let her be safe.*

As he stepped into his son's room, Liam stiffened and let out a wail. Colton cupped the back of his head. "It's okay, buddy."

He looked around the room. Drawers hung open, their contents tossed to the floor. Nearby, a Lego village sat in a state of incompletion. Maybe this was where Liam had been playing when the man grabbed him.

Jasmine stepped up behind him. "Cops are on the way. I checked on your dog. He's unconscious, but his breathing is steady. What happened?"

"Someone just tried to kidnap my son. My house is ransacked and my babysitter's missing." He spun to walk from the room.

She stepped out of his way. "Maybe she escaped when the men broke in."

"And left Liam inside? Not Meagan."

"Or she could have slipped out to call the police."

He walked into the bathroom across the hall. "They'd have been here long before now." The destruction they were looking at didn't happen in minutes. "She's here somewhere. She'd never abandon Liam to save—"

Colton cut off his own thought. Had he just heard a thud? His gaze snapped to his neighbor. She'd obviously heard it, too.

He jogged down the hall toward the master bedroom. When he called Meagan's name again, the thuds grew louder, more insistent. As he entered the room, there was another thud, and the door on the large walk-in closet jumped. He shifted Liam to one hip and swung it back on the hinges.

Meagan lay curled on the floor, hands tied behind her back, ankles bound. Tape covered her mouth. An angry bruise was already forming on her left cheek. When her fear-filled eyes met his, they welled with tears.

Colton tried to pry his son loose, but Liam released a wail that built into a scream of pure terror.

"Here, let me." Jasmine pushed Colton aside and dropped to her knees. "This is going to hurt."

When she ripped the tape from the girl's face, Meagan winced. "I tried to protect him." The tears flowed in earnest now.

"He's fine." Jasmine looked at Colton. "Get me something to cut the rope."

He pulled a pocketknife from the drawer in his bedside stand. Jasmine had stepped in and taken charge. With a terrified child and a babysitter on the verge of hysteria, he was thankful for the help.

"Why did you come?"

"You." Without looking up, she continued sawing through the ropes binding Meagan's ankles. "When Cade was leaving, you started acting weird, like you were worried about something. I figured I'd stay outside and watch you."

Colton shook his head. He'd just met the woman. How could she identify *weird* when she had nothing to base *normal* on? Had to be women's intuition. After seven years of marriage, he still didn't understand it.

"When you left your front door wide-open, I knew something was up." The last rope gave way. Jasmine helped a sobbing Meagan to her feet and led her to the bed. "It's okay. You're safe now."

Colton sat next to his babysitter, Liam in his lap. "What happened?"

"Liam and I were sitting on the floor playing with his Legos when I heard glass shatter." She drew in a shuddering breath, struggling to pull herself together. "I jumped up to get my phone. I'd left it on the coffee table in the living room."

She swiped at her tears. "I got halfway back to the bedroom when someone tackled me from behind. He was straddling me, flipped me over and punched me in the head. Everything went black. I just woke up a few minutes ago."

She squeezed her eyes shut. Today's events would likely trigger some terrifying nightmares.

He put a hand on her shoulder. "Do you know who attacked you?"

"He was wearing a ski mask." The tears started anew. "All I could think about was Liam." She stroked his back. "Is he all right?"

"Just frightened."

Colton had no idea what his son had witnessed and probably wouldn't anytime soon. Liam had stopped speaking shortly after his mother died.

"Uh, Colton?"

Something in Jasmine's tone sent fingers of dread crawling down his spine. He followed her gaze toward the door.

His mahogany dresser occupied a sizable section of the wall to the right of it, the massive mirror framed by curved shelves on either side. Letters were scrawled across the glass in his dead wife's lipstick.

His foundation shifted, and the room seemed to tilt sideways as the message dived deep into his heart.

"The sins of the fathers…"

From the time he was adopted at age fifteen, he'd attended church. He knew his Bible. The next words went something like "…are visited on the children to the third and fourth generation." Whoever wrote the phrase was taking the verse out of context, but the intended meaning was clear.

Colton tightened his hold on Liam and buried his face in the boy's hair, soft and silky like his mother's had been. Determination surged through him. No one was going to get to his son ever again. He'd see to it.

Sirens wailed outside, growing in volume. Soon the police would be there. He'd give his report. And he'd insist that Meagan go to the hospital.

Then he'd find a bodyguard. Someone big and tough and mean.

The fence encircling the yard, with its electronic gate, the rottweiler prowling the property, the alarm when they were asleep. It wasn't enough. What had previously been empty threats had just taken on flesh and blood.

He'd do whatever he must to ensure Liam's safety. Even if it meant paying for around-the-clock protection.

Or leaving Atlanta and starting over somewhere else. Maybe both.

Yes, definitely both.

Jasmine strode down the hall of Burch Security Specialists, her gait heavier than normal. She still had another week blocked off, which would have given her enough time to finish the interior painting before the scheduled carpet installation began. So much for plans. Less than an hour ago, she'd gotten a call from her boss and former commander—she needed to show up pronto for a new assignment.

Gunn didn't tell her what the assignment was, but something in his tone warned her. She was about to meet another idiot who had his doubts about whether a woman could handle the job. After doing two tours with her in Afghanistan, Gunn didn't have any of those reservations.

She stopped at the end of the hall. A plaque was affixed next to a closed door—*Gunter Burch, Owner* in engraved black letters. At her two soft raps, Gunn's voice boomed a command to enter.

A man sat facing Gunn's desk, his back to her. He was wearing a suit, sandy-blond hair brushing the jacket's collar.

"Colton Gale, Jasmine McNeal." Gunn indicated her with a tilt of his head.

Her jaw slackened when Gunn gave the visitor's name. "We've met." They spoke the words simultaneously.

"It's good to see you again." Colton stood and extended his hand, pinning her with his blue gaze.

Yesterday, his eyes had held panic, desperation, protectiveness. Now a sadness she hadn't noticed swam in their depths. When he smiled, there was a tightness to it, as if it had been so long since he'd given the gesture a try it no longer came naturally. He and Cade were identical twins, but they wore their personality differences on their faces.

Jasmine accepted the handshake, her grip firm and confident. Colton probably had her five feet two inches beat by a solid foot. The one-inch heel on her boots didn't make any appreciable difference. He still towered over her.

He wasn't in bad shape, either, especially for a business type. His jacket hung open. Beneath the dress shirt and narrow tie, the guy was obviously fit. Of course, she'd suspected that yesterday, too.

Colton released her hand. "I take it you work here?"

"For the past three years." They hadn't exchanged personal details yesterday. He'd helped her carry in a bucket of paint, then left. At his place, they'd been occupied with more important things.

"What do you do for the company?"

*Great.* He probably thought she did clerical work. Gunn did that on purpose—referred to her by her nickname when talking to potentially difficult clients and introduced her by her legal name in person.

She straightened the zippered black jacket she wore and lifted her chin. "Bodyguard. Former MP."

He cocked a brow for a half second before understanding flooded his eyes. "Jaz. Jasmine." His jaw tightened, and his gaze went to Gunn. "This isn't what I had in mind."

Jasmine bristled. "I'm sure he told you my qualifications."

Those blue eyes turned to her again. But the sadness she'd seen was buried under layers of determination. "He did. But I'd assumed Jaz was a man."

Heat built in her chest and spread. "You felt those qualifications were impressive until you found out they belonged to a woman."

"I know this sounds sexist. I don't mean it that way." He heaved a sigh. "You know what I came home to yesterday. No offense, but I'm looking for someone a little more…intimidating."

Yeah, someone like her coworker Dom. But Gunn knew what he was doing. Other than the fact that the former sniper was assigned elsewhere, he was built like a linebacker and unintentionally terrified small children.

She drew in a calming breath. Colton was trying to protect his little boy. The reminder was like water splashed on a fire. Enough to slow it down but a long way from dousing it completely.

He continued before she had a chance to respond. "I'm an assistant district attorney, and I've put away some really bad dudes. One has decided to go after my son." He crossed his arms. "I'm sure you're good at what you do, but I need somebody big and mean."

He stared down at her, exuding an unmistakable sense of power. In the courtroom, he was probably a force to be reckoned with.

But when it came to protection, so was she. "A thirty-eight stops a man cold, regardless of the size of the hand holding it."

"What if someone sneaks up behind you?"

"They'd better hit me with a tranquilizer dart first."

"That's exactly what they did to my dog."

*Oh.* "You're assuming they could get close enough. Not gonna happen."

He dropped his arms to his sides. His gaze swept downward to her feet and back up again. Something changed. His eyes held a momentary flash of indecision, then coldness.

She stepped back with her right foot, weight distributed equally between both legs, knees slightly bent.

She didn't get where she was by not being able to read people. Unless she'd completely lost her touch, Colton Gale was preparing to administer a test.

One she was determined to pass.

He lunged toward her, arms swinging upward to capture her. She didn't give him the opportunity to complete the maneuver. In one smooth motion, she grasped his arm, twisted, crouched and thrust one hip into his legs. Using his own weight and momentum against him, she jerked him forward as she straightened.

He sailed over her, did a flip and landed hard on his back, the plush carpet muffling the thud. Before he could recover, she rolled him over, dropped to one knee and wrenched his right arm behind his back.

He slapped the floor like a wrestler conceding a match. "Okay." His voice sounded strained. "Point taken."

She held him a moment longer before releasing him, then rose and watched him get to his feet. "So, tell me about my assignment." The words were for Gunn, but she kept her gaze locked on her tall neighbor.

"You're going to live at their home. While Mr. Gale is there, you'll be responsible for protecting both of them."

Colton settled himself in the chair where he'd been when she first entered. "But Liam will be your first responsibility."

"Understood."

She tamped down her annoyance and sank into the chair next to him. Dom likely never had potential clients doubt his competence. The other three Burch Security people probably didn't, either. Though not as large as Dom, they were all men.

Colton continued. "Tomorrow morning, we're heading to Murphy, North Carolina, two hours north. We moved from there a year ago." He heaved a tension-filled sigh. "Probably should have never left."

The last words were soft, like a private thought that spilled out without him realizing it. Life had apparently not gone the way he'd hoped. Of course, that was typical for those who walked through Burch Security's door. People didn't need a bodyguard when everything was sunshine and roses.

"Where is Liam now?"

"With Cade."

Colton's brother rather than his wife. Maybe he was a single parent.

She frowned. She wasn't good with kids, particularly ones that young. At least, that was what she assumed. In actuality, she'd managed to avoid them. With the exception of a sixteen-year-old amateur model who'd picked up a stalker, all her assignments had involved adults.

"When do I start?"

"Tonight." Gunn tapped a pen on his desk. "I'll fill you in on what you need to know. Then you can get your personal belongings together. Corine will be in touch with you after she checks out the leads Mr. Gale gave us."

She nodded. Corine had worked for Burch Security since a month after Gunn opened shop, and she was a whiz on the computer. If there was information available, she'd find it.

Colton continued. "By nine tomorrow morning, I want to be on my way to Murphy. The sooner we leave Atlanta, the better I'll feel. Whoever's threatening us likely doesn't know about the Murphy house."

A good reason to go there. But likely not Colton's

only reason. Whenever he spoke of Murphy, his tone held a solid dose of nostalgia. It wasn't just a physical haven. It was likely an emotional one, too.

But beyond providing a safe place to stay, relocating wouldn't fix anything. Whatever had transpired over the past year, Colton couldn't make it *un*happen. Time went forward, never backward. Water that flowed under the bridge never came back.

How well she knew.

"Then I guess it's settled." He pushed himself to his feet. "You know where I live. See you in two hours?"

"Two hours." She stood and extended her hand.

After finishing the handshake, he reached across his torso to massage his right arm. One side of his mouth lifted almost imperceptibly. "Do you always rough up your new clients?"

"Only the ones who need it."

The smile broadened just a tad. "Staying in Murphy should make your job a lot easier." That thread of a smile disappeared completely. "As long as we're not followed."

She gave a sharp nod. "It'll be my responsibility to make sure we're not."

# TWO

The security system's high-pitched beep punctuated the thunk of the dead bolt as Colton locked the front door. He had no idea when he'd return. After one week back on the job following an almost five-month leave of absence, he'd resigned his position with the district attorney's office.

Cade had come back after his appointment Thursday afternoon and done a thorough search of the house, making sure he'd moved the last of his possessions. The break-in had shaken him. Apparently, it had taken almost losing his nephew to make him realize life wasn't just one cosmic joke.

Colton turned from the door, Liam perched on his hip. This time, the house would sit empty. Not only had Cade gotten an apartment, he wasn't even going to be in town for the next month. He'd teased that he didn't want to be mistaken for Colton.

In reality, he'd gotten leads on some collections to be auctioned off. Cade's plans often changed at the last moment. The lifestyle suited him well. He didn't let anything tie him down, which was why he'd never bought

a house, even though he could afford it. Home owner-
ship felt too much like commitment.

Colton headed down the porch steps. A black Suburban waited behind his Highlander. Jasmine stood next
to the driver's door.

Her eyes shifted to him briefly before she went back
to scanning their surroundings, ever vigilant. She'd
spent the night and slept on the daybed in Liam's room.
Thursday night, Liam had awoken screaming so many
times Colton had lost count. Last night's sleep had been
blissfully free of nightmares, at least for his son. Unfortunately, he'd had a few of his own.

As Colton swung open his rear driver door, Jasmine
continued to stand guard. Her presence brought just the
sense of security he'd hoped.

Before leaving Burch Security yesterday, he'd signed
the necessary paperwork. As he had written the check
for the first payment, Gunter Burch had reassured him
of Jasmine's qualifications. Between her military background, her civilian assignments and all the advanced
training in both capacities, he and Liam were going to
be in good hands. Of course, eating carpet fibers had
already dispelled whatever doubts he'd had.

Jasmine's eyes shifted to him, and he nodded. Yes,
he was ready. More than ready.

She opened the Suburban's door. "I'll be behind
you, but I might hang back on the interstate. Keep your
phone plugged into your car's stereo system. Anything
suspicious, I'll let you know."

"Thank you." She was only doing her job, a job that
was costing him a pretty penny. But that didn't stop
him from appreciating everything she was doing to
protect them.

He leaned into the vehicle to secure Liam in his car seat. Brutus sat next to him, tail thumping against leather. Huge brown eyes seemed to hold sadness, maybe even guilt, as if the dog sensed he'd failed in his job to protect.

Colton fastened the last latch, then leaned across Liam to pet Brutus. "It's okay, buddy. It wasn't your fault."

He straightened and closed the door. Yesterday morning, before going to Burch Security, he'd taken care of the things he hadn't gotten to on Thursday. Mandy's jewelry was now locked in his safety deposit box.

Then he'd gone to a thrift store and parked at the open bay door in back. It had taken all the strength he had to climb from the vehicle and pull out the first box. With each one he passed to the volunteer, he'd felt as if he was handing over a piece of his heart.

Now it was done, and several suitcases holding his and Liam's possessions occupied the space behind the back seat. He'd packed everything he could think of. Anything he'd forgotten, he'd buy in Murphy.

The investigation was far from complete. Cops had viewed the security footage. Besides the knit masks, the intruders had worn gloves, so the likelihood of recovering prints was nil.

As he drove through the subdivision's exit gate, some of the tension flowed out of him. In two more hours, he'd be pulling up the drive and stopping in front of the log home with its soaring windows and steeply pitched roof.

Warm, cozy and filled with love, it had always held a special place in his heart. He and Mandy had purchased it six years earlier for a weekend getaway and built so many memories.

Four years ago, he and his pregnant wife had decided Murphy was a perfect place to raise children, and they'd made the move. Until the district attorney's office had lured him back.

Now he was going home.

After several turns, he accelerated up the I-285 ramp. The black Suburban was right behind him, Jasmine at the wheel. Dark sunglasses shielded her eyes. But he didn't need to see them to know she was watching traffic in more than a defensive-driving sense.

He craned his neck to glance at his son in the rear-view mirror. As expected, he was awake, left arm clutching his plush rabbit, right thumb in his mouth. Another change Colton had noticed. As Liam's speech had gotten less, soon stopping completely, his thumb sucking had gone from only when sleeping to almost all the time. Colton would have to address it eventually, but certainly not now.

He moved into the left lane and accelerated. Varying his speed would make it harder for someone to follow him, at least without Jasmine noticing. He checked his mirrors. On a Saturday morning, traffic was moderate. The Suburban was some distance back, traveling in the right lane. He signaled and prepared to merge onto I-75. As he decreased his speed, several vehicles went around him. He moved into the far-right lane and exited 285 in front of a slow-moving dump truck.

After several miles, he picked up speed again. Soon he'd be on 575, headed toward Murphy. An unexpected sense of anticipation wove through him.

He'd made this move twice before. Each time, it had represented a fresh start, and he'd found freedom, happiness, a sense of belonging.

The first time, he'd been fifteen, leaving behind years in foster care to become part of a real family. The second time, he'd been filled with excitement, ready to start his own family.

This would be a new start also, one he'd never hoped to make. He and Liam, facing an uncertain future, their family unit shattered. Hoping to stay hidden from someone who might want them dead.

The phone's ringtone cut across his thoughts. It was Jasmine.

"Don't take the 575 exit. I think you have a tail."

His pulse picked up speed, and an instant sheet of moisture coated his palms. "Which vehicle?"

"The silver Mustang."

He looked in his rearview mirror. There it was, one lane to his left, about five cars back. "Can you slow down, get a tag number?"

"I've tried. I think he knows I'm with you. Whenever I drop back, he does, too. Won't give me an opportunity to read his tag."

"What do you have in mind?"

"Ernest Barrett Parkway is the next exit. Easy off, easy on."

After he disconnected the call, Jasmine slowed down so much he almost lost sight of her. Several cars moved between them. The Mustang didn't.

As he approached 575, the GPS told him to exit. He ignored it. Jasmine was in charge and he had no problem letting her call the shots.

After he exited I-75, the light ahead was red. He eased to a stop, then dialed her back. "Did our friend follow?"

"I'm not sure, but I think he's behind the box truck."

He counted the vehicles lined up in his rearview mirror. In their lane, three waited between him and Jasmine, two more between her and the box truck. Likely every one of them would turn left on Ernest Barrett. If the Mustang followed him and Jasmine back onto 75, they'd know for sure.

The light changed, and he moved forward. As he made his way up the on-ramp, two vehicles followed from Ernest Barrett, a semitruck blocking any farther view.

He completed his merge and touched the phone, still clipped into the dash mount. Jasmine's rang four times, then went to voice mail.

Maybe she was calling the police, which meant someone was following them. A sense of protectiveness gripped him, an urge to wrap Liam in his arms so tightly no one could pry him loose.

Colton lifted his chin until the rearview mirror framed his son's face. Sad eyes looked back at him. Brown, just like his mother's. Liam had gotten Mandy's eyes and Colton's blond hair.

When his phone rang a few minutes later, he swiped the screen, heart racing while he waited for Jasmine's update.

"Sorry, I was on the phone with 911 when you called. He followed us back onto the interstate, hanging back like before. But he knew we were onto him. He got off on Chastain Road, no signal, just whipped it over. The police know to look for the car there, but I'm not holding out high hopes."

He wasn't, either. "What now? Exit, then head back south to pick up 575?"

"Not knowing where that Mustang is, I say we continue north and take 411 near Cartersville. It might be a little out of the way, but it's better than running across those guys again."

The next two hours were uneventful. When he finally pulled onto Hilltop Road, several miles southwest of town, all of nature seemed to wrap him in a comforting embrace. He was home. The quaintness, the low crime rate, the small-town atmosphere, the feeling of having stepped back into a safer, slower, less complicated time—Murphy was still a great place to raise a child.

He stayed left where the road forked and wound his way upward. He hadn't been back since Mandy died. For weeks, he'd stumbled around in a grief-induced fog, somehow managing after a two-week bereavement leave to return to his duties and care for Liam when he wasn't working.

A week later, he'd gotten word that Mandy's father had had a heart attack. Though he'd survived, it was going to be a long road to recovery. Having just lost their only child, they'd had no one to turn to.

So Colton had taken a leave of absence, loaded up Liam and headed to Montana. He wasn't sure who had benefited the most from his trip out West. He'd gone to help his in-laws. But in those quiet moments, sitting on the back deck as the sun sank behind the mountains and daylight turned to dusk, then darkness, God had ministered to him. Little by little the frayed pieces of his heart had begun to heal.

Near the top of the hill, he pulled into a gravel drive. A huge hemlock rose from the center of the front yard, hiding the majority of the A-frame log cabin from the view of the road. Trees huddled around the other three sides of the house. The hardwoods' limbs were bare except for the most stubborn leaves. Brown and curled, they were determined to hang on until they had no choice but to succumb to winter's fury.

Colton put the vehicle in Park and turned in his seat. "We're here, buddy. Our favorite place."

The excitement he tried to inject into his tone had no effect on Liam. He didn't expect it to. Every week, his little boy seemed to retreat a bit more into himself. And Colton had no idea how to help him. Apparently, his counselors hadn't, either, because nothing had seemed to work.

Colton climbed from the vehicle and removed his son from the car seat. After retrieving one of the suitcases, he walked up the sidewalk, Liam's hand in his. Halfway there, Liam broke away and ran toward the house. When he reached the front deck, he looked over one shoulder. Hope had replaced the vacancy in his eyes.

Colton's heart swelled with emotion. Liam remembered the place.

Of course he did. It was where he'd lived the first year and a half of his life and where they'd spent almost every weekend after that until the past six months.

As soon as Colton opened the door, Liam burst through. He crossed the living room at a full run, skidded around the bar that marked the boundary of the kitchen and disappeared into the bedroom to the right. Colton smiled, laughter bubbling up inside. It was the first glimpse he'd seen of the carefree little boy he used to have. Coming back to Murphy was the best thing he could have done for his son.

Liam reappeared moments later. After running into the master bedroom, he returned to the living room. His gait was shuffling, every bit of excitement gone. Had he worn himself out that quickly?

Colton dropped to one knee in front of him. "What's the matter, buddy?"

Liam's lower lip quivered, and his eyes filled with tears.

Colton sank the rest of the way to the floor, realization kicking him hard in the chest.

Liam wasn't happy to be back in Murphy.

He was looking for his mother.

Colton stretched out his arms and grasped his son's hands. "Sweetheart, Mommy's not here."

When he'd pulled him onto his lap, he wrapped his arms around his little body and held him tightly, rocking side to side, seeking to comfort himself as much as his son.

Movement drew his attention to the left. Jasmine stood in the open doorway, her purse hanging from her shoulder and a suitcase in each hand. She didn't say a word, but the sympathy in her gaze spoke volumes. She'd had her own heartaches.

Maybe having her there would help ease some of Liam's sorrow and loneliness. Maybe it would help ease some of his own.

No, Jasmine wasn't a mother figure. And she certainly wasn't a wife. That wasn't why he'd hired her. He'd hired her to protect him and his son.

Once the assignment was over, she'd be gone.

No one would ever take Mandy's place.

Not in his life or his son's.


Jasmine parted the curtains and peered into the front yard. Late afternoon shadows stretched across the landscape. Security here was minimal. Actually, it was non-existent, something that would be remedied this week.

Shortly after arriving at the Murphy house three days ago, she'd walked the premises and come up with a security plan. An alarm system was a minimum requirement. Before the weekend, all windows and doors would be wired and motion-sensing lights installed on the perimeter of the house. For the time being, camera installation was on hold. But it would be scheduled immediately if she felt the need.

She let the cloth panel drop. For the past thirty minutes, she'd made her rounds to several of the house's windows, checking on Liam in between. This residence wasn't elegant like Colton's Atlanta home. But with hardwood floors, tongue-and-groove walls and a fireplace tucked into one side of the living room, it was nice—cozy and rustic. And as long as Colton's enemies didn't know he was here, it was safe.

Ideally, she'd have backup, a second or third bodyguard to help patrol and provide relief. But Colton didn't have as deep pockets as Burch's celebrity and big-business clients, especially after the extended leave of absence to care for his in-laws—one of the things she'd learned from Gunn after Colton had left the office Friday. If he'd remained in Atlanta, they wouldn't have given him a choice.

The ringtone sounded on her phone, and she released it from the clip on her belt. The screen ID'd Burch Security as the caller.

Corine's Southern twang came through the phone. "I've checked out some of the names Mr. Gale gave Gunn. I'm still working on it, but there are two people who match the description of the men who tried to kidnap his son. At least their size. Since they were wearing ski masks, that's all we've got to go on."

"Who?"

"Richard Perez is the first name Gale gave us. Turns out, he has regular visits from his brothers. Both have records, but they're out now. The older one is tall and lanky. The younger one is close to the same height but built like an offensive lineman."

Jasmine nodded. "It fits."

"Another name Gale gave us is Broderick 'Ace' Hoffman, who was released three weeks ago. He's roughly the same size as the thinner guy. We're checking out people he's known to associate with to see if any of them fit the other guy's description."

As Corine continued to provide information, Jasmine moved to the back door and peered through the paned glass inset. Finally, the admin fell silent.

"Anyone else?" Corine had given her six possible matches.

"That's it for now. You know Gale's wife died of natural causes, right?"

"Yeah, Gunn gave me all the history."

After ending the call, she glanced through the open doorway to Liam's room. Keeping track of the boy was the easy part of her assignment. He wasn't a typical preschooler, with boundless energy and a touch of mischievousness. Instead, he seemed perfectly content to play quietly on the floor.

He was also spending his days in preschool. Colton had enrolled him yesterday, after securing his former job with the district attorney's office for Cherokee County. He'd given her two reasons for the preschool decision. One, he hadn't hired her to be a babysitter. She couldn't agree more.

Two, he didn't want his son spending so much time with her that he'd get attached. More good thinking. Liam's mother was no longer in the picture, and he wasn't handling it well.

She'd abide by Colton's wishes and not let Liam get attached to her. But the sad little boy she'd been charged with protecting stirred something in her. Twenty-five years ago, that had been her—quiet, withdrawn, tormented by nightmares. Unlike Liam, she'd had a mother throughout most of her childhood. And her mother loved her. She'd just been too young and dysfunctional to know how to raise a child.

Jasmine leaned against Liam's doorjamb, and his eyes met hers. He sat amid a sea of Legos, an almost completed rectangular object in front of him.

She stepped into the room. "What are you building?"

He lowered his gaze and searched through the pieces until he found a truss-shaped one, then snapped it onto an end.

"Are you building a house?"

Liam continued his project without making eye contact again. She turned to leave the room. She'd never been good at one-sided conversations.

At the door, she hesitated. A chest of drawers sat to its right, a framed eight-by-ten photograph on top. She'd noticed it there before but hadn't taken the time to look at it closely. Now she took the frame down and held it in front of her.

It was one of those studio portraits, with a Christmas background. Colton sat on a stool. A woman was nestled in front of him, Liam on her lap. Colton's wife. Her hair was a medium brown, the same color as her eyes. Though she wore makeup, it was understated. There was nothing striking about her individual features.

But she was gorgeous. She radiated warmth and friendliness, her easy smile an outward expression of inner joy. If one could deduce personality from a photograph, Mandy Gale was the type of person every woman wanted to have as a best friend. The world had lost someone special.

A key rattled in the front door lock and she set the frame back on the dresser feeling as if she'd almost been caught eavesdropping. Colton was home, with dinner. He'd called forty minutes ago to take her order.

She stepped into the kitchen as the door swung open. Colton held up two plastic bags. "Chinese takeout. Courtesy of China Town Buffet."

She drew in a fragrant breath. "Smells wonderful."

Colton carried the bags to the kitchen table. "How did everything go today?"

"Fine." He wasn't asking about *her* day. He was asking about Liam's. Colton Gale wasn't a man for small talk. "When I took him to day care, he went from me to his teacher without any fuss."

"Good."

He disappeared through the door behind him, then returned a minute later, holding Liam. By the time he had him strapped in to his high chair, she'd filled two water glasses and put milk in a sippy cup.

He removed the foam containers from the plastic bags. "I'm guessing there weren't any threats."

"No. Just like yesterday."

"Good."

He'd wanted her close but not conspicuous. Although

he'd explained the situation to the owner of the day care, he didn't want to alarm the workers or the other parents. So she'd parked a short distance down the road and watched the activity through binoculars.

After laying a cellophane-wrapped package of plastic silverware at each place, Colton sat adjacent to his son at the four-person table, and Jasmine took the chair opposite Colton. Pleasant aromas wafted up from the container in front of her, and her stomach rumbled.

But she waited. She'd learned her first night there that the Gales never ate without saying grace.

Colton took his son's hand, then hers. The first time, he'd asked if she minded. She'd said no. Praying before meals was a sweet tradition.

When he bowed his head and began to pray, even Liam closed his eyes. Jasmine did, too, but only out of respect for the man sitting across from her. The God Colton worshipped was one she didn't like very much— an ever-present, all-powerful God who saw the suffering in the world but chose to ignore it. It was much less disturbing to imagine a distant God who set everything in motion, then turned His back to let nature take its course.

For the fourth night in a row, she listened to Colton thank God for His protection over them. *She* was the one providing the protection, but whatever.

When he finished his prayer, he tore into the cellophane package that held his plastic silverware and napkin. "I called a fencing contractor at lunchtime. I'm meeting him here at noon tomorrow."

"Good." The backyard was fenced, and that was currently where Brutus was. But the entire front was unguarded.

Colton continued in his professional no-nonsense tone. "They'll connect to the existing fence and take it all the way to the road. They told me if I go ahead with the contract tomorrow, they'll do the work this weekend."

"Good. Brutus is our first line of defense. It's best if he can access the entire yard."

Colton turned his attention to eating, all topics of business thoroughly covered. But the silence wasn't uncomfortable. Though they were all living under the same roof, Colton was keeping that professional distance.

That was fine with her. She wasn't any more interested in a relationship than he was. When the sting of her latest disaster finally faded and she was ready to put herself out there again, it certainly wouldn't be for a man who was still grieving the loss of his wife.

Frenzied barking from outside sent her into fight mode, and she sprang to her feet. From what she'd gathered, the dog didn't bark unless he had a reason to. Colton's clenched jaw and the lines of worry around his eyes confirmed her suspicions.

She retrieved a flashlight from the kitchen drawer and reached the back door the same time he did. He planted his hand against it, his other arm extended palm up for the flashlight. "I'll check it out."

"You need to stay inside. And keep away from the windows."

He bristled. He was probably used to being the protector, especially with women and children.

But that was the job he'd hired her to do. "I'm the one who's armed and wearing Kevlar."

His eyes narrowed. "You're supposed to stay with Liam."

"No, I'm supposed to *protect* Liam and, in the process, also protect you. Right now, there may be a threat out there. I'd suggest you let me go investigate."

His jaw was still tight, but he dropped his hand and gave her a sharp nod.

She opened the door enough to slip through. "Lock this behind me. Don't open it unless I give you an *all clear*."

After a glance around, she stepped onto the back deck and drew her weapon. Dusk had passed and full night was fast approaching. Brutus was on the side of the house, to her right, still barking.

She crept that direction, dried leaves crunching beneath her feet. A chilly breeze cut right through her, and a shiver shook her shoulders. The light jacket she always wore hid her holster from view but offered little protection against the winter cold. She should have grabbed her coat.

When she rounded the corner, Brutus stood with his back to her, facing the front yard. He'd stopped barking, but deep growls rumbled in his chest, and his body rippled with tension.

A rustle sounded a few yards to the side of them, raising the fine hairs on the back of her neck. Every sense shot to full alert with the impending threat of an ambush.

She wasn't in Afghanistan anymore. But she didn't try to shake off the sensation. That state of being constantly on guard, trying to anticipate potential threats before they could become imminent, made her good at what she did.

She clicked on the flashlight and directed its beam into the woods. There was no sign of movement. Had she just heard the wind? Or was someone out there?

After stepping through the gate, she closed it behind her, then approached the tree line. Except for the rustle of leaves in the breeze and Brutus's low-pitched growls, the night was quiet.

She swept the beam back and forth, studying the ground in front of her. Light reflected against underbrush brown and dried after a couple of winter freezes.

Her hand stilled. At the edge of the woods, decaying growth was pressed down and lying against the ground. Someone had recently come through there.

Whoever it had been was likely long gone. He'd apparently come out of the woods, then run across the front yard, since that was the direction Brutus was looking when she'd first come out.

After making a final rotation with the flashlight, she walked back to the house. The key Colton had given her when they'd arrived was in her pocket. Instead of using it, she rapped on the door. "Let me in."

It swung inward moments later. As soon as she was safely inside, she spun on him. "I told you not to unlock the door unless I gave you an *all clear*."

"You did."

"No, I said 'let me in.' There's a difference. What if someone was holding a gun to my head?"

His lips pressed into a thin line. "Okay, I get it."

"In that case, you'd take Liam, run out a different way and pray to your God that no one sees you."

He sank into his chair, the weight of her words reflected on his face. "Did you see anything?"

"Someone came out of the woods and left through the front yard."

His eyebrows shot up. "You saw him?"

"No. The underbrush was pressed down. When I got to Brutus, he was staring into the front yard, growling."

She cast a glance at Liam, who was sitting at the table, munching on a rangoon, oblivious to the tension of the adults in the room.

Colton nodded. "It's possible it was nothing, some teenagers trying to make their way home by dark, not realizing this place is now occupied." He frowned, wrapping a protective arm around his son's shoulders. "Or maybe someone was checking to see how secure we are."

She took her seat opposite him, and he continued.

"We need to keep our guard up."

"No problem."

Her guard was always up. Night or day. Sleeping or awake.

Three years ago, she'd left behind the dangers of Afghanistan. But she'd swapped them for other threats, not as constant, but just as real.

If there was one thing Colton would never have to worry about, it was her state of readiness.

# THREE

A single lamp burned in the living room, its glow not quite reaching the far corners of the space. The fire that had blazed in the fireplace earlier that evening had long since turned to ash.

Colton sat in the overstuffed chair, silent and alone. How many hours had Mandy occupied this exact spot, curled up in an afghan, an open book in her lap? This had been her favorite place to read.

Now he'd taken over her spot. Except his reading wasn't for pleasure. A bulging expandable folder sat on the end table next to him, and a bound document occupied his lap. It was the deposition of a store clerk held up at gunpoint.

He flipped the last page, then closed the plastic binder. When he'd slid it back into the expandable folder, he removed the next item for review.

Tomorrow was Friday, the end of his first week back at the Cherokee County district attorney's office. After almost losing his son, nothing could have kept him in Atlanta. But he'd been blessed that someone was leaving his old office and he'd been able to step immediately into a job. After his extended leave of absence, his savings account was reaching dangerously low levels.

He opened the next piece of discovery, then let his gaze drift to the front wall. Curtains covered all the lower windows, but beyond the edge of the hemlock outside, stars were visible through some of the high trapezoid-shaped windows.

Liam had been in bed for some time. So had Jasmine. Since it was nearing midnight, that was where he should be. Eventually he'd head there—when he was beyond exhaustion and the blessed oblivion of sleep was within reach.

*God is in control.* It was a fact he'd known since age fifteen. But for the past six months, he'd had to recite those four words again and again. Even more in the past week. Unfortunately, all the reminders didn't seem to penetrate those inner spaces where peace resided. His world had fallen apart, and he hadn't been able to regain his footing.

With a sigh, he lowered his eyes to the document in his lap. Sometime later, he stuffed the pages he'd been reading into the folder and rose from the chair. He couldn't say he'd reached the point of exhaustion, but if he stayed up much later, he'd be worthless tomorrow.

When he turned off the light, a faint glow shone from the partially open door off the side of the kitchen. Burning a night-light was the only way he could get Liam to sleep. If it bothered Jasmine, she hadn't mentioned it.

He padded silently in that direction, then paused at the open door. Liam lay in the small bed at the far side of the room, eyes closed and thumb in his mouth. A thin curtain of wispy blond hair had fallen over one side of his face. His mouth moved in a series of sucking motions, then again grew still.

Colton drew in a shaky breath. Love swelled inside him, mingled with a sadness that pierced his heart. He was trying his hardest to be both mother and father. But as he'd watched his little boy retreat further into himself, he'd known it wasn't enough.

He started to turn away, then hesitated. He'd wanted to keep Liam with him during the night, but Jasmine wouldn't hear of it. She'd said she wouldn't risk someone again tranquilizing the dog, then slipping in to whisk Liam away while she slept in another room. She was the security expert, so he'd given in, even though he didn't like it. Having his son sleeping on the opposite side of the house upset every protective instinct he possessed.

But *opposite side of the house* wasn't as bad as it sounded. The two bedroom doors were less than twenty feet apart, Liam's off the side of the kitchen, his off the opposite side of the living room. The house was also equipped with a security system now. According to Jasmine, Tri State had finished the installation at three that afternoon.

Poking his head into the room, he sought out the other bed, against the wall to his right. Jasmine was curled on her side, back toward the wall, blanket tucked under her chin. Instead of resting in its usual soft layers, her short hair jutted outward in disarray, as if she'd done some tossing and turning.

One hand lay near her face. But it wasn't relaxed and open. Instead, her fingers were curled into a fist. Even in sleep, she projected a tense readiness. Not good for her, but great for his son. And a huge comfort for him.

Allowing Jasmine to be responsible for his son's safety had been a good choice.

He backed away and crept silently through the kitchen. It wouldn't do to have Jasmine awaken to find him staring at her. She'd probably think he was some kind of a creep. But it wasn't like that. He didn't think of her as anything more than his and Liam's bodyguard.

And he never would. The complete opposite of Mandy, she was so not his type. Where Mandy was soft and relaxed, Jasmine was hard and rigid. The warmth and openness that had always drawn him to Mandy seemed to be lacking in Jasmine. He'd never witnessed anything but cool professionalism. As far as openness, something told him she guarded her personal details like the Secret Service guarded the president.

When he stepped into his room, he left the door open. Ten minutes later, he was lying in bed, staring at the darkened ceiling. Another thirty minutes passed before sleep crept close enough to brush against consciousness. His thoughts slowed, growing more and more random.

A terror-filled wail split the silence. He stumbled from bed, heart in his throat. It took almost landing on his face to realize one foot was still tangled in the sheets. No matter how many times it happened, he'd never get used to Liam's middle-of-the-night screams. He'd hoped the intensity and frequency would lessen with time, but so far, they hadn't.

A second shriek set his teeth on edge. Then sobs followed, wails of sorrow rather than fear. He burst into Liam's room, flipping the switch as he passed. Stark white light obliterated every shadow.

He skidded to a stop. Liam's bed was empty. Jasmine had already scooped him up and sat in the wooden rocking chair. She held him tightly, his head resting against her chest. Her face was tilted downward as she whispered soothing words into his hair.

She glanced up, meeting Colton's gaze. Her eyes seemed to hold a lingering wildness of their own. Before he could analyze what he was seeing, she returned her attention to the sobbing boy in her lap.

Liam took a shuddering breath, then lifted one arm to partially circle her waist.

Colton clenched his fists. Jasmine shouldn't be the one comforting him. Mandy should. The boy needed his mother.

An inner voice told him he was being irrational. On some level he agreed. But he was powerless against the emotions bombarding him.

"I'll take him." His tone was stiff and cold.

Jasmine looked up again, her brows drawn together. When she tried to move Liam, his hand tightened around the fabric of her silk pajamas.

Colton reached for him. "Come here, buddy. Daddy's here."

Liam finally released his hold. When Colton took him, Liam's arms went around his neck. He eased himself down onto Jasmine's bed, since she was still occupying the rocking chair. Already, guilt was pricking him.

"I appreciate what you did for him." It probably hadn't been easy. Jasmine didn't seem like the gentle, motherly type.

"I didn't mind."

He owed her an apology, as well as an explanation. *Sorry I snapped at you. I was angry that you were here instead of my dead wife.*

Okay, maybe not.

"I'm sorry he woke you up." That was an apology. Sort of.

"I was already awake."

He wasn't surprised. When he'd checked on them, she hadn't looked to be in a sound sleep. At least not a relaxed one.

She looked away. "Nightmares are the pits, especially for kids."

Her words seemed to be more than an opinion. Her tone held a *been there, done that* sentiment.

He nodded. "They're pretty regular, have been ever since... For the past six months."

"Since your wife's death."

"Yeah." He shook his head. "It was sudden. Brain aneurysm. We had no time to prepare." Not that it would have done any good. No amount of preparation would lessen the blow of saying goodbye to one's soul mate.

"I'm sorry." Her eyes held the same sympathy he'd seen when they'd first arrived at the Murphy house. Not just sympathy. Empathy. Like she'd walked in his shoes. Or some that fit in a far too similar way.

"Thanks." He forced a smile, but only one side of his mouth cooperated. "I've tried to keep things as normal for Liam as possible." Normalcy when one's entire world had shifted wasn't easy to accomplish.

Actually, *normal* was gone. Trying to recapture the life they used to have was pointless. Instead, he was settling in to a new life, defining a new normal, while still holding on to the few constants. Though it was often the last thing he felt like doing, he'd continued with church, trips to the park and other activities Liam enjoyed, even during their stay in Montana.

Tomorrow would be the first Friday in December, the night of the Murphy Christmas Art Walk. The event had been one of his and Mandy's traditions and what kicked off the decorating they'd done at the Murphy house, even when they'd lived in Atlanta.

"Tomorrow night…" He started the thought aloud before he could change his mind. He wasn't kidding himself. Holidays were going to be pure torture. Getting through them would require every ounce of strength he possessed. "I'm taking Liam to the Christmas Art Walk. We'll need you to come along."

No way was he taking his son out without Jasmine's protection. Since arriving in Murphy, he'd felt safe, except for the incident two nights ago when Brutus had caught someone prowling around. Since nothing had happened since, it was probably just kids passing through.

Jasmine shrugged. "Sure. What's the Christmas Art Walk?"

"We stroll around downtown Murphy, where they have art, food, live music and, of course, the lighting of the tree in the square. We'll go out for supper first, my treat."

She gave a sharp nod. "Will do."

He rose and moved to his son's bed. As he and Jasmine had talked, Liam's arms had slowly slid from around his neck. He positioned the boy in his bed and tucked the stuffed rabbit into the crook of one elbow. Liam's other thumb slipped into his mouth.

Colton straightened and tilted his head toward his son. "His nightmares, they usually only happen once in any given night."

"No problem, even if it's more."

He left the room and headed toward his own. Tomorrow night, he'd be tackling the first of their Christmas traditions.

Same time, same event, same location. There'd even be three of them, like before. But instead of Mandy, Jasmine would be with them.

It just wasn't right.

But they weren't a family unit, not the three of them. They were a father and son with their bodyguard. He wasn't even trying to pretend there was anything more.

It still somehow felt all wrong.


Jasmine stood in Hiwassee Valley rec center's playground, straight-legged jeans disappearing into the tops of her boots and her jacket hiding both her weapon and her Kevlar vest. Liam sat in one of the swings, fists clutching the chains as she pushed him. He was dressed the same as she was, minus the vest and in tennis shoes instead of boots. Heavier coats waited for them in the car. When the sun went down, they'd need them. Right now, the temperature was pleasant.

Colton had called an hour ago with a change of plans. They were still doing supper and the Christmas Art Walk, but he wouldn't make it home first. So he'd asked her to meet him at five at the Cherokee County Courthouse downtown. Since she was running early, the park offered a fun detour. Maybe it would not only distract Liam for a short time but also wear him out enough to sleep well tonight.

"Would you like to try out the slide?" Though Liam didn't respond, she brought him to a slow stop and lifted him from the swing.

Colton had apologized for him disturbing her sleep.

In actuality, he hadn't. She'd awoken from a nightmare herself shortly before he'd started screaming. When she'd scooped him up, she'd still been shaking from her own private terrors.

Then something unexpected had happened. As she'd held and soothed him, an odd sense of comfort had woven through her, shattering the images flashing in her mind and calming her spinning thoughts. The whole experience had caught her off guard. She didn't seek comfort from anyone. She dealt with everything on her own.

As a child, she'd had no choice. Often, she'd been left alone while her mother partied through the night. Or her mother left her with random people for days on end. Most didn't want to be bothered. Some did, men who tried to do things she didn't understand but somehow sensed were wrong.

As an adult, keeping herself closed off had been a hard habit to break. She'd even been tight-lipped with the counselors the army had assigned to help her process the horrors she'd seen and adjust to civilian life.

She led Liam to one of the slides, searching the perimeter as she'd been doing since they arrived fifteen minutes ago. Nothing raised any red flags. Several moms and a couple of dads stood or sat on benches. Jasmine had already matched the adults to their charges.

She was just finishing her three-hundred-sixty-degree observation when something over her left shoulder snagged her gaze. A man stood under the pavilion outside the fence, leaning against one of the posts, watching the activity on the playground. Was he one of those creeps who liked to hang out where young children played? Or was he interested in one child in particular?

Liam climbed the stairs, and she moved around to the base of the slide, keeping the man in her peripheral vision. He continued to watch. The fine hairs on the back of her neck stood up.

She shifted position, the weight of her weapon in its holster now more pronounced against her hip. She likely wouldn't have to draw it. If the man represented any kind of threat, he'd be crazy to act in a public place in broad daylight.

When it came time to leave, he hadn't moved. Liam walked with her to the Suburban without any objection. As she pulled into the courthouse parking lot, her phone buzzed with an incoming text. Colton was finished. Perfect timing. Two or three minutes later, he approached the passenger side, and she lowered the window.

He leaned inside. "Are you okay with taking your vehicle, or shall we transfer the car seat?"

"I can drive. Hop in."

He directed her through a turn onto Valley River Avenue. The art walk appeared to be in full swing, with every parking space occupied and people roaming the sidewalks. An alleyway between two buildings opened up into a parking area. If Colton hadn't been with her, she'd have never found it.

When they'd walked back to the front of the building, a sign overhead announced The Daily Grind.

She looked up at Colton. "A coffee shop?"

"And more. Salads, soups and sandwiches. Fast, but good. One of the favorite places around for people to congregate."

He opened the door, then walked in behind her, carrying Liam. In front of her, a wide hallway separated the Curiosity Shop Bookstore on the right from The

Daily Grind on the left. They joined the end of a short line. Above and behind those working the counter, the menu was displayed on boards. She decided on a grilled panini sandwich with hot roast beef and Swiss.

After placing their orders, they found an empty table at the front. Colton positioned Liam in a booster seat and took the chair next to him. Jasmine sat opposite them. Large windows offered a clear view of Valley River Avenue. People strolled by just outside.

Jasmine shifted her attention to Colton. "Are you working tomorrow?"

"Not at the office, but I did put some files in my vehicle before walking over to where you'd parked."

"Are you always this much of a workaholic?"

He shrugged. "I've got a lot of catching up to do. I'm taking over someone else's caseload."

She nodded, even though he hadn't answered her question. She glanced around the interior space, then looked out the window again. A group of people had stopped to converse, blocking her view of anything beyond.

After they moved on, she scanned the area. The sun had set, and the last rays of light were fading. Her gaze fell on a figure across the street, and she tensed. Shadows hid his face, but the baseball cap, jeans and bulky coat matched the clothing of the man at the playground.

"Is everything okay?"

Colton's words pulled her attention back inside. For a nonmilitary, nonsecurity guy, he was pretty observant.

She cast a glance back out the window. The guy was gone.

"Everything's fine." She wouldn't alarm him yet. Based on what she'd seen, most of Murphy turned out for this event. The man across the street might not even be the same person. If he was, he hadn't followed her. She'd been watching too closely.

When they finished eating, Colton looked at his watch. "If we want to make it to the tree lighting, we'll have to walk fast."

"I'm up for it if you are." She stood. "So, what happens at the tree lighting? Other than lighting the tree."

"There's children's music and dance and a kids' jingle bell walk. Then Santa arrives on a fire truck."

"Sounds like fun."

Especially for a kid. She hoped Liam would enjoy it. She would have at that age. If the small town she grew up in had had activities like that, she hadn't known about them.

Her mother apparently had, at least the adult parties. More than once Jasmine had gotten up in the morning to find that her mother had come in during the night and passed out on the living room floor still wearing a Christmas hat.

When they reached the town square, a good-size crowd was already gathered. Jasmine scanned those standing around, searching for the man she'd seen at the park. Throughout each activity, she continued to look. If he was there, he was staying hidden.

When the last activity ended, Colton shifted his son to his other hip. Liam didn't participate in the jingle bell walk with the other kids, but his eyes were alert, taking in everything that was going on around him. Maybe next year.

Of course, she wouldn't be there to witness it.

An unexpected sense of loss settled in her core. She mentally shook herself. Being part of a real family, albeit temporarily, was messing with her. She had no intention of putting down any kind of roots. She loved the transient nature of what she did. The crazy pace helped her stay ahead of the memories.

Unfortunately, the nightmares always managed to catch up with her. No matter what she'd done or where she'd gone, she had never gotten rid of them. After years of fighting, all she'd managed to do was trade childhood terrors for adult-size ones.

As the crowd began to spread out, Colton moved down the sidewalk. "Now for the art walk."

For some time, they wandered in and out of the shops. Several stores down, a variety of paintings were on display. The artist sat to the side. Jasmine stopped to watch as the woman dipped a brush into one of the globs of paint on her palette, then spread it with sure strokes onto the canvas in front of her.

It looked like a local scene, as did the others around the room. This one was a park with mountains in the background, silhouetted against a striking sunset.

Jasmine stepped away to look at the other paintings more closely. "I've always envied artistic people. I never progressed past Paint by Numbers."

Colton stood next to her. "Mandy painted, watercolor."

"Your wife." Colton hadn't mentioned her name previously, but Gunn had.

"Yeah. She did it as a hobby, but she was good."

So Liam's mother wasn't just loved and needed. She was talented, too. With so many rotten people walking around, why did someone like Mandy Gale have to die? Why did any good people die young? Men and women serving their country, sent home in caskets. What kind of God made those decisions?

When she reached the door, bluegrass music drifted to her from somewhere nearby, probably a local band entertaining the attendees. She stepped out onto the sidewalk, glancing up and down the street.

A man stood about twenty feet away, the glow of a streetlamp spilling over him. The bill of his cap cast his face in shadow, but this time she was sure. It was the man from the park.

She reached for her phone. "Pick up Liam. I want to take your picture."

When he'd done as she asked, she turned the phone sideways and touched the screen, focusing on the figure to the right. After snapping three pictures, she scrolled through them.

Colton peered over her shoulder. "Usually it's better to center the subjects you're taking a picture of. You got Liam, but you cut me in half. I'm glad you're a better bodyguard than photographer."

She ignored his teasing criticism and expanded the picture, moving it to the side until a grainy face occupied the center of the screen.

"Do you recognize this man?"

"No, why?" His eyes lit with understanding, then respect. "Who is he?"

She looked back toward the streetlight. As expected, the man was gone.

"I was hoping you could tell me. I took Liam to the park before meeting you. I noticed him standing some distance away, watching the activity on the playground."

"And you saw him when we were in the Grind." It was a statement rather than a question.

"I wasn't sure. He was across the street, in shadow. But when I saw him this time, I knew it was the same guy. Are you sure you've never seen him?"

He looked at the picture again. "It's hard to tell. His face is dark."

Yeah, the shadows were even more pronounced than what she'd seen. Maybe the authorities could enhance the photos enough to identify him.

She shrank the picture until the man's full length displayed on the screen. "Could he be one of the guys who tried to take Liam?"

Colton studied the image. "I didn't see their faces, but this could be the thinner guy."

She pocketed the phone. Maybe he *was* one of the kidnappers. Or maybe he was just a Murphy resident who liked to hang out at the park and attend the town's activities.

But that wasn't what her gut told her. She'd gotten icky vibes all three times she'd seen him.

When she looked up at Colton, his jaw was tight and his lips were compressed into a thin line. "Are you dead set on finishing the art walk?"

"No."

"Good."

Because if there was one thing she'd learned over the years, it was to always listen to her instincts.

# FOUR

Colton hauled a large empty box out of the middle of the living room and stood it against the wall. Jasmine sat on the rug, back against the coffee table, piles of plastic branches surrounding her.

Walmart bags lined the couch. Liam had pulled boxes of Christmas lights out of one and set them on the floor. Now he was tackling a second bag, pulling out ornaments. At least he was engaged. Maybe he was even enjoying himself.

Colton lowered himself to the floor and assembled the tree stand. He and Mandy had always had a live tree. This year's would be artificial. And though the attic held boxes of decorations, he wouldn't use them. He was committed to making Christmas meaningful for Liam, but he didn't have to let each strand of garland, every ornament, even the fresh pine scent of a live tree, be a reminder of what he'd lost.

Last night, he'd barely gotten through the activities in town. Cutting out early had been a relief, both to escape possible danger and to no longer have to pretend he was having a great time when he was dying inside.

Jasmine unfolded a piece of paper and smoothed out

the creases against the coffee table. "Okay, bottom row, blue." She passed him a handful of branches.

Colton smiled. "So, you're a follow-the-directions kind of girl."

"Yeah. Saves time in the long run."

His thoughts exactly. "Someone needs to explain that to my brother. Step-by-step instructions feel too much like structure, something he avoids like Black Death."

"And you're a by-the-book guy."

"Totally." One year, a church had taken on his group home as a project and bought every child a Christmas gift. He and Cade had received model cars. Cade had finished his in half the time, but some of the components never made it into the car because he'd glued together the exterior before finishing the inside. Cade was bright, but an innate impulsiveness had gotten him into trouble more than once.

Jasmine nodded. "Didn't take me long to pick up on the fact you guys are polar opposites."

The tree took form as they progressed up the inner pole, each series of branches shorter than the last. Liam stayed busy with the contents of the bags. Across the room, Brutus lay against the wall, silently watching the activity.

The guys from Western Carolina Fence had arrived that morning and were still hard at work. The dog hadn't been happy to have strangers tromping around his yard. Keeping him inside was less stressful, all the way around.

When they finished assembling the tree, Colton stepped back. "Now for the lights."

He retrieved a box from the haphazard stack against the couch. Liam handed him an ornament, still in its packaging, a teddy bear holding a bouquet of candy canes.

"You like this one?"

Liam's mouth curved in a small smile, and Colton swallowed around a sudden lump in his throat. *Thank You, Lord.* It was just a smile, one minuscule step on the path back to the happy child he used to be. But every bit of progress, no matter how small, felt like cause for celebration.

And he'd do whatever it took to see the progress continue. He'd keep up the cheery front. He'd gotten good at stuffing the grief beneath layers of *I've got it all together* for the benefit of his son.

He knelt in front of Liam and placed the ornament on the coffee table. "The lights have to go on first, then the garland. How about if you get the rest of the ornaments out and put them with this one?"

Liam nodded and went to work tackling the task he'd been given. By the time Colton had placed the last strand of lights, boxes of ornaments were spread across the coffee table. Garland went on next, while Liam watched.

Colton crouched at the table in front of his son. "Now the ornaments."

Another smile, this one a little bigger. It tugged a matching one out of Colton. They'd been back in Murphy for one week, and already he was seeing his son slowly reengage with his world. The move had been a good choice, one he'd never have considered if not for the events of last week.

Another thought slid through the back of his mind, the fact that the move to Murphy wasn't the only change in his son's life. There was also Jasmine's presence.

He didn't want to credit any of Liam's progress to her being there. She was a temporary addition to their lives. If Liam became too attached, his behavior would revert right back once she left.

He scooped up his son, a sense of protectiveness surging through him. Somehow, he'd make sure that didn't happen. "We'll let Miss Jasmine put the hooks on them, and you can hang them."

After tearing into the perforated back of the package, Jasmine removed a handful of wire hooks and laid them on the coffee table. One by one, she affixed them to the ornaments and handed them to Liam. Colton held him up to adorn the higher branches, gradually working their way around and down the tree.

Each time Liam placed ornaments side by side, Colton let them be. He wasn't going for perfection. Everything he was doing was for his son's benefit. And Liam didn't care that the decorations weren't evenly spaced. Although he didn't say a word, several spontaneous smiles revealed how much he was enjoying himself.

Jasmine was smiling, too. But the spontaneity Liam displayed was lacking in her. Now that she wasn't task-focused, her features held tightness. He wasn't the only one feigning enthusiasm.

He placed Liam on the floor. After directing him to one of the lower branches, he glanced up at Jasmine. "You seem to be trying as hard as I am."

She didn't have to ask him what he meant, confirmation he'd pegged her right. Instead, she shrugged. "I've never made a big deal out of Christmas. As a child, I was forgotten. As an adult, I don't see the purpose.

That whole 'peace on earth, goodwill to men' message is nothing but a pipe dream."

"And I thought *I* was jaded."

She shrugged again but didn't comment.

"How about you?" She swept her hand toward the newly decorated tree. "Is this how you grew up?"

"Till age seven and from age fifteen forward. Between seven and fifteen, how I celebrated Christmas depended on what foster or group home I was in."

She lifted her brows. "You were in foster care?"

"For a while. The Gales adopted me when I was fifteen."

"What happened to your birth parents?"

"My mom died." When he was seven, the breast cancer she'd defeated three years earlier came back with a vengeance. Six months later, she was gone. "What happened to my dad is anybody's guess. They divorced when I was young."

What he said was true, but there was more to the story. He and Cade had both ended up with their father. But after he'd left them alone too many times, Child Protective Services had stepped in, and they'd landed in foster care. Though the state worked with his father, he never did get his act together and eventually signed away his parental rights.

She handed Liam another ornament. "That had to have been rough."

Colton met her gaze, and the words he was going to say stuck in his throat. He'd seen it again—that empathy, the silent message that said she'd been there. Close enough to understand, anyway.

He shrugged. "It was rough. But Cade and I at least

got adopted. My friend Tanner aged out of the system. A lot of teenagers do."

"They kept you and Cade together?"

"Through foster care, they did. They tried to get us adopted together, but there weren't many adoptive parents up to the task of handling two messed-up boys, one brooding, angry and destructive, and the other with a mischievous streak a mile wide."

She gave him a wry smile. "Let me guess who was who."

He returned her smile. "Pretty obvious, huh? Although, I think I've obliterated any destructive tendencies. And anger isn't so much an issue anymore, either." He pursed his lips. "As far as Cade's mischievousness… that just manifests itself in other ways now."

"You were adopted separately? But you have the same last name."

"Another family started adoption proceedings for Cade." The more serious, studious twin, Colton had always been a little envious of his outgoing, carefree brother. When Cade went to a permanent home at age fourteen, that slight envy became full-blown jealousy.

"A week before the adoption would have been final, the adoptive parents backed out."

Jasmine's eyes widened. "How awful."

"The family realized the charming, fun-loving personality that had drawn them in came with some characteristics that weren't so pleasant, especially when the police got involved."

Cade had seemed to handle the rejection well. But Colton knew better. After that, his brother's mischievousness and impulsiveness sometimes bordered on self-destruction.

"I'd already gone to the Gales by that time, so that made things worse for him. But once my adoption was final, the Gales adopted Cade, too."

She threaded a hook into the last ornament and handed it to Liam. "They must be amazing people." The wistfulness in her tone left Colton wondering what had been missing from her own childhood.

"They are." He'd never seen two finer examples of Christians. "They were in the process of making retirement plans when my grandfather was diagnosed with Alzheimer's and my grandmother had a stroke. So a year ago, they put their travel plans on hold and moved to upper New York to care for my grandparents."

Liam raised his arms toward Jasmine. The softest whisper reached Colton's ears.

His pulse kicked into overdrive. "Did he just say something?"

"I think he said 'more.'"

Colton scooped him up and spun him around, heart still pounding. "You want more? Sorry, buddy, you hung them all up."

Liam's thumb went into his mouth, but the vacancy Colton had grown accustomed to seeing in his eyes wasn't there. Instead, they sparked with life. He moved to the couch and sat, positioning his son on his lap facing the tree. "You did such a good job. That's the prettiest Christmas tree ever."

The thumb came out, and Liam pointed toward the tree. Colton's heart sang. If the smile had been a small step, the single word had been a giant leap.

When he shifted his gaze to Jasmine, she was watching him. For one unguarded moment, he saw in her eyes the same wistfulness he'd heard in her tone. But there was something else, too. Longing. It threaded a path right to his heart.

The next moment, it was gone, hidden behind that veil of self-sufficiency that seemed to always cloak her. She moved to the front window next to the tree and pulled the drapes aside. "They've got the posts and top rail up and are starting to run the fence."

"Good." He tamped down whatever it was he'd felt moments earlier. Her rotten childhood, the traumas she'd faced as an adult—they were none of his business. Just as his personal struggles were none of hers.

He joined her at the window. He didn't envy the men their job. Mixed in with the rich topsoil and clay were varying sizes of rocks. Lots of them. He'd learned that when Mandy had wanted decorative ornamentals planted around the house. Of course, the men currently working outside were professionals and far better equipped than he'd been.

The ringtone sounded on his phone. The screen displayed a familiar number. He swiped it and greeted his brother.

Static interrupted Cade's voice. "I've wanted…several times…insane hour."

Colton stepped outside, even though the problem was likely on Cade's end. "Where are you?"

"Egypt…driving… Cairo."

"Your satellite cell service stinks."

"Hold on."

Colton waited. When Cade came back on, the background noise he'd heard earlier was gone. So was the majority of the static.

"That's much better." He'd apparently stopped, maybe even gotten out of the vehicle and climbed a hill.

If the area surrounding Cairo had hills. Colton wouldn't know. His brother was the world traveler.

"I've wanted to call several times, but it's always been some insane hour in the States. Are you and Liam okay?"

He leaned against the deck railing. "We're fine. We've had a couple of small scares, but nothing came of them."

"What kind of scares?" Worry laced Cade's tone, strongly enough that the thousands of miles separating them didn't dilute it.

"Someone cutting across the yard, which we decided was probably a teenager from the neighborhood."

"And?"

"And someone hanging out near the park yesterday afternoon and the Christmas Art Walk last night. I don't think he posed any threat." No sense in saying otherwise. None of this was Cade's deal. Half a world away, he couldn't do anything about it anyway.

"You've got to stay away from Atlanta."

Colton lifted his brows at the urgency in his brother's tone. His philosophy in life had always been "Nothing's gonna happen." Apparently, he wasn't so optimistic when his nephew's safety was at stake.

"Trust me, I'm not going anywhere near there until whoever tried to take Liam has been locked up."

"Good." Cade heaved a sigh of relief. "You know, I already miss the little guy."

"Look at the bright side. There's no one to spill juice all over you."

Cade's laughter held a heavy dose of affection. "Would you believe I even miss the mishaps?"

The last mishap had given Cade a lot more time with

his nephew than he'd planned. The evening before the break-in and attempted kidnapping, Cade had stopped by for dinner, then ended up spending the night after Liam had loosened the top on his sippy cup and spilled the entire contents over him. Colton had loaned him some sweats and thrown both shirt and pants into the washer before the red juice could leave a stain.

Cade continued, his tone turning from playful to eager. "So how are things progressing with the hot bodyguard? It's been a week. I hope you've moved from the protector/protectee relationship to something much more interesting."

Colton groaned. After his meeting at Burch Security Specialists, he'd filled Cade in on the fact that his pretty neighbor was going to be the one providing the bodyguard services. Maybe he should have kept that detail to himself.

"Our relationship is strictly professional, as it will remain."

Sure, he admired her. Although she hadn't elaborated, she'd provided enough hints for him to know she hadn't had an easy life. But she'd survived whatever rough upbringing she'd had. Not just survived. Overcome.

She was strong, physically and emotionally. She'd risked her life serving her country and continued putting herself in danger serving those she protected. But she had no problem setting aside that strength and toughness to comfort a frightened little boy.

Yeah, he admired her. But that was as far as it would go. From what he'd gathered, Jasmine wasn't any more in the market for a relationship than he was.

Cade heaved a sigh. "Whatever. But I think you're passing up a golden opportunity."

When Colton didn't respond, Cade let the subject drop. "I've got to get to an appointment." The same urgency entered his tone. "No matter what, don't go back home. You've got to stay in Murphy. You hear me?"

"Yeah, loud and clear." Something dark fell over him, drawing his stomach into a knot. "What aren't you telling me?"

"I'm just worried. Somebody's threatening my nephew. Stay away from Atlanta. Lie low. Keep Jasmine close, Liam closer." A hum came through the phone. Cade had apparently gotten back in the car and cranked the engine. "I'll call you in a couple days."

The line went dead. Colton looked at his phone, brows dipping together. What was up with his brother? He never stressed about anything, even when stress was warranted. He took the adage "Don't worry, be happy" to extremes.

But no one had ever threatened Liam before. Cade obviously wasn't handling it any better than Colton was. Colton wasn't surprised. He and his brother were close, in spite of their differences. But if not for Cade's desire to talk to his nephew every week or two, the adults' interactions wouldn't be nearly as frequent.

He pushed himself away from the railing. The men were unrolling chain-link fence, affixing it to the framework they'd already installed. By the end of the day, they'd be finished. Brutus would be back outside with free run of the entire yard. Anyone trying to approach the house would find himself with a bite-size chunk taken out of his rear end.

The thought brought him some comfort. But not

enough to soothe the lingering anxiety that still coursed through him.

He stepped back inside, where Liam was stuffing empty ornament boxes into a bag that Jasmine held open. A few minutes earlier, the sight would have warmed him. But a cold knot of worry had settled in his chest.

He didn't plan to go back to Atlanta anyway. But Cade's dire warnings had shaken him.

Was Cade afraid that if they returned, the kidnappers would try again? Or was it more than that?

Maybe someone got to him. Maybe before Cade left town, the kidnappers made some kind of threat.

And Cade was trying to protect him, to keep him from worrying.

It wasn't working.

Unfortunately, Cade's silence was doing just the opposite.

Jasmine fought the urge to retch. There was smoke, dust, screams.

And blood. So much blood.

Zach lay on the ground, clutching his stomach, his wails fraying her nerves. She added her own hands to the gaping wound, trying to help stanch the stream of blood. It didn't help. The river kept flowing, warm and sticky.

She'd been standing in front of him moments earlier. They'd kissed goodbye, then walked opposite directions to get ready to report for duty.

Then there was a shout of warning and the sound that struck terror deep into the core of every soldier—the whistle of an incoming mortar round. The nearby blast knocked her to the ground. When she'd gathered her wits enough to rise and search for Zach, the scene before her was what she'd found.

"Hang on, Zach. Help's coming."

But it was hopeless. She'd encountered Death enough times to know when it had gone from crouching at the door to leaping over the threshold.

Zach went suddenly still, eyes no longer focused. She opened her mouth, her own wail traveling up her throat. A warning sounded deep in her subconscious, and she squeezed off the scream.

A hand gripped her shoulder, and what she'd stifled moments earlier found full release.

"Shh, Jasmine. It's okay. You're safe."

*Zach!* She snapped her eyes open with a gasp.

But Zach wasn't there. She was no longer at the post in Afghanistan, chaos all around her, the stench of fear and death. She was in Liam's bedroom, his father standing over her.

"What are you doing in here?" Her tone was shrill and laced with panic, partly from the remnants of the nightmare, partly from the thought that Colton had been able to walk into the room and approach her bed without her knowing.

Nearby, Liam rolled over. She tried to sit up, but she was restrained. Fresh panic surged through her. She worked a hand free and heaved a sigh of relief. It was just the sheet and blanket. One side was still tucked between the mattress and box springs, the rest wound tightly around her.

Colton helped to pull the bedding from under her. "I was having trouble sleeping." His tone was low, soothing. The glow of the night-light washed over him, softening his features. "I went to the kitchen to get a drink and heard you thrashing around."

She pushed herself to an upright position as Liam started to cry. Colton moved that direction, and she sprang to her feet.

"Let me get him." It was only fair.

"You're not his babysitter."

"I'm the one who woke him up. Besides, it's Monday, the start of a new week. You need your sleep."

She scooped Liam from his bed. In a matter of seconds, he'd worked himself up to a full wail. She settled herself in the rocking chair, his legs draped over her right thigh. He calmed down and snuggled against her, thumb in his mouth.

As she rocked him, she rubbed his back, making slow circles with her palm. He drew in several shuddering breaths, then lifted his other arm to grip her silk pajamas.

She closed her eyes, letting her pulse slow and the images fade. Something cleansing washed over her, leaving behind an odd sense of calm. How could the comfort she tried to give flow both ways? How could the act of soothing Liam's fears be a balm for her own?

"What did you dream?"

The question jarred her eyes open. "Nothing important, just a nightmare."

"From your military days?"

He sat on her bed, fingers intertwined in his lap. Great. He was planning to stay awhile.

"Yeah." If he expected her to elaborate, he was going to be disappointed. She didn't discuss the memories that haunted her with anyone.

"You want to talk about it?"

"No." He wasn't her counselor.

But she *was* tasked with protecting his son. He needed to know that she wasn't in danger of flipping out and hurting Liam.

She drew in a stabilizing breath. "I've been out of the army for three years, living a fairly normal life. The horror of combat is behind me."

Sort of. The things she witnessed would never go away. But the nightmares had gradually decreased in frequency. More important, she was getting better at waking herself up before reaching the state that had drawn Colton into the room.

Not all her assignments had been in war zones. Only two had. During those deployments, she'd witnessed dozens of deaths. Every one of them had bothered her. Zach's had almost killed her. Their relationship hadn't been perfect. But it had been less dysfunctional than her previous ones.

Colton nodded. "If you ever want to talk about it, I'm a good listener."

"Thanks." But that wasn't how she did things.

He dipped his head toward his son. "Looks like he might be going back to sleep."

"I think you're right." Except for the occasional shuddering breath, he hadn't moved in several minutes.

Colton rose. "I'm going to take you up on your offer to let me get some sleep."

As she watched him walk from the room, tenderness wove through her. In spite of all of her toughness, sad stories got to her. And his was tragic on so many levels.

Suffering the death of his mother at age seven. Unwanted by his father. Bounced between foster and group homes for the next eight years. Left behind when his brother was adopted.

He'd overcome all of it, then had his family shattered again when his wife died. If anyone had grounds for claiming life wasn't fair, it was Colton.

But he didn't. During quiet times, he projected a sense of grief that was almost palpable. But an unexplainable peace seemed to run beneath it.

If she asked him about the peace he seemed to possess, he'd probably credit his faith in God. That didn't make sense, either. If Colton believed God was close enough to provide any type of comfort, he'd also have to believe that God was close enough to see what was happening and intervene.

Liam released a soft sigh, and his hand fell to his lap. He was fully asleep. She could lay him in his bed and return to her own.

Instead, she sat for a few more minutes, relishing his warmth against her and letting the soothing movement of the rocker continue to relax her. She tipped her face downward and pressed a soft kiss to the top of his head. Colton didn't want his son getting attached to her. He didn't express any concerns about her getting attached to the little boy.

Finally, she rose and laid him in his bed next to the stuffed rabbit. The thumb that had fallen out of his mouth went back in.

Her chest squeezed. Every child should be loved and cherished like Liam. Instead, too many grew up like her and Liam's father—unwanted, shuffled from place to place, fed but not nourished, cared for but not loved. Maybe Colton didn't feel life was unfair, but she certainly did.

She moved to her bed and crawled between the rumpled sheets. Watching Colton hold Liam Saturday, praising him for the job he'd done decorating the tree, had stirred something in her. It was something she desperately wanted, a longing she didn't even know she'd had.

It wasn't that she wanted it with Colton. Or even his sad, sweet little boy. She just wanted it. Period. That sense of home. Family. Maybe she'd find it eventually.

But not with Colton. The last thing she wanted to do was to try to step into the shoes of his dead wife. She'd never measure up to those standards.

Amazing mother. Loving wife. Artistic, talented and creative. Beautiful inside and out.

No way could she compete with that.

She wouldn't even try.

# FIVE

Colton walked from the courthouse into late dusk. The parking lot lights and streetlights along Alpine had already come on.

As he made his way toward his vehicle, he scanned the area. There hadn't been any possible threats since the art walk a week ago, but he couldn't bring himself to fully relax. If life continued to be safe and uneventful, though, he'd have to eventually let Jasmine go. He couldn't afford to keep her on indefinitely.

In the meantime, her presence was a comfort, and not just for the security she provided. She was at least partially responsible for the improvement he was seeing in Liam.

Over the past week, several more words had slipped from his mouth. No full sentences, yet. He was still a long way from the chatty little boy he used to be. But it was a start.

Colton's cell phone vibrated at his side. A second, then third buzz told him it was a call rather than a text. Not Cade again. He was starting to sound like an audio clip on automatic replay. He'd called twice this week, and Colton had had to reassure him both times that he and Liam weren't going back to Atlanta, even for a brief visit.

He removed his phone from its clip, shaking his head. He was still trying to get used to the mature, somber side of Cade. When he swiped the screen, though, it wasn't his brother's name and number there.

Colton smiled. He and Doug Blanton hadn't just worked together since Colton's return to Atlanta. They'd gone to the same church and become good friends over the past couple of years.

Doug's booming voice came through the phone. "How is Murphy?"

"Good."

"No kidnappers or creepy stalker dudes?"

Doug knew the reasons behind the sudden move. Colton had caught up with him when he'd gone into the office to resign his position.

"Nope. Just a couple of false alarms." He pressed the key fob and approached the Highlander. Beyond its nose, a chain-link fence marked the edge of the parking lot, the guardrail inside an extra layer of protection from the ten-or twelve-foot drop-off to the road. "I did hire a bodyguard."

"That makes me feel better. Is he out of Atlanta?"

"Yeah, Burch Security. But it's a she rather than a he."

"Good." That fact obviously didn't bother Doug like it had him at first. Of course, it didn't bother him anymore. God had a way of placing people exactly where they needed to be.

As Doug caught him up on happenings around the DA's office, Colton settled into the driver's seat. Something white snagged his gaze—a sheet of paper tucked under the right wiper blade.

Uneasiness settled over him, and he shook it off. Kidnappers didn't leave notes on windshields. It was probably a flyer from one of the local businesses. He just needed to remove it before he pulled from the parking lot.

After ending the call a few minutes later, he stepped out to retrieve the page. As soon as he unfolded it, a bolt of panic shot up his spine. The paper fluttered to the ground. Bold, dark letters screamed out their message—*You can run, but you can't hide.*

His heart pounded, sending blood roaring through his ears. The men he fled from in Atlanta had found him. They knew where he worked. They probably also knew where he lived.

He had to warn Jasmine.

He bent to pick up the paper at the same time a shot rang out. Glass shattered, and he hit the pavement, facedown, heart pounding.

As he retrieved his phone and dialed 911, his thoughts spun. If his enemy was here in town, firing on him, that meant he wasn't at the house threatening his son.

Unless he'd gone there first.

The dispatcher picked up before the last thought could lodge too deeply. As he filled her in on what had happened, he doubled back to collect the paper, staying in a crouch. The light breeze had carried it across an empty parking space and pressed it against a car's tire two spaces over.

Handling just the corner, he picked it up and carried it to his vehicle. The bullet had entered the driver side of the windshield and exited the rear passenger window. Judging from the angle, it had likely come from the direction of the library. The trees lining that side of the road would have offered a handy place for a shooter to hide.

As soon as he ended the call, he brought up Jasmine's number. Sirens sounded nearby. Right downtown, he'd expected as much.

When the call went straight to voice mail, his stomach tightened. Why didn't she have her phone on? The sirens were moving closer. Maybe he should ask the police to dispatch another unit to his house.

Or maybe he had a better idea. It would take the police a good ten minutes to get there, but his friend Bryce lived one street over, on Ranger Road. Tanner lived a mile farther, on 294. Both worked in law enforcement, Tanner with Murphy PD and Bryce with Cherokee County.

Bryce answered on the second ring. He was on duty several miles the opposite direction. Colton ended the call without an explanation and brought up Tanner's number. A police cruiser turned onto Peachtree as his friend answered.

Colton dispensed with the formalities. "Where are you?"

"At Ingles, tackling the grocery list Paige texted me. Why?"

"I was going to have you check on Jasmine and Liam. Someone just shot at me, and I can't get ahold of her."

"Call 911."

"I have."

"I'm leaving my cart."

"No, go ahead and finish your shopping." Even if Tanner left the store immediately, he wouldn't make it to Colton's house until long after the on-duty officers arrived.

"On second thought, how about stopping by the courthouse and giving me a ride home?" His vehicle was evidence. He'd probably have to leave it there for some time.

As he disconnected the call, the cruiser made its way up the narrow drive into the courthouse parking lot. Its siren fell silent, but others still sounded nearby. Probably units searching for the shooter.

Before the officer could exit, Colton stepped up to his open door. "Will you please send a unit to my house?" He rattled off the address. "With this attack on me, I'm worried about my son and his bodyguard."

The officer raised a brow but immediately reached for his radio. As he spoke, a little of Colton's tension eased. A unit would be dispatched from Cherokee County. When the officer finished, he turned his attention to Colton. "Show me where you were and where this shot came from."

Colton walked to his vehicle and relayed everything as it had happened. After donning latex gloves he'd retrieved from the car, the officer took the note into evidence.

"Any idea who'd want to take a shot at you?"

"I've made a few enemies during my time as an assistant DA." He gave the officer the same names he'd given Gunter Burch two weeks ago.

"Did you see or hear anything before the shot was fired? A vehicle speeding by or anything?"

"No. But it seemed to have come from over there." He nodded toward the library. Though it wasn't situated as high as the courthouse, its grounds sloped upward from the road. Not an ideal position, but doable.

He continued. "I didn't notice anything suspicious. But I'd just found the note, and I was pretty shaken. Someone tried to kidnap my son two weeks ago in Atlanta, so I came up here. The note tells me they've found me."

He shifted his weight, impatience tightening his shoulders. He needed to get home and check on Liam and Jasmine.

He drew in a steadying breath. Law enforcement was already on its way and would likely arrive within minutes. Meanwhile, he'd left Liam in Jasmine's care. She was sharp. She never let down her guard.

*God, please protect them both.*

A Silverado pickup pulled into one of the streetside parking spaces below, Tanner at the wheel. As he drew to a stop, the officer's radio came to life.

"The woman and child on Hilltop are unharmed."

Colton's knees buckled, and he clutched the Highlander for support. *Thank You, God.*

The officer finished his report and Colton descended the stairs to the street. He'd been right. The detectives wanted to look at his vehicle before he moved it. Which was fine with him. He didn't want to drive it until the damaged glass was replaced anyway.

After he slid into the passenger seat of the Silverado, Tanner made his way toward the four-lane. Little by little, the last remnants of fear and panic slowly dissipated, leaving room for annoyance, then anger.

He crossed his arms. "Jasmine had better have a really good reason for her phone being off."

He'd had a major scare and hadn't even been able to

check on his son. That wasn't acceptable. As long as Jasmine was responsible for protecting Liam, he needed to be able to reach her.

Tanner shot him a sideways glance. "Maybe the battery went dead."

If that was the case, that wasn't acceptable, either. She needed to be able to call out in case of an emergency. Allowing her phone to go dead would be totally irresponsible.

When Tanner approached Colton's property, a Cherokee County cruiser was parked on the road, lights still flashing. The gate was closed, but Brutus wasn't in the front yard. Maybe Jasmine had brought him inside when the deputies arrived. But why were they still there, twenty minutes after radioing that Liam and Jasmine were safe?

Colton jumped from the Silverado. "Thanks for the ride."

When he swung open the gate, Tanner pulled inside. Colton wasn't surprised. Tanner wouldn't leave until he knew everything was all right. That was the kind of friend he'd been ever since the two of them had landed in the same group home at age thirteen.

The door swung open and Jasmine stepped onto the deck.

Colton stalked toward her. "Where is Liam?"

"Watching a movie."

"Why isn't your phone on?" His tone was several decibels louder than normal and filled with accusation.

Jasmine's brows drew together. "It *is* on. It's sitting on the kitchen counter, where I was cooking."

*Cooking?* He hadn't hired her to be cook or maid

any more than he'd hired her to be babysitter. But that would be a conversation for later.

She frowned. "I was just getting ready to call you to ask why you sent cops to check on us. Is this all because you couldn't get ahold of me?"

"Someone left a note on my windshield at the court-house this afternoon. That was before they shot at me."

Jasmine blanched. Her eyes swept over him, then bounced back up to his face. "Are you all right?"

"I wasn't hit. I'd dropped the note and bent to pick it up just as he fired."

The last of the color leached from her face. "If you hadn't bent over when you did…"

Tanner approached and stepped onto the deck with them. "Where are the officers?"

"They're checking the perimeter. When I filled them in on everything, they wanted to make sure no one was prowling around."

Tanner nodded. "I'll see if they found anything."

Jasmine watched him disappear around the side of the house, then opened the door to step back inside. A pleasant aroma drifted to him, along with a child-ish voice he instantly recognized—Liam was watching *Finding Dory*.

When Colton followed Jasmine into the living room, Brutus met them, tail wagging. The Christmas tree twinkled with hundreds of lights, and Liam was lying on the floor, a throw pillow he'd pulled from the couch beneath him. Colton closed the door, and Liam swiv-eled his head. "Daddy!"

Colton almost stumbled. He'd waited nearly six months to hear his name from his son's lips. Ignoring the dog, he scooped Liam up and held him close, heart swelling as a lump formed in his throat.

His eyes met Jasmine's. The joy filling his chest was reflected on her face. When the assignment was over, and he and Liam were safe again, how was he going to be able to let her go? What was her leaving going to do to Liam?

He placed his son back on the floor and straightened. "What happened with your phone?"

"I don't know, but I guarantee you it's on."

She marched into the kitchen and Colton followed. Two covered pots sat on the stove, but the burners under them were off. One held spaghetti sauce, based on the pleasant aroma that had wrapped around him the moment she opened the door.

Jasmine snatched her phone from the counter, swiped the screen and turned it to face him. "See, no missed calls."

He squinted. "And one bar." Cell service wasn't always reliable in the mountains. He'd have thought of that if he hadn't been so panicked. "We need to either get you a different provider or I need to program the landline number into my phone." He'd had it installed last week, for the sole purpose of monitoring the alarm.

She nodded. "If you ever can't reach me, call the landline. I'll answer it." She leaned back against the counter. "The note on your windshield, what did it say?"

"'You can run, but you can't hide.' Not very original, but he got his point across."

Determination entered her gaze. "I don't want you leaving the house without protection."

He closed his eyes, nausea churning in his gut. Jasmine was right. He and Liam were no longer safe here.

But he had nowhere else to go. They'd be just as vulnerable at his home in Atlanta as they were in Murphy. Heading back to his in-laws' place in Montana wasn't an option. He wouldn't put them in danger. He wasn't licensed to practice there, anyway, and he couldn't afford to take any more time off.

"I have to work."

"Then it's time to call in more help. We need someone on you and someone on your son twenty-four-seven."

She was right. His son was his first priority. But if something happened to *him*, where would Liam be? Cade was far too irresponsible to raise a child. But Colton couldn't afford any more security. At least not the paid kind.

"Let me talk to Tanner and Bryce. I know they'll be glad to help out however they can." Neither Murphy nor Cherokee County had the manpower to provide twenty-four-hour protection. But one or both agencies would probably make regular patrols through the area. And Tanner and Bryce would drive by even more frequently, both on and off duty.

A knock sounded on the door. When Colton opened it, one of the deputies stood on the deck, Tanner next to him. His partner was walking toward the car.

"We checked all the way around. No one was there. There aren't any signs that anyone has been snooping around here recently, either. But Tanner told us about what happened in town today, so we're going to try to make regular passes."

Colton thanked him, and he walked away to join his partner. Tanner held up a hand in farewell. "Since everything's good here, I'm going to go back to Ingles and pick up where I left off." He dropped his hand and let it rest on Colton's shoulder. "I'll be circling up Hill-top every time I pass by, but if you need me, just call. I don't care if it's the middle of the night."

"Thanks." Without even asking, Colton knew Bryce would say the same thing. When he'd moved to Murphy at age fifteen, Bryce had been his first friend.

After Tanner left, Colton closed the gate and let Brutus back outside. When he joined Jasmine in the kitchen, one burner was on High, the other on Medium.

"As good as this smells, I'm hesitant to have this conversation, but I only hired you to be our bodyguard."

"No offense, but if I have to eat takeout once more, I'm going to scream."

Colton winced. He'd never been a great cook. Though he'd done some cooking for Liam before and after the trip to Montana, he'd tried to take pity on Jasmine.

She removed the lid from a pot and peeked inside. It was two-thirds full of water, a thin layer of oil pooled on the surface. Tiny bubbles collected at the bottom.

She put the lid back on, then stirred the contents of the other pot. Just as he'd guessed, spaghetti sauce.

"By the way, you owe me $42.67."

He lifted a brow. "For what?"

"Groceries."

Tension spiked through him. "You took Liam to the grocery store?"

"I took him to the park last Friday, too. And we took him to the art walk and to church and a number of other places. And I've taken him to day care every weekday for the past two weeks."

He released a pent-up breath. She was right. Leaving the house had become dangerous only an hour ago.

The water finally came to a boil, and she stirred in half a bag of pasta. When it had resumed boiling, she turned the burner down and faced him.

"Why warn you?"

"What?"

"The note. If someone really intended to kill you this afternoon, why put the note on your windshield?"

She had a point. "Do you think the shooter missed me on purpose?"

"I don't know. It just doesn't fit. Who warns their victims before attacking?"

Colton sank into one of the kitchen chairs, dread settling over him.

*Perez.*

That was his MO. He toyed with all of his victims—stalking and terrorizing them. The games sometimes went on for weeks. But they always ended the same.

Perez was locked up. For life. No chance of parole.

But it didn't matter. He had thugs to do his bidding—two brothers, according to what Jasmine had learned. He'd see to it that they followed his pattern, so there'd be no doubt about who was behind every attack.

Colton had fought with every bit of legal expertise he had to secure a death sentence for Perez.

Instead, he'd secured his own.

He was on Perez's hit list.

And no one made it off alive.

Jasmine stalked from the kitchen into the living room, heading toward the front door. She'd already been outside a half dozen times to circle the yard, scan the woods and look up and down the road. Each time she'd seen nothing but a rural mountain neighborhood—safe, quiet and still.

Even though it was Sunday, they hadn't left the house. The past two weekends, Colton had insisted on taking Liam to church. Which meant she'd had to go, too. So she'd alternated between watching from the back of the sanctuary and patrolling outside the building.

This afternoon, Colton was viewing the service online. And she was doing almost as well avoiding it as she'd done the past two weeks.

Nothing against MountainView Community Church in particular. The people were friendly, the music inspiring and the pastor's message engaging. But she didn't do church. For good reason.

While she'd stood in the back listening to the band play and the attendees sing, something had tugged at her. She'd looked away several times, but the song lyrics projected on the screen up front kept drawing her gaze back.

Too many spoke of an intimate God, a God who so wanted a personal relationship with His creation that He sent His son to earth in the form of a baby.

The Christmas story had never bothered her before. Of course, she'd never taken the time to fully analyze its meaning. Now that she was doing that, she found the whole idea disconcerting. If she wasn't careful, the messages of those songs and the pastor's words were going to upend her long-held beliefs.

On her way to the front door, she cast a glance at Colton. He sat on the couch with Liam nestled against his side clutching his little rabbit. If it wasn't so close to nap time, Liam probably wouldn't be so content.

Colton tilted his head toward the empty spot next to him. "You can join us if you'd like."

"Thanks. But I'm going to check things outside again." She probably wouldn't see anything different from what she'd seen the first six times.

Colton had talked to her about his enemy Friday night. For the next days and weeks, the two of them were going to be continually on edge, waiting for Perez's next move. Meanwhile, all they could do was wait.

After a peek out the front window, she opened the door and slipped outside. For the indeterminable future, she was going to be stuck at the house. Colton was even pulling Liam out of day care.

Jasmine glanced around the yard, then headed down the steps. Brutus plodded toward her. He'd made her a little nervous when she'd first met him, just because of his sheer size. The way he'd lowered his ears and eyed her warily hadn't helped, either.

After that initial greeting, he'd moved her from the *foe* to the *friend* category. Or more likely, *unknown* to *friend*.

When Brutus reached her, she sat on the top step, which put her face even with his. She scratched his cheeks and neck, and his tail wagged.

"You like that?"

In response, the tail wagged harder. She sometimes felt sorry for him, roaming the yard alone. But that was the reason Colton had gotten him—for protection, not as a house pet.

Brutus bounded off, then returned to lay a partially chewed tennis ball at her feet. She picked it up, hoping the moisture was left over from this morning's rain rather than dog slobber. When she tossed the ball, Brutus took off after it, catching it in midair.

Her phone buzzed in her back pocket, notification of an incoming text. She smiled at the name on the screen. Dom was more than a coworker. He was a friend. She had a good relationship with all Burch Security bodyguards, but she'd always felt closest to Dom. He was the big brother she'd never had.

His text was short—Good time to call?

She texted back a yes.

Moments later her ringtone sounded. As soon as she answered, Dom's voice came through the phone, tough but with an edge of playfulness.

"How's the second-best security guard in all of America?"

She grinned. She was second best because he'd claimed the number one slot a long time ago. "Fine." She picked up Brutus's ball and tossed it again. "Enjoying the clean mountain air. This assignment is getting me out of the city."

"Good for you. I just finished mine. Boyfriend-turned-blackmailer. The client decided she was tired of paying out. I caught the creep trying to climb in her second-story bedroom window. He got a little surprise."

Jasmine's lips lifted in a wry smile. That surprise probably came in the form of Dom's fist. He'd always been protective of women, sometimes in an extreme, obsessive way. He'd almost gotten himself in trouble a few times.

Except for a six-year stint with the Marines, until moving to Atlanta, he'd lived in Massachusetts. Or "Mass," as he called it. The heavy New England accent just added to his tough-guy persona. He was one of only two men on the planet that she'd trust with her life. The other was Gunn.

"Don't know what's next. How's yours going?"

"Not sure. The guy's a district attorney, has made some enemies. One of them is going after him and his son."

"No wife in the picture?"

"No wife." Just a handsome, heartbroken father and a little boy who was touching her heart in a way no one else ever had. Oh, to have an assignment like Dom just finished—uncomplicated and unemotional.

She picked up the ball again. Brutus wasn't showing any signs of winding down. As he took off after it, a Silverado pickup drew to a stop outside the fence. This time Tanner's wife, Paige, was with him. Jasmine had met them both at church her first Sunday there, along with several of Colton's other friends.

She disconnected the call with Dom, then opened the gate and motioned them inside. When they'd parked, she closed the gate behind them.

While his wife exited the passenger's side, Tanner climbed out from behind the wheel. "We went out to eat at ShoeBootie's with Andi and Bryce. Figured we'd stop by here and check in with you guys on our way home."

Jasmine led them toward the house. "Colton will be glad to see you."

Tanner stepped onto the deck behind her. "Any more threats?"

"No. But it's only been two days."

When she swung open the door, Colton shut off the TV. "I thought I heard voices outside."

Soon Tanner was positioned on the love seat with

his arm around his wife, and Jasmine had taken a seat beside Colton.

Tanner crossed an ankle over the opposite knee. "I don't suppose there've been any new developments in the case."

Colton shook his head. "Not yet."

Liam climbed over his father to get into Jasmine's lap. She wrapped him in her arms and gave him a tight squeeze. When she glanced at Colton, conflicting emotions tumbled across his face. The concern she understood. When it came to his son, there was plenty to be concerned about.

She *didn't* understand the warmth. Or maybe she did and didn't want to acknowledge it. Somehow, it made her want to put distance between them, yet draw closer at the same time.

But accusation? As if she'd intentionally wormed her way into his son's heart?

She gritted her teeth. He'd said he didn't want his son getting attached to her. But she'd only been doing her job. Well, maybe comforting him during his nightmares fell a little outside of those job responsibilities.

But how could she deny him what she'd longed for at his age when it was within her power to give?

He slid from her lap and ran toward the kitchen. When he disappeared into his room, Colton crossed his arms, his gaze shifting to his friend. "The authorities in Atlanta have been working to identify the men responsible for the break-in and attempted kidnapping. I've had several conversations with them. My former administrative assistant has, too. We've given them the names of everyone we can think of who might want to exact some vengeance. They're also looking at recently released inmates, seeing if I was involved in any of their cases."

Tanner nodded. "From what I hear, Cherokee County is throwing in some of their resources now, too."

"Good," Colton said. "Since that note, Atlanta PD is putting special focus on one defendant in particular. We wrapped up his case the week before Mandy died. At that time, he made some pretty serious threats."

"That was seven months ago. Why wait till now to act?"

"Four weeks after he made his threats, I left for Montana. Then I was back home only a week before coming up here."

Tanner pursed his lips. "The reference to you running."

"My thoughts exactly. Ransacking my house, trying to take my son, leaving threatening notes that let me know he's watching—that's his style. He stalks his victims, making them almost crazy with fear before he finally takes them out."

Liam returned to the room holding his stuffed rabbit. This time he made a beeline for Paige, whose face lit with a broad smile. She obviously loved kids. The boy lifted his arms, the rabbit dangling from one hand, and she dragged him onto her lap. When he snuggled against her chest, she rocked him back and forth.

Colton nodded toward his son. "I'm pulling him out of day care. I think it'll be easier for Jasmine to protect him if he stays here in the house. But I have to hire a babysitter. Jasmine needs to be free to patrol without distractions."

He rose and began to pace. "After my last babysitter ended up bound and gagged in the closet, I'm a little hesitant. I still haven't come up with a solution."

Paige wrapped her hand around one of Liam's. "I can do it. At least until the next term starts."

Tanner stared her down, a tic in his jaw. "Colton knows I'd do almost anything for him, but putting my wife in danger is where I draw the line."

Paige shifted her position to face him more fully. "It sounds like the creep is still in the stalking stage."

"He tried to kidnap Liam." Exasperation filled Tanner's tone.

"Now Liam has a bodyguard. And in case you've forgotten, I can pretty well hold my own."

"Two wom—" Tanner cut himself off midphrase, apparently second-guessing the opinion he was about to express.

Paige sighed. "Look, it's only during the day, while Colton is at work. Won't you guys and Cherokee County be doing some drive-bys anyway?"

"Occasionally." Tanner still didn't look happy. "What about in between times?"

"There are still two lines of defense—Brutus and Jasmine."

"What if someone shoots her?"

Jasmine lifted her brows.

"Sorry, but it's a possibility."

"I'll be wearing Kevlar."

She was stating a fact, not taking sides. She wasn't sure whose side to take in the argument. She tended to agree with Paige, that Perez, or whoever, was still in the stalking stage.

Colton was right about needing to hire a babysitter. She couldn't effectively do her job if all her attention was on watching Liam. Paige was as good a choice as anyone. Probably better. Jasmine didn't know anything about her background, but that statement about being able to hold her own was encouraging.

When Tanner and Paige left a short time later, Liam climbed back onto Jasmine's lap. Colton patted his son's back.

"Okay, buddy, it's nap time."

Liam wrapped his little arms around her waist and squeezed. "No."

"How about if Miss Jasmine puts you to bed?"

He was silent for several moments, as if thinking about his answer. "'Kay."

Colton helped her to her feet, Liam still wrapped around her. After laying him on his side in his bed, she positioned the rabbit in his arms, then rubbed his back for several moments. "Sleep good."

His thumb slipped into his mouth, and she straightened. Colton stood leaning against the chest of drawers next to the door, arms crossed. His posture said *restrained*, maybe even a little defensive.

But that was not what his eyes said. His gaze was warm, filled with admiration. Something else, too. As if he was looking at her, not simply as his son's protector. But as a woman.

She swallowed hard. She was seeing what she wanted to see. She'd found Colton attractive right from the start. Cade, too, since their looks were identical. But Colton's depth and seriousness appealed to her far more than Cade's flippancy.

Her eyes shifted to the framed portrait sitting atop the dresser. The perfect happy family—successful husband and father, beautiful wife and mother, sweet child, the product of their love.

She didn't belong in that picture. Even with Mandy gone, that empty slot was one she could never hope to fill.

She strode toward the door. When her gaze met Colton's, whatever she thought she'd seen was gone.

"I'm going outside." This time she'd stay out for a while, throwing the ball for Brutus, circling the yard however many times she had to. Whatever it took, she'd crush the feelings Colton stirred in her and end this longing for something she could never have.

She stepped onto the deck, again envious of Dom's easy assignment. But no matter how difficult this one was turning out to be on a personal level, something told her she was exactly what Liam needed at this point in his life.

As far as Liam's handsome father, she didn't know what he needed.

But she was pretty sure she didn't have it.

# SIX

A terrified scream pierced the quiet.

Colton clawed his way to consciousness. The shriek that had jarred him awake wasn't the first. There'd been at least one other. It hovered in the back of his mind, like the remnant of a dream.

He sprang from the bed and darted into the living room. Why hadn't he come instantly awake? He certainly wasn't letting down his guard.

Or maybe he was, on a subconscious level. Maybe after six months of middle-of-the-night screams, having someone else to ease the burden was working its way into his psyche. Knowing Jasmine never let down her guard, he was slowly letting down his, at least in sleep.

When he shot through Liam's open door, Jasmine was sitting in the rocking chair, already holding him. Brutus lay nearby. Yesterday morning's rain had ushered in a cold front. With temperatures expected to dip near freezing, Colton hadn't had the heart to leave him outside.

He knelt in front of the chair to cup his son's head. Except for some quiet whimpers, he was still. "You okay, buddy?"

Liam drew in a shuddering breath through his nose,

not willing to give up the security of his thumb. His free arm was stretched along Jasmine's side.

When Colton had first met her, he'd pegged her as not the motherly type. He'd obviously been wrong.

He glanced behind him to check the digital clock on the dresser—5:12. His own alarm would be going off in another forty-five minutes. It wouldn't be worth trying to go back to sleep. "Sorry about the short night."

"No problem. I was awake anyway." Her voice was a soft murmur.

He matched her tone. Liam seemed to be going back to sleep. "You've said that before."

"I sleep in bursts. I've never required a lot."

Maybe she didn't, but she probably needed more than she got. She'd likely just conditioned her body to function well in a continuously sleep-deprived state.

"You should try to work in another burst before daylight."

She gave him a half smile. "I might do that."

He'd get ready for work, have his quiet time, then whip up some breakfast. He wasn't a great cook, but he made some mean scrambled eggs. And he could usually manage toast without burning it.

He leaned back to sit on the floor, giving his knees a break. "I appreciate what you're doing for him. You're really good with him."

"I don't mind. He's an easy kid to love." She closed her eyes and placed a soft kiss on the top of his head.

Colton's heart swelled. Watching Jasmine play a motherly role, treating Liam with such tenderness, did funny things to his insides. He was still having a hard time reconciling the tough ex-MP who put him on the floor in Gunter Burch's office with the gentle woman whose presence was bringing such healing to his son.

God had brought her into their lives. When Colton had walked into Burch Security, he'd known what he wanted—a burly monster of a guy no one would mess with. Instead, God gave him five-foot-two-inch Jasmine, tough as nails but with an unexpected gentleness, sympathetic with their struggles because she'd had plenty of her own.

When Jasmine opened her eyes, her gaze locked with his and held. Something he couldn't put a name to passed between them. He'd seen it yesterday, too, when they'd put Liam down for his nap—a hint that she might need them as much as they needed her. Then she'd looked away, walked from the room and escaped outside.

She continued her gentle rocking motion. "You're an amazing father. I know it's got to be tough."

He nodded. He wouldn't try to downplay what he'd been through. Trying to keep his son from retreating completely while drowning in his own grief. Struggling to be both father and mother and feeling he was failing miserably at both.

Since she'd come, some of that overwhelming burden had lifted. Now her expressive brown eyes tugged at him. Encouragement and respect swam in their depths, along with the same sense of longing he'd briefly witnessed during those rare unguarded moments.

"I sense that you've been through your own traumas. I can see it in your eyes."

She shrugged, her eyes shifting sideways. "Everyone has their burdens to bear."

"And some burdens are especially heavy."

She pulled her lower lip between her teeth. For several

moments, the only sound was the gentle creak of the rocking chair. When she finally spoke, she didn't look at him. "His name was Zach, one of the few guys I ever loved."

Silence stretched between them again. "We were stationed together in Afghanistan. It was early in the morning. Everyone was getting ready to start their day. Someone shouted 'Incoming.' Then total chaos. Zach was hit. He died in my arms."

Colton rested a hand on her knee. "I'm sorry."

She shrugged again. "I think Liam's asleep."

Colton wasn't surprised at the abrupt subject change. "I'll put him back in bed."

When he tried to lift Liam from her lap, the boy pulled his thumb from his mouth. That arm joined the other to partially circle Jasmine's body, and he tightened his hold.

"Mommy."

The single word was barely audible. But it left Colton with the sensation that someone had thrown a bucket of ice water in his face.

Jasmine's reaction was the same. Her lips parted, and her brows drew together. He might have even seen panic flash in her eyes.

Colton turned away, trying to rein in his emotions. Maybe Liam was remembering his mother, pretending that was who held him. Or maybe he'd already made the substitution in his mind. If the latter, memories of Mandy would quickly fade. Maybe they would anyway.

His gaze locked on the framed eight-by-ten photograph atop the dresser. It sat in shadow, barely touched by the soft glow of the night-light.

But he didn't need light to see the picture clearly in his mind. It had been taken at Christmastime a year ago, the last professional one they'd had done. Mandy was hugging a laughing Liam, her eyes shining with love and joy.

She'd loved their son more than life itself. Colton couldn't let Liam forget her. He had to help him hang on to her memory as long as possible. He just didn't know how.

There was rustling behind him as Jasmine rose and a soft creak when she placed Liam in his bed.

Colton swallowed hard and spoke without turning around. "I'll wake you up well before I have to leave."

Even as he spoke the words, he knew he wouldn't have to. No matter how rough the night, Jasmine never slept past sunup.

He left the room and returned to his own. He was having to rely on Bryce for a ride to work. But tonight he'd have his vehicle back. Curtis Home & Auto Glass had the windshield and window replacements scheduled for today.

After dressing, he slipped his wallet and keys into his pocket, then picked up his phone. Sometime during the night, two texts had come through. He touched the icon. Both were from the same unknown number.

His chest tightened. Who would text him in the middle of the night from an unknown number?

He touched the screen again to bring up the messages. The first was short—Sleeping well? The simple question held a sinister undertone.

The second text was an all-out threat—Instead you should be watching your back.

He struggled in a constricted breath, the sense of being watched so powerful it almost paralyzed him. He'd had the same personal cell number for years. It was private, known only to friends and family.

But Perez had a long reach, with control over people

in high places. And he used those connections to strike terror into the hearts of his victims.

Colton spurred his legs to action, his phone still gripped in one white-knuckled fist. He needed to wake up Jasmine so she could be alert and armed. Or maybe they should all get in the Highlander and run.

Outside Liam's room, he skidded to a stop. He needed to get a grip. He knew Perez well enough to know how he worked. When he was ready to strike, it would be without warning.

When Brutus plodded into the kitchen, Colton led him to the front and disarmed the alarm. After letting the dog out, he started the coffeepot. He'd nurse his two cups while enjoying his morning prayer and Bible reading. Then he'd make breakfast.

Paige would be arriving around the time he'd have to leave. The thought sent conflicting emotions tumbling through him—guilt over allowing his friend to put herself in possible danger, and relief that she'd be here backing up Jasmine.

Paige was right. She could hold her own. He hadn't seen her in action, but he'd heard enough stories to know she wasn't bluffing.

He added some flavored creamer to his coffee and headed into the living room. Before moving to his favorite chair, he stepped on the floor switch at the other end of the room, and the lights blanketing the Christmas tree's branches woke up. He didn't know about Jasmine, but Liam was enjoying the tree. Colton was, too. The decorations lent warmth and cheer to the house, qualities that were augmented by Jasmine's presence.

He settled into his chair and clicked on the floor

lamp. His Kindle sat on the end table next to him, but his Bible reading would wait a few minutes.

Tipping back his head and closing his eyes, he thanked God that Paige would soon be on her way over.

And he thanked God for sending Jasmine.

Both to protect him and his son and to help them heal.

And since God had sent her, he asked Him to also help them pick up the pieces when it was time for her to leave.

Pleasant aromas drifted into the room, and Jasmine opened her eyes. Light seeped in around the Captain America curtains, too bright to be the first glimpse of daybreak.

She bolted upright with a gasp, searching out the clock. It was just past 7:30. Liam was still asleep, curled on his side with one thumb in his mouth, his other arm wrapped around his little rabbit. The bedroom door was closed. Colton must have shut it so he wouldn't disturb her.

After gathering a change of clothes, along with her vest and holster, she eased the door open. The scent of breakfast hit her full force. Colton stood in front of the stove, pushing scrambled eggs around a skillet with a wooden spoon. Contents of another pot simmered on the small back burner. Several pieces of fried bacon sat on a paper-towel-lined plate.

Jasmine leaned against the doorjamb, not ready to announce her presence. She was used to the professional Colton, dressed in a suit, heading out to continue his fight for justice. And she'd seen him in the role of father numerous times.

But watching the domestic Colton move about the kitchen preparing breakfast for her and his son warmed her inside. The problem with that warmth was how longing always followed, the desire for things that were out of her reach. At least with the man in front of her.

"Brutus is outside?"

Colton turned, brows lifted in surprise. "I let him out as soon as I got up."

"I'm getting dressed, then taking a look around before breakfast."

"Be careful." He laid down the spoon and pulled his phone from his pocket.

She hesitated. There was a stiffness to his movements. "Is everything okay?"

Instead of answering, he touched the screen a couple times and handed her the phone.

She skimmed the words, her tension increasing with each one. "You should have woken me up."

"I started to, then decided to let you get your rest." He returned to his breakfast preparations. "He's still playing with me. If this is Perez, that's how he works. He's an expert in fear and manipulation."

"It's disconcerting he has your cell number."

Leaving Colton in the kitchen, she headed toward the bathroom off the side of the living room. It was a full bath rather than a partial, but instead of a tub/shower combo, it had one of those small walk-in shower units. But it was her own space. Much more comfortable than sharing the larger master bath with Colton.

Two minutes later, she emerged dressed in jeans, boots and a sweater, her bulletproof vest hidden beneath and her holster affixed to her belt. She crossed the living room and looked out one of the front windows. From her vantage point, no one was there. All was still under a gloomy, gray sky. Brutus was apparently around one of the sides or in the back. As she watched, a gust swept through, blowing dead leaves across the yard.

She lifted her heavy coat from the hook by the door, slipped into it and walked outside, locking the door behind her. After scanning her surroundings, she moved down the steps. Before she reached the bottom, Brutus appeared at the corner of the house, body rigid with tension. He immediately relaxed and bounded up to her.

She bent to pet him. She wasn't letting down her guard, but if anyone was out there, Brutus would have let her know. He seemed to share her constant state of alertness. She straightened. Her rounds would be abbreviated this morning, since Colton would be ready for breakfast once he'd gotten Liam up.

She released a sigh. She'd told Colton that Liam was an easy kid to love. That was exactly what had happened. She'd fallen in love with the sad little boy.

But she was trying hard to keep her distance from Liam's handsome, hurting father, no matter how much her heart wanted to do otherwise. Colton and Liam needed stability, something she would never be able to provide.

Her own history proved it. From her mom's string of boyfriends who screamed curses and slapped her around to her own failed relationships, anything more than friendship never turned out well. Even her latest. Although she'd loved Zach, she'd had to admit that her relationship with him wasn't much less dysfunctional than the others.

Colton deserved better. Someday, someone as amazing as Mandy would walk into his life. When that happened, she hoped he'd be ready. For both his sake and Liam's.

She moved toward the side, gaze scanning the mix of evergreens and mostly bare hardwoods that made up the scenery there. As she did her rounds, Brutus walked beside her.

This assignment was turning out to be a mistake, all the way around. Colton had feared that his little boy would get attached to her. He'd done what he could to make sure that didn't happen, enrolling him in day care and taking care of Liam himself evenings and weekends.

Unfortunately, it hadn't worked. And early this morning, Liam had called her Mommy. Instead of finding the name endearing, she'd felt like she'd been punched in the gut. Colton had turned away, but not before she'd seen the hurt on his face.

During her time in the Gale household, she'd watched Liam take small steps and slowly reengage with his surroundings. In trying to help the little boy heal, she'd thought she was doing a good thing.

Now she knew better. In the end, her involvement would do more harm than good.

Over the past two and a half weeks, Liam had already started viewing her as a mother figure. No matter what she and Colton did, he was only going to get more attached. When the assignment ended, he'd find his little world shattered for a second time.

She followed the back fence, Brutus still walking next to her. Breakfast could wait a few more minutes. She needed to call Gunn. Dom was finished with his assignment. Although he wasn't ideal for this one, he was a better choice than she was.

Jasmine sighed. She'd never given up on a job, no matter how difficult. She wasn't a quitter. But this was different. She'd been fighting her attraction toward Colton almost from the moment she'd met him. And she was losing the battle.

But it was more than that. A child's emotional health was at stake.

She glanced at the house. Colton had opened the curtains over the sink and now stood framed in the window, watching her. He lifted a hand, and she waved back. Her heart squeezed.

When she turned the corner to head toward the front, she pulled her phone from her pocket and brought up Gunn's cell number. He answered on the second ring.

She skipped the pleasantries. "I'm the wrong person for this job. You need to put Dom on it."

"Two and a half weeks ago, you showed Mr. Gale you were the *right* person for the job. Did something change?"

"It's not Colt—Mr. Gale. It's his son."

"You're letting a three-year-old run you off?" Gunn's tone held barely restrained humor.

She heaved an exasperated sigh. "It's not like that at all. Liam is precious."

"And what about his father?"

"He's...fine." Several other adjectives flitted through her mind, but she wasn't about to pass any of those along to Gunn. If her former commander had any inkling of the feelings she was developing for her client, she'd never hear the end of it.

Gunn was only twelve years her senior, but too often, he tried to slip into a father role. He'd been there when Zach was killed and over the following months had helped her come to grips with it. She owed him a lot.

But as well as he knew her, sometimes he was totally off base. Just because he'd been happily married for most of his adult life didn't mean she was cut out for a stable relationship.

She pulled her thoughts from Colton and focused

on his son. "Less than seven months ago, Liam lost his mother. Now he's getting attached to me." She paused, closing her eyes. "He called me Mommy."

"You're worried that the boy is getting attached to you, but it sounds like that's already happened. What does his father think?"

"He hasn't said."

"And he hasn't spoken with me, either. If he's worried about it, he'll give me a call. Until then, I think you might be exactly where you need to be."

She tightened her hand around the phone. Gunn was probably thinking he'd found her a ready-made family. Another example of him believing he knew what was best for her when he had no clue.

"You're not old enough to be my father, so stop trying to act like one."

The clipped tone obviously didn't annoy her boss. Instead of a reprimand, she got good-natured laughter. She reached the end of the front fence and headed toward the house. Beside her, Brutus stiffened, then shot away.

"Gotta run." She ended the call with Gunn and hurried after the dog, weapon drawn.

Brutus had stopped at the back fence and stood staring into the woods. The hair on his back was raised, and a low growl rumbled in his chest.

"What is it, boy? Do you see something?"

She scanned the woods, but whatever he'd seen was gone.

Finally, Brutus relaxed. Jasmine had just started to walk away when a loud rustle sounded nearby. She spun, swinging her weapon around. Two squirrels chased each other along the outside of the fence and up a nearby pine.

She released a nervous laugh, scratching the back

of Brutus's neck. "We're going into fight mode over a couple of squirrels."

She shook her head and walked toward the house. When she entered the kitchen, Colton already had Liam dressed and in his high chair and was dishing up their plates. He turned and gave her a half smile that was in direct conflict with the worry in his eyes. "Everything okay out there?"

"Yeah. Brutus's meltdown was nothing more than a couple of squirrels playing."

After an especially somber breakfast, Colton disappeared into the master bedroom, then returned ready for work, blond hair combed into soft layers. He'd already been wearing his suit pants and long-sleeved dress shirt. Now a jacket and tie completed the ensemble.

Her heart stuttered. It wasn't just his good looks. It was the whole scenario—the man of the house heading off to work to provide a stable home for his family.

He approached the table, then bent over the high chair to hug and kiss his son. Suddenly she wanted one, too—a hug or a kiss. Or both.

Instead, she got a wave and a caution to be careful.

A horn tooted outside and Colton crossed the living room to peer out the front window. "Bryce is here. Paige should be arriving any minute, but I'm still going to close the gate behind me."

"Sounds good. She'll let herself in."

Jasmine spooned the last of the grits into her mouth. When Liam finished, she took him down from the high chair and wiped his hands. Sudden barking set her nerves on edge. Her hand stilled, Liam's fingers still wrapped inside the washcloth. She straightened, every sense on alert.

Brutus wasn't letting her know Paige had arrived. Paige would be stopping at the front gate. Brutus was in the back. Maybe what he'd seen before had been a real threat and not simply squirrels.

She moved to the kitchen sink and peered past the edge of the curtain, which Colton had closed. Brutus stood at the back fence staring into the woods. His head and body jerked in time with the barks. He fell silent for several seconds, then resumed the ferocious barking. Judging from his stiff stance, and the way the fur stood up on the back of his neck, the periods between rounds of barking were probably filled with deep-throated growls.

From her vantage point, she couldn't see anything suspicious. Other than a highly agitated dog. And she couldn't go out to investigate. Not with Liam inside the house alone.

Letting the curtains fall, she moved into the living room. She'd heard Colton lock the dead bolt with his key but couldn't ignore the compulsion to double-check. When that was done, she headed back to the kitchen, then into Liam's room. His window offered the same view as the kitchen one, just a slightly different angle. Whatever Brutus was barking at, she couldn't see it from inside the house.

Where was Paige? She was supposed to arrive close to the time Colton left. Of course, it *was* close to the time Colton left. He hadn't been gone more than five minutes.

When she turned from the window, Liam was standing in the doorway.

"Legos?" His voice sounded so sweet. Knowing his history, every word he spoke warmed her heart.

"Sure, sweetie. You can play with your Legos."

He picked up the plastic bin and poured its contents onto the bedroom floor. She didn't know what he planned to make, and she wasn't going to stay there long enough to find out.

"I'm going to see if Miss Paige is here yet. Call me if you need me, okay?"

Liam didn't look up from his activities. "Okay."

She stepped back into the kitchen. Brutus was still barking. It didn't sound like he'd changed positions, either. The barking was reassuring. If someone came into the yard, he'd just attack. So whoever had him in such an uproar was still outside the fence. And he apparently didn't have a tranquilizer dart.

She moved into the living room and peered out one of the front windows. The gate was ajar. Colton would have closed it. And Paige would open it fully so she could park her vehicle in the driveway. Instead, it was open about two feet—just enough for someone to slip through.

Was the commotion in the back a decoy, a way to draw Brutus to the rear fence while someone accessed the house from the front?

Jasmine reset the alarm and put her hand on her weapon. She hadn't drawn it yet, because she hadn't wanted to startle Liam. But she was alert and ready.

She scanned the yard, looking for signs of movement. There were plenty of hiding places. Like behind that huge hemlock. But intruders wouldn't be able to get to the front door without her seeing them. If they broke a window, she'd hear the glass shatter.

She leaned closer to the windowpane. Paige suddenly shot out from behind the hemlock and sprinted the few yards to the driveway. She ran around the Suburban and disappeared from view.

Jasmine disarmed the alarm, then swung open the door and stepped onto the deck, weapon drawn. A man sprang to his feet on the other side of the SUV. A ski mask hid his face, but the eyes peering through the holes were wide.

A second later, Paige was on him, fists swinging. Though the guy tried to block her punches, several found their mark.

Jasmine raised her weapon. "Hands in the air, or I'll shoot."

The intruder spun and ran toward the fence. Three steps later, Paige tackled him, and they both disappeared from view, the vehicle blocking them.

Jasmine hesitated. The man Paige had tackled wasn't the only threat. Someone else was in back. Maybe they intended to lure her away from the house so Liam would be unprotected.

It wasn't going to work. As concerned as she was for Paige's safety, she wasn't going to abandon her responsibility to Colton's little boy.

Several seconds passed before she realized that Brutus had stopped barking. Except for some thumps and grunts from the other side of the vehicle, the morning was eerily quiet.

When the man rose, his mask was cockeyed. But Jasmine didn't get a good look at him. He again made a beeline for the fence.

Paige charged off after him, and Brutus resumed barking, louder and closer. He appeared around the side of the house as the man slung himself over the top rail of the fence. Paige grabbed his leg, but he slipped through her grasp and disappeared into the woods. When she made her way around the Suburban, she was limping.

Jasmine frowned. "You're hurt." It was amazing she wasn't dead. Whatever had possessed her to attack someone half again her size?

"I'm all right." She motioned toward the road. "I need to bring my car into the yard."

Jasmine glanced that direction, but the hemlock blocked the view of whatever she'd driven.

Paige continued. "As I was coming up on Colton's place, the creep was walking along the other side of your car. Then he squatted down. I pulled off the road, slipped through the gate and tackled him." She frowned. "I think I got to him before he had a chance to do anything, but I'm going to look at your brake lines to be sure."

"You're a mechanic, too?" Nothing would surprise her at this point.

She shrugged. "I've picked up bits and pieces over the years, enough to recognize if brakes have been tampered with."

Paige went to retrieve her vehicle, and Jasmine headed back inside to call 911 and check on Liam. She unclipped her phone from her belt, then picked up Colton's cordless instead. She'd had one bar. Her signal was better outside than inside.

While she waited for her 911 call to connect, she stood in Liam's doorway. He fished through the colorful pile on his floor and picked up a rectangular piece. "This one."

She smiled. He was even starting to talk to himself. A good sign, something she'd share with Colton when he got home.

Leaving Liam to his play, she moved to the front of the house. When she finished relaying everything to the 911 dispatcher, she stepped onto the deck. A Dodge Charger sat in the drive. Paige was limping toward the opposite side of the Suburban, favoring the injured leg. She disappeared, rose a half minute later, then disappeared again.

As she walked back around, she made a fist, thumb raised. "So far, so good."

She again lowered herself to the ground, gripping the front wheel well for support. Jasmine shook her head. Tanner wasn't going to be happy with either of them.

Once she'd checked the rear, she straightened. "Everything's fine."

Jasmine released a pent-up breath. If Paige hadn't come when she had…

The commotion in the back was definitely a decoy, something to distract the dog and get Jasmine to focus her attention behind the house. She wouldn't fall for that ploy again.

Paige followed her inside and sank onto the couch.

Jasmine stared down at her, hands on her hips. "I don't know whether to scold you or thank you."

Paige shifted position and winced. "How about neither?"

"You'd probably rather I don't say anything to Tanner, too."

"Yeah, that would be good."

Jasmine sat on the opposite end of the couch. "I was going to ask you what your superpower was. I don't think that's necessary now."

"My superpower?"

"You reminded Tanner you could hold your own, so I knew there's more to you than meets the eye."

Paige gave a sharp nod. "Street fighting. Hand-to-hand combat."

"You good with a gun?"

She shrugged. "Not bad."

"Did you bring one?"

"Can't."

Jasmine cocked a brow, but Paige didn't explain.

"How long have you and Tanner been together?" She'd give Paige a reprieve for now. But that didn't mean she wouldn't circle back to the topic before the end of the day. If the woman was going to be around Colton and Liam, it was her job to know what secrets she harbored.

"Married eight months. Dated almost two years before that." Paige gave her a crooked smile. "Took me a while to give in and take the plunge."

Liam padded into the room, his stockinged feet almost silent against the hardwood floor. "Water, peez."

"Sure, sweetie." Her response came in unison with Paige's.

Paige held up a hand. "I'm the babysitter, remember?"

Jasmine nodded. "I'll be outside."

She'd make her rounds until the police arrived, then take over the babysitter role while Paige came out and talked to them.

After scanning the front yard through one of the windows, she opened the door and stepped onto the deck. For the next ten minutes, she walked the yard, studying the woods beyond the fence. The man who'd run from Paige had trampled down underbrush and kicked up leaves in his rush to escape. Whoever had had Brutus in an uproar hadn't left so obvious a trail.

Approaching sirens drew her eyes to the road. An emergency vehicle was making its way up Hilltop. She opened the gate and flagged in a Cherokee County sheriff cruiser.

The uniformed deputy stepped out and introduced himself. "You called about someone tampering with a vehicle?"

"I did." She relayed what little she'd witnessed. "But the lady you really need to speak with is inside."

She jogged to the house and sent Paige out. When she checked on Liam, he'd returned to his Legos. He looked up at her, and his mouth lifted in a smile. "Movie?"

"Which one do you want to see?"

*"Cars."*

Two minutes later, she'd located the DVD and had the credits rolling. As soon as she laid the remote on the coffee table, a small hand slipped into hers.

"You want me to watch it with you?"

He nodded. When she sank onto the couch, he climbed up next to her. She put her arm around him, and he snuggled against her side.

She closed her eyes and dipped her head, breathing in his strawberry-scented shampoo. Her chest tightened in a combination of love and longing.

This was precisely the reason she'd tried so hard to get Gunn to reassign her. Whatever he was trying to do, it was likely to turn out poorly for both her and Liam.

When a soft knock sounded sometime later, she rose to let Paige in.

Paige locked the door behind her. "I closed and latched the gate."

"Good. I don't suppose the deputy found anything."

"No. He headed into the woods the same direction the guy had gone, then came back a few minutes later. Didn't see anything. The other one found where it looked like someone had tromped through the woods in the back, but didn't find anyone there, either."

Paige returned to her babysitting duties, and Jasmine stepped back outside. After spending the morning alternating between patrolling the yard and checking on things inside, she sat down to grilled ham-and-cheese sandwiches Paige had prepared.

"Thanks for lunch." She picked up her sandwich, still hot from the griddle. "So, what are we keeping you from? What do you normally do with your days?"

"I'm taking classes at the community college, but as of today, I'm on Christmas break."

"What are you studying?"

"My Gen Eds now, but next term I'll start education classes. I'm working toward getting my teaching certificate."

"I didn't think you could teach school if you were a felon."

"Who said I was a felon?"

"You did, but not in so many words."

Paige shrugged. "That was another lifetime."

"Considering you're married to a cop and are a regular church attender, I gathered as much."

Paige gave her a half smile. "Back to the teacher question, it depends on the felony. I never killed or molested anyone." The smile widened. "Although I was tempted to run that creep's head into the ground this morning." She sobered and a fierceness entered her eyes. "Thinking about anyone threatening Liam just about makes me lose it."

Jasmine nodded. She liked Paige. Tough and no-nonsense. She was a good one to have around.

She'd told Tanner she could hold her own.

After watching her this morning, Jasmine agreed wholeheartedly.

# SEVEN

Colton stepped from the courthouse under a steel-gray sky. The weather had been cold and dreary for the past two days.

But that wasn't the reason for his dark mood. When he'd gotten home yesterday evening, Jasmine had told him about the events of the morning. His enemies had been watching, waiting until he left and Jasmine was alone with Liam.

It all about drove him nuts—waiting for the next strike, unable to predict when or where it was going to happen.

He didn't do well with helplessness. It had been a constant companion through most of his childhood as he'd been shuffled from one foster home to the next. He'd thought that once he became an adult, he'd never feel helpless again.

But it wasn't a malady reserved for unwanted children. For the past six months, he'd suffered through more than his fair share, at a loss as to how to help his son and defenseless against the grief that threatened to drown them both.

Last night, he'd taken out his fear and frustration on

Jasmine, demanding to know why she hadn't called him immediately. She'd stood her ground, and she'd been right. There'd been no reason to intrude into his workday. No one was hurt, and there was nothing he could have done anyway.

He hurried through the parking lot, glancing around him. Next on the agenda was a trip to the grocery store, with Tanner accompanying him. According to Tanner's text, he was already there, probably inspecting the Highlander.

Colton had gotten it back yesterday afternoon. Now it was parked at the rear of the courthouse next to the parking for the senior center. The area was open, with no trees for someone to hide behind.

When Colton approached, Tanner was lying next to the SUV, looking beneath. After Jasmine and Paige's experience, they'd all agreed—no cranking vehicles without first checking them.

Tanner rose. "So far, so good."

As he circled around to the front, Colton's phone rang. He frowned. Cade was calling. Three days had passed since the last warning. Apparently, it was time for another one.

Colton put the phone to his ear and greeted his twin. Cade's "how are you?" seemed to hold more meaning than the three words usually did.

"We're all fine. How is your trip going?"

"Could be better. I've been looking for a particular piece. Everything similar seems to be locked away in someone's private collection."

"I'm sure you'll find what you're looking for." He always did.

Colton was smart, but he'd always had to work for

what he got. Cade was brilliant. Everything seemed to come easily to him, gift wrapped and delivered on a golden platter. He'd partied his way through college and still managed to maintain a 3.8 GPA.

And no one could deny that he was good at what he did. He had a knack for finding the deals and turning everything he touched to gold. Their adoptive father had always been able to make a nice profit, but Cade's success lately had been phenomenal.

Tanner finished his inspection and held up both thumbs.

Colton opened the driver door. "I've got to run. Tanner and I are getting ready to do some grocery shopping."

"You guys actually made plans to grocery shop together?" Cade released a throaty laugh. "That's as bad as some of the girls I've dated who won't go to the restroom without a friend."

Colton winced. "We're keeping Liam inside, and I'm trying to avoid going anywhere alone at night." In fact, if he hadn't had a midafternoon appointment across town, Tanner would have insisted on dropping him off in the morning and picking him up at the end of the day.

He stepped into the opening but didn't get in. "We've had some threats."

"What kind of threats?"

"Just random stuff." He didn't need to worry his brother. Colton almost laughed at the absurdity of the thought. Until two and a half weeks ago, it wouldn't have crossed his mind. He'd never seen Cade worry about anything.

"You've got to get Liam out of there." Cade spoke with urgency bordering on panic.

Colton sighed. So much for not worrying his brother. "I don't have anywhere to go. Even if those guys have found us, it's different now. Liam doesn't have a baby-sitter. He has a bodyguard."

Actually, he had both. And the babysitter could almost double as a bodyguard.

Colton ended the call. "Thanks for checking it out."

"No problem. It pays to be careful." Tanner's jaw tightened. "I have to admit, I spent most of my day off at your house."

Colton nodded. Tanner knew about someone tampering with Jasmine's car, but Paige probably hadn't told him she'd accosted the guy. And Colton wasn't about to spill any secrets. That was between Paige and Tanner. "Ready for that Ingles run?"

"Ready as I'll ever be. Swing around front, and I'll follow you."

Colton watched his friend head toward the steps leading down to Alpine and slid into the driver's seat. When he turned into Ingles's parking lot a short time later, the sky had darkened from gray to deep charcoal. He pulled into a space a short distance from one of the parking lot lights, and Tanner stopped next to him. By the time they finished their shopping, the darkness would be complete.

Colton snagged a cart and pulled out his cell phone. When he looked at his friend, Tanner had done the same thing.

Tanner held his up. "List from Paige."

He nodded. Jasmine had texted hers early that morning. At least Tanner was doing more than following him around the grocery store.

When they stepped back through the automatic doors a half hour later, each of their carts held four bags.

"That was relatively painless." Tanner's words held a touch of humor, but he didn't meet Colton's eyes. Instead, he scanned the parking lot, lines of concern on his face and tension radiating from him.

When they reached the SUV, Colton opened the back door.

Tanner passed him two of the bags. "Once we return the carts, I'm going to do a quick check of your vehicle again."

Colton nodded, his jaw tightening. It had been only four days since the note and the shot. Already that state of being constantly on guard was wearing on him.

When the last bag was loaded, he wheeled his cart toward the corral several spaces down, Tanner next to him. Away from the relative safety of his vehicle, a sense of vulnerability swept over him. Were his enemies out there somewhere, watching from the shadows?

He shook off the sensation. It was past dark, but the parking lot was well lit. It wasn't deserted, either. He wasn't the only one making an after-work stop before heading home.

He wheeled his cart between the parallel metal rails, then watched Tanner do the same. "Thanks for coming with me."

Tanner shrugged. "I had to come anyway. Besides, you're feeding me."

"Paige is feeding all five of us."

"With your food."

True. The ladies had planned it that morning, and Jasmine had informed him at lunchtime that they'd have company for dinner.

Tanner slid him a sideways glance. "Liam's starting to talk again."

"I know."

"Jasmine spent a lot of the day outside, but every time she came back in, Liam seemed to light up. I think she's good for him."

Colton gave him a sharp look. What was he getting at? "She's his bodyguard. Liam getting attached to her isn't a good thing, because once this is over—"

Tanner's eyes dipped downward several inches and widened in a momentary flash of panic. Colton's words stuck in his throat.

The next moment, his muscled six-foot-two-inch friend slammed into him, knocking him to the asphalt behind the Highlander. Pain stabbed through his wrist and elbow.

"What—" He couldn't move. Tanner was on top of him, the injured arm pinned beneath him.

The weight lessened, then was gone.

"Stay low." Tanner hissed the words. "Get between the vehicles and call 911."

Colton's thoughts were spinning, but he forced himself into a crawl. When he put pressure on his left hand, the pain in his wrist intensified, and his arm buckled. Definitely sprained.

He finished the short trek in an awkward one-armed crawl. His elbow was on fire. He sank back on his heels and cupped it with the opposite hand. When he drew it away, blood dotted his palm. His suit coat was probably history. So was the dress shirt. The pants were likely shot, too, because now that he thought about it, his left knee had started to throb.

He unclipped his phone from his belt and looked

for his friend. Tanner was positioned two feet away in a partial crouch, weapon drawn, peering through the Highlander's windows.

What had he seen?

No one had tried to shoot at them. There'd been no crack of gunfire, not even the *pfsst* of a weapon with a silencer.

Colton dropped his gaze to his phone. It looked undamaged. Good thing he carried it on the right. Otherwise it might not have fared so well.

"What am I reporting?" All he knew was one of his best friends had just tackled him.

"I'm pretty sure someone aimed a rifle at you. I saw the red light of the laser on your chest."

Strength drained from Colton's body, and he leaned against his vehicle. If he'd been alone, chances were good he'd be dead right now.

Or maybe he wouldn't. Whoever was out there took aim but didn't pull the trigger. Maybe leveling that laser on his chest was part of the terror, one more way to make him crazy before delivering the final blow.

The scenario fit Perez perfectly. Once he had a target, he never lost interest until he'd seen his plans through to completion. Being on the receiving end of Perez's wrath was like walking around with a bomb strapped to one's chest.

For Colton, the timer had been triggered. It had happened the moment the jury delivered the verdict. Colton had put it on pause during his time at his in-laws'.

But the moment he came back to Atlanta, the countdown had resumed. And now nothing could stop it. Perez was likely orchestrating the whole thing from inside the maximum-security facility where he'd spend the rest of his life.

Through his goons on the outside, Perez would keep toying with him until he grew bored or decided Colton's time was up.

Then it would be over.

The clock would click to zero and…

Boom!

Jasmine stepped from the front deck into Colton's living room. This was the third time in the past twenty minutes.

Paige wasn't doing any better. She was pacing the living room with a whimpering Liam in her arms.

Jasmine shut and locked the door. "Any improvement?"

"He's burning up." Paige jiggled him, and Liam cried harder.

"Bryce should arrive with Colton any minute." Since nothing on Colton's schedule was to take him away from his desk, Tanner had dropped him off at the courthouse that morning, then headed to the station with plans to pick him up at the end of the day. But Liam had changed that.

He'd been fine when he'd gotten up. By late morning, he'd started to feel a little warm. When he threw up his lunch, she'd called Colton. Tanner was still at work, but since Bryce's shift wouldn't start until later, he'd agreed to shuttle Colton home.

Jasmine started her own pacing. Over the past thirty minutes, Liam's temperature had risen even more. Once Colton arrived, he'd decide how to proceed. Two days had passed since the incident in the Ingles parking lot, and nothing had happened since. But leaving the house with Liam made them all much more vulnerable.

Jasmine stepped back outside. Brutus stood at the bottom of the deck steps, stiff and alert. He'd apparently picked up on her tension.

When Bryce's Sorento came into view, she hurried to open the gate. As soon as the vehicle stopped, Colton jumped out and ran for the house, an elastic bandage peeking out from one jacket sleeve. All he'd gotten out of Tuesday night's scare was a sprained wrist and some asphalt scrapes.

"How's Liam?" He threw the words over his shoulder.

She hurried after him. "Really uncomfortable. His temperature has gone up a half degree since I called you."

Paige opened the door, still holding Liam. She'd apparently been watching for Colton and Bryce's return, too.

Jasmine followed him inside, Bryce right behind her. When Colton reached his son, he cupped the boy's face with both hands. "Liam, look at Daddy."

Panic laced his tone. Jasmine understood why. Liam had stopped fussing. Instead, he was listless, his eyes unfocused.

Colton ran to Liam's room and returned with a child-size afghan. "We're going to the emergency room."

Paige hesitated. "Shouldn't we call an ambulance?"

"I'd rather have armed escort." He wrapped the blanket around his son and took him from Paige.

Bryce unclipped his phone as they headed out the door. By the time Colton had fastened Liam into his car seat in the Highlander, Bryce had finished his conversation.

"A Cherokee County unit is headed this way."

Paige climbed in next to Liam, and Colton slid into the driver's seat. "We'll meet up on the four-lane."

Jasmine moved toward her own vehicle, calling instructions to Bryce as she walked. "Can you close the gate, then bring up the rear?"

The situation wasn't ideal. She'd feel better if they'd waited for Cherokee County. But even though Bryce was off duty, he was armed. He'd guaranteed them of that before he'd gone to pick up Colton. Of course, she was, too.

At the end of Hilltop, traffic was clear in both directions. She followed Colton through the left turn onto 64. Or "the four-lane," according to the locals. Since it was the only four-lane road in all of Murphy, the name worked.

She finished the turn and accelerated, checking her rearview mirror. Bryce should catch up with them shortly. She hoped he wasn't a slow driver. Colton had almost hit the speed limit and was still accelerating.

On the right, A-1 Mini Storage came into view. An older model Sunfire sat at an angle, as if ready to pull out. She strained to see if the car was occupied, but the windows were too tinted.

She shot past, then cast repeated glances in her rearview mirror. The car eased onto 64 and accelerated. Soon it was gaining on her. Uneasiness trickled through her.

She moved into the left lane. She didn't want anyone to get too close to Colton's Highlander, but if there was a threat, she'd rather it be behind him than beside him.

When she checked again, a Sorento traveled some distance back. The Sunfire was gaining on her, but so was Bryce. *Please hurry.*

As the small car drew closer to Colton's vehicle, Jasmine squeezed the wheel more tightly. Maybe the other driver only wanted to get around her. She couldn't take that chance. She was traveling just off Colton's left rear quarter panel, the gap not large enough for another vehicle to fit between them.

The Sunfire disappeared from her rearview mirror and appeared in her side mirror. It was now only two or three car lengths from Colton's vehicle, close enough to be considered tailgating.

The other car's engine revved, and the vehicle surged forward. Jasmine glanced over her right shoulder, hoping she was facing a case of road rage rather than a killer.

The rear window lowered, and in the midafternoon sun, something metallic glinted. She did a double take, and her heart leaped into her throat.

The rear passenger held a pistol, and it was aimed at her.

She jammed on her brakes and jerked the wheel to the right. The crash of metal against metal reverberated through her vehicle, with the simultaneous explosion of the airbags. The impact set her spinning, tires making a shrill squeal that seemed to go on and on.

*Don't roll the car, don't roll the car.* She squeezed the wheel with every bit of strength she possessed, as if that would somehow keep all four tires on the pavement.

Over the top of the deflating airbags, trees whizzed past. She'd lost sight of the Sunfire. Colton's Highlander, too.

She slipped off the shoulder and bounced over the uneven surface, momentarily becoming airborne before hitting the ground with enough force to jar every bone in her body.

Through the front windshield, a stand of trees seemed to move toward her at lightning speed.

The next moment, her scream mingled with the sound of twisting metal and shattering glass.

Then everything fell silent.

Colton jammed on his brakes and pulled off the road, bouncing along the grassy shoulder until he came to a full stop. "Call 911. We need an ambulance."

He twisted in his seat to look at Liam. His eyes were closed. Was he asleep or unconscious?

"Make that two ambulances."

One would be for his son, the other for Jasmine. He didn't know her condition, but it didn't look good.

With his eyes on the road ahead of him, he hadn't seen the crash. But he'd heard it and looked in the mirror in time to watch the car that had been tailgating him disappear off the road and Jasmine's Suburban begin a series of donuts. Now her vehicle was sitting thirty or forty feet behind him where a copse of trees had brought it to an abrupt stop. It rested at an angle, the windshield and driver window shattered.

*God, please let her be okay. Please let Liam be okay.*

Paige ended the call with the dispatcher and reached for the door handle. "Stay with Liam. I'll check on Jasmine."

Colton reached into the back seat and took his son's hand. Liam stirred. Though his eyelids lifted halfway, he didn't make eye contact. Colton's chest tightened. *God, please bring the ambulance quickly.*

He wouldn't remove his son from the car seat until the men who'd attacked Jasmine were in custody. Which should be soon. An SUV had turned around at a break in the median, a strobing light on its dash.

Some distance behind Jasmine's Suburban, the vehicle that had tailgated him sat with its front end wrapped around a tree, steam rising from beneath its hood. Bryce had stopped behind it and was approaching slowly, weapon raised.

Colton released Liam's hand to put the Highlander in Reverse and ease backward. Paige had reached Jasmine's SUV and was giving the driver door several hard yanks. He couldn't see well through the shattered glass, but there hadn't been any signs of movement.

Jasmine's driver door finally creaked open a foot. Paige gave it another forceful pull and it swung back fully.

When Colton eased up next to the Suburban, his heart almost stopped. Jasmine was slumped forward, head resting against the steering wheel. Two rivulets of blood traced paths down the side of her face.

As he lowered the passenger window, Paige reached into the vehicle and pressed her fingers against Jasmine's throat. She was checking for a pulse. *Dear God, she can't be...*

A lump formed in his throat. Jasmine would say putting her life in danger was part of the job. But she'd done this for him and his son. If anything happened to her, he'd never forgive himself.

A distant squeal pierced the silence. Paige put a hand on Jasmine's shoulder and murmured something to her.

The soft timbre of her voice reached him, but not the words.

Colton killed the engine. When Jasmine lifted her head, he released a breath he hadn't realized he'd been holding. *Thank You, Lord.*

She rubbed the back of her neck, then stiffened. "Liam—"

"—is safe." Paige straightened. "You should stay put. There's an ambulance on the way."

"No." She released the seat belt and struggled to her feet. Once standing, she put a hand on her weapon and swayed. "I need to check on Liam."

"You need to sit." Paige grasped her arm and helped her into the Highlander's back seat.

Jasmine took Liam's hands in hers. "He needs a doctor. He's burning up."

"Help is on the way."

She leaned back against the seat, the tension draining out of her.

Colton studied her. Her head was cut and bleeding. She also likely had a concussion. But there apparently weren't any broken bones.

"What happened? Did he hit you?"

"I hit him…after I saw the passenger had a pistol pointed at me."

Colton's gut filled with lead. The gunman had intended to take out Jasmine to get to him.

A shout from Bryce drew Colton's attention toward the Sunfire. He still stood facing the car, his posture stiff, weapon trained on the man in the back seat. "Hands in the air."

For several tense moments, Bryce didn't move. Colton held his breath. He couldn't see into the car at that distance, but he had a good idea of what was going on. According to Jasmine, the man had aimed a pistol at her. That weapon was somewhere inside.

The sirens grew closer, and Colton looked toward town. Flashing blue lights appeared around a gentle bend in the road. Two ambulances trailed behind.

The sheriff cruiser flew past, then turned around at the first break in the median. After stopping behind the wrecked Sunfire, a deputy jumped out. Bryce gestured toward the rear driver's-side door, and the deputy swung it open, weapon pointed inside. After pulling a cloth from his back pocket, he reached in and removed a pistol.

When Colton looked at Jasmine again, her hands had fallen into her lap and her head was tipped back against the seat. Her eyes were closed.

"Hey, don't go to sleep."

She roused herself to look at him. It seemed to take a lot of effort.

"You've probably got a concussion." He glanced back up the four-lane, where the ambulances were completing their U-turn. "Help will be here in a minute."

"No, I don't need to go to the hospital. It's just a bump on the head." She touched the side of her face. When she saw blood smearing her palm, her eyes widened.

"You've got to go, let them check you out."

She touched her head again. "This is nothing. Head wounds always bleed profusely. A wet cloth and a couple of Band-Aids, and I'll be fine. I just need rest."

Colton heaved a sigh. He'd never gone head-to-head with Jasmine. She definitely had a stubborn streak.

"If you won't listen to me, maybe you'll listen to

someone else." He snatched his phone from his side and pulled up his contacts. Burch Security's administrative assistant answered after the first ring. A half minute later, Colton had Gunter Burch on the line.

After briefly relaying what had happened, he looked at Jasmine. "She got seriously whacked in the head and is insisting she's fine. I think she needs some tough love." He handed Jasmine his phone.

After a brief pause, Jasmine spoke. "Colton's exaggerating. I've got a few cuts, nothing that can't be remedied with some butterfly bandages." Another pause. "So I'll have a headache. I'm not confused. I know my name and my address and what day it is. I can even go into all kinds of detail about my overprotective boss, who's under the deluded assumption that he's been commissioned to play the role of my father."

Colton bit back a smile.

Finally, Jasmine heaved a sigh. "Okay, I'll get checked out."

She ended the call, then frowned at the phone before handing it back to him. "I hate hospitals."

"They'll just look at you, probably run some tests. They may not even keep you overnight."

"They'd better not."

She unfastened the straps on Liam's car seat and pulled him onto her lap. For several moments, she held him close, rubbing his back with one hand. Emergency medical personnel would soon take him away from her. One ambulance had stopped behind the Highlander and two paramedics were moving their direction. The other ambulance was parked near the Sunfire.

When Jasmine's gaze met Colton's, it held a softness he'd never seen. Her guard was down, every barrier crumbled. Emotion rushed through him with the force of a tidal wave.

She'd risked her life to save his and Liam's. She could have simply evaded the men, but slamming into them ensured they wouldn't be able to reach him and his son.

And he'd almost lost her.

A black hole opened up inside him. It was more than guilt, deeper than a feeling of responsibility.

He closed his eyes, trying to get a grip on his runaway emotions. This couldn't be happening. He couldn't be falling for his son's bodyguard.

The job was ending. The men who'd threatened them for the past three weeks were heading to the hospital for treatment, then straight to jail. It was time for Jasmine to go back to Atlanta and move on to her next assignment.

He tried to tell himself that was okay. He wasn't looking for someone to replace Mandy. If he was, it wouldn't be Jasmine. Not that she wouldn't make a great wife for someone. She would. But she wasn't his type.

He wasn't hers, either. Young and full of life, she'd probably go for someone more like his fun-loving brother.

He stepped from the vehicle to meet the paramedics. His mental arguments were logical. Persuasive.

Of course they were. That was his specialty. He could convince judges and sway jurors with his words.

But his own heart wasn't even listening.

# EIGHT

Jasmine stepped out the double doors of MountainView Community Church and squinted in the midday sunshine. Liam was in her arms, Colton behind her carrying their coats. The temperature had risen considerably since early that morning.

Liam was a different boy than he'd been three days earlier. He'd been treated in the emergency room, then released once his temperature had come down to a less scary level. He'd had a bad virus. Fortunately, it was the twenty-four-hour kind, or more like thirty-six hours. He'd gotten up yesterday morning ready to play between naps. This morning he'd insisted on going to church.

Her own emergency room visit hadn't gone as well as Liam's had. The doctor had been concerned about the possibility of a concussion and ordered a CAT scan. The cuts had needed nothing more than butterfly bandages. But the visit had evolved into an overnight stay, and it had been late in the day Friday before she'd been able to convince everyone she was fine.

Andi slipped a hand into Bryce's. "See you at our place in a few."

They'd talked yesterday about the seven of them,

Paige and Tanner included, having Sunday dinner in town, then decided instead to do a cookout at Bryce's. For the time being, everyone was remaining on alert. The men who'd threatened them on the highway were in custody. They weren't Perez's brothers, according to their identification. Of course, those names could be aliases.

After strapping Liam into his car seat, Jasmine climbed into the front. Colton cranked the engine and glanced over at her. "I'm glad you sat with us today."

She shrugged. Liam hadn't given her a choice. Instead of going to children's church, he'd insisted on sitting with the "big people." In Liam's mind, "big people" had included her. As Colton had carried him down the aisle, he'd stretched out his arms and pleaded in that sweet little voice, "I want Jasmine." How was she supposed to resist that?

So she'd sat in the third row, nestled between Liam and Paige, Colton on his son's other side. Sitting that close to the worship band, the song lyrics and the meaning behind them had been hard to ignore. And too many times, she'd found the pastor's message unsettling.

As expected, it had a Christmas theme—"Emmanuel, God with Us." He made it relevant to today by talking about God's presence through the storms of life. But she wasn't looking for a God who promised to be with her through the storms. She wanted to avoid them altogether.

Colton drove down the steep drive, then smiled over at her. "You look like you're deep in thought."

She tilted her head to the side. "Do you believe God saw your wife's aneurysm before it ruptured?"

"Of course He did." He stepped on the gas, pulling onto Fall Branch Road. "Nothing catches Him by surprise."

"Then why didn't he do anything to stop it? He's all-powerful, right? He could have intervened but chose not to."

"I don't have all the answers. But I do know God is right here and will carry me through whatever trials I have to face."

Jasmine chewed her lower lip. She'd never experienced that kind of faith. But something told her if she ever found it, the peace she'd sought all her life might be somewhere in the midst of it.

Colton eased to a stop at the end of the road, then turned right toward 64. "I'm not saying it's been easy. It hasn't. Losing Mandy is one of the hardest things I've ever experienced, right up there with losing my mother."

"And you believe God has helped you through it."

He nodded. "I have no doubt. I've felt His presence, seen Him at work."

"How?"

For several moments, he didn't respond. The light ahead turned red, and he eased to a stop. When he finally looked at her, his eyes were serious, filled with meaning. "Most recently? I asked for someone big and mean and scary, and He sent me you."

The words floored her. "You think God sent me?"

"Absolutely." He craned his neck to look at his son in the rearview mirror. "Look at the change that's happened in Liam in three short weeks."

The light changed and Colton stepped on the gas. "You were exactly what he needed. I didn't know that, but God did."

She swallowed hard. He'd said she was what Liam needed. What about what Colton needed?

"So you believe God orchestrated events so I'd be the one to guard you two."

"Without a doubt."

She shook her head. "If He did all that, why not just seal up the aneurysm? Then the other stuff wouldn't have been necessary."

"Sometimes God stills the storm, like He did for the disciples on the Sea of Galilee. Other times He carries us through it."

"Like He did for Paul and the other two-hundred-something passengers on the ship that wrecked." She'd been listening. If she thought about it, she could probably even recite several of the pastor's sermon points.

She crossed her arms. "The whole thing bugs me."

"What bugs you?"

"How all this works. I mean, you're a nice guy, a family man, church attender, a good, moral person. If God should spare anyone from having to go through something horrible, I would think it would be someone like you."

"That's not the way life works. At least not *this* life."

And now he was going to tell her he had heaven to look forward to. Jasmine frowned. She'd always believed in an afterlife, but heaven had never felt real. It seemed more the stuff of fairy tales, a way to explain death to a child.

But when she looked over at Colton, he was well-grounded. That peace she coveted was evident on his face, along with a genuine acceptance of his circumstances. But there was more than that. A sense of contentment seemed to weave through his whole being.

He pulled up to his gate a short time later. "Stay with Liam. I'll run in and get the potato salad." That would be their contribution to the meal.

Brutus met Colton at the gate, wagging his tail. Although he was still playing the part of guard dog, he was getting to spend more time inside the house, and not just when the weather was bad. Though he'd tear apart anyone who threatened his pack, his gentleness with Liam warmed her heart.

After giving the dog two pats on the head, Colton jogged toward the house. Jasmine stepped from the SUV and scanned the surrounding woods, leaving the door open.

Liam's voice came from inside the vehicle. "Jasmine?"

She leaned inside. "Jasmine's right here, sweetie. I'm not going anywhere."

Her assurances seemed to satisfy him. How was he going to handle it when she finally left for good? A vise clamped down on her chest.

That day was coming. Soon. Colton didn't seem to be in any hurry to send her back to Atlanta. And she wasn't in any hurry to go. Waiting to find out who the men were and why they'd attacked was a great reason to extend the assignment. Their names weren't familiar to Colton. And neither of them was talking.

But detectives were working on it. Eventually they'd find the connection, and Colton would have to decide whether he and his son still needed her protection.

She turned in a slow circle, scanning her surroundings. She'd been identifying and guarding against threats for enough years to have developed a sixth sense.

Now there was nothing, not even a blip on her radar. The danger here was over.

Colton stepped out the front door, then locked the dead bolt with the key. He was still taking precautions and probably would for the rest of his life. The experiences he'd had tended to leave a permanent mark.

He closed the gate, and she climbed back into the SUV. After sliding into the driver's seat, he handed her the cold container. He'd said he'd pick up some potato salad somewhere. She'd insisted his friends deserved homemade.

"I've enjoyed getting to know Paige this week."

Colton smiled. "I'm glad you two hit it off so well."

Although she didn't know Paige's whole story, she'd learned enough to know they had a lot in common, including their dysfunctional childhoods. As adults, they shared that toughness that only comes with the struggle to survive. It wouldn't take much for them to become best friends.

There was one difference between them, though. After a bunch of bad relationships, Paige had found the love of her life in Tanner.

Jasmine wasn't there yet. She had the bad relationship part down pat, but finding true love seemed more of a distant dream.

She slid a sideways glance toward Colton. His eyes were on the road ahead of him as he drove down Hilltop toward the four-lane. The tightness that his features had held since the day she met him had disappeared.

She'd found him attractive from the moment he'd walked up her driveway and insisted on helping her haul in buckets of paint. But his appeal went much deeper than his physical attractiveness.

He was kind, compassionate and selfless, the type of man who'd do anything for those he loved. He didn't project the carefree abandon that his brother always seemed to display, but that wasn't what drew her to him. He had depth, integrity. Even his faith tugged at her in a way she hadn't expected.

What would it be like to be a permanent part of Colton's and Liam's lives? Was there even the slightest possibility that she could find with him what Paige had experienced with Tanner?

Colton braked at the stop sign at the end of Hilltop and looked over at her. His lips lifted in an amused smile. He'd caught her staring at him.

"And what are you thinking about now?"

Heat crept up her cheeks. No way was she going to admit the direction her thoughts had taken. Not only were her feelings for him unprofessional, putting them out there would make the rest of their interactions stiff and uncomfortable.

She shrugged. "I was thinking about how much more relaxed you look."

Not a lie. In fact, that was the observation that had started her whole train of thought.

His smile deepened as he turned onto 64. "I'm *feeling* more relaxed. I'm not ready to totally let down my guard, but I'm not expecting someone to start shooting at me, either."

He cast her a quick glance. "I owe you a lot."

Their eyes had met for the briefest of moments, but the sincerity in his sent a surge of warmth through her insides. She shrugged. "Just doing my job."

"You saved our lives, probably more than once. I

want you to know how much I appreciate everything you've done."

When he stopped in Bryce's driveway a minute or so later, his phone was ringing. He frowned down at a number he apparently didn't recognize. Moments after answering, the frown gave way to eagerness.

When he ended the call, he clipped the phone back onto his belt.

She looked at him with raised brows. "That sounded like good news."

He nodded. "Perez was behind the attacks. The guys had several aliases, but they're his brothers."

"Do the detectives think there are others out there who want to see you dead?"

"No one can say for sure, but Perez doesn't have any other relatives. Male ones, anyway. His father was killed by rival gang members when Perez was a boy, and he doesn't have any other brothers."

"Friends, acquaintances?"

"As near as they can tell, none close enough to put their own lives in jeopardy to do his dirty work. So it looks like, starting tomorrow, you'll be able to go back home and move on to your next assignment."

Jasmine studied him as he spoke. Did his shoulders slouch a little? No, that was her imagination. The news he'd gotten was cause for celebration.

He pulled the keys from the ignition. "Today you're still on duty. And your assignment for the rest of the afternoon is to relax and have fun getting to know my friends."

He stepped from the SUV, then leaned into the back to unbuckle Liam. "Are you ready to go in and see Aunt

Andi and Uncle Bryce?" His tone was cheery. But it seemed forced.

Maybe he *would* be sad to see her go. Was it possible he was feeling at least some of what she'd been fighting?

No, she needed to stop trying to see things that weren't there. Colton was still mourning the loss of his wife. And he wasn't looking for a replacement. Even if he were, she'd never be able to fill Mandy's shoes.

Perfect wife and perfect mother. She and Colton had probably had a near perfect marriage.

Jasmine had never even had a dating relationship that didn't fall squarely into the realm of dysfunctional. If she couldn't make men who were as messed up as she was happy, how would she have any hope of making Colton happy when she had to follow in the footsteps of a woman like Mandy?

She climbed from the SUV and walked with Colton toward the porch. This afternoon, she was going to do exactly what he'd ordered—relax and have a good time with his friends.

Tomorrow she'd head back to Atlanta. If Gunn didn't have an immediate assignment, maybe she could get the work finished at the house. She'd been close when she'd had to pull off for the Gale assignment.

Maybe she could convince Gunn to give her the last two weeks of the vacation she'd earned. She'd again pour her time and energy into making the reality of her new house match the pictures she'd conjured in her mind. It would be fun watching it take shape and all come together.

She heaved a sigh. All her efforts to rouse some enthusiasm for her plans fell flat.

That was because everything she looked forward

to involved leaving the man who made her dream of things she'd thought impossible and the little boy who'd stolen her heart.

Liam sat on the floor amid scattered toys and crumpled wrapping paper. Behind him, several hundred mini lights shone from the tree.

There was still one wrapped gift lying beneath. It had Jasmine's name on it. After the cookout at Bryce's, she'd packed her belongings and Colton had driven her back to Atlanta. He should have given it to her then, but he'd forgotten.

Or maybe the oversight was a subconscious effort to make sure he'd have to see her again.

He rose from the floor, where he'd helped Liam open his gifts, and collected the discarded paper. It was his first Christmas without Mandy, Liam's first without his mother.

But it wasn't Mandy that Liam had been asking for. It was Jasmine.

At least, he'd asked for her Sunday night and most of the day yesterday. By last night, he'd stopped. Because he'd stopped talking altogether.

This was what he'd been afraid of. He hadn't wanted his son getting attached to her. But it had happened anyway. And now Liam had lost a second mother figure.

After throwing away the paper, he returned to the living room and stared out the front window. The sun was still low on the horizon, hidden behind the trees. He moved away and squatted next to his son. "How about some breakfast?"

Liam loaded a double handful of plastic rocks onto the dump truck without looking up. When he pressed the button on the side, the bed rose and the rocks tumbled onto the rug.

Colton tried again. "We'll have pancakes, your favorite."

Liam's eyes met his, and his chest clenched at the vacancy he saw there.

He ruffled Liam's hair. "I'll make you a Mickey Mouse one. Would you like that?"

Liam nodded, and Colton rose. On his way through the room, he stopped at the coffee table. A sterling silver bookmark lay on the polished oak surface, engraved with the words *Keep the Faith*.

When he'd pulled Liam's gifts out from beneath the tree, he'd found a small wrapped box with his name on it. The tag said, "Thanks for letting me be a part of your family. Jaz."

Since she'd spent most of the past two weeks sequestered in the house with Liam, she had to have gotten some help. Probably from Paige. That made the gift all the more thoughtful.

He was going to miss her. Actually, he'd started missing her five minutes after she left. Her going home didn't just leave a hole in his son's life. It also left a hole in his own.

He trudged into the kitchen. No need to feign the excitement he was trying to display for his son's benefit. He plugged in the griddle and pulled the pancake mix from the cupboard. An easy meal.

Christmas dinner was going to be even more effortless. It was in the fridge, waiting to be moved to the oven and warmed. He'd picked it up at Ingles yesterday. Instead of turkey, he'd selected a Cornish game hen. A ten-pound turkey was a little overkill for one man and a thirty-pound boy.

But it was going to be just the two of them. Bryce and Andi were having Christmas dinner with Andi's family in Asheville, and Tanner and Paige, both without any real family connections, had left yesterday morning for a week in a Florida beach condo.

Not that he hadn't had other invitations. He had. Mandy's parents had invited him to spend the holidays in Montana. His own had asked him to come to New York to be with them and his grandparents. He'd even gotten invitations from a couple of his Atlanta friends, the most insistent coming from his former coworker Doug.

As Colton added the wet ingredients, sounds of play came from the living room. There was no chatter, or vocalizing of any kind, just the hum of the mechanism that raised the dump truck bed and the muffled clatter of plastic rocks.

Colton had just ladled the first spoonful of batter onto the griddle when his phone rang. Doug's voice came through the line, a little subdued.

"I'm hesitant to wish you a merry Christmas, but I'm praying it's a little easier than we'd expect."

"Thanks." He added two dollops of batter to the larger one to form Mickey's ears. "At least I no longer have someone trying to kill me." He'd spoken with Doug while Jasmine was still in the hospital, letting him know what had happened.

"That should make for at least a little Christmas cheer. Have you learned who they were?"

"Perez's brothers."

"Oh, no. How—"

The line went silent. "Doug?"

When his friend spoke, his voice was tight. "Did you get a gift basket delivery a few days after you left?"

"No. Why?"

"I might know how they found you. Friday, I got a card in the mail from the victim's family in a case I just tried, thanking me for all my efforts. A new intern we have was there when I opened it. He said we probably get that a lot."

Doug drew in a deep breath and continued. "He said someone tried to deliver one of those candy-and-nut gift baskets to you three weeks or so ago. When he said you were no longer working there, the delivery person asked if he knew where you'd gone. He said he thought you'd gone to Cherokee County, North Carolina, but wasn't sure."

Colton leaned against the counter, the pieces falling into place. No wonder they'd found him so quickly. The first time he'd left, it had been different. Most of the office staff knew where he'd gone, but even if that information had gotten back to Perez, his brothers had probably decided against following him to Montana, knowing he'd be back eventually.

Colton created another Mickey Mouse, then started four more pancakes cooking, boring round ones. By the time the conversation was winding down, all six were golden brown and stacked on two plates.

Doug sighed. "Are you sure you don't want to spend the day in Atlanta? We'd love for you to join us."

"Thanks, but we're just going to have a quiet Christmas at home."

Doug came from a big family. At last count, there

were going to be thirty people at his gathering. That was more chaos than Colton wanted to deal with.

After ending the call, he opened the fridge to remove the maple syrup from the door. Three covered containers sat on the second shelf. Christmas dinner.

He'd turned down Doug's invitation because a gathering with thirty-plus people had sounded more grueling than fun. But three would be perfect.

He walked back to the counter where he'd left his phone. Jasmine didn't have plans. He'd already asked what she was going to be doing. She'd reiterated that she'd never been big on holiday celebrations.

She answered after three rings, sounding a little breathless. She was apparently happy to hear from him. Or maybe she'd had to run for the phone.

Whatever her reason, everything inside him responded to her sweet voice. They'd agreed to keep in touch, but he hadn't spoken with her since he and Liam had said goodbye to her Sunday night.

Now something tugged at him, the longing to be with her again, even if only for the day. Maybe it would help Liam. Maybe he needed regular visits to know that Jasmine wasn't gone like Mandy.

He cleared his throat. "What are you up to?"

"Painting."

"That's dedication. Liam and I haven't even eaten breakfast yet."

"What are you having?"

"Pancakes, complete with mouse ears. His, anyway."

"You're a good dad." There was a smile in her tone.

It tugged one out of him. "Thanks. How about doing a late Christmas dinner with us?"

"In Murphy?"

"No, I'll bring it to you. You'll just have to walk across the street."

"That sounds good. I'd love to see Liam again."

"What about his grumpy father?"

"Him, too."

"It's not going to feel like Christmas. There won't be any decorations."

"At least the company will be good."

"We'll try. I'm afraid you won't get much interaction out of Liam, though." He drew in a breath and released it in a sigh. "He's regressed. As of last night, he's completely stopped talking again."

"Oh, no. I was afraid of that." She paused. "If you want to maintain regular contact, I don't mind. If we FaceTimed or Skyped on a regular basis, that might help him adjust."

He closed his eyes, that tug stronger than ever. Jasmine was a special person. The assignment was over. She owed them nothing more. But she was willing to do whatever she could to help ease Liam into the next phase of his life.

After settling on a time for dinner, he disconnected the call and carried plates and utensils to the table. Last was the maple syrup and a milk-filled sippy cup.

When he returned to the living room, the dump truck was parked, and his son was playing with a set of Lincoln Logs.

"Are you ready to eat?"

Liam didn't look up.

"We need to eat our breakfast. Then we're going to have dinner with Miss Jasmine."

Liam's head swiveled toward him. Hope filled his eyes and his mouth lifted in a one-sided smile.

Colton scooped him up and walked to the kitchen. His son wasn't the only one whose day had gotten brighter. Colton was now looking forward to a meal he'd dreaded for the past two days.

He put Liam in the high chair and placed his plate on the tray. Although Liam eyed the pancakes hungrily, he waited until Colton sat, then held out his hands. When Colton had finished praying, Liam's eyes met his.

And they held life.

As Colton cut the Mickey Mouse pancakes into bite-size pieces, his stomach twisted in a mixture of anguish and hope. For almost seven months, he'd tried to be everything for his son. But it wasn't enough. Liam needed more.

He needed Jasmine.

As long as she was willing, Colton would see to it that they maintained regular contact. He'd drive to Atlanta on weekends and holidays. During the week and anytime he couldn't make it, they'd FaceTime or Skype.

Anything to help ease Liam's loneliness.

But what about his own?

# NINE

Colton opened the oven door and a blast of heat hit him in the face. Cartoon voices drifted in to him from the living room, where Liam was occupied with *Rudolph the Red-Nosed Reindeer*. Jasmine would arrive in thirty minutes. They'd scheduled Christmas dinner for three to give her extra time to paint.

Satisfied that the food was progressing as it should, he closed the oven door and walked from the room. When he entered the living room, Liam was standing at the front window, vertical blind slats resting on each shoulder, head holding them apart. He seemed to have been watching for Jasmine almost from the moment they arrived. Colton had lost count of how many times Liam had run to the window to peer out, then returned to the movie.

"Dinner isn't ready yet, but when it is, she'll be here." He carried Liam to the couch and settled in next to him. The movie continued to play, and he hugged his son close, a sense of contentment swelling inside. *Thank You, God.* He'd brought them through a scary time. They still had healing to do. And Jasmine's place in their futures was a big unknown. But they were safe.

The ringtone sounded on his phone. Rather than trying to talk over *Rudolph*, he strode into the kitchen to take the call. It was Jasmine. When she spoke, she sounded breathless. "I just finished the living room, which was a chore with the cathedral ceilings."

"At least you got your workout today."

She groaned. "Stretches, check. Quads, check. And a few other muscles I didn't know I had, check, check and check. I'm going to feel this tomorrow."

"I can imagine." Although, she was probably exaggerating. As physically fit as she was, her body likely wouldn't even register the additional activity. Jasmine was no couch potato.

"Anyhow, I'm running about twenty minutes late. I've got to clean my brush and rollers and then myself." The humor returned to her voice. "I'm a three-coat painter—one on the wall, one on the floor and one on me."

He laughed. "Take your time. Liam is occupied with Christmas movies, and I can always turn the temperature down on the oven."

He laid the phone on the counter and removed a glass from the cupboard. After filling it with ice, he poured some of the sweetened tea he'd picked up yesterday.

When he returned to his spot on the couch, he kissed Liam on the head and gave him another squeeze. For the next several minutes, he sipped his tea while watching the animated movie.

*Rudolph* had just been chosen to be the head reindeer guiding the sleigh. The turning point. The start of the happy ending. Was there one in store for him and his son? Actually, they'd had one, with the arrest of the

Perez brothers. But what about the hole that Mandy's death had left in their lives?

Whenever he tried to envision that happy ending, Jasmine figured prominently in every image. He'd already decided to maintain regular contact. And she'd agreed.

But Liam didn't just need occasional visits. He needed a constant in his life. Someone to kiss away the boo-boos with the tenderness that only a woman could provide. Someone to hold and comfort him after a nightmare. He needed a mother.

And Colton needed more than a friend. The loneliness had been more acute in the past two days than it had in several months. He'd gotten used to having Jasmine around and never dreamed that the house would feel so empty without her.

Now that the assignment was over, their relationship had moved easily from strictly professional to friends. Was there any chance it could move from friends to something deeper?

He couldn't deny the attraction he felt. She was completely different from Mandy, but every bit as beautiful. He already respected and admired her. Strong in spite of a fractured past. Tough when needed, but surprisingly tender. Caring and selfless, putting others' needs above her own. It wouldn't take much for the admiration and respect he felt to grow into love.

Jasmine would be an amazing mother to Liam. And a good wife to him.

The thought was like having a bucket of cold water thrown in his face. He rose from the couch and started to pace. Over the past few minutes, he'd taken the leap from being glad they could visit regularly to thinking about making her his wife. How had that happened?

He stopped in the foyer and leaned against the front door. What he was thinking wasn't even practical. Jasmine liked him as a friend, and she'd connected with his son in a powerful and unexpected way. But she'd never hinted at feeling any kind of attraction toward him.

He returned to the living room in time to see Liam disappear into the hall, headed toward his room. He'd apparently lost interest in the movie.

Colton continued to pace. Once he got used to Jasmine not being there and they settled into the routine of regular visits, he'd get his head back on straight. It was just that the loneliness was getting to him. The time of year didn't help, either—the holidays with their constant focus on family, the continual reminders of what was missing in his life.

He walked into the foyer again and paused. Did he just hear the kitchen door rattle? He couldn't have. Brutus had been inside with them earlier, but Colton had let him out an hour ago to do his business and enjoy the outdoors. As long as he was outside, no one would get anywhere near the house.

Unless they had a tranquilizer dart.

His gut filled with lead. Perez's brothers were off the street. But what if there was someone else?

His eyes went to the alarm panel two feet to his right, and he pressed the button to arm the system. When he reached for his phone, he winced. He'd never picked it back up after pouring his tea.

The next moment, the sharp snap of splitting wood sent a bolt of panic through him. Someone had just kicked in the back door. The ear-piercing squeal of the alarm filled the house, setting his teeth on edge.

He ran toward the back, reaching the living room the same time two men entered from the direction of the kitchen. A sick sense of déjà vu swept over him. Two men in ski masks and gloves. One larger and one smaller.

He continued his panicked dash into the hall. He had to get to Liam before they did. The police would have already been notified. The alarm was still monitored. He just had to hang on until they arrived.

But Jasmine would get there sooner. She was probably already in action. She'd have heard the squeal of the alarm from across the street, grabbed her weapon and dashed out the door.

As he ran down the hall, heavy footsteps pounded behind him. He'd just bolted through his son's door when a large body crashed into him, tackling him from behind. He hit the floor, his assailant landing on top of him. The impact knocked the air from his lungs, and he struggled in a constricted breath.

Liam released a terrified scream as piercing as the wail of the alarm. The man rolled Colton onto his back while the second man entered the room. Colton twisted, reaching for his son. A meaty fist moved toward the side of his face at lightning speed, connecting almost before the threat registered. Stars exploded across his vision.

The thinner man lifted Liam from the floor and Colton struggled to rise. But the larger man tightened his hold, keeping him pinned to the floor.

As the man carrying Liam moved past him, Colton lifted an arm toward his son. "No."

The word sounded far away, as if it came from somewhere else. Someone was taking his son, and there was no one to stop him. Why hadn't Jasmine come?

Suddenly he was free. He rolled onto his stomach, then rose to his hands and knees. Blackness encroached from all directions, and a watery weakness filled his limbs.

He lifted one knee, placing that foot flat on the floor. He couldn't let the men take his son. He had to get up.

He reached for Liam's dresser, but his perception was off. His hand found nothing but air. A boot met his ribs, and pain shot through his side. The blow knocked him back onto the floor. The men disappeared from the room.

He pushed himself back into a crawling position. He couldn't lose consciousness. He had to save his son. *God, please help me.*

He forced a hand forward, then a knee, then the other hand, rotating his body as he moved. The open doorway was in front of him. Inch by inch he crawled through, his circle of vision growing smaller by the second. The alarm still squealed, but there was another squeal, even closer. It was inside his head.

He flopped onto his side, the last vestiges of consciousness slipping away.

He'd made a terrible mistake. The capture of Perez's brothers wasn't the end. There were other men determined to bring him down.

Men every bit as dangerous.

And now they had Liam.

A roar filled the bathroom, and Jasmine's hair danced in the hot stream of air coming from the blow-dryer.

Before cleaning her brushes and rollers, she'd set the

light/heater/exhaust fan combo to heat. So the room had been warm and cozy by the time she'd stepped into the shower.

Now she was dressed in a sweater and a nice pair of jeans. She didn't have a Christmas sweater, or even any holiday jewelry, but this one was at least red.

She pressed the off switch and laid the blow-dryer on the counter, then fluffed her hair with her fingers. She hadn't always worn it short. When she was a teenager, it had hung almost to her waist. As a young adult, she'd worn it shoulder length. While deployed, she'd wanted easy. Wash and wear. The style had stuck.

A lot of men liked long, flowing locks. Fortunately, she wasn't looking to please any men.

After winding up the cord on the blow-dryer, she dropped it into one of the vanity drawers. Eventually it would hang on the back of the bathroom door. Once she got a hook installed. One of many small projects still undone.

She took a final look in the mirror, then reached for the heater switch. She was ready except for putting on her boots. And it was five minutes earlier than the estimate she'd given Colton.

When she flipped the switch, the heater motor died. But she didn't get the silence she'd expected. There seemed to be a faint squeal coming from somewhere else in the house.

She frowned. What was she hearing? She opened the bathroom door and moved through her room, down the hall and into the living room.

The squeal was louder now. A siren? No, the pitch was too constant. It was more like an alarm.

*Colton's alarm.*

When she swung open the front door, she had no doubt. The shrill squeal was coming from across the street.

She raced to retrieve her weapon from where she'd laid it on her nightstand, but didn't take the time to don her jacket or her boots. Seconds later, she was running down her driveway in her stockinged feet, weapon stuck into the waistband of her jeans.

Colton's driveway was empty, the front gate still closed. His own vehicle was likely parked in the garage. Law enforcement hadn't responded yet. So maybe the alarm had been triggered right before she shut off the bathroom heater. Whoever had tripped it could still be inside.

She pulled out her weapon and slipped through the gate. Brutus didn't come to greet her. And he wasn't barking.

A sick sense of dread wrapped around her.

What if the men who'd tried to kidnap Liam weren't the same two who'd come after them in Murphy?

What if they'd let down their guard too soon?

She crept closer to the house, every sense on full alert. When she stepped onto the porch, she tried the door. Locked. None of the windows appeared to have been tampered with, either.

She moved across the front, rounded the corner and walked along the side. When she stepped into the back, she picked up her pace. Something didn't look right. A dark shape stood out at the base of the shrubs lining the rear wall.

Brutus. Now she had no doubt. That dark, unmoving blob was the dog, likely the victim of another tranquilizer dart.

Which meant Liam's kidnappers had returned.

Her gut burned with a cocktail of worry and fear. As she crept along the back of the house, another sound seemed to blend with the screech of the alarm, the pitch rising and falling. Help should be there within minutes. But Colton and Liam might not have that long.

She approached the kitchen door. It was open. The side of the jamb that was visible from her vantage point was splintered. Everything inside her demanded that she rush through, shouting Colton's name. Instead, she shut down her emotions and called on her extensive training. She couldn't lose her wits now.

She tiptoed toward the door, shifting to a crouch at each window. When she reached the nearest edge of the doorway, she stopped. A moment later, she leaped across the opening to disappear behind the opposite side, weapon still raised. During that brief span of time, she'd taken in the view of the kitchen and dining area. No one was there.

She jumped through the doorway and spun around the edge of the kitchen counter, then cleared each area the same way. The living room offered an unobstructed view down the hall, where a crumpled form lay half in, half out of Liam's bedroom.

Once again, she had to corral her feelings. Heedlessly rushing in could get her killed. She stood frozen for several moments, listening. But the wailing alarm drowned out any possible sounds of movement inside the house.

So did the sirens. They were closer now, probably right at the entrance to the subdivision. In another half minute or so, backup would arrive. In the meantime,

Colton's life could be ebbing away. And she still didn't know Liam's whereabouts.

Colton stirred and released a moan. Relief shot through her. He was hurt, but he was alive.

He pushed himself to a seated position but didn't try to rise. As she rushed toward him, conflicting emotions flitted across his face—relief mixed with agony. "They took Liam."

"Who?"

"The same men as before. I don't know. They had ski masks." He grimaced and pressed a hand to the side of his head. "The alarm."

"What's your code?"

"Nine-four-three-six."

As she made her way to the front of the house, sirens rose in volume, then fell abruptly silent. She'd just punched in the four numbers when a loud knock sounded on the front door.

She swung it open. Two Atlanta police officers stood on Colton's front porch. She invited them in and told them what she knew, which wasn't much.

When she led them into the hall, Colton was rising, clinging to the doorjamb for support. "They took my son."

He stood shaking his head, his shoulders hunched. He wasn't just hurt. He was defeated. Her heart clenched.

The older of the two officers spoke. Posner, according to his nameplate. "Did you see which way they went?"

"No. The bigger guy knocked me out."

Jasmine stepped forward. "Since the front door was still locked, they probably left the same way they came in—through the back. Then over the wall with the help of the oak tree."

The younger officer took off in that direction while Officer Posner spoke into his radio. When he'd finished calling for backup and instructing them to comb the woods behind the subdivision, he turned to Colton again.

"Any idea who these men were?"

"No."

"Or what they want?"

"My son, but I don't know why. This is their second visit. The first time they weren't successful."

Over the next hour, several people were in and out of Colton's house, including two detectives. Since the men had worn gloves, the detectives had decided against dusting for prints.

Liam's information was going immediately into the missing persons database. Soon his photo would be all over Atlanta and beyond, disseminated throughout the law enforcement agencies.

At one point, Jasmine had found Colton texting both Tanner and Bryce, asking them to pray for Liam's return. The extra prayers wouldn't hurt. But she didn't put much confidence in them. If God intended to offer any kind of intervention on Liam's or Colton's behalf, He'd have prevented the kidnapping to begin with.

Finally, she and Colton were alone in the living room. Christmas dinner was still in the oven. She'd turned it off after the police arrived, but it was probably too dried-up to eat. Not that it mattered. Colton's appetite wouldn't be any better than hers.

Colton sank onto the couch and put his face in his

hands. "I should have stayed in Murphy. I could have invited you there."

She rested a palm on his knee. "Don't blame yourself. Hindsight's twenty-twenty. We both thought that once Perez's brothers were captured, you were safe. Everybody did."

He lowered his hands and looked at her. Moisture pooled against his lower lashes. "What am I going to do if they don't find him? I can't lose him, Jasmine."

Her heart twisted at the grief in his eyes. She wrapped both arms around him and squeezed, her face pressed to the side of his head.

Maybe her actions weren't professional. But this was what Colton needed. Besides, she wasn't his bodyguard anymore. The assignment was over. Now she was acting solely in the capacity of a friend.

When his arms circled her waist, the action silenced all her doubts. He held on to her in the same desperate way a drowning man clings to a life ring.

"They're going to find him." His breath was warm against the side of her neck. His tone held more hope than confidence.

She dropped her arms from around him and gripped his hands. "The guys who took him had to have a reason. When we find out what it is, we'll know better how to proceed."

"I can't imagine someone is holding him for ransom. There are lots of kids easier to get to than Liam and plenty of dads with more money than I have."

Colton was right. Finding a ransom note in the morning would be an easy resolution. But that wasn't likely to happen.

He drew in a deep breath. "The authorities are doing

everything they can to find him. In the meantime, I'm trusting God to protect him. I've been praying for that since the moment I woke up."

The confidence she'd looked for earlier crept into his tone. He seemed sure prayer could make a difference.

But would God really hear him, one man among millions? What if God was busy elsewhere, doing important things, like preventing massive natural disasters or keeping the planets in their orbits?

Or maybe God did hear him, but instead of deliverance, this was one of those storms he was supposed to go through.

She tightened her fingers over his. No, she wasn't going to allow thoughts like that to stay in her mind. After losing his wife, Colton couldn't lose his son, too.

If only she'd been there. The score would have been more even—two against two. The thirty-eight at her hip would have made it even more so. Depending on how long Colton had been out, she might have missed the kidnapping by only ten or fifteen minutes.

The amount of time she'd taken to finish the last wall. The realization was like a steel-toed boot to the gut.

If she had stuck to the original plan and gotten to Colton's at three, Liam would possibly still be home. She closed her eyes and said a prayer of her own.

*God, I don't have any reason to expect You to listen to me. But I'm begging You, for Colton's sake, please bring Liam back home.*

Her prayers wouldn't hold any special power. She'd ignored God all her life.

But maybe, when combined with Colton's, they could have the ability to move the hand of God.

# TEN

The jangling of the phone sent Colton's pulse into overdrive.

He pulled his hands from Jasmine's and rose. "My landline number is unlisted. I only have it to monitor the alarm."

He reached the kitchen at a half jog. Before snatching the receiver from the wall, he glanced at the caller ID. Blocked number displayed on the small screen, sending his tension skyrocketing. He pressed the phone to his ear and gave a breathless "Hello."

"You're not answering your cell phone."

The voice was gruff. Definitely not a friendly call. He glanced over his shoulder at Jasmine, who'd followed him into the kitchen. If he could keep the caller on the line long enough, maybe Jasmine could have the call traced.

He pulled a pen and sheet of paper from a drawer. "It didn't ring."

While he jotted down his phone number, the caller continued. "You thought you'd get away with it, didn't you?"

*Get away with what?* Making sure another criminal paid for his crimes?

He handed the paper to Jasmine. She was a step ahead of him and already had her cell phone in hand.

"Who is this?"

"You know who I'm calling for."

"Perez." The name slipped out before he could stop it.

The man laughed, the sound hard and cruel. "You've got so many people after you, you can't keep them straight."

Jasmine's soft voice came from the living room. She was probably on the phone with police. He needed to keep the caller on the line.

"Tell me what you want." Whatever it was, he'd find a way to give it to him. Anything to get his son back.

"I'm through waiting. Return what you took, or the boy dies."

His brain shut down. The man's last three words branded themselves on his mind. He was threatening to kill Liam.

Several moments passed before the first part of the sentence even registered. Return what he'd taken?

"What are you talking about?" This couldn't be connected with his job. Those decisions were irreversible, at least by him.

"I'll text instructions tomorrow morning. Make sure your phone is charged and working. If you don't show up at the appointed place and time with what you took in hand, the boy dies."

Panic pounded up his spine, scrambling his thoughts. How was he supposed to return something he didn't have? "I didn't take anything."

"If you want to see the boy alive, you'll follow my instructions explicitly. Don't involve the police or anyone else."

"Tell me what you want." His voice was several decibels louder than normal. But it didn't do any good, because he was talking to dead air.

He stared at the phone for several moments before placing it back on the hook. When he walked into the living room, Jasmine was pacing silently, phone still pressed to her ear. Her eyes met his, and he shook his head.

Her shoulders dropped. "He's gone. Were you able to get anything?" After a short pause, she disconnected the call. "The kidnappers?"

He nodded.

"Did they make a ransom demand?"

"They said if I don't return what I took, Liam dies."

"What did you take?"

"Nothing." He flung his arms wide, all the fear and frustration coming out in his tone. "How am I supposed to give them something when I have no idea what it is?"

"How long do you have?"

"I don't know. He's texting further instructions in the morning."

*To his cell phone.*

He charged into the kitchen and swiped it from the counter. "When I first picked up the call, he chided me for not answering my cell phone. I told him it didn't ring."

He checked his log. The last call was from Jasmine. Maybe it went straight to voice mail. He didn't know how, since he had full signal strength. After all, this was Atlanta, not rural Smoky Mountains.

But that explanation was better than the alterna-tive, that the kidnappers had the wrong number and he wouldn't even get the text.

While he waited for his voice mail to connect, worry, fear and hopelessness melded into one toxic concoction. Moments later, a computerized voice said the words he dreaded—*You have no messages.*

Okay, maybe the kidnapper hung up when the call went to voice mail instead of leaving a message. He laid his phone back on the counter and squeezed his eyes shut. He was grasping at straws.

"The kidnappers have the wrong number. He hung up without giving me a chance to check it."

Jasmine put a hand on his arm, and he opened his eyes.

"When you don't respond to the text, he's going to figure it out. He'll call you on the landline again. And when he does, we need to be ready. Call the police. I'm calling Gunn."

She swiped her screen and pulled up her contacts.

"No." He covered her phone with his hand. "I can't involve anyone else. If I do, they'll kill Liam."

Her brows dipped toward her nose. "If you try to handle this alone, you could get both you and your son killed."

"But if they find out that I've involved the police or anyone from Burch Security, Liam is as good as dead. That's a chance I'm not willing to take."

She heaved a sigh, indecision flashing in her eyes. "Let me call Gunn, at least get his input. There might be a way to give you and Liam some security without the kidnappers finding out."

Colton stalked into the living room, unable to remain

still. He didn't like it at all. The kidnapper had made himself clear—no one except Colton.

But bringing in other minds might be a good thing. "Advice only, right?"

"Yes. Tomorrow when he calls back, we'll figure out how to proceed. The final decision will be yours."

Colton's cell ringtone sounded from the kitchen, and his breath caught in his throat. For a split second, he stood frozen, then ran from the room, Jasmine right behind him. When he swiped his phone from the counter, Cade's name and number displayed on the screen.

His heart fell, and he gave his brother a weary "Hello."

Cade apparently didn't notice the heaviness in his voice. He didn't even try to temper that characteristic playfulness. "If you're spending Christmas with your hot new neighbor, I don't want to interrupt anything. But I did want to wish my favorite brother and nephew a merry Christmas."

Colton winced. The mention of Liam was like a red-hot poker through his heart.

"You can't talk to Liam. They took him." His tone was flat, in spite of the maelstrom of emotion swirling inside. If he didn't keep tight reins on it, he'd fall apart and never be able to pull himself back together.

"Who took him?"

"I don't know. The same guys as before."

"They found you in Murphy?"

"No, I'm in Atlanta." His gaze met Jasmine's. The sympathy and support he saw there bolstered him.

"What?" Cade's voice was almost shrill. "I told you not to come back to Atlanta."

"It was supposed to be safe. The authorities caught Perez's guys."

"These aren't Perez's guys." Cade screamed so loudly Colton held the phone away from his ear. "I told you to stay in Murphy."

He matched his brother's tone. "And I assured you I wasn't going anywhere until the people after us had been caught. They were caught last Thursday."

There was a muffled thud, like a boot hitting a wall. Or a fist. Cade wasn't just sick with worry. He was furious. He blew out a breath. "Has anyone made contact with you?"

"Someone called my landline and said if I don't return what I took, Liam dies."

"Oh, no. Oh, no. Oh, no." Cade released a long moan.

Colton's gut tightened. His brother's reaction didn't make him feel any better. Cade knew something. He'd said these weren't Perez's guys. Did he know who they were?

"Is there something you're not telling me?"

The pause that followed stretched out so long Colton thought the call dropped. "Cade?"

"I'm here." He released a long sigh. "I acquired a collection for a buyer, five Roman signet rings, circa second century. One was gold and oval-shaped eye agate, a beautiful piece. The agate was cone-shaped, with three color layers and an inscription on the face."

Colton curled his free hand into a fist. "Get to the point."

"It was exactly what I'd been searching for, for another buyer." After a brief pause, the rest of the words tumbled out. "I pulled it from the collection and replaced it with a fake."

Colton closed his eyes, clutching the counter for support. Cade had made some poor decisions in his life. But Colton had never known him to do something this stupid. "What were you thinking?"

"It was one piece out of five. And the fake was such high quality, *I* almost couldn't tell. I didn't think anyone would notice."

He clenched his teeth. If his brother were standing in front of him, Colton would have his fingers around his throat.

"Why did they go after Liam? I have nothing to do with the antiquities business."

"It's a case of mistaken identity."

Colton shook his head. That didn't explain anything. "How? I'm never at your business. It's on the opposite side of Atlanta from where I live and nowhere near where I used to work. Other than the fact that we look alike, there's nothing to lead them to me."

"While I was living at your house, I had some of my meetings there instead of in my office. It was more comfortable. We could kick back, have drinks, socialize. Your place is good for that, makes a good impression. Classy without being ostentatious."

Jasmine put a hand on his shoulder and squeezed. He needed it. He was probably growing paler by the second. The only thing keeping him on his feet was anger with his brother.

Cade continued. "They disabled the alarm at the business and ransacked it the night before coming to your place. I didn't learn that until later. When they didn't find the ring there, they came to the house."

The pieces of the puzzle were falling into place. And they weren't forming a pretty picture. Their father had made a good living dealing in antiquities. But that hadn't been enough for Cade. He'd wanted more. And he'd resorted to dishonesty to get it.

This probably hadn't been the first time he'd done something like this. He'd apparently had the connections in place when the need to quickly create a quality fake had presented itself.

Whatever stupid choices Cade made were his business. But how could he even think about pulling anything shady with people he'd brought into Colton's home? But that was just it. Cade didn't think. That had always been his MO—acting without weighing the consequences.

Colton pursed his lips. Cade had created the problem, and Cade would have to fix it. Colton was not going to lose his son to his brother's greed.

"You have to get the original back from the other customer. Buy it back. Pay double if you have to."

"I can't. It disappeared from your house the day they tried to take Liam."

"What was it doing at *my* house?"

"I had it in my pocket in a small cloth bag when I stopped to see you and Liam the day before. I was meeting the other customer at his hotel room the following afternoon. Since I'd be running around with you in the morning and had the other appointment in the middle of the day, I took it out of the safe to bring home with me. I figured I'd save time backtracking to the south side of the city."

"And you stashed it at my house in the meantime."

"Not intentionally. Remember, I ended up having dinner with you, then staying the night. When Liam spilled his juice on me and you loaned me your sweats, I needed to put it somewhere safe."

"And why didn't you take it with you when you left?"

"Would you want to carry around a $20,000 artifact while running errands? I figured I'd pick it up when we got home, but I had to leave for my appointment right away. When I came back to get it, that's when I found out you'd been robbed, and it was gone."

"If they took it, why are they demanding I return it?"

"Maybe the guy that wants it doesn't know that."

"The guy you ripped off." His tone was heavy with disdain.

"The buyer. Maybe his goons decided to pick up some quick cash and pawn it themselves, then told him they couldn't recover it." Cade heaved another sigh. "I tried to make it right. I figured if I could get a similar piece, the problem would go away. I've made dozens of phone calls. I've got dealers all over the world searching. But until I had it in hand, I knew I didn't dare come back. And you couldn't, either."

"But you didn't bother to tell me."

"I did. I told you to stay away from Atlanta."

"But you didn't tell me why. You let me think all this time that Liam's attempted kidnapping had to do with one of my defendants."

"You were supposed to stay—"

"Don't try to place any of the blame for this on me." His angry outburst shut his brother up instantly. "If anything happens to Liam, I'll—"

He'd what? There was nothing he could do. Even if he never spoke to his brother again, it wouldn't bring his son back.

Rustling came through the phone. "I'm packing up now. I'll be at your place before morning."

"Where are you?"

"Grand Cayman. I'm catching the first flight out. I'll charter one if I have to."

"There's nothing you can do."

"There is. Marino tried to call me a half hour ago. I'm waiting to hear back from one other dealer. I wanted to have that answer before I took Marino's call."

*Cade's cell phone.* That was the number the kidnapper had. The phone where he'd text instructions tomorrow morning.

But he'd called Colton's landline. "How did he get the number to my house phone?"

"I made a few calls from it when my cell battery was low."

Colton closed his eyes again. His home and his phone. Cade hadn't used Colton's name, but with their identical looks, he'd inadvertently impersonated him.

"I'll make this right." The urgency in Cade's voice pulled Colton's thoughts back to the conversation. "If I have to trade my own life for Liam's, I'll do it. If I'd had the piece, I'd have given it back immediately. I should have hidden it better."

No, he shouldn't have ripped anyone off to begin with. And he certainly shouldn't have involved his family.

"A jewelry box is the first place a thief looks for valuables."

Cade's words seemed to be an afterthought. But they slammed into Colton with the force of a freight train.

"Jewelry box?"

"Your closet door was open partway. When I was

looking for a safe place to temporarily stash the piece, I saw Mandy's jewelry box on your shelf and dropped it into there."

Colton's heart beat so hard his chest felt ready to explode. "The intruders didn't empty the jewelry box. I did."

"What?" The single word held shock infused with hope.

"Remember the boxes I loaded into the back of the SUV before heading to the bank?"

"Mandy's clothes and things you were donating."

"I'd also transferred her jewelry to a zippered plastic bag and taken it with me, planning to put it in my safety deposit box while we were out. I ran out of time but stopped by both the ministry and the bank on my way to Burch Security the next day."

"The piece is in your safety deposit box?" Amazement filled his tone. A door slammed in the background. "I'm going to find a flight out of here. As soon as I land, I'll call you. Then I'll take a cab straight to your place."

Colton ended the call, ready to fill Jasmine in on everything he'd learned. He was still almost frantic. But now a wide river of hope flowed through the worry that had almost debilitated him.

Cade's motto had always been "Nothing's going to happen." It was how he lived his life. Now Liam was taking the brunt of those bad decisions. But come tomorrow, Colton would be at the bank the moment the doors opened and he'd retrieve what Cade had stolen. Then he'd meet Liam's kidnappers. He'd give them the piece and they'd return Liam to him.

Unless something spooked them.

Or they decided to take revenge on Cade for what he'd done.

*God, please make everything go as planned.*
*And protect Liam until he's back safe in my care.*

Jasmine sat in the front passenger seat of Gunn's Range Rover. Black with tinted windows, it looked like something that might be used for surveillance. Currently, they were waiting in the shade of an oak at the far end of the bank parking lot, Gunn behind the wheel, Dom in the back. Her Suburban was parked two spaces away.

Convincing Colton to let the two men come had taken some effort. What part he'd allow them to play still remained to be seen.

Colton was inside the bank. So was Cade. Cade had driven his Corvette, while Colton had taken his own vehicle. Jasmine had followed at a distance to make sure they didn't pick up a tail. When they arrived, Dom and Gunn were already there.

Although they'd tossed around ideas and run through scenarios, no one knew for sure what any of them would be doing. They couldn't formulate a plan until they heard from the kidnappers.

Gunn had pulled in some support, unbeknownst to Colton. He'd never have approved it. But they'd made other preparations, measures that Colton *did* approve. Cade's phone now had a tracker. Dom had installed the app. They'd also hidden a small tracking device inside the Corvette's dashboard.

From the moment the car left the bank parking lot, Dom would be viewing both the phone's and the car's movements on the laptop in the seat next to him. But the argument over who would meet the kidnappers was unresolved.

She'd rather it be her, or even Gunn or Dom. Any one of them would have a chance of finagling their way out of the situation. But Cade was too impulsive, and Colton, though good with persuasive words, had too much at stake to think clearly. Neither of them would know what to do if things went seriously south.

The bank's glass doors swung open, and Jasmine straightened. "Here they come."

At that distance, she couldn't tell them apart. Actually, she couldn't up close, either. They'd both dressed in blue jeans and black button-up shirts, if for nothing more than to create a moment of confusion should the opportunity present itself.

As the two men approached the passenger side of the Range Rover, Gunn turned the key and lowered the window. Jasmine studied them. The one on the right was Colton.

Maybe. The depth and seriousness she usually saw in Colton was present in both of them. The situation weighed on Cade enough that the carefree air he always projected was gone.

They moved between her and Gunn's vehicles, and one of them nodded at her. "We got it. Now we wait for the text."

Definitely Colton. She'd been right. His voice had a slightly different timbre from Cade's.

Cade frowned. "You need to give me the ring."

"No, *you* give *me* the phone."

"We talked about this at the house. I have to do this. It's bad enough I got you guys into this. If something happened to you, I'd never forgive myself."

"He's my son, so I'm going. If anything bad happens, you'll have to live with it." Colton's voice held a hardness she'd never heard before. This was likely to put a long-lasting wedge in his and Cade's relationship. If Colton lost Liam, that wedge would become a chasm, forever uncrossable.

"He's your son, but he's my nephew. And I'm the sole reason his life's in danger right now." Cade flung his arms wide, his whole body radiating his worry and frustration. "You go in and you could get yourself killed. You're not law enforcement. You don't know self-defense. The only fighting you've done is in the courtroom."

"And the only fighting you've done is on a mat in high school wrestling. You aren't any more qualified for this than I am."

Gunn let out a sharp whistle, making a *T* with his hands. "Time-out."

Everyone's attention went to him, and he continued.

"I don't like the idea of either of you doing this, but we don't have a choice. Colton is the boy's father, so it's his decision."

Cade looked ready to argue, but a text notification silenced him. His eyebrows shot up and he reached into his pocket. When he pulled out his phone, the screen was lit with recent activity.

Colton stepped closer, and his jaw tightened as he read. When he looked up, a vein throbbed in his temple.

"I'm to meet them at 148 Auburn Avenue with the ring. They reiterated that I'm to come alone. If they even *think* I've involved anyone else, Liam's dead." A steely hardness entered his eyes and he held out a hand, palm up. "Keys."

Cade pulled them from his pocket and turned them over. But he clearly wasn't happy. When Colton handed over his own keys, Cade took them with a frown.

"Don't try to follow me." Colton's tone was stern, discouraging any argument. "You can meet me back at the house later."

Jasmine's chest tightened. It was time. She stepped from the Range Rover with a lump in her throat and a sudden urge to wrap him in a tight hug.

She restrained the urge and simply took his hands in hers. "Be careful. Just focus on getting your son back. No heroics. Leave taking out the bad guys to the professionals."

He gave a sharp nod. He didn't seem the type to do anything stupid. He was levelheaded to the extreme.

But people sometimes lost capacity for rational thought when their loved ones were threatened. Restraining that need for vengeance wasn't easy. Colton especially would want the kidnappers to pay for their crimes. If he didn't have a strong sense of justice, he'd have chosen a different career.

Colton pulled his hands free of hers and pressed the fob. A corresponding beep sounded several spaces away, and the Vette's lights flashed. After sliding Cade's phone into his pocket, his gaze locked with hers.

"I'll call you when Liam and I are safe. Until then, I don't want you within a mile of the place. At this point, I don't even care if these guys are caught. I know I won't feel that way when it's over, but right now, I just want my son back."

"You should be wearing a wire, or at least a tracker."

"No." They'd discussed it last night, and he was as adamant now as he'd been then.

She touched her earpiece. No matter what happened, she'd have radio contact with Gunn and Dom. "We could conceal it."

"Unless it was something I could swallow, I'm not willing to take a chance."

Arguing with him was pointless, but she had to give it one last shot. "If they make you get in their vehicle and ditch your phone, we've lost you."

"Come on, Jasmine." The tension in his tone said he didn't like it any more than she did. "You heard the text. These guys don't play around. If they even *think* I'm pulling something, they're going to kill Liam. What do you think they'd do if they found a wire or tracking device on me?"

As he walked toward his brother's Corvette, a vise clamped down on her chest. But Colton wasn't alone in this, whether he wanted to be or not.

As soon as he'd relayed the location given in the text, she'd heard the click of the computer keys from the back seat. Even now, Dom was probably staring at a satellite image of the area, searching for a way to approach unseen.

But even with backup, there were a hundred things that could go wrong, snafus that could get Liam or his father killed.

She drew in a stabilizing breath. She'd do anything to protect her clients. But Colton had become more than that. He'd even become more than a friend. She watched him back from the space, feeling as if someone was ripping her heart from her chest.

She reined in her thoughts. She had a job to do and was already at an extreme disadvantage. She needed to keep a clear head and be in top form, which meant operating like a machine—no emotion.

As Colton drove from the lot, she leaned down to look through the passenger window at Gunn. He already had the address programmed into the vehicle's GPS. She tilted her head. "What's the plan?"

He had to have one. He always did. So did Dom. She'd worked enough jobs with both of them to know.

"We follow. Stay out of sight. Assess when we arrive. See how close we can get without jeopardizing the safety of Colton or his son."

Beyond her boss, Cade had almost reached the Highlander three spaces away.

She straightened. "Hey." Her voice stopped Cade in his tracks. After waiting for him to turn, she continued. "You're with me."

Cade unleashed would be more of a liability than they could afford. As determined as he'd been to play the hero, she wouldn't put it past him to do something reckless.

Gunn cranked the engine. As she walked toward her own vehicle, she tilted her head toward Cade. "In the back."

"Why?"

"If you have to hit the floorboard, you can. Hiding is easier than in the front."

The explanation seemed to satisfy him. Which was good. Considering he was the sole reason they were there, if he decided to be argumentative, she might brain him.

She programmed the address into her own GPS and backed from the space. By the time she pulled into traffic, Gunn was several vehicles ahead of her. Colton would be too far away for even Gunn to see.

She slipped between two cars in the center lane, hoping to close the distance. "So where are we going?"

When Cade started to answer, she motioned toward her earpiece, and he fell silent. Dom's voice flowed through the wire, sounding as if he was much closer than several vehicles away. "148 Auburn Avenue is the old office of the Atlanta Life Insurance Company. The building's been vacant for decades."

"Is there a back way in?"

"I don't know. John Calhoun Park is right across Piedmont, which runs along the side of the building. Might be able to see something from there. Can't park there, though."

Jasmine changed lanes again. Now there were only two vehicles between them.

"I'll have a better chance of slipping in undetected than either of you." Besides, Colton was *her* client.

A few minutes later, she followed Gunn and another vehicle up the ramp onto I-85 South. The Corvette was still out of sight. If everything went smoothly, either she or Gunn would pass by the abandoned building early enough to see Colton exit the vehicle but late enough to avoid arousing suspicion. Everything else they were going to have to play by ear.

Not the way she preferred to operate.

After taking the John Wesley Dobbs exit, one more turn put them on Auburn, a single vehicle between them. According to the GPS, they were less than a quarter mile from their destination.

The radio came to life again. "That's it, up ahead on the right."

Cade's Corvette was parked in the lot next to the building. Three stories, with neoclassical architecture, it had probably been pretty impressive in its day. But time had taken a toll. The brick was dingy; plywood covered the arched window openings and chunks of plaster were missing on some of the pillars.

"They're up ahead." It was Gunn who spotted them.

She saw them almost immediately also—two men moving down the sidewalk away from her, Colton on the right. The man next to him looked to be the same height but probably outweighed him by seventy-five pounds. They'd almost reached the next crossroad.

She chewed her lower lip. "Where is he taking Colton?"

Gunn didn't answer. She didn't expect him to. And Cade was being exceptionally quiet. The man walking with Colton swiveled his head slowly, glancing over his shoulder. His gaze seemed to lock on the Range Rover, but she couldn't see his eyes. He wore a cap pulled low, casting his face in shadow. If he was armed, his weapon was likely hidden under his lightweight jacket.

He wouldn't need it. Colton was no threat. As long as they held his son, he'd do exactly as instructed.

"Go around the block," she said. "I'm pulling over." Eight or ten parallel parking spaces bordered the edge of Auburn, starting just ahead of her and stretching almost to where Courtland crossed. "I'm following on foot."

"Don't let them see you." Gunn's tone held a note of warning.

She didn't need it. Having Colton spot her would be just as dangerous as the kidnapper discovering her. He'd never be able to hide his reaction.

She cast a glance in the rearview mirror, peering at Cade through her sunglasses. "Get down."

Cade complied immediately. She slowed to a crawl and maneuvered into an empty space as Colton and his escort crossed the side street. Instead of continuing on Auburn, they turned right.

"They're headed north on Courtland now."

Jasmine looked around her. A modern building sat to her right—Georgia State University, Centennial Hall. Though she was five or six years past college age, she could probably blend in. Except the day after Christmas, the area was deserted.

She waited until Colton and the other man had disappeared around the side of the building, then opened her driver door. "I've got quarters in the console. Give it a minute, and if the coast is clear, feed the meter. Then get back in the vehicle."

Instead of staying on the sidewalk, she climbed the handful of stairs leading to Centennial Hall, then followed the perimeter of the building. Colton walked thirty or forty feet ahead of her on the opposite side of the street. The man with him regularly peered over his shoulder, scanning his surroundings.

For a short distance, she was able to keep to the school grounds until a fenced parking area stretched in front of her, giving her no choice but to follow the sidewalk. Trees lined her side of the road, but they weren't large enough to hide behind. And the five lanes of traffic moving toward her down the one-way street was sparse.

She slowed, letting the distance between her and the men lengthen, and pulled out her phone. With her head down, she slid her thumbs over the screen. If the man noticed her, he'd assume she was a student who didn't go home for the holidays. Colton hadn't turned around since she first saw him on Auburn. They'd almost reached the next crossroad when they changed direction.

"There's a parking lot on the west side of Courtland. They just walked into there." She stopped to lean against a tree. Her face was still tilted downward, but behind the sunglasses, her eyes shifted between her phone and where the men had gone.

"I don't like this." Gunn's tone was laced with concern.

A single beep sounded, and lights flashed on a red sports car. Her pulse kicked into high gear. The Atlanta Life Insurance Company wasn't the destination. The men had Liam somewhere else. And since Colton wasn't going there in Cade's Corvette, the tracking device would be worthless. They'd have to rely on what Dom had installed on the phone.

After a hand motion from the other man, Colton moved to the driver's side.

"They're getting into a vehicle, and Colton's driving."

"What kind of vehicle?"

"A red sports car. I'll give you the make in a minute. Where are you?"

"Three or four blocks away, on John Wesley Dobbs."

The engine turned over, and Colton backed from the space. Just before he made his right turn onto Courtland Street, the passenger window lowered. An object arced through the opening and landed on the sidewalk.

"The passenger just threw something out of the car."

"What?"

"I don't know yet."

Colton stepped on the gas and made his turn into

the far-right lane. As the car approached, the man's gaze landed on her for the briefest moment before he looked away, apparently confident she didn't pose a threat. Colton stared straight ahead.

When they passed, she turned. Another vehicle overtook it, blocking her view. "I think it's a Mazda Miata, newer model. I couldn't get the tag."

She resumed walking again.

"See what he threw," Gunn said.

"Headed that way now."

She glanced over her shoulder. The Miata was making a left turn onto Auburn. Moments later, it was out of sight. As she drew closer to the parking lot, she picked up her pace, heart pounding. "Dom, are you showing movement on Cade's phone?"

What lay on the asphalt looked an awful lot like a cell phone.

Which meant the Miata was moving away with Colton inside. And no way to track him.

Time to call in some of those connections Gunn had put on standby. And hope that circumstances didn't throw them any other curveballs.

At least ones they weren't prepared to handle.

# ELEVEN

Colton made his way east on Auburn, hands moist against the steering wheel.

The man in the passenger seat pressed his phone to his ear. "I've got him. We're headed your way."

Just like that, the conversation was over. He touched the screen and dropped the phone into his lap.

When Colton had arrived fifteen minutes ago, the parking lot next to the vacant building was empty. It wasn't until he got out and approached the door that the man stepped around the corner and led him to the other side of the building.

Moments later, he was thanking the Lord that he hadn't allowed any of the Burch Security people to fit him with a wire or tracking device. In the small space between that building and the next, the guy frisked him so thoroughly he would have found it. He even made him take off his shoes and empty his pockets.

The precautions hadn't ended there. When they'd reached the car, the man had demanded he hand over his cell phone. He'd spent the next minute scrolling through calls and texts.

And Colton had sweated bullets the entire time. He had no clue what was there. It wasn't his phone.

Apparently, nothing had set off alarms. The only thing the man had wanted to know was who he'd talked to last night. Colton had said he'd wished his brother a merry Christmas.

He hadn't, but Cade had. Since he was playing the part of Cade, what he'd said was true. The man had seemed satisfied with the explanation.

Then he'd thrown the phone out the window.

"Turn right up here." The command cut into Colton's thoughts.

He signaled, looking at the street sign as he approached. Boulevard. He knew the area. He knew most of Atlanta. But he had no idea where the man was taking him.

The Burch Security people wouldn't, either. Neither the tracking device in Cade's car nor the app installed on Cade's phone were going to do him any good. Whatever happened, he'd be facing it alone.

No, he wasn't alone. He needed to keep reminding himself of that. He was never alone.

*God, please protect Liam and be with me. Help me get him back and please don't let either of us get hurt.*

He braked leading up to the turn, then accelerated as he straightened the wheel. Sporty and low to the ground, the car handled well. Under other circumstances, he'd enjoy the snazzy ride. Now he just wanted to get to wherever they were holding Liam.

The man directed him through a couple more turns until he was traveling east on Dekalb Avenue. A low rumble sounded in the distance, somewhere behind them.

Colton checked the rearview mirror. A box truck occupied the majority of the rectangular space.

He shifted his gaze to the side mirror. In the upper part of the glass, a helicopter hovered against a partly cloudy sky. It seemed to be flying lower than normal.

His heart pounded as an odd mixture of hope and dread swirled inside him. Jasmine and her partners had wanted to implement more security measures, and he hadn't let them.

Maybe they'd moved ahead with their plans anyway. If so, there would be professionals on his side.

And all kinds of things that could go wrong. The men had warned him—if he involved anyone else, Liam would die.

He slid a nervous glance toward the man next to him. He'd noticed the helicopter, too. He sat staring at his own side mirror, tension radiating from him.

He picked up his phone and touched the screen. "We might have company. There's a chopper headed right toward us."

In the pause that followed, he kept his gaze fixed on the side mirror. "Don't worry, we're not coming to you till I know it's clear."

He slid Colton a sideways glance. "I don't think he's that stupid. He knows we mean business."

He dropped the phone back into his lap. "I'm right, aren't I? You didn't do anything stupid like calling the police?"

"Of course not." Actually, that wasn't true. "I called them when it first happened, but that was before you made contact. They know nothing of this meeting."

He struggled to keep the nervousness from his voice.

He didn't have anything to hide. He wasn't the one who summoned that chopper. Maybe no one had.

He watched it until it disappeared from view, now too high to be visible in the mirror. The rumble increased in volume until it seemed to come from all around them.

The man removed a weapon from beneath his jacket and pointed it at him. "If you've pulled something, the boy won't be the only one who dies. You're going to join him."

"I'm not pulling anything." The panic ricocheting through him made the words come out louder than he intended. "I didn't call anyone."

He leaned toward the window and cast a quick glance over his left shoulder. The chopper was gaining on them, poised to pass almost over them.

He released a sudden sigh of relief. "That's not the police." He should have thought of it sooner. "Atlanta's choppers are black."

That one was white. As it moved past them, he read the letters painted on the side and bottom.

"It's from one of the local news stations. They might even be doing traffic."

The man seemed to relax. Colton almost crumpled. One disaster averted. The man was jittery. Likely, both kidnappers were.

Colton gripped the wheel more tightly. If he could get through the entire exchange with nothing spooking them, he and Liam might have a chance of surviving the day.

The chopper moved ahead, and the man pointed. "Take the next right."

Colton did as told. It looked like they were proceeding as planned. Since they didn't seem to be heading toward any of the large roads leading away from Atlanta, the meeting location was probably somewhere nearby.

When the man directed him through another turn, the sign at the corner triggered a vague sense of familiarity. Rogers Street. Why did it ring a bell?

He followed a ninety-degree curve and scanned his surroundings. The Circus Arts Institute stood on the right. On the left, a chain-link fence ran parallel to the road, barbed wire on top. Red no-trespassing signs were affixed at points along its length. Beyond, metal buildings were spread out over the landscape, towering, barnlike structures that obviously hadn't seen any activity in decades.

The Pullman train yard. Now he knew why the street name sounded familiar. He'd read a news piece about the place, that a film production company had purchased the long-abandoned complex with big plans to turn it into a mini city with a boutique hotel, restaurants and a public gathering space for movies and concerts.

But none of those improvements had begun. Even in broad daylight, an eerie air of abandonment hung over the property. Any one of those graffiti-covered buildings would be the perfect place for an exchange like this to go down.

"Pull over here."

Just ahead on the right was a cleared area, large enough for a vehicle to turn around. Beyond a chain-link fence, grassy fields were visible in a break between trees. A sign next to the locked gate announced Welcome to the Arizona Avenue Fields.

Colton pulled off the road and eased to a stop in front of the gate. Maybe someone would question the car being parked illegally and call the police.

Not likely. Since they were on Rogers rather than Arizona, the entrance he was blocking was likely a back way in.

Colton turned off the engine. The Miata was the only vehicle there. "Where is Liam?"

Instead of answering the question, the man spoke into his phone. "We're here...no, we weren't followed."

As he spoke, he wrapped a handkerchief around the door handle and opened it. He'd done the same thing getting in, careful to not leave prints. Maybe he planned to ditch the car when everything was over. It was likely a rental, obtained with fake identification.

Colton stepped from the car. "Where are we going?" The gates to the train yard and the athletic fields were chained and padlocked.

The man didn't answer that question, either. "Open the trunk."

Colton did as instructed. It was empty except for some bolt cutters. So that was how they'd get inside the fence, likely the one across the street. He picked up the tool and held it out.

The man leaned against the car, then motioned toward the train yard. "You cut. I'll keep watch."

Yeah, he wasn't going to leave prints on the bolt cutters, either. Colton crossed the street and knelt on the narrow strip of grass in front of the fence. He'd completed several snips in a horizontal path when the man stopped him.

"Get over here. Someone's coming. Act like you're getting something out of the trunk."

Colton's stomach tightened. He didn't need a Good Samaritan stopping to lend a helping hand. Contact with anyone, even random strangers, could spook the men.

Leaving the cutters in the grass, he rose and walked toward the Miata. A white minivan moved toward them. A short distance behind it was an SUV.

Two for one. Good. The fewer interruptions he had, the sooner he'd see his son.

He leaned into the trunk, not straightening until the second vehicle had passed. When the road was clear again, he returned to his task. Soon the cuts formed a decent-sized upside-down *L* that ended at the ground.

When he turned for further instructions, the man was crossing the street.

"Crawl through."

Colton pushed on the cut section, forcing it inward. As he slipped through the opening, a sharp piece of fence grabbed his sleeve, ripping the fabric and scraping his shoulder. After a final glance in both directions, the man struggled to follow him inside. The opening was almost too small.

He got to his feet, and Colton followed him toward the graffiti-covered buildings. Every square foot of reachable surface showcased the creativity of local urban artists. Even though he didn't approve of defacing property, he had an appreciation for the talent displayed.

Instead of walking into the nearest building, the man led him past it. Ahead was a hodgepodge of brick-and-steel structures. Wide bay doors spanned the side of the nearest one.

Once sure of their destination, he picked up his pace. Liam was likely inside.

He stepped beneath one of the partially raised doors and scanned the huge open space. Metal framework supported a pitched roof probably thirty feet high at its center. Sunshine struggled in through dirt-streaked skylights. Graffiti decorated the lower portions of the walls and metal posts, and rainwater had pooled in places on the concrete floor.

A rustle of movement drew his attention, and he turned. It was just the man who'd brought him here.

"Where is Liam?" He fought to keep the panic from his voice. Someone was supposed to be there waiting with his son.

What if Liam wasn't there? What if the men had lured him to the abandoned train yard with plans to kill him and take the ring?

*God, please protect us both.*

"Be patient. They're here." He crossed his arms and leaned against one of the metal support posts. The pose highlighted the size of his chest and biceps, even through the jacket. "But they're not going to show themselves until they know it's safe."

Colton's panic lessened, but not by much. He wouldn't relax until he and Liam were far away from here. For the past few weeks, wherever he'd gone, Jasmine had had his back. What he wouldn't give now to know she was somewhere close.

A sound set his pulse pounding. Did he hear a child's whimper? He froze, hope tumbling through him.

When he heard it again, he turned in that direction. Windows encrusted with decades of dirt lined the wall adjacent to where he'd entered. Trees stood a short distance beyond them.

A figure moved past. Then another. The silhouette of the first one was bulkier, as if the person was carrying something.

Like a small child.

Now he had no doubt. What he'd heard was a child's

soft cry. The whimpering was closer now, filled with loneliness and despair.

A vise clamped down on his chest, squeezing the air from his lungs. When someone holding his son entered through one of the bay doors, his knees almost buckled.

Liam was safe. He was scared, but he appeared unhurt.

Colton took several stumbling steps forward. Now that Liam had seen him, his whimpers had escalated to wails. He was kicking and twisting, trying to get down, both arms stretched toward Colton.

"Hey."

The shout didn't register until too late. The larger man thrust out an arm, lightning fast. The back of his fist caught Colton in the stomach.

Colton skidded to a stop, doubled over at the waist. Liam screamed more loudly.

A third man entered. "Shut him up."

Colton straightened, his heart in his throat. "It's okay, buddy. Daddy's here." He shouted the words, but Liam seemed not to hear him. A good thirty feet separated them, and Liam was as distraught and terrified as he was after one of his nightmares.

The man holding him started to bounce him, and Colton continued.

"Don't cry, buddy. Daddy's going to take you home."

The screams settled into sobs, and Colton released a pent-up breath.

The last man who entered spoke. "You have what I told you to bring?"

Colton nodded. Since all his attention had been on his son, he hadn't given the man more than a passing glance.

Now he did. This was Marino. Even without the description Cade had given him early this morning, he'd have known. The other two seemed like enforcers, thugs who carried out the orders of others. Marino didn't.

He was bald, stocky and short—probably only five-six or five-seven. But he projected an aura of power. He was used to giving orders and having them obeyed.

"I have it." He removed the item from his pocket. "Take it, and let me have my son."

Marino stayed where he was. "Boulder, bring me the ring."

*Boulder.* Obviously a nickname, probably a reference to his size. Colton placed the small cloth bag into the man's extended hand. Boulder carried it to Marino without opening it.

"I have to make sure it's the real thing." Marino opened the bag, then nailed Colton with a cold glare. "Since the dealer has no integrity."

Colton felt an odd sense of shame that wasn't his to bear. He fought the urge to defend himself, to set the record straight.

But he had no defense. What Cade did was inexcusable. And all three men believed he was Cade.

"This is the original. I guarantee it." Not that Cade's promises meant anything.

Marino removed the ring from its protective bag. As he studied it, Colton fidgeted. What if the original was a fake? What if someone had slipped a reproduction into the collection before Cade acquired it?

No, Cade would have recognized it. He was too good at what he did.

Seconds stretched into a half minute. Everything was

silent except for Liam's muffled sobs. And something a lot more distant. The squeal of sirens.

As the volume increased, Colton stopped breathing. Jasmine wouldn't have called the police. Even if she had, they wouldn't descend on the place with their sirens screaming. Atlanta PD was much better at stealth than that.

Colton studied the men. He wasn't the only one who was nervous. Boulder and the man holding Liam shifted from one foot to the other, their stance alert, as if ready for a quick exit. The only one unruffled by the approaching sirens was Marino.

Boulder drew his weapon. "Come on, let's dump the kid and get out of here."

"Not so fast." Marino walked slowly toward the other side of the building, his dress shoes making rhythmic taps against the concrete. Halfway across, he turned to retrace his steps. Rather than to calm himself, the pacing seemed more for the purpose of putting others on edge.

"Mr. Gale here had his instructions." His speech was as lazy as his mannerisms. "If he chose to ignore those instructions, the kid will pay."

Colton gasped. "I didn't call anyone." As hard as he tried, he couldn't keep the quiver out of his voice. Or the desperation. "Those sirens have nothing to do with me."

Acres of overgrowth and abandoned steel-and-brick buildings gave the impression of complete solitude. But it was an illusion. The bustle of the city was only a few blocks away.

"This is Atlanta. You hear sirens twenty-four hours a day."

As emergency vehicles moved even closer, the lankier man placed Liam on the floor but kept a tight grip on his hand. He, too, drew his weapon.

The squeals reached their loudest, then started a slow fade. Judging from the direction and closeness of the sirens, they had likely passed by on Dekalb.

Colton drew in a shaky breath, every nerve frayed. "Come on, I've held up my end. I brought you what you wanted and I didn't involve anyone else. Let me have my son."

Marino stared at him, and a shiver skittered down Colton's spine. There was something about the set of the other man's jaw, the hardness that had entered his features. His eyes held coldness, even cruelty.

"Move to the other end of the building."

"What?"

"You heard me."

Colton hesitated, not wanting to put even more distance between him and his son. But he had no choice. Marino had all the power. He had none.

He walked, casting repeated glances backward. The building was long, probably close to three hundred feet from end to end.

"You made a promise." He flung the words over his left shoulder. "You said if your terms were met, you'd return my son unharmed."

When he reached the far end, he turned. Bay doors occupied the entire wall to his right. The three men were spread out in front of two of the doors near the opposite end.

His gaze shifted to the windows several hundred feet in front of him. Had he just seen movement? A brief silhouette of someone moving against the woods?

No, that was wishful thinking. No one was coming to rescue him.

He prayed he wouldn't need it. Maybe Marino had an innocent reason for sending him so far from his son. Maybe their plan was to release Liam to go to him while they ran from the building to whatever means of escape they had waiting.

It wouldn't be the Miata. He was sure of that. Otherwise Boulder wouldn't have been so careful about not leaving behind prints.

Marino gave a slight nod. "Let him go."

The man dropped Liam's hand. For several moments, Liam stood unmoving, eyes wide, thumb in his mouth.

"Come on, buddy." Colton held out both arms, relief and joy colliding inside him. It was almost over. Within a minute or two, he and Liam would walk from the building.

He had no phone, no way to get in touch with Jasmine and the others. But he'd find a way. He could walk to a nearby business. Or flag down a motorist.

Liam pulled his thumb from his mouth and began moving toward him, picking up speed as he went. Colton struggled to remain where he was. Marino had made him walk to the far end of the building and probably expected him to stay there.

But everything inside him demanded that he run to his son, scoop him up and disappear out the nearest door. Instead, he dropped to one knee and spread his arms wider.

Moments later, Liam tripped and crashed to the floor. He remained on his hands and knees as renewed sobs shook his little shoulders.

That protective instinct took over, and Colton shot

to his feet. He'd covered about half the distance when Marino spoke, voice devoid of emotion. "Shoot the kid."

Colton's heart stuttered as he skidded to a stop. "What?"

Several seconds passed before he realized he'd heard his question in chorus. He wasn't the only one who'd voiced an objection. Boulder still held his weapon poised but was shaking his head.

"I said shoot the kid. Mr. Gale needs to learn there are consequences for trying to rip people off. Especially people like me."

Colton shifted his gaze to the windows, then immediately snapped it back again. Someone was out there.

Was it kids doing unauthorized exploration? Or trained people who were qualified to lend a hand? If the latter, was there any chance they'd get there in time?

The larger man lowered his weapon. "No way. I don't kill kids."

A figure bolted past the first opening. The bay door was raised only a couple of feet, but he recognized those boots.

*Jasmine!*

How had she found him? If she was there, that probably meant Gunn and Dom were there, too.

"You'll do as I say."

Colton's mind spun. He needed to give them time to get into position to stop the men before anyone opened fire.

"You've got what you want." He spoke with more boldness than he felt. "You need to leave while you can."

He hesitated, thoughts still swirling. "That helicopter we saw, they weren't just looking for news. They were tracking me."

Okay, that was pretty far-fetched. But it was the best he could come up with on the spur of the moment.

"I'm sure the authorities have already located the car and are moving in as we speak. If anyone fires a weapon, guys with guns are going to be all over this place."

Marino gave a derisive laugh. "You're full of it. Just like you were when you tried to pass off a fake Roman signet ring for a real one."

Marino's words were convincing, but a seed of doubt had crept in, tainting that air of confidence. If there was anything Colton had learned as a prosecutor over the years, it was how to read people.

"You don't know that for sure. Do you really want to stake your freedom on it? What if you're wrong?"

Two more figures slipped past the opening, likely Gunn and Dom.

Marino shifted his attention back to Boulder. "Now do what I said."

Colton held up a hand. "Wait." The three bodyguards were just outside, making their way closer along the side of the building. The next two doors were closed, the fourth being the first open enough to walk under without ducking. They needed a few more seconds to reach it.

Suddenly, another set of legs appeared in front of the first door. The next second, Cade dropped to the ground and rolled beneath it. A moment later, he was on his feet, creeping silently toward the three men.

What was he doing? He'd probably been instructed to stay in the vehicle. Instead, he was going to try to play the hero. It was a good way to get them all killed.

"No more stalling." Ice tinged Marino's tone. "Do it."

"I told you, I don't kill kids. I won't live with that on my conscience."

"No, I guess you won't." Marino reached beneath his jacket. In one smooth motion, he withdrew his weapon, aimed it and fired.

Boulder twisted and lunged, but not quickly enough to avoid the bullet. He clutched his side and dropped to his knees.

Cade charged Marino the same time Colton ran full bore toward his son. Liam had sat back on his heels and was screaming, eyes squeezed shut and hands pressed to his ears.

Marino brought the weapon around and pointed it at Liam.

The next several seconds played out in slow motion. Colton shot forward in a final burst of speed. Jasmine, Dom and Gunn ran through the open door, and Cade slammed into Marino.

Gunfire exploded a second time. Colton's leg buckled, and he crashed to the concrete. Pain ricocheted through his body, the keenest agony centered in his right thigh.

He covered the final few feet at a sloppy crawl while chaos erupted a few yards away. Another shot rang out. A quick glance that direction confirmed that neither Cade nor any of the Burch Security people had been hit.

He sat and scooped Liam into his lap. His pants leg was soaked. He was losing blood fast. While he put pressure on the wound with one hand, he held Liam to his chest with the other, rocking him back and forth and whispering soothing words into his ear.

Sirens sounded in the distance, filling him with relief instead of fear. This time, they were probably for him.

He looked up to see both Marino and the thinner man lying on the floor facedown, their hands behind their heads. Gunn's and Dom's weapons were trained on them. Boulder was lying nearby with Cade kneeling over him trying to staunch the flow of blood. The man was still conscious, but just barely. He'd refused to kill Liam. Colton hoped he made it.

Jasmine had just risen and was walking toward him and Liam. Sunlight washed over her as she passed under one of the skylights.

Never had he seen anything so beautiful.

If not for her and the other Burch Security people, Liam would be dead. Colton likely would be, too. He owed her everything.

When she dropped to her knees in front of him, he wrapped his arms around her, Liam pressed between them. The next moment, his lips were on hers and he was pouring everything he felt into the kiss—respect, admiration, appreciation.

And love.

*Love?*

He stiffened. Mandy had been gone for just seven months. How could he even think about letting go of what he'd had with her and giving it to someone else?

He pulled away, letting his arms fall from around her. "I'm sorry. I was with my wife for seven years. I haven't even dated anyone since she died."

Jasmine brought a hand to her mouth. Her fingers quivered, and her eyes held confusion. "It's okay. I'm not any more ready for this than you are." She looked down at his leg. "Are you all right?"

His leg. Yes. No. "I got shot."

She'd been quick to dismiss what had just happened between them. Good. It was for the best.

"I know how bad it hurts. I've been there." She gave him a weak smile. "Help is almost here."

The sirens were louder now, almost ear-piercing. They'd likely turned off Dekalb and were now on Rogers. Someone needed to tell them where they were.

Colton searched for Cade, but he was gone. Maybe he'd gone out to meet law enforcement and emergency medical personnel. Today he'd taken a small step toward atoning for his wrongs. But he still had a long way to go.

"Are you staying with me?" Jasmine's hands pushed his aside to press down on his leg, and he grimaced.

"Yeah." At least he was trying. His stomach threatened to hurl its contents and shadows danced on the edges of his vision.

He wasn't going to pass out. Not with Jasmine watching. If their roles were reversed and she was the one lying there with a bullet in her leg, she'd stoically bear both the pain and the blood loss. She was one tough lady. She'd served on the front lines in one of the scariest places on earth. And she'd been shot, probably more than once.

The shadows darkened. No, he was *not* going to pass out.

Keeping pressure on his leg with one hand, Jasmine reached for Liam with the other. "You'd better lie down. You're looking really pale."

"I'm all right." Beyond her, four police officers and two paramedics entered the building. He seemed to be watching them through a tube that was growing smaller by the second.

"You're not all right." She wrapped an arm around Liam and dragged him onto her lap.

Colton allowed her to gently push him backward. From this perspective, everything looked different, the ceiling a maze of metal trusses and beams, maybe even a couple of catwalks.

"Is anyone else hurt?" The male voice likely belonged to one of the paramedics. He couldn't look to see. The clouds had moved across his entire field of vision.

"Over here. Gunshot wound to the thigh." Jasmine sounded far away. But she was there. He could still feel the pressure of her hand on his leg.

He wasn't going to pass out, but someone would have to watch Liam during the ambulance ride and his time at the hospital.

Cade would gladly do it, but as far as Colton was concerned, he'd lost that privilege.

He reached for Jasmine. "Please take care of Liam."

She squeezed his hand. "Of course I will."

A sense of peace settled over him. His son was finally safe. It really was over.

*Thank You, Lord.*

He released a long sigh and gave in to the oblivion overtaking him.

# TWELVE

Colton shifted his position and wasn't quite able to stifle a grimace.

Jasmine gave him a sympathetic smile. "Does it hurt bad?"

"Not as badly as I'd expect it to."

He probably had some heavy-duty pain meds to thank for that. He'd woken up in Recovery an hour ago and eventually been moved to a semiprivate room.

The other bed was empty, which was a good thing. It hadn't taken long for the room to fill with visitors. Jasmine, Gunn and Dom had come into the room within minutes of the nurses getting him settled in the bed.

His Murphy friends were lending their support, too. Jasmine had texted Paige, who'd relayed what had happened to Tanner, who'd passed the information on to Andi and Bryce. Tanner and Paige had walked in a few minutes ago. Andi and Bryce hadn't arrived yet but were on their way.

Jasmine had even been allowed to bring Liam into the room. He'd immediately wanted to climb up into the bed, and Colton had let him. For the past several minutes, Liam had lain with his head on Colton's shoulder, his arm stretched across his chest.

When the nurses eventually ran out all the visitors, Liam wasn't going to be happy. Colton wasn't, either. Liam would be in good hands with Jasmine, but after coming so close to losing him, Colton wanted to hold on to him forever.

He looked at Dom and Gunn, then let his gaze settle on Jasmine. "I need to tell you guys thanks for not listening to me. I don't even want to think about what would have happened if you hadn't gotten involved."

Jasmine shrugged. "That's what we do. What kind of bodyguard would I be if I let you meet kidnappers alone? I'm just glad it worked out."

His eyes shifted to the corner. His brother stood several feet away, back against the wall. He'd ridden there with Jasmine and Liam. But when the others had gathered around the hospital bed, Cade had hung back, face lined with fatigue and eyes projecting sadness.

Yeah, he blew it. And he knew it.

Colton winced as compassion tugged at him. He tamped it down. Cade had acted heroically in the end, but he didn't deserve to be welcomed back into their lives as if the events of the past twenty-four hours hadn't happened.

He pulled his attention back to Jasmine. He had a whole slew of unanswered questions. In the few minutes they'd been there, the conversation hadn't progressed beyond them asking how he felt and his checking on his son.

"How did you find us?"

"I guess you could say we know people in high places." She smiled. "None of us were comfortable with not being able to track you except through your phone and car. We knew we needed a plan B. So Gunn got ahold of a friend who covers traffic for one of the local news stations. He told her the situation, that we might need some help."

"The helicopter." Colton released a laugh. "When the men were going to shoot Liam, I said the helicopter had been tracking me. I was making something up, trying to convince them to take the ring and disappear."

"That was a pretty good guess. When I realized they'd ditched your phone, Gunn placed a call to someone at the station. His friend kept an eye on you until she knew where you were going."

He nodded. "Liam and I both owe our lives to you three."

Jasmine shrugged. "Everyone played a part."

Colton frowned. "I didn't do much."

"You did. It was your trying to persuade the guy to not shoot that bought us the time we needed."

Yeah, persuasive argument. That was his specialty. He wasn't good with a firearm, and he probably wouldn't fare well in hand-to-hand combat. But thinking on his feet? That was something he could do.

"Cade was supposed to wait in the car." She cast a quick glance over her shoulder. "But it's a good thing he didn't. He'd slipped up behind us, so we didn't even realize what he'd done until we rushed into the building."

She was right. Cade's actions had been reckless. But they'd saved Liam's life.

"Who fired the last shot?"

"The thinner guy. It was intended for Cade, but Dom tackled him first. Dressing alike had been a good idea."

Gunn nodded. "When the guy saw Cade, his mouth

dropped open. He looked at you, then back at Cade. By the time he recovered enough to fire, Dom was taking him down. So the shot went wide."

God had allowed all the pieces to fall perfectly into place. The extra set of eyes in the sky, the Burch Security people arriving when they did, Cade's reckless but heroic actions, even the man refusing to shoot Liam.

"What about the bigger guy who got shot? How is he?"

Jasmine shrugged. "He was still alive at the time they took him away from the scene, but that's all I know."

"I hope he makes it."

She shook her head. "You and Liam almost died today. But you're concerned about the condition of one of the bad guys. Somehow that doesn't surprise me."

There was no criticism in her tone. Instead, her eyes held respect and admiration. She'd hinted at it before— she'd been observing him, watching how he lived out his faith, searching for the same peace he'd found.

But having a soft spot in his heart for the man who'd chosen to let his son live was easy. Letting go of the anger with his brother wasn't. He'd put Liam in grave danger, for nothing except greed.

Colton's gaze wandered again to the lone figure against the wall. Cade's eyes held a silent plea for forgiveness. That same nudge poked at him again, harder to ignore than before.

He curled his hand into a fist. He didn't want to make amends with his brother. Not right now. He wanted to nurse his anger a little longer.

Maybe Cade had learned his lesson. Maybe not. Frankly, it wasn't Colton's concern. What Cade had done was between him and God.

And whether Colton chose to forgive was between *him* and God. He knew what God required. Hating his brother or even remaining angry wasn't an option.

Andi and Bryce walked into the room and joined the other five gathered around the hospital bed.

Bryce clasped Colton's hand in a firm grip. "You'll do anything for attention, won't you? But almost getting yourself killed is going too far."

Colton laughed. "I think I've had enough attention for a while. I'm looking forward to returning to Murphy for a quiet and uneventful life."

Gunn gave him a high five. "I'll second that. Here's to the hope that you'll never need our services again, and that all future interactions with Jasmine will be strictly personal."

Gunn and Dom made their farewells, but before they could leave, a nurse walked in. With her salt-and-pepper hair pulled into a tight bun and a stern set to her jaw, she looked like an old-time schoolteacher. The kind that carried a thick ruler.

"Looks like there's a party going on in here."

Andi stepped aside to allow her to approach the bed. In spite of the no-nonsense demeanor, her touch was gentle. She checked his temperature and made a notation in the chart.

"How are you feeling?"

"I've had better days, but I've also had worse." Like yesterday, when he hadn't known whether he was going to see his son again. He offered up another prayer of thanks.

When the nurse finished checking his vitals, she scanned the faces of his friends. "Mr. Gale just got shot. He needs his rest."

She was probably right. They'd told him he'd lost a lot of blood. Besides the pain medication, they had him on some heavy antibiotics and were keeping him overnight for observation.

The rest she'd ordered sounded good. Maybe it was the effects of the anesthesia. Or not sleeping in more than twenty-four hours. Or the fact he'd just gone through the scariest experience of his life. But exhaustion was quickly overtaking him.

Dom lifted a hand. "At least two of us are on our way out."

Jasmine reached for Liam. "And this little guy looks like he's ready for a nap."

Liam gave brief half-hearted resistance before wrapping his arms around Jasmine's neck. As she walked toward the door, Cade followed.

Colton's jaw tightened. He wasn't ready to welcome his brother back into his life, but he had to begin the healing process. "Cade?"

Cade turned. The hope in his eyes squeezed Colton's chest further.

"Thanks for what you did today."

"It was the least I could do."

"It was brave and selfless."

Maybe today's events *would* be a turning point for Cade. *Selfless* wasn't an adjective he'd ever expected to use to describe his brother.

Colton watched them walk away, then motioned toward his Murphy friends. "These guys just drove two hours to get here. I'll run them out when I get tired."

The nurse gave a sharp nod, then left the room.

Bryce moved closer. "So what happened? All Jasmine's text said was that Liam had been recovered and everyone was okay, but you'd been shot."

Colton relayed the entire story, starting with last night's phone call from the kidnappers.

When he'd finished, Andi shook her head. "That's scary. At least it's over."

Colton released a sigh. "Thank You, Lord."

"So what now?" Bryce asked.

"When I get out of here, Liam and I will head back to Murphy."

"What about Jasmine?"

"She'll move on to her next assignment."

"And that's it?"

Colton shrugged. "We've talked about staying in touch, for Liam's sake. Unfortunately, he's gotten attached to her."

Tanner cocked his head to the side. "What about you?"

Colton shifted position and pain ripped through his thigh. Whatever they'd given him in Recovery was starting to wear off.

But the wound wasn't his only discomfort. Tanner and Bryce were ganging up on him. And he knew where they were headed.

"We're friends. That's all."

Tanner frowned. "That's what you say, but it's not how you feel. And there's no sense trying to deny it. It's obvious every time you look at her."

"My focus is on my son. He comes first."

Bryce shook his head. "Doing what makes you happy and what's best for Liam aren't mutually exclusive."

He crossed his arms and glared at his friends. He

was outnumbered. Though neither of the women had spoken, they'd nodded their agreement.

"Give me a break. I just got shot."

"Hey, turnabout's fair play."

He narrowed his eyes at Tanner. "What's that supposed to mean?"

"Remember when I was ready to let Paige walk out of my life? You were the one who talked some sense into me. I'm returning the favor."

"I don't need either of you meddling in my business."

Bryce held up both hands. "All right. We won't bother you anymore. At least until you get out of the hospital."

Great. They were giving him a reprieve, but it was only temporary.

He and Bryce had been friends since he was fifteen, he and Tanner longer than that. Those guys knew him better than his own parents did. But that didn't mean they had all the insight into his love life.

Bryce had said to think about it. He already had. There'd been that kiss, initiated during a time of extreme emotional stress. But they'd both agreed it was a mistake. Jasmine wasn't interested, and he didn't blame her. Why would she give up her freedom to take on the responsibility of another woman's child? And the thought of allowing someone else to take Mandy's place in his or Liam's life still tied his insides into knots.

His curt response had ended the conversation with his friends. But long after they left, their words still circled through his mind.

And each argument he posed seemed less and less convincing.

* * *

Jasmine turned onto Hilltop Road and released a sigh. Today started a new year. A year filled with uncertainty. Colton had insisted that she come up and join him and Liam for lunch. He'd said he needed to make up for the Christmas dinner that had never materialized.

Returning to the cozy house, even for a visit, was a bittersweet experience. She'd come here a month ago, ready for another typical assignment. She'd approached this one like she had all her others—with confidence and cool professionalism, emotionally detached.

No assignment was "just a job." Whether she was providing extra security for a visiting celebrity or protecting a woman from a crazed ex-boyfriend, she gave it her all, throwing herself into the line of fire to protect her charge from harm.

But she always kept a distinct line between her professional and her personal life. No, not a line—a chasm, a virtual Grand Canyon. Or a wall. The Great Wall of China.

Until this time. Somehow, one sad little boy and his grieving father had changed that.

Maybe it was all the times she'd rocked Liam, soothing away his fears after a terrifying nightmare. The way he'd snuggled against her and wrapped his arms around her waist. Those times he'd called her Mommy and melted her heart.

Maybe it was the late-night talks with his father, talks that had gradually transitioned from superficial to levels of sharing she'd never experienced with anyone else.

Whatever the reason, the barriers she'd kept up for years had gradually crumbled. Now she found herself head over heels in love with a man she'd never have, because his heart still belonged to someone else.

That kiss had proved it. At first, it was amazement, anticipation and joy all rolled into one heart-pounding, ground-shifting experience. Then everything changed. She knew the moment it shifted. The kiss was no longer hers. It was borrowed, maybe even stolen. Because it belonged to his deceased wife.

She slowed the rental car as she approached Colton's property. The insurance adjuster had notified her yesterday that they'd be totaling hers. Tomorrow she'd begin the search for a new one.

When she reached Colton's driveway, he'd already opened the gate for her. She killed the engine and stepped from the vehicle, pulse pounding with a mix of nervousness and excitement. She'd hadn't seen them since they'd returned to Murphy after Colton's twenty-four-hour hospital stay. But they'd had daily phone conversations and even Skyped a few times.

She made her way up the front walk to the deck. The living room curtains were open, framing the still-decorated Christmas tree. Maybe that was one of Colton's traditions—putting away Christmas on New Year's Day. They'd decorated together; maybe they'd undecorate together.

Moments after she rapped on the door, it swung open. Colton stood inside, weight shifted to his left leg, a crutch tucked under each arm.

He extended both arms. "Happy New Year."

If the strength of his embrace was any indication, he'd missed her as much as she'd missed him.

"Jasmine!"

She pulled away from Colton to find Liam running

full speed toward her. He didn't stop until he'd slammed into her and wound both arms around her legs.

Laughing, she clutched the doorjamb for support, then disentangled herself so she could pick him up. "Have you been a good boy for your daddy?"

Liam nodded.

When her gaze met Colton's, his eyes held seriousness. "Your name is the first thing he's said since the kidnapping."

Her heart fluttered, partly from Colton's words and partly from the warmth in his gaze.

She put Liam down and bent to pet Brutus. His greeting was less exuberant than Liam's, but just as joyful. Since the moment she entered, he'd stood staring up at her, tail wagging.

Colton retrieved a small package from under the tree and handed it to her. "Today is happy New Year and belated merry Christmas all in one. I forgot to give it to you before you left. I brought it to Atlanta with me on Christmas, but with everything that happened, I forgot again."

After putting Liam on the floor, she tore off the wrapping paper to reveal a small hinged box. It held a gold locket, Liam's picture inside. "I love it." She worked the fine chain free of the slots and held it up.

After Colton had fastened it around her neck, he extended an arm toward the kitchen. "Lunch is ready."

When she turned that way, she drew in a sharp breath. A white tablecloth covered the small table. A dozen red roses occupied a vase at one end, candles burning on both sides. The places were set with china, even Liam's.

"Wow, this is a bit fancy for just lunch, isn't it?"

"It's not 'just lunch.'"

Ignoring her raised brows, he removed a covered casserole from the oven and placed it on one of the three pot holders on the table.

She strapped Liam into his high chair. "What can I do to help?"

"You can pour our tea and put some milk into one of Liam's sippy cups."

When finished, she moved to the table, where three hot baking dishes waited. Colton removed their lids, and a variety of aromas wrapped around her. Her stomach rumbled. There was some kind of chicken dish, a potato casserole and green beans with sliced almonds.

After Colton slid serving spoons into each, he sat next to Liam. She took a seat opposite Colton. An envelope lay facedown on the table in front of the roses. She eyed it, curious about what was inside. With all he'd done to make a beautiful presentation, he wouldn't have left a piece of mail lying on the table. It was there for a reason.

Colton grasped his son's hand, then reached across the table to take hers. When he'd finished blessing the food, he indicated the serving spoon in the chicken. "Help yourself."

She dished up a large breast swimming in some kind of delectable sauce.

"Did you make all this?" Either his cooking skills had improved in the past few weeks or he'd gotten some help.

"Okay, I admit it. I enlisted some help from Paige. I was hoping to impress you. Have I succeeded?"

"If it tastes half as good as it smells, you have." After

spooning the other two items onto her plate, she looked across the table at Colton. "I went to church yesterday."

A smile climbed up his cheeks. "Awesome."

"When those guys had Liam and we'd lost you, I prayed. And God answered. I figured it was time to look more seriously into this faith you have."

"And how was the service?"

"Good. I'll definitely be back."

The conversation over lunch was light. Colton hadn't gone back to work yet but hoped the doctor would release him in another week or two, even if he needed the help of crutches. By then Paige would have returned to school, so Liam would go back to day care.

Liam had had two nightmares since they'd come home several days ago. At least the frequency hadn't increased from what it had been before. Maybe the kidnapping didn't traumatize him as much as they'd feared. Apparently, the kidnappers had treated him well.

As they conversed, she shifted her gaze to the envelope several times, unable to shake the feeling that the light conversation was a prequel to something much weightier. Apparently, Colton planned to make her wait until the end of the meal to find out what.

After lunch, she cleared the dishes while Colton served up three pieces of cheesecake and poured a blueberry glaze over them. Ten minutes later, all the plates were empty.

Colton sat back and rubbed his stomach. "That hit the spot."

"That did more than hit the spot. I feel like I've just been served a gourmet meal."

"I have to give Paige all the credit."

"Not *all* the credit. I doubt she did all this on her own initiative."

The smile he gave her made her chest constrict. It figured. After a history of falling for guys who were bad news, she'd finally found one perfect for her and someone else had gotten him first.

Colton stood and returned moments later with a wet cloth. After cleaning the blueberry glaze from his son's fingers, he handed the envelope to Liam. "How about giving Miss Jasmine her card?"

A smile spread across Liam's face as he passed it to her.

She removed the card from the envelope and read the script. "May the year ahead be filled with unexpected blessings…"

When she opened it, a folded piece of paper fell to the table. Before picking it up, she read the words on the inside of the card. "…and joy beyond measure."

It was signed, "Love, Colton and Liam."

She looked at Liam, then his father. "Thank you."

When she picked up what had fallen to the table, Liam clapped his hands, excitement radiating from him. It was a piece of computer paper, folded in fourths. She opened it slowly.

Large crayon letters filled the page—

*Will you please marry my daddy?*

Her heart stuttered to a stop, then kick-started in a crazy rhythm. She longed to say yes. Colton was everything she wanted in a man. He was the answer to what she'd longed for even before she could put it into words. And even though she'd fought it with everything in her, she'd fallen hopelessly in love with him.

His grief over the loss of his wife drew her to him in

a way she'd never expected. They'd both lost someone dear to them, and it had created a special bond.

But there was a difference. She'd moved past her loss. He hadn't.

She met Colton's gaze. "And how does his daddy feel?"

"His daddy wants this as much as Liam does."

She shook her head. Colton wanted it because he felt it was best for his son.

"I'm not Mandy. And I can't live under her shadow. From what I've gathered, she was everything I'm not. I can't compete. I won't even try."

"No, you're not Mandy."

She flinched at the words, even though she'd just said them herself. Even though they were true. She lowered her gaze to her hands, folded on the table over the card.

"You're Jasmine. And you're every bit as incredible."

She again met his eyes.

"You have qualities she didn't have, qualities that I admire just as much. Although you had no nurturing yourself, you have an innate sense of how to make Liam feel loved and secure. In spite of your upbringing, you've become an amazing woman. You're strong and brave. You'd throw yourself in front of a train if it meant protecting someone you cared about."

She shook her head. "You'll never have with me what you had with your wife. Every relationship I've had has failed."

"Maybe you were looking for the wrong things with the wrong guys." He reached for the crutches he'd leaned against the wall.

As soon as he stood, Liam raised both arms. "Down?"

His attention shifted to his son, and she expelled a

relieved sigh. She needed space, the opportunity to digest everything he'd just said.

She didn't have long. Within moments, Colton had wiped his son's hands and placed him on the floor. Two seconds later, Liam was running for his room.

Colton circled the table and pulled out the chair next to her. "I've been fighting feelings for you since the first time I saw you comforting my son. I believed if I gave in, I wouldn't be honoring Mandy's memory."

"What changed?"

"A stern talking-to by some meddling friends. When Tanner and Bryce came to see me in the hospital, they said things I didn't want to hear. But they got me thinking."

He took her hands in his. "Over the last few days, I've come to realize some things. First, Liam isn't going to remember his mother, no matter what I do to keep her memory alive. He's just too young."

He drew in a deep breath. "Second, in trying to honor my wife's memory, I've neglected what I know her wishes would be."

"And what's that?"

"To do what's best for both Liam and me. That's having you in our lives."

He squeezed her hands. "I love you, Jasmine. And I'm asking if you'll marry me. If you won't say yes to Liam's cute little note, will you say yes to my heartfelt proposal?"

Warmth surged through her as if a geyser had erupted inside. Behind her eyes, pressure built. And heat. Several seconds passed before she recognized the sensation for what it was.

No, she wasn't going to cry. She'd experienced hardship and sorrow. She'd seen death. Many times. She railed in anger. She punched things. She stormed off to be alone and gain control over her emotions.

But she didn't cry. Not ever.

That was exactly what was happening, though.

The heat built. Tears overflowed her lashes and trickled down her face.

"Jasmine? What did I say?"

"I'm sorry." At least she wasn't doing the ugly cry she'd seen on some women, eyes squeezed shut and face contorted. It was just these silent, stubborn tears making rivulets down her cheeks. "I'm not upset. I'm happy."

And that was the problem.

She handled adversity with amazing strength. But this wasn't adversity. It was joy. Maybe one reason she never cried was because she'd never been this deliriously happy.

She swiped at the tears streaming down her face. "How about if I say yes to both?"

As he pulled her to her feet, Liam returned to the kitchen holding his latest Lego creation. He raised it for their inspection.

Colton took it from him and looked at it from every angle. "This is a pretty amazing house. Did you do this all by yourself?"

Liam nodded, a big smile climbing up his cheeks, and Jasmine offered her own praise.

Courtship was going to be different with a little one. And when she and Colton entered marriage, it would be as a threesome. Not what she'd envisioned for her life.

But she wouldn't have it any other way.

She watched Colton hand him back the miniature house. "What are you going to have him call me?"

"Anything he wants."

"Even if it's *Mommy*?"

"Especially if it's *Mommy*."

Liam ran off to his room to play. After wrapping her in his arms, Colton pressed his lips to hers, then pulled back. Hesitation filled his eyes. "Are you sure you're ready for this?"

"I'm positive."

"You're giving up your freedom."

"It's a small price to pay for what I'm getting in return."

He searched her eyes. "And this is what you want?"

"I want you. And I want Liam." She heaved a sigh. "Shut up and kiss me."

All his hesitation dissolved. He pulled her closer. When he slanted his mouth across hers, her knees went weak.

There was nothing borrowed about this kiss. It was hers and hers alone.

Colton was hers.

And he always would be.

One hundred percent.

# EPILOGUE

Colton walked down the sidewalk with Jasmine's hand in his. The Valley River flowed lazily by on his left. On his right, a soft blanket of lawn stretched upward. A brief shower had passed through while they'd been in church, and the landscape now shone with a post-rain brilliance.

Behind them, Bryce and Andi carried on a conversation. Paige and Tanner brought up the rear. Four children danced down the path ahead of them, one several heads taller than the other three. They'd all finished a picnic at Konehete Park. Now the kids were having trouble containing their excitement over a promised playground visit.

"Slow down." Colton used his authoritative parent voice. "You're getting too far ahead of us."

Liam cast a quick glance over his shoulder before turning back around to corral his younger playmates. As Colton watched his son give directions, then shift from instructor to buddy, he couldn't stop his smile. If he hadn't lived those agonizing months himself, he'd never believe the joyful, energetic boy in front of him had ever been the sad, silent child who'd occupied his home three and a half years ago.

And during those dark weeks after Mandy's death, he would never have anticipated that in a few short years Liam would have a perky, dark-haired little sister.

Just past the tennis courts, the kids made a sharp right to follow the path that led away from the river. They knew the way to the playground. They'd been there often enough. Picnics in the park, followed by playtime, were a regular occurrence for all of them.

Andi and Bryce had been the first to announce their good news. Three months later, Paige had learned she was expecting. Three months after that, Jasmine had awoken nauseated.

For a full trimester, all three women were in one stage or another of expanding bellies and raging hormones. Tanner had insisted it was something in the water. Colton had sat back in wonder, amazed at the unexpected blessings God had brought into his life.

When they reached the fenced playground, Colton's little girl slid her hand into his and pointed.

Liam stepped up next to her. "Lacey wants you to push her on the swings."

Although she was two years old, Colton's daughter spoke very little. It wasn't that she didn't know how. With a protective big brother who anticipated her every desire, she probably didn't feel the need.

Paige grinned. "Swing time with Daddy sounds like a great idea." She turned toward Tanner and waved her hands in a shooing motion. "The ladies have more scheming to do."

Colton laughed. It was that time again. The three couples had done combined family vacations for the past three years. From what he'd overheard, this year's plans involved renting a motorhome.

He led his two friends toward the swings, then lifted Lacey into one. Soon Tanner's son swung on one side of her, Bryce's on the other. Being the only girl in their foursome had never seemed to bother Lacey.

When Colton sought out the women, they were seated on one of the park benches, huddled over their cell phones. Paige said something and passed hers to Andi, who then showed it to Jasmine. Probably an interesting travel destination.

Paige had completed her degree and gotten her teaching certification. Next week, she would finish her first year as a fifth-grade teacher. Andi was still managing her party store and doing special events decorating.

Of the three women, it was Jasmine's path that had taken the greatest deviation. After she and Colton had gotten married, she'd given up her job with Burch Security and gone to work part-time for the Cherokee County Sheriff's Office. Nine months later, Lacey showed up. Jasmine took temporary leave and never went back. She'd said she would. Someday.

Colton hadn't pushed. She stayed plenty busy chasing around two active children, besides volunteering at MountainView and assisting Andi with the occasional decorating job. During the time she'd been a full-time mom, Liam had flourished. Lacey also seemed to enjoy having her around.

When Colton looked at Bryce, he, too, was watching the three women.

Bryce spoke without looking at him. "What do you think they're planning?"

"A cross-country trip. Or maybe Canada. Just a guess."

Tanner nodded. "I wouldn't mind seeing Canada again."

"Yeah." Colton knew where his friend's mind had gone. The same place his own had—the two-week rafting and backpacking trip the three of them had taken years ago. That had been when they were young, single guys, without the responsibilities of wives and children.

Bryce sighed. "Remember when vacations meant hang gliding, rock climbing or finding some other way to pit ourselves against the forces of nature?"

Tanner's response held a touch of nostalgia. "Yeah."

"You guys ever miss it?"

Colton didn't have to think about his answer for long. "Miss it? Sometimes. Regret where I am now? Not a chance."

He was married to an amazing woman. He had a happy, well-adjusted son. Both were blessings he'd never expected to receive. As if that wasn't enough, his world was enriched even further by a beautiful little girl.

Regrets? Not a one.

He wouldn't trade the life he had now for all the wealth in the world.

\* \* \* \* \*

**Lisa Phillips** is a British-born, tea-drinking, guitar-playing wife and mom of two. She and her husband lead worship together at their local church. Lisa pens high-stakes stories of mayhem and disaster where you can find made-for-each-other love that always ends in a happily-ever-after. She understands that faith is a work in progress more exciting than any story she can dream up. You can find out more about her books at authorlisaphillips.com.

### Books by Lisa Phillips

### Love Inspired Suspense

#### Secret Service Agents

*Security Detail*
*Homefront Defenders*
*Yuletide Suspect*
*Witness in Hiding*
*Defense Breach*
*Murder Mix-Up*

*Double Agent*
*Star Witness*
*Manhunt*
*Easy Prey*
*Sudden Recall*
*Dead End*

Visit the Author Profile page
at Harlequin.com for more titles.

# YULETIDE SUSPECT

Lisa Phillips

And when he comes home, he calls together his friends and neighbors, saying to them, "Rejoice with me, for I have found my sheep, which was lost!"

—*Luke* 15:6

To all my readers.
Have a very merry and blessed Christmas season.

# ONE

Arrest him. Or apologize.

Liberty Westmark gripped the steering wheel, not sure which she was going to do first. If she ever got there. She peered out the windshield, where fat flakes of snow obscured both lanes of the highway beyond her high beams.

"In six hundred yards, turn right."

The voice of her GPS was loud and clear, but the way was not. She'd probably wind up turning into a ditch. It would serve her right to end up the sad conclusion of an obscure news article about the snowstorm of the century. Heartwarming. She rolled her eyes and muttered, "Lone Secret Service agent who left ahead of her team gets lost and freezes to death chasing a dream."

She froze. A *suspect*.

Not a dream.

Where had that come from, anyway? The fact that Tate Almers had been her fiancé a year ago was absolutely not relevant anymore—unless she got the chance to apologize. Otherwise this was just work, and once she had Tate in custody she could drop him off at the nearest federal agency office and go back to her cozy DC condo and her hairless cat.

Job done.

It was a courtesy, nothing more. Tate might have done something bad—really bad—but the qualifier was what made her unable to believe it was actually his doing. A plane had gone down, and three people were missing—two White House staffers and a senator. The man she had known and worked with—okay, and loved—would never have done something like this. That history was why she'd convinced the director she should come here ahead of the rest of the team.

Liberty was going to give Tate the courtesy of explaining, and then he could tell his former Secret Service team the same thing.

The turn came up faster than she was expecting. Liberty hit the brakes and took the corner too fast. The back end of her car hit ice and fishtailed. Stupid man, living in the middle of stupid nowhere. The car kept spinning. Liberty gripped the wheel harder, like it was going to help.

She squealed.

When the car came to a stop, she was sideways on the single-track road.

Liberty sighed. "No one heard that squeal."

She was still the fully fledged Secret Service agent her teammates respected. Just a little ice that threw her for a minute. No big deal. She was fine.

Liberty shook off the rush of adrenaline that had set her heart racing and righted the car on the road. A single lane, probably dirt or gravel, but right now it was covered in a layer of snow and ice. Liberty drove slower than she needed to down to the house.

It was more of a cabin, really. The roofline was lit up with Christmas lights, and she could see a Christmas tree in the front window, the only light in the house. Tears filled her eyes. It was beautiful, like a Christmas card. Tate was a no-nonsense kind of guy, and this was anything but. What on earth? Then it hit her. What if he was married now? What if he'd found someone else, and this was all for *her*?

Liberty nearly turned around and left, but the Secret Service would be here soon and she wanted answers. After it was done, she'd be able to move on for good. Sure, he might be married, but actually that was better. It would help sever those few lingering ties, right?

Liberty cracked the car door and braced against the cold as she got out, then leaned back in and grabbed her gloves. The wool wouldn't protect her much against this temperature. Cold cut through the layers of her clothing, and the wind chafed her cheeks. Her coat covered her badge, but maybe there would be time to really talk before she told him she was here for work reasons.

A couple of dogs barked, but not in the house. The sound came from the barn. Liberty waded through snow and banged her fist on the barn door. It swung open and two dogs raced toward her, barking louder. Liberty took a step back.

Tate stepped out of the barn, but she couldn't take her focus off the dogs, even as she backed up more across the stretch of snow over the driveway between the barn and the house. They barked and circled her, their attention imposing enough that Liberty didn't move.

"Good boys. Sit."

Both dogs sat, one on either side of her. Liberty wanted to slump onto the packed down snow between them. The sound of Tate's voice cut through her and left a ragged wound in its wake. She glanced up, and her eyes locked with his. It was too dark to get a good look, but in the glow of the Christmas lights the line of his jaw was set. He wasn't happy.

One of the dogs broke his sit and barked.

Tate's eyes widened, fixed on some point beyond her, away from the house. "What…" He lunged and grabbed her arm, dragged her the ten feet or so back toward the barn and yelled, "Bubblegum!"

A gunshot went off. Liberty ducked, having no idea where the shot had come from. She skidded on the barn floor, reached the end of Tate's grasp and snapped back toward him. She grimaced. Tate didn't let go. Outside the dogs barked, and someone yelled.

"Intruder," he said. "I thought it was you who set off the alarm, but there was a man out there with a gun." A gunshot went off outside. "Do you have your weapon?"

Liberty pulled her gun from the holster at her back, under her jacket. He grabbed it from her. "Hey—"

Tate stepped outside and shut the door behind him. The dogs continued to bark. Outside, Tate yelled, "Hey!"

A gunshot followed.

Liberty pulled the backup weapon from her ankle holster and moved to the door. She was the Secret Service agent. Sure, Tate had been one, too, over a year ago. But he'd quit, and Liberty didn't have time to think through all of that—or the fact that it was basically her fault.

Liberty wanted to pray, but that part of her life was long gone, just like her love life. Neither had ever done her any favors or bettered her in any way. She'd given up on God and romance both in the last eighteen months.

This was one last favor to Tate, and then she was done. Liberty was going to live her life her way, on her terms.

The door swung open before she reached it. Tate strode to her, and the dogs raced in around him. Liberty shook her head. "What on earth was that? And why did you shut me in here?"

"Man outside," he said, without handing her weapon back to her. "An intruder, which I already mentioned." He didn't look happy. "He ran off. The dogs did their job."

As though they knew he'd complimented them, the two dogs returned to his side and sat to be petted. One was a German shepherd, lean enough that Liberty wanted to feed the animal treats. The other was a stocky Airedale who came to her next. She didn't pet him.

Tate raised his eyebrow. "You still have that ugly cat?"

She ignored the question. Loki was alive and well, not that it was any of his business. "Bubblegum?" They had to talk about something; otherwise she'd just stare at the blond hair sticking out the bottom of his knit beanie. His hair grew fast and had to be cut frequently, but it seemed Tate no longer cared. He wore the mountain man uniform of jeans and a checkered shirt under a padded denim jacket. No gloves. Wasn't he cold?

"Bubblegum is a command. If the person attacking you doesn't know what you just asked your dog to do, they'll think twice." Tate's jaw was hard again. "He shot at them, saw me and then ran off."

"Are you going to give me my gun back?"

Tate stood stunned for a second before he forced himself to snap out of it. He motioned for her to back up. "You have one, and mine are all in the house. I'll be keeping this until I know for sure he's gone."

He had to focus on the intruder who'd just tried to kill him. Otherwise he'd stare at her blond hair. Those blue-green eyes. *Focus.*

"That is against policy and you know it." She used her most snooty voice, and it almost made him smile. Almost. "I can't lend out my duty weapon."

"I'll be sure to write that on the form I fill out explaining why you're dead." Tate swept past her and moved toward the door again. Liberty huffed behind him, but he figured she didn't argue because she knew he wasn't wrong.

Tate cracked open the door, peered out into the night and tried to tamp down the boiling rage. Shoot at him? Whatever. Shoot at his dogs? Unacceptable. Tate adjusted his grip on the gun, though using it would deny him the fight he was itching for. He'd always had a temper problem. He'd learned in the army how to channel it into discipline, and during his time with the Secret Service, Tate had rarely lost his cool. It never went well when he did.

He sucked in a breath of icy air and counted to ten in his head. One of the dog's muzzles touched his leg, and he reached down to pet Joey. His Airedale boy loved life and thought everything was a game. The German shepherd, Gem, was more task oriented. Wake up. Eat. Work. Sleep. Repeat.

"Looks clear."

He shoved the door wider and walked out. Snow was thick on the ground and falling fast. They'd have another two feet by tomorrow, but that wasn't what had his attention. He pointed at the far end of his front yard where the dense trees began. They blocked his view of the land, but he much preferred being in a cocoon of privacy.

Tate pointed. "That's where he ran off to."

"And you shoved me in the barn so you could take care of it?"

She was still stuck on that? "Guess it was a reflex. All those years of protection duty for the Secret Service ingrained in me. I'm the one who faces the danger."

"And the dogs."

She really was intent on arguing, wasn't she? Tate sighed. "They're trained."

"And I'm not? I'm still a Secret Service agent, Tate."

He turned to her. "That's not what I meant." Not that he'd have heard from out here if she'd quit or not.

He didn't know how to get himself out of this one, and why did he even feel like he needed to? He didn't owe her anything, and he didn't want her to owe him anything back. Whatever they'd had was done now. She'd killed it when she gave him his ring back and sent him packing.

Tate had lost it a couple of days later and gotten pushed into early retirement from the Secret Service over it, but this life was better. Simpler. He knew who he was out here, with the dogs.

Tate scanned the area but couldn't see any sign of the gunman. The man might return. He could scout out the area and see if the guy was still here, but he'd have to do it after Liberty left.

The dogs trotted along. Gem scanned the area, but Joey ran in circles, ready to play. Tate motioned with his hand and gave them the command to head for the porch and wait for him there. He used it mostly when the UPS guy delivered packages, but it came in handy at other times as well.

Tate didn't even want to contemplate what it meant

that Liberty was here. He'd do so later, when he was alone again. The way he preferred it.

*Liar.*

Okay, so it wasn't his choice, but life was life. She'd broken up with him. Called off the whole thing, and he didn't even know why, so he'd simply concluded it was him. He'd always known there was something defective in him, and she'd tried to make it work. Until she realized it never would.

Tate stopped beside her car and opened the driver's-side door. Waited. She didn't move, just stood there looking like she had so much to say. He really didn't want to hear any of it. What was the point? He took her in. All her blond hair, even softer than it looked, was secured back in a business ponytail. Dress slacks. Completely the wrong shoes to be traipsing around in snow. The bottom few inches of her pants were wet, but it wasn't his problem, now was it? Not anymore.

Liberty's eyebrows pinched together. She wore makeup, but not much. The top curve of her lip had a bump he'd always thought was adorable, as she'd been born with a cleft palate. The scar where it had been repaired was barely visible now. Still cute, though.

"We should call the police and report that man. He tried to kill you."

Tate said, "Maybe he was here to kill *you*."

Liberty blinked. "I… No, I don't think so." Still, there was a question in her eyes as she considered it.

Tate didn't want to think about her being in danger. It was a reality of being a Secret Service agent, but not one he was going to dwell on. "He can't have known you'd be here, unless he followed you, and how could he do it through this terrain, on foot?" Only her car was out here. His truck was under the carport.

Liberty pulled out her phone. "I'll call emergency services. Get a sheriff, or whoever is the law around here, to come over."

"Give me your phone. I'll call him." Even if her cell actually worked up here, she shouldn't do the talking. That was more involvement than she needed to have in this situation.

Then again, if she left now, he could make the report to the sheriff and perhaps pretend she'd never even been here. It wasn't exactly honest, but tell that to his heart.

Liberty clutched the phone. "I've given you enough already."

She had no idea. "I don't have a signal, and I don't have a landline either."

"So how do you communicate with people?"

Tate said, "Shortwave radio."

Liberty glanced up from her phone. Evidently she had the one carrier that actually got a signal up here. "There's no reason to be rude."

She thought he was lying? Tate just enjoyed his privacy.

She said, "I know you want me to leave, but there's a reason I'm here, so I'm not going to go. I came to tell you the Secret Service is on their way here to talk with you."

"About what?" He had even less to say to his former employer than he did to his former fiancée.

"A plane went missing a hundred miles from here. Two White House staffers and a senator were on board."

"I haven't heard anything about it." Not that he watched the news much. His aerial only got half a dozen channels, and he didn't listen to the police band all the time on his scanner.

She kept talking. "It happened in the early hours of this morning. They lost contact right after the pilot sent out a distress call. We don't know if the plane went down or if they were hijacked. Everyone is out looking for it."

"I'm sure I can lend some assistance with the search," he said. "For old times' sake."

"That isn't why the Secret Service wants to talk with you."

Tate didn't know what else there would be to say. It didn't seem like this had anything to do with him. "They'll have to get in line. I need to make a report with the sheriff about a gunman on my property."

Liberty let him change the subject. "Did you see who it was?"

Tate shook his head, still leaning his forearms on her open car door. Was she ever going to get in and drive away? This was painful enough without her drawing it out.

Tate sighed. "I didn't get a good look at his face, but he didn't seem familiar to me." And it had definitely been a man. "Joey nearly chased him to the trees."

Liberty didn't smile. He knew she liked dogs, so he figured the problem was him. Tate glanced at the dogs. Joey wasn't sitting the way Gem was. Instead, the Airedale paced the porch by the front door with his nose to the mat. He pawed at the door and then barked once.

Tate saw the flash of movement through the living room window.

He started running toward his cabin. "Someone's in the house."

# TWO

Tate ran to the front door, so Liberty circled the house in case the intruder ran out the back. It was slow going, wading through thick snow, but she was already soaked and there would be time later to thaw out her toes. Liberty pulled out her cell phone and dialed emergency services. She requested the police, and was told the sheriff was on his way. The dispatcher seemed to know exactly where Tate's house was, but this was a small town. Maybe they knew each other. Maybe she—it had been a woman—was his girlfriend.

Liberty stuffed her phone back in her jacket pocket and huffed out a breath at the workout she was getting. Okay, not only at the workout. Who cared if there was someone in Tate's life now? It wasn't like she had any claim on him. Not since she'd broken it off and severed the tie between them. As much as it had pained her to do it—and the reason for it hurt almost more than the act of doing it—Liberty hadn't had another choice.

There was no future for them.

Still, if she got the chance, then she might tell him she regretted hurting him. But Liberty was never, ever going to tell him why. She could barely even think about it herself.

She reached the rear corner of the cabin, and the back door slammed. Liberty brought her gun up as the man flew out the door, stumbled and then started to run.

"Secret Service! Freeze!" Her voice barely carried.

He didn't even slow down.

She ran after him. Tate rushed out the back door and got to the man first, launched himself at the guy and tackled his legs. The two went down in the snow like an ugly version of a snow angel. Tate grunted, and the two men struggled.

Liberty stopped six feet away and planted her now-numb feet. "Freeze, or I'll shoot!" Tate would have to get out of the way first, but the man didn't know.

Tate shifted and she saw the man's face. He was probably in his midthirties.

He gritted his teeth and struggled. Tate jammed his arm up under the man's chin. "Who are you?"

The man jerked his head around, trying to get away. "Get off me." His gaze found hers, and she saw the moment he realized he'd lost this fight to the two of them. His eyes flashed. "Let me go."

If he was going to try to get her to shoot him, Liberty wasn't going to oblige. Suicide by cop might be something the police had to face, but it wasn't part of her résumé. "Tate."

He lifted the man off the snow to his feet. "Who are you?"

The guy looked like he was about to bolt. He wore jeans, boots and a heavy jacket. The men had both dressed for the weather, while Liberty was dressed for a mild winter in DC. Which was exactly what they'd been having. How was she to know this part of Montana was freezing and buried under four feet of snow?

When the man didn't answer, Tate said, "Find me something to secure him with."

Liberty went inside and found a dog leash hanging by the front door, beside where a big duffel sat on the floor. He'd always carried a bag to his workouts. The two animals were on dog beds in the living room, making the Christmas picture complete. They watched her move through the cabin, but thankfully didn't come over expecting her to pet them. Liberty couldn't handle that, when they would only remind her of her favorite dog. She'd had only cats since Beauregard died.

Hurrying back to Tate, Liberty held out the leash. He motioned to the guy with a tilt of his head. "You do it."

"Put your hands behind your back." She stowed her weapon and stepped behind him, where she secured his hands with the leash. "The sheriff is on his way."

"Good." Tate tugged on the man's elbow, took him into the kitchen and deposited the man on a chair. "Don't move."

Liberty shut the back door and took off her gloves, so thin they were pointless. She blew on one hand, then the other, switching off the hand holding her gun as she attempted to impart some warmth back in her stiff fingers. Tate frowned and then hit the power icon on the display of his coffee maker. Fancy. She used a four-cup coffeepot, the cheapest she could find, but he'd always been particular about what brand he drank. Liberty didn't care, so long as it was thick, hot and strong.

The man in the chair glanced between them but didn't say anything. Under the LED kitchen lights his clothes looked worn, his hair matted to the top of his head.

Liberty disliked silence. She motioned to the man but asked Tate, "Is this the guy from outside the barn?" He could have come back and gotten inside somehow. Though he'd had a gun before.

Tate shook his head. "This is a different guy." He pushed off the counter and took a step toward the man. "Come here with your partner. Come here to kill me. Why? Who am I to you?"

The guy looked away. Liberty had to wonder where the other man had disappeared to. Two assailants at Tate's house tonight, within minutes of each other? It seemed impossible they weren't connected.

Tate slammed both palms on his table. Liberty started and the seated man's eyes widened. Tate said, "Why did you come here to kill me?"

"I want my lawyer."

Liberty said, "We're not cops."

The minute the words were out of her mouth, Tate glanced at her. What? What had she said? He was being hard on the man. Yes, he had a right to be angry. But it was as though he'd forgotten everything they'd learned about questioning and just gone with what was in his gut: anger.

The last time she'd seen him, Tate had been so angry it had taken two of their fellow agents to pull him back from punching the director. He hadn't been fired; it'd been more like a mutual decision between both parties that he should move on from the Secret Service. Liberty's heart had broken even more than it already was that day, as she'd realized it was all her fault. Those tendencies he'd had as a kid to get mad instead of working through his problems had resurfaced through no fault of his own. Only hers.

Liberty strode to the intruder, because if she didn't she'd start crying, thinking about how everything between her and Tate had gone wrong. She didn't want to contemplate *again* how it was all her fault.

She said, "Stand up," and glanced at Tate. He nodded to indicate he had her back. Liberty stowed her gun, but the man hadn't moved. She hauled him up by his elbow and patted his pockets.

She found a cell phone, then a knife, and laid both on the table. She kept searching but found nothing else. Liberty grabbed the phone and stepped back. It wasn't locked, and it had no apps downloaded. There were no contacts listed, and if there were any messages, those had been deleted as well.

"It's clean." She tossed the phone on the table.

"Our friend here can talk to the sheriff."

"And it doesn't bother you that *his* friend tried to kill you?" She couldn't believe he was acting so blasé about this.

Tate shrugged. Was this his default now, when he'd decided he wasn't mad? The indifference almost hurt more than the anger.

One of the dogs started barking. Tate said, "Sheriff's here."

Liberty left him with the intruder and went to the front door.

Tate waited where he was until Liberty walked back in with the sheriff. He lifted his chin at Dane Winters, a good friend since peewee football. "This guy is all yours." Tate explained what had happened. The more he talked, the wider Dane's eyes grew.

"And you have a guest." Dane smiled. Because, yes,

Tate had shared about Liberty. But Dane could fish all he wanted, Tate wasn't going to spill.

"She was just leaving." His only guest except Dane in months.

He pushed off the counter and didn't offer anyone a cup of coffee, even though it was done brewing. He could drink it later and stay up all night brooding about the mess his life was now.

"Don't you want to know why I'm here?" Liberty asked.

She might think he should be curious about this missing plane. She likely would be if things were reversed and he'd shown up at her house after so long. They'd been engaged. Tate had honestly figured it meant something, but apparently not. It was a good thing she wasn't here for a reunion, or she would have been sorely disappointed.

Liberty looked almost sad. "Like I said, I'm here because a small aircraft, a business jet, went down not far from here. On board was a senator from Oklahoma and two White House staffers. Twelve hours ago we lost contact with them. We think the plane might've crashed somewhere close to here, and it's believed there was foul play involved, possibly with the pilot. At least, as much was indicated from the last radio call before communication was cut off." She paused. "We need to find those people."

"That should be an FBI investigation, shouldn't it?"

"They're on it. But at the top of the list of suspects who might be involved is a certain former Secret Service agent I happen to know personally. So I figured, why not? For old times' sake I'll visit this former agent and let him know the Secret Service and the FBI are all on their way here to ask you a whole lot of uncomfortable questions you aren't going to want to answer."

She couldn't seriously think he might be part of it. "You think I have something to hide? Something to do with this?"

"Do you?" She lifted her chin, like there was no history between them and she had every right to suspect him of something heinous. "It's a valid question."

"You really think I've changed that much?"

She didn't answer. Instead, she said, "The FBI and the Secret Service want to know if you're involved. But they're betting on the fact that a disgruntled former Secret Service agent—"

"Disgruntled?" Why would they think he harbored resentment? Tate had moved on. Wasn't it obvious?

Liberty shrugged. "Despite the cute cabin all decorated for a family Christmas, there is evidence against you. Seems to me from the blog, at least, that in the last few months your attitude has deteriorated. And it's the basis of their evidence."

"What blog?"

The sheriff shifted, but Dane couldn't hide the fact that he was listening to their conversation. They were friends, and Dane was curious. Tate didn't fault him for it. Even beyond this missing plane, there was a lot to talk about. Too bad there wasn't time.

And good thing he didn't want to talk about it anyway. His life now was none of her business.

Except the blog thing. What was that about?

When the sheriff peered at a tattoo on the man's neck—one Tate hadn't noticed until now—Tate went over to look as well. They glanced at each other, and Tate said, "Russians."

"Like the mob?" Liberty asked. "In backwoods Montana?"

The sheriff stepped back and shrugged. "It happens. Not often, but all kinds of people travel through this town on the way to somewhere. Some of them even like it and stay, and not all are law-abiding citizens." He glanced at Tate. "I got an update about this missing plane an hour ago. We should talk about it."

Tate didn't like the look on Dane's face at all. He'd known, and he stood there and let Liberty give her whole speech about him being a criminal.

"You want to take my badge for being involved, and keep it until I'm out from under suspicion?" The idea of losing the job as well, when he'd already lost so much, sat like a bad burrito in his stomach.

Liberty gasped. "His badge?"

He nearly kicked himself for saying it while she was here.

Dane said, "Tate is a deputy with the county sheriff's department. He only works shifts occasionally, and I pay him so much less than he's worth it's not even funny. But technically he's an employee. And as a sounding board, he's been invaluable."

Tate shook his head and pulled the badge from his drawer. "More like it's your attempt to make sure I'm not cooped up here all the time. Like it's a bad thing."

The sheriff shrugged again, pocketed the badge and then took the now-cuffed intruder out to his car where he'd be secure.

Liberty nodded. "The FBI doesn't know you're a deputy sheriff. It will strengthen our argument."

Tate said, "We don't have an argument, Liberty. We don't have anything. You took care of that." He saw the blow the words inflicted, but couldn't let himself care about it. She'd ripped him to shreds when she'd given his ring back and started the cascading fall of his life into this pit. A pit he tried to pretty up, just so he didn't dwell on the fact that it was kind of pathetic.

Now the Secret Service was here investigating a missing plane and three people, and they thought he was involved? He needed to get out in front of this, or he could wind up spending the rest of his life in prison for a crime he didn't commit.

If he cared enough, he'd ask her about the blog she'd mentioned. But Tate figured he'd find out soon enough. After she left his house.

He opened the hall closet and started to put his coat on.

Liberty had followed. "You're going out now?"

He looked at her, trying hard to hide everything he was feeling. "Lock the door before you leave."

"Where are you even going? You should stay here, help me convince the FBI you had nothing to do with this."

"Or I could go and find the plane and those missing people instead."

The sheriff walked back in. "If they think you're involved with this, it's going to be messy to unravel. But I'll do what I can. I've got your back, Tate. You know that."

He held out his hand, and Tate shook it.

Liberty didn't wait long before she asked, "Where are you going to look? Do you have an idea of where it might be?"

"Maybe." Tate pulled on a pair of gloves. "I know where I'm going to look first, at least." He turned away from their huddle toward the door. Yeah, this likely wasn't turning out the way she'd thought it would, but at least if he was gone looking for the plane, then the Secret Service might be convinced he wasn't involved.

Dane followed Tate to the door. Liberty walked over, her hand out for the sheriff to shake, but Dane didn't see it. His attention was on a black duffel leaned against the wall. The sheriff stepped toward the bag. "What is this?"

They worked out together, and Dane had never seen that bag before…because Tate had never seen that bag before. "It's not mine."

The bag was partially unzipped. The sheriff pulled the zipper back all the way as Liberty moved closer to them. Inside the duffel were bundles of cash secured by rubber bands, and an orange box the size of a lockbox like the one he kept his gun in. The sheriff lifted it out of the bag.

On the side of the box it said, FLIGHT RECORDER. DO NOT OPEN.

# THREE

"That's not mine." Tate said the words before he'd even thought them through.

The sheriff glanced over his shoulder at Tate, looking like he wanted to kick him. "Of course I know this isn't yours, dude. Except now what we have are two Russian intruders—one in my car, one who's fled—and a bag of money, along with what I'm guessing is the voice recorder for the plane that's currently missing. Which means any search the FBI has going for this thing—if it's active—is going to lead them right here. To the home of their lead suspect."

Liberty paled. "He's being framed."

Tate almost thought she might have cared for him just then as he studied her face and heard the soft tone of her words. Too bad he knew that wasn't the case. He didn't believe she'd come here because of any lingering feelings for him. She probably just wanted to save her reputation at work by convincing everyone she was prepared to do her job and arrest Tate—who was about to be labeled a traitor to his country.

Liberty looked at him, saw he was staring at her and glanced away.

"You should get your coat on," he said. Like he was going to hang around here so she could arrest him? She'd said the Secret Service were on their way. "And you should also switch out your shoes for boots."

Tate didn't wait around for her to comply. He strode to the closet and pulled out another set of gloves that would actually keep her hands warm, along with a hat, and turned back to her in time to see her plant one hand on her hip.

"What do you mean put my coat on? Why do I need my coat?"

"Because you're coming with me." He put all the outerwear in her hands and then turned to the sheriff. "You're good, right? I can leave?"

"Sure," Dane said with a distinct smirk on his face. "Just keep your phone on you."

"Good idea." Who knew how far away the plane was.

Tate strode to the kitchen and opened the junk drawer, not worried anyone would be able to use the thing to track him. It was almost useless, capable of making calls and sending texts—not that he ever did— and that was all.

He pulled out his cell phone and pressed the power button. Hopefully he'd charged it before he turned it off last time. He only kept it with him when he was on shift as a deputy sheriff. There was no signal on this mountain, so there was no point in having it on up here. One of these days he would switch to the carrier that actually got a tiny signal in this area, but he hadn't done it yet.

Tate slid the phone into his front pocket and found the keys to the snowmobile. He wasn't about to hang around and have this whole thing pinned on him. Not when he might be able to find the plane and prove his innocence. He'd have to deal with Liberty being with him—as opposed to somewhere else, probably causing trouble for him.

She wouldn't be causing him trouble on purpose, but she would have to do her job, and that wouldn't be good for him. If she was with Tate, he could keep an eye on her. And keep her safe in case that man had been here to hurt *her*.

The thoughts spun in his head like a tornado.

"Are you going to tell me where we're going?" Liberty asked.

"To find the plane," Tate said. Like that wasn't perfectly obvious. "If the Russian mob, or whoever is sitting in the back of the sheriff's car, is trying to frame me for this, then I'm not about to stay here and try to convince the feds and the Secret Service that I'm not involved." He'd burned those bridges to the ground when he'd tried to punch Locke his last day on the job. "There's no way I'm going to trust them to believe me when I can prove I'm innocent myself."

Locke had known exactly why Tate lost his cool and hadn't blamed him one bit. Which only made the whole situation all the more infuriating. His anger needed an outlet. It wasn't good if he bottled it up, so he had to channel it somewhere. There wasn't much to get mad about on this mountain, so he'd been fine.

Until Liberty showed up.

Now he wanted to kick a wall, because prison would *not* be good for him.

He trailed to his bedroom and got his Beretta from the safe. Two extra clips. He dropped them in a backpack as he walked to the entryway, where he handed it to Liberty. She'd need to carry it.

She raised her brows at his offering. "Is there a reason I have to come?"

Tate figured it was probably a valid question. Apparently Liberty was all about questions these days. The truth was he'd kind of missed her, which was totally messed up. But he had loved her, and she'd thrown it away. Maybe he didn't want to pass up this opportunity to hang out with her, even under the circumstances.

Instead of actually telling her, Tate waved toward the window. "Have you seen the weather out here? You don't go out in that alone. You take a buddy."

Tate thought he might have heard the sheriff snort, but he ignored it. Dane had figured out what it was about even if Liberty hadn't. She would eventually, and then he would be done for. She'd never liked being tricked.

Tate opened the door, stepped outside and headed for the shed. Joey barked and raced out into the snow behind him, ready for whatever adventure they were going on.

Tate turned to the house and called for Joey to follow him back inside. The dog bounded up the porch steps where Liberty stood, while Tate stayed at the bottom. Liberty jumped aside at the last minute, a nervous look on her face. Was she scared of dogs? He hadn't thought so. Hadn't she had a dog once? It was possible something had happened recently that he didn't know about. Tate figured it was just another indication of their incompatibility.

"You still have that ugly cat?"

Liberty's mouth dropped open. "Yes. You've already asked me that, Tate."

The sheriff stepped out with them and shut the door,

almost choking in an attempt to hide his laughter. "I'll wait for the Secret Service and then take that guy in." He motioned to his car, where the intruder sat.

Liberty walked down the porch steps after Tate. "Just answer one question before we go find the plane."

Tate waited.

"What is up with the Christmas decorations? Your house looks like a postcard."

"It was a wreck, so I fixed it up. The Realtor's coming by first thing tomorrow morning for a showing."

She looked like he'd kicked her ugly bald cat.

Tate flicked two fingers toward the sheriff, who drove away with the intruder, and then stepped into the dark of the shed. He fired up the snowmobile and drove it out. Liberty walked over on black boots. She gaped. Tate just ignored it and said, "Get on. We've got a plane to find."

That got her moving. She jumped on behind him and set her hands on his shoulders. Tate reached back and pulled her arms around him. Before the feeling of her being so close could take root, he set off. Liberty squealed and held on tighter. She would get the hang of it pretty soon, and until then he would ignore the fact that she was holding on to him for dear life.

Tate found the path through the trees and headed up the mountain, toward the valley to the west of town. The snow was a thick covering, but the temperature wasn't too bad. He'd been out in colder weather than this, when the wind beat against him and he'd felt like he was frozen down to his bones.

As he drove, he prayed they would find the plane and the missing people—and that when this was done and Liberty went home, his heart would still be intact.

Four miles later her grip on his waist began to loosen. Half a mile after that she started to slide to the side. Tate shook his head. She'd fallen asleep, probably exhausted from a day of travel and then showing up at his house only to face intruders. Tate slowed the snowmobile to a stop and left it to idle while he reached back and shifted Liberty so she was sitting upright.

She looked even paler in the moonlight. He held her with one arm and then put his free hand on her face. When her eyebrows twitched, he took off his glove and touched the cool of her skin with his warm fingers. This would turn out to be a mistake, but he couldn't seem to stop himself from hugging her. It had been too long since he'd received any kind of affection from anyone. Dog slobber didn't count.

Liberty roused. Tate shifted her so he could see her face and said, "Are you okay?"

She nodded, but couldn't quite hide the wince. "Headache, but that's all."

"Aside from the fact that you're exhausted." She always downplayed it when she was hurting. "Can you hang on some more? It's not much farther."

She looked up at him as though he'd paid her the nicest of compliments. Tate had seriously missed that look in the last year but didn't want to dwell too much on the fact that he was soaking it up now. It wasn't going to help him when she left if all he could do was remember what she looked like. What she felt like. How she smelled. He had to get this woman out of his head if he was going to survive alone for the rest of his life.

Liberty straightened. "I'm good."

"Okay then." Tate turned back around to face forward and set off again.

* * *

For the first time since she'd shown up at his house, Liberty had seen the man she'd fallen in love with. She hugged his middle again, and felt the prick of tears in her eyes. Everything good they'd ever had between them…she'd ruined it all when she gave him back his ring and said she'd realized it wasn't going to work.

Which was true. Considering what she'd learned, there was no way a relationship between them would've worked. There was just so much unsaid now. She'd seen the question in his eyes, the pain of their relationship being torn apart when there was nothing either of them could do about it.

And nothing had changed since.

They'd both found some semblance of peace. Liberty could hardly believe that their lives now were what God had wanted for them, but what else were they supposed to have done? This was what God had given them, and it simply didn't work for them to share their lives.

Liberty wanted to ask Tate if he'd moved on, if he'd found someone to care about, but she couldn't voice the words out in the cold, dark night, silent except for the rumble of the snowmobile's engine. She hoped he'd found someone else.

Because she never could.

Tate revved the engine. Liberty saw something out of the corner of her eye and glanced over. Her whole body solidified as she spotted a man dressed in dark clothes, a weapon pointed at them.

"Gun!"

Tate shot forward even faster as the man opened fire. They both ducked and the shots rang out, each one as loud as a firework.

Blast after blast flashed in the dark, illuminating his position. His aim chased the snowmobile's path as Tate flew across the terrain. Liberty pulled her own gun out and fired back two shots, but the ride was too bumpy. She would never be able to hit him. Still, she gripped Tate tighter with her other arm and both knees and tried not to fall off.

Unless…

The shots continued. Liberty shifted back and launched herself off the snowmobile. She landed on her back in a berm of snow and heard Tate yell. He gunned the snowmobile, then turned it in a wide arc, coming back for her.

Liberty ran for the nearest tree so that at least there'd be some cover from the shots. While Tate raced back to her, she returned fire at the man who now sent bullets at both her and Tate in turn. Then he swung his arm back and fired at her.

Liberty ducked and the bullet took out a chunk of bark. She raced for the next tree, moving closer to the man.

The roar of the snowmobile engine raced up behind her. She glanced over, but Tate wasn't coming for her. He drove the snowmobile past her, toward the man trying to kill them. What was he doing? His weapon was in the backpack on her back.

Liberty shifted for a better position and fired to give him the cover he needed. Over and over. One shot managed to clip the gunman in the shoulder, and then Tate was in her line of fire and right on top of the man. He launched himself from the snowmobile and tackled the guy to the snow.

The vehicle they'd been riding continued on, but the engine lost power fast and careened into a tree.

Liberty raced over while they fought. The gun went off. She ducked and went to one knee. Tate had the man on the ground. He shifted, put his knee on the guy's elbow and grabbed the weapon.

Liberty relaxed one tiny notch.

Gun at the ready, she made her way to them. "You good?"

Tate didn't look at her. The man on the ground was bleeding, but Tate hauled him to his feet. Liberty pulled out her phone.

"Won't get any signal out here."

"So what do we do with him then?"

Tate shifted the man's collar. "Same tattoo. Russian as well, I'm guessing. Maybe the first guy from my house. He's wearing the right clothes."

The words weren't directed at her, but the man didn't answer. Didn't say anything. His face was deadpan, with no expression. No movement whatsoever.

"Guess we're walking back to town," Tate said. "We can turn him over to the sheriff, and Dane can get some answers."

That got a reaction.

Liberty saw the slightest movement. "Tate—"

But the man was already in motion. He launched himself at Tate.

Liberty hardly had time to react, but she was a Secret Service agent.

A shot went off.

Liberty fired as well, her aim true, and the bullet hit the gunman square in the chest. Tate fell back and the man landed on top of him. He rolled the man so their attacker lay in the snow. Two choppy breaths later, he was dead.

"Lib."

She stepped back, even though he hadn't moved.

Tate got to his feet. He stepped toward her, and she held out a hand, palm up. "We're okay, Lib."

She shook her head. "The snowmobile is trashed and we're in the middle of nowhere."

"We don't have to walk back to town now. The mine isn't far from here. Come on," he coaxed. "It isn't far, Lib."

"Don't call me that." She lifted her gaze and looked him square in the face. "Don't ever call me that."

They weren't a team. They would never be a team again, as good as it felt working together. Protecting each other. Taking down their assailant. Liberty had to let go of all her memories with him. Again. As much as it hurt, she had to walk away from Tate and let him live his life. Because one of them should have a future.

And it wasn't going to be her.

# FOUR

Tate wanted to hold her hand. He also wanted to yell at her and get her to tell him why she'd jumped off the snowmobile. He'd nearly had a heart attack when he realized what she'd done. Yes, she was a Secret Service agent. He'd been one as well, and that stuff didn't just disappear. He was wired to protect, and that meant Liberty along with everyone else. Feelings didn't matter. Even after she'd torn his life apart. Maybe especially. They didn't get to pick and choose who they protected.

*Thank You for keeping us safe.* God had protected them. That man had tried to kill them, and in the end had chosen to end his life by forcing her hand. He'd known what it meant to attack Tate one last time. It couldn't have ended another way.

Now there was a dead man in the woods. Liberty had taken a million pictures of the body while he checked for ID and found nothing, then noted as many details as he could in a text to the sheriff that would send just as soon as he got a signal. Liberty had said she would email the photos to Dane later after she downloaded them to her laptop.

Aside from that, there wasn't much they could do

about a dead body in the woods. Tate needed to find the plane so he could prove to the Secret Service—and anyone else—that he hadn't been involved in its disappearance.

Then there were the two men at his house. One had tried to kill him, and the other had planted evidence by leaving the plane's black box by his front door. The first had come back and tried again. It couldn't be a coincidence; there was no such thing in their line of work, he had learned. So it wasn't just the Secret Service pointing a finger at him. Someone else wanted to make sure he was implicated in this. But who? And what did they have to gain, getting him arrested and thrown in prison?

Liberty was silent beside him, and Tate didn't try to draw her out of it. He had no idea what was going on in her head, but when she was ready to talk to him she would. That had always been their way. What would be the point of making her talk?

Even though it had been more than a year since he'd seen her, a lot of who they had been together still seemed to fit. Despite that, he couldn't imagine them working as a couple after everything. But then, Tate couldn't imagine it working with *anyone* now. Clearly he wasn't the kind of guy any woman kept around.

Soon enough they were at the old mine, the place Tate had thought of immediately when she'd mentioned a missing plane in this area.

Assuming it hadn't crashed and there wasn't debris splayed across the terrain somewhere around here just waiting to be found.

If this was indeed a case of foul play, the plane had to have landed somewhere close to here. After all, the black box had been removed and was intact. It hadn't been destroyed or crashed with the plane and buried in the debris.

If the people who were doing this truly wanted the plane to remain undiscovered, it meant they had to be hiding it somewhere. The front part of this system of caves and tunnels making up the entirety of the mine was an opening big enough to taxi a plane into. It would not be completely closed in, but it would at least hide the aircraft for a while.

Tate couldn't think of a better place to put it.

Liberty stopped and looked across the clearing, at least eight acres of snowfall. "This is it?"

"It's where I would hide a plane." When she shot him a look, Tate added, "*If* I was the one who was behind this. Which I am not, and you know that. Or at least you should."

Maybe she'd never had total faith in him, and their relationship had been shakier than he'd known. But he'd thought they were good. Preparing for the future, making plans together for when they were no longer Secret Service agents. They'd been busy all the time, out on the road campaigning every few years. On overseas details, protecting the secretary of state and other dignitaries.

They had lived in some amazing places and seen some amazing things, but the strain of that life weighed a person down until they felt old beyond their years. He knew he felt it, but Liberty didn't look it. Her mom didn't look her age either, so he figured it was probably inherited.

"How are your parents?" Tate set off toward the mine.

Liberty strode through the snow beside him. "They're good. My dad won a golf tournament last weekend, beat all of his friends and everything. He was seriously proud.

They even got him a little trophy." She grinned, and her teeth flashed white in the moonlight. "Have you seen your brother at all?"

He'd told her the story about his parents' car crash when he was in college. It was the first time he remembered being really, truly angry. Tate's younger brother had been sixteen at the time and had spiraled on a downward descent since then. Braden had hit rock bottom so many times Tate had lost count.

"He doesn't return my calls. I invited him to Christmas, but I figure he'll probably just ignore the holidays." Tate paused, unsure whether or not to add this next part. In the end, he decided to brave the potential heartbreak. "The house I'm living in right now is actually our family's vacation cabin. I fixed it up so I could live there."

"But you told me it's for sale."

"I tried. I really did. I just can't face it by myself, Lib. I can't live with all those happy family memories and be by myself."

Liberty stared at him with some kind of wonder he didn't understand. "Tate, why haven't you found someone?" Her voice was full of so much pain it almost hurt to hear it. Like she couldn't believe he didn't meet eligible women every day.

It wasn't like they just showed up on his mountain.

She cleared her throat, and he let her change the subject. "Your Christmas tree is very nice. And the place looks great." She spoke tentatively, like she wasn't sure how the words would be received. "I haven't even had time to get mine up yet. And I was planning on going down to Florida anyway, but that isn't going to happen now."

"I'm sorry this has ruined your Christmas plans."

"I might still be able to get them back on track. I have a few days of travel left before Christmas Eve. If this gets wrapped up before then, I'll probably still try to head down to see my parents if I can." Liberty tucked some hair behind her ear, the way she did when she was avoiding something.

Tate figured she didn't want him to know her Christmas wouldn't be anything special, just a visit with her parents. It would be more than what he was looking forward to—assuming his house didn't sell in the next week.

A fire in his fireplace, hot coffee and a book. Sounded about perfect, but it wasn't anywhere near as enjoyable as the years they'd meet up on Christmas Eve at one of their homes and watch an old movie together. It had been a tradition, a part of their life together. One he'd dearly missed last Christmas Eve.

Right now wasn't the time to dwell on memories. Not when they had a plane to find.

"I'm sure that'll be great," he said.

She shot him a funny look, but he didn't have time to figure out what it was about. Tate led Liberty over to the mine's entrance. Once one of the most prominent sources of coal in this entire area, the cave had an opening big enough to accommodate heavy equipment. It stretched above their heads and to their left and right. The inside was a dark cavern he could barely see into. Good thing he'd brought a flashlight.

When they were close enough for her to see just how big it was, Liberty gasped. "You could totally hide a small aircraft in there."

"Me, specifically?"

"You know what I mean, Tate. This place is big

enough to hide a business jet like the one that disappeared. I really hope we find it and the people who are missing. I can't imagine what they're going through." She started to walk fast.

Fifteen feet from the mine's opening, a rumble shook the ground. Before Tate could register the fact that it was an earthquake, an orange fireball split the space between the roof of the mine and the walls.

The force of the explosion pushed them back onto the snow with a rush of hot air and flames.

Dirt and rocks rained down over the entrance like a tsunami of earth as the mine exploded in on itself. Tate grabbed her arm, but Liberty was already climbing to her feet and running. The roar was almost as loud as the deafening explosion. Her ears rang, and she thought he might be yelling instructions to her, but she couldn't hear. Thankfully, the terrain wasn't sloped, or there quite likely would have been an avalanche.

The ground started to shift under her as she ran. Liberty stumbled, and Tate scooped her up like the hero he'd been to her for years. Underneath he was still the same protective guy she'd loved. Being in his arms had been the safest place, second only to right at his back during a fire fight. And she knew which she preferred.

Tate picked up the pace, forcing her to keep up. Liberty ran until sweat chilled on her temple and ran down her back. She estimated it was almost half a mile before they were clear of the explosion and the debris it had caused, and Tate slowed.

Liberty set her hands on her knees and bent forward, sucking in breaths.

Tate set his hand on her back. When she looked up

he was scanning the area. Then he looked at her. "I think we're clear."

Liberty straightened. "What do you want to do now?" She could barely think. They'd nearly died. Her head spun, and it was entirely possible she was going to fall over. Just swoon and pass out, like she wasn't a Secret Service agent.

She sucked in a breath and squared her shoulders. Then gasped. The mine was *gone*. The mountain had caved in on itself like an empty burlap sack. Tate stepped toward it, but she waylaid him with a hand on his arm. "We'll be careful," he said.

"You want to go over there?" Was it even safe to walk over the debris?

"We need to see if the plane was in the mine. We might be able to get a look."

"We should tell the Secret Service." Not to mention the FBI and the sheriff. "There's no way that explosion was missed, even if it is the middle of the night."

"It's only one in the morning."

She glanced at him. He'd always been Mr. Night Owl, while she was an early riser. Something about the dark had always creeped her out. She didn't like being outside in the middle of nowhere at night. But even though she wasn't alone, she still couldn't relax too much. He would protect her, and she would hold up her end, but it wouldn't last.

Liberty looked at her phone, just so she could do something unrelated to Tate. His presence had always filled a room. When he was calm, that calmness seemed to permeate the air. When he was agitated, like he was now, she had to let him work through it. He'd told her he had tools he used to process his emotions. Methods for reining it in while he thought through what needed to be worked out.

She couldn't imagine it had been easy to lose his parents so young and suddenly have to take care of his brother full-time. He'd said it was going into the military that saved him and gave him the structure and discipline he'd so badly needed back then. He'd thrived, making it all the way to a senior NCO. The Secret Service had been a good move, though he'd brushed up against the bureaucracy more than once.

Tate was all about improving methodology instead of doing things the same way over and over. If it could be improved, it should be. Liberty agreed, though she was more of a follower than a leader. Some people were naturally take-charge people. She could do it if she had to, and she had in her personal life. But only when it was a necessity.

"No signal?"

She sighed. "Nothing."

"I figured as much. The whole mountain where my cabin is, I get nothing." He held up his own device—one of those ancient flip phones.

"I didn't even know they sold those anymore. Does it even connect to the internet?"

Tate shrugged. She knew he'd never enjoyed email and probably hadn't done a Google search in his life. The man still used a phone book to look up numbers. She'd called him a "dinosaur" about technology more than once.

Tate stepped over snow mingled with dirt and rocks, testing each step to make sure it would hold his weight. Liberty did the same, carving out her own path to his right. "The ground seems pretty stable."

"But the mine is toast."

She nodded. "We aren't going to be able to see inside."

"Still, the explosion might have made the plane visible. We at least have to look at it from all angles, in case we can see something."

"The FBI and the Secret Service are going to have to bring earth movers up here to clear it out if they really want to find out if the plane was here. *Is* here."

He pointed left, past the mouth of the mine that was no more. "There's a road on the other side. We can follow it out and get to town, get the word out that we think we know where the plane might be."

Liberty nodded. "That's a good idea. We can start convincing them you don't have anything to do with this."

"Is that why you came by yourself?"

She glanced at him.

"There has to be a reason you didn't come with your team. You drove out by yourself to my cabin." He paused. "I didn't think about it until now, since we've been busy fighting off guys. But now that I think about it, shouldn't you be working *with* the Secret Service instead of flying solo?"

"Locke knows where I am." Liberty figured it was time to admit the truth. "He wanted to wait out the snow, but I said I was leaving right away. So yeah, it was bad and I almost didn't make it. But I got to your cabin, and they should have been maybe an hour behind me. They were going to check into the hotel first." She shrugged. "I figured I could get a jump on proving you weren't part of it."

"So you *didn't* think I was guilty."

"Your mental state isn't the best, but it doesn't exactly scream 'domestic terrorist.'"

He gave her a dark look. "What exactly do you know about my mental state?"

"The blog—"

"Right, the blog." He lifted both hands, palms up. "I have no idea what blog you're talking about. I'm not even sure what one *is*."

She had thought it was weird that a technologically inept man such as Tate would suddenly start a blog. "About eight months ago you started posting monthly rants. At first they were just generally disgruntled, stuff about the government and how it's run. Federal agencies. Budgets."

"And you thought that was me?"

"It was all stuff we've talked about." What else was she supposed to have thought?

"I don't own a computer, Liberty. I have no internet access."

"I didn't know. It seemed like you, kind of."

"Kind of?"

Liberty shrugged. She'd hurt him, and when he had started the blog—or when the blog had started—it'd made sense to her he'd feel that way. She just hadn't figured he'd spew his feelings online. "What do you want me to say? I thought you were lashing out because I hurt you."

"And you came here to what...apologize?"

"Would that be so awful?" she asked. "I felt like I owed you something at least."

Tate didn't react. Not in his face, and not in his stiff body language. "The last thing I want to hear from you is that you're sorry. At least have the guts to stand by what you did. You tore us apart for whatever reason was in your head." He paused. "Does the reason still apply?"

Liberty nodded, unable to speak past the lump in her throat.

"Then there's nothing more to say about us."

Liberty nodded again. "It's good you think so. You'll be able to move on with no ties to us or anything else in your past." It hurt to say those words, but she wanted him to know he was free. He needed to believe she would be happy for him. "Is there anyone in town you're…interested in? Have you met someone?" Maybe he would answer now.

Tate's eyebrows drew together. "You *want* me to be with someone else?"

"I want you to be happy, Tate." It was why she'd let him go.

"Guess I'm just not wired for happily-ever-after."

Liberty blinked. "Of course you are. Why would you say that?"

"You made it pretty clear we weren't going to work, so why would it work with someone else?"

"Why would it not?" She hated that he thought this. She had to change his mind. "Of course you can be happy."

"And waste months—maybe even years—trying to find out? I'm done with relationships. Otherwise I'd have figured it out by now."

"Plenty of people find happiness in their thirties."

"Yeah? Like you?"

Liberty wanted to say something. Instead she just closed her mouth. What was there to say? Relationships were great, but she wanted more for Tate than she could give anyone, and a man who didn't realize the demands on Secret Service agents would never understand her life. It wouldn't work, and since Tate was gone from her life, she hadn't even been looking. She had thought he was her future, but that wasn't the path God had set before her.

A car engine revved.

Liberty spun around to see a truck round the corner over where Tate had pointed out the road. The vehicle rumbled fast over the ruts of debris, right toward them.

Tate set one hand on her stomach and moved her back so he was in front of her. Liberty glanced around the breadth of his shoulders. "It's coming right for us."

"Give me the backpack."

She did so, and they started to run. But before Tate could get it open gunshots exploded the dirt around them.

"Freeze!"

Liberty halted. Tate slammed into her, backpack first. He dropped it and slid his arms around her. She lifted her hands.

"Both of you, in the truck."

# FIVE

Liberty didn't ever want to move, and not because she would be shot by the men in this truck. Tate's arms were around her. Strong arms she had missed so much, it made her want to cry at the chance to feel them again after being alone for months. Just over a year.

"I said, in the truck." The man wore boots, jeans, a wool sweater and a leather jacket, and held a revolver on them. "That means now." Beyond where he stood at the open door, another man sat in the driver's seat.

Tate took his arms from around her and held his hands up. "No worries."

The man didn't look like he agreed. Tate put his hand on her back, and they moved slowly toward the truck. Liberty climbed in first, over the fast-food wrappers and the blanket strewn on the seat. It smelled bad. She glanced, once, at the backpack as Tate slid in beside her, and the gunman got in the front. The man turned, his gun still pointed at them.

He motioned with it to Liberty, and she saw Tate stiffen out of the corner of her eye.

The driver turned around. He was older, and also wore a leather jacket covered in patches. He had the same tattoo as the man in Tate's kitchen. They didn't have accents but were evidently affiliated with the Russians in some way. "Don't worry, you probably won't catch a disease from the truck."

Liberty had been attempting to ignore the state of it, especially the sticky thing under her shoe, but now it was impossible.

The gunman said, "Hands."

She lifted them, and the driver put a zip tie on her wrists, securing them together. He did the same with Tate, tying them so tight the strap cut off her blood circulation. Liberty glanced at Tate as the older man, the driver, turned the truck around. It was hard to stay upright, and she had to grab the seat back to keep from falling into Tate's lap.

She glanced at him again.

Still nothing. Tate's face was blank, but his gaze studied every inch of these men. The tattoos, the patches. All of it. She tried to see what he might be seeing, but couldn't. After a minute or so, she slid her coat pocket onto her lap and eased her phone out gently. If she suddenly got a signal it wouldn't be good. The phone would come alive with incoming messages, emails and missed calls. The beeping notifications would be a giveaway for sure.

No signal.

She turned her ringer to silent and slid the phone back into her pocket before the passenger with the gun saw her.

Kidnapped. What was Locke going to think?

Her boss *always* had an opinion, but first he'd have to realize what had happened to her. They might think she was part of this as well, and she would be implicated in the plane's disappearance. Liberty was a woman in a male-dominated profession. She was used to having to prove herself, and this would be no exception. Especially when it was not just her reputation on the line but Tate's as well.

No one else except her team cared where Liberty was, or what she was doing. No one would be calling to check up on her, and she hadn't told anyone but her neighbor—who fed her cat when she was gone—that she would be leaving.

The pang in the vicinity of her heart wasn't unexpected, but the strength of it was what hurt. And why? It shouldn't hurt when this was the way it was supposed to be. She should be used to it by now. This was the road God had called her to walk. But it was *hard*. She couldn't believe how hard it was turning out to be. Not that she'd thought being alone would be easy, but for it to hit her this intensely? Liberty blew out a breath.

The driver let his foot off the gas a split second at the stop sign, and then pulled out onto the highway.

The gunman turned back, and Liberty caught his gaze. She looked away, not wanting to have some kind of wordless communication with him. He would know he'd gotten to her. Yes, she was a trained Secret Service agent. But that didn't mean Liberty never got scared. The day she'd told Tate she was overwhelmed by it, years ago after a member of their team had been killed by an out-of-control truck, he'd told her fear was good. And how it was normal to be scared, but courage would show in what she did with the fear.

Liberty looked at him now. Tate still didn't look at her. Maybe he was scared, too. But he didn't look like he was. He almost looked as though he was…waiting for something.

She shifted on her seat and said, "Where are you guys taking us?"

Maybe these men were just looking for a lone stretch of highway where they could kill them and dump the bodies out of sight. But maybe not. It was worth trying to find out, if she could.

The gunman grinned, his teeth bright in the dark interior of the car. "Got a mess to fix."

"Are you going to kill us?"

"Maybe," he said. "Maybe not." The man tipped his head back and cackled his laughter. There was no other way to describe it. She'd always been the "good girl" and never acted out. Her parents had considered her wanting to be a Secret Service agent as doing exactly that. Like she should be a kindergarten teacher or a nurse instead.

Maybe they were right. Though, would a safer profession even help her? Liberty had never done anything really bad, even though she knew she was a sinner who'd been saved. No one was perfect, but what had doing the right thing gotten her? She had no life, no family. No real, true close friends. And not much faith anymore.

Nothing.

Tate had two problems. First was the gun pointed at Liberty, and the second was the fact that he was 90 percent sure the child locks on the back doors of the truck were engaged, because it's what he'd have done. Even if he subdued these two guys, they'd have to climb in the front seat to get out. Or roll down their windows and open the doors from the outside. Zip ties didn't count as a problem; Tate just had to decide whether to snap them before he went for the gun and waste a second in which the passenger could realize what he was doing, or wait until after they were out of the car.

*Mile marker sixteen.*

Rage burned in him at the idea that Liberty might get shot, but he continued to breathe through it. And count. His time would come, but getting angry only led to mistakes. Success was all about control. He'd learned that lesson by failing over and over again.

These guys were not professional kidnappers. They were, however, professional heavies. Whoever the Russians were being paid by—because guys like this never did anything that didn't come with a possible paycheck—wanted to get at Tate and Liberty. One or both of them. Did it matter? And whoever it was might not want them alive.

*Mile marker seventeen.*

"In a minute we should have enough signal to call in," the driver said.

Tate figured now was as good a time as any. Besides, the turn was coming up. The passenger who held the gun on them turned his head slightly. Big mistake. Tate silently thanked the Lord for the space to move in a crew-cab truck and launched himself forward. His bound hands went over the headrest and his stomach slammed into it just as he shoved the passenger forward, hard enough his head bounced off the dash. Out cold.

Before the driver could react, Tate grabbed the gun from the passenger and shot him in the thigh.

Liberty made a surprised sound, but Tate didn't have

time to explain it to her. If she was going to object, she could keep it to herself until he was done.

While the man screamed, Tate yanked the wheel hard to the right. The driver had let off the gas, but the truck hit the guardrail with enough force to bust through it and head down the ravine. This valley was shallow enough that they weren't going to tumble to a fiery death, but it was probably going to hurt.

Liberty gasped. "We're going to crash."

Tate held on to the steering wheel, his stomach still pressed against the passenger's headrest.

The driver, hands bloody from holding his leg, reached around. Before he could find a gun, or knife, or whatever, Tate did the only thing he had room to do. He elbowed the guy in the face. The man's head slumped to one side.

The truck bounced on a rock, headed for the river.

Tate yelled, "Hold on!"

"I am!" She sounded mad. Seriously? He was getting them un-kidnapped, and she couldn't be grateful? The woman had some serious problems. But he already knew that, so he just ignored her. Again.

The truck glanced off a tree, and the windshield splintered. Tate grabbed the gearshift and moved it to third to try to slow their momentum. Thankfully, it was enough; they didn't hit the water at full speed. Tate moved it down to first, and when they'd slowed enough he put it in Park.

In the middle of a rushing river.

He sat back. The truck shifted like it was going to start floating downstream. Liberty whimpered. He glanced around but couldn't see beyond what the headlights illuminated. Which wasn't much.

He lifted his hands above his head, then pulled them down over his raised knee. The momentum snapped the zip ties. It worked, but it also hurt. Getting out of tape or rope was way less painful.

Liberty did the same move, and her zip ties snapped as well. She hissed between her teeth and didn't look at him, just leaned forward and searched the driver's pockets. When she pulled out a phone, Tate commandeered it. She didn't say anything, but displeasure screamed from her shoulders and the angle of her mouth. No signal.

Tate used her phone again to take more pictures, this time of the two unconscious guys. "Come on. We can hike out and call the sheriff, have him pick these two up."

Like Dane was a trash collector, picking up the debris of Tate's life. He almost smiled, because it wasn't exactly wrong. It just wasn't what Tate had planned for his nice, quiet Montana life of dog training, taking shifts as a deputy sheriff and fixing up his house. Some extra construction work in those long days of summer, just to stay busy. Certainly not traipsing around in the snow in the middle of the night in December.

Liberty didn't move. Tate climbed over the passenger to get out the front door. Water rushed in at the gunman's feet. He jumped into the water, which was knee high, and winced. It was freezing. He waded around the truck and opened Liberty's door for her. "I can carry you, if you want. No point in both of us hiking with soaking wet feet."

Liberty didn't say anything. Tate touched her cheek so he could peer closer at her face in the dim light. "Did you get hurt?"

She shook her head.

"Then what is it?"

"You could have gotten shot. I can't believe you started a fight in a truck cab and sent us careening off a cliff."

"It wasn't a cliff. The stretch past mile marker seventeen is a shallow valley." He paused. "I knew what I was doing, Lib." She had to know. He'd been in danger before, and she hadn't reacted like this.

"I couldn't even help."

She was a help just being there, but he couldn't tell her. There was way too much history between them for him to actually tell her he appreciated her presence. It wouldn't help either of them to say that stuff.

Tate turned, and Liberty held on for a piggyback ride out of the river. When he set her on her feet, he took her hand. Her eyes widened. "It's dark out. I don't want you to get lost."

Sure. That was the *only* reason he wanted to hold her hand.

Liberty wiggled her hand out of his as soon as they stepped onto the blacktop of the highway. She couldn't allow herself to get used to him being close to her. Not again. He was just being nice because they were in a crazy situation. Obviously there wasn't more to it. How could there be?

As soon as they had a phone signal, they called the sheriff. Dane drove out and picked them up. When he pulled into the driveway of a yellow house, he said, "Make coffee, and make breakfast. I'll go get those guys and be back in an hour."

Tate nodded and got out. Liberty said, "Thank you,"

because that was the way her mother had raised her, and then followed him inside. The house was cute, and the front walk had been shoveled. The snow was up to her elbows in a bank at the edge of where the lawn should be.

Tate was in the kitchen. Liberty found a bathroom, then entered the kitchen, where he was cracking eggs into a pan. Coffee was already dripping into the carafe.

Her stomach turned over. "I'm not really hungry."

"Me neither, but we need calories."

"We need sleep." She didn't want to argue about food because she was actually hungry, but it was after three in the morning and she was so tired she'd stopped having a filter. That was why she had to be so careful about not touching him; otherwise she would launch herself into his arms and start bawling about how they could never be together.

Instead, Liberty kept the kitchen island between them and sat on a bar stool. Tate loved to cook, and she'd missed watching him move around in a kitchen. Liberty glanced about and saw a picture of Dane with a woman in a navy uniform.

"Is the sheriff married?"

"Yup." Tate didn't turn from his pan. The smell of sausage made her stomach rumble. "She's the NCIS agent afloat on the USS Blue Ridge."

"Oh. Wow. So they're both cops then?"

Tate nodded.

"That's cool."

"Yeah, she's stationed out of Seattle, and he's the sheriff here. Long-distance, but they make it work. Dane actually said all the time apart makes them value the time they do spend together more. Instead of taking it for granted." Tate paused. "Some people know it's going to be hard, but they figure out how to make their relationship work." His tone had an edge to it.

Any comfort she'd felt over Dane's happy relationship—though she didn't know anything about it and was just assuming it was happy—now dissipated. Was she really going to rise to his bait? He was definitely baiting her. She knew Tate wanted answers. He'd had plenty of questions when she broke off their engagement, but Liberty couldn't think of how on earth to answer them. She couldn't just come out and say it, when she didn't even want to contemplate the truth herself.

Tate was just tired, as she was. It had probably come out inadvertently and she should just ignore it.

Still, Liberty couldn't help saying, "Some things you can't work past. Sometimes you have to let a relationship go because it's the best thing for everyone involved."

"So you live alone in DC, working all the time." He turned. "And I survive here, keeping busy and trying not to think about what should have been."

Liberty swallowed. He looked so hurt, and she'd done it to him. "This is the best way."

"You really believe that?"

"I have to." She tried to think of more to say, to explain it. "Because if I don't…"

Then all this pain would have been for nothing. Liberty had to believe this was best, or at least what God had asked of her. To let Tate go so he could live his life and have everything they should have had, just with someone else.

But Tate wasn't keeping up his end of the bargain he didn't know he'd made. He hadn't met anyone else yet, and he wasn't even trying! Tears pricked her eyes. One trailed down her cheek, and she swiped it away.

"Crying isn't going to garner you any sympathy, Lib."

"That isn't why I'm doing it," she said, reaching for a paper towel. "I'm just tired."

"When the sheriff gets back, maybe he can give you a ride somewhere. To your car. A hotel. Whatever." Like it was no big deal to him.

"Maybe I'll do that."

Tate shrugged, his back to her.

More tears fell, and she wiped those away, too. "Clearly you don't need me here, getting in your way. So I'll just go." She jumped off the stool. "I don't need to wait for the sheriff. I can walk." She didn't have her purse or keys and there was hardly a cell signal anywhere in this town, but she was resourceful. She'd figure it out. "I'll just leave you to your federal charges and prison time. Have a nice life, Tate."

Liberty strode to the door. Before she got there the sheriff walked back in. "Whoa. Where are you going?"

"I'm leaving."

Dane looked over her shoulder. His eyes flashed, some male communication she didn't much care to figure out. Then he looked at her. "The truck was still there, but those men were gone."

Tate's voice came from the kitchen. "They must have woken up and hiked out like we did."

Liberty winced. She was leaving, and that was all Tate had to say?

Dane looked down at her with soft eyes. "Stay for breakfast, Liberty. Stay so we can figure this out."

His wife probably loved when he spoke to her like

that. It made Liberty want to do whatever he said just to see if she could make those eyes smile. Too bad she would never have the same kind of look to call her own, not ever in her life.

Liberty shut her eyes and ran her hands through her ratty hair. She probably looked like a total mess. Why wasn't it Tate asking her to stay? It could be, if she hadn't done what she had.

Dane said, "There's more to tell you."

# SIX

Tate stared at her back. Did he want her to leave? It had started to feel natural all over again, having her here with him. Facing danger together. He set the pan on the tile countertop, and even though his stomach rumbled with the idea of food, Tate didn't move to serve it into the bowls he'd set out.

Part of him wanted to yell at her to stay. To demand she give him…something, after she'd taken away everything he'd had. Okay, so she hadn't taken his job. It'd been a mutual agreement, and the best decision for everyone. Still, if he looked at the root cause, it was Liberty. And Tate wanted to know the answer to his most pressing question.

Why?

There had to be a reason she had broken it off with him. It had taken months to realize it, mostly because he'd been busy nursing his own hurt. Then he'd begun the process of going back over everything she'd said. Then everything *beneath* what she'd said. Because if Liberty didn't want to think about something, or talk about it, then she didn't. She just ignored the problem, even while she claimed she was "dealing with it." There hadn't been many ups or downs in their relationship. The first hurdle they'd had, it seemed like she had refused to face it. She'd just given up and told him to move on.

But if she was going to stay and face this, it had to be her choice.

"Okay, fine." She turned and walked back to the table.

Tate dished out the food like there wasn't a war going on in his head, trying to figure out whether or not he was glad she had stayed.

As they ate, the sheriff described what he'd found in the river. Dane blew out a breath. "I sure am glad you guys are okay."

Tate nodded.

"Just a couple of bruises, but I'm good," Liberty said.

Tate whipped his head around to where she sat across from him. "What bruises?" She was hurt and she hadn't told him?

Liberty frowned. "I'm fine. Like I said."

Dane continued, "Since there was no one there to arrest, I ran the plates on the truck first. Got a hit on a Vance Turin." He lifted his phone and showed them a picture.

Tate nodded. "That was the driver."

"Vance is the leader of a motorcycle club out of Great Falls. It's supposed to have close ties with the Russians."

"He has their tattoo," Tate said. "But what are they doing way out here? Does their territory stretch this far?"

Dane shook his head. "Not as far as I can see, though I'm going to call the police in Great Falls this morning and get the lowdown."

"Ask them if they know why Vance and his friends might be involved with a missing plane. After you ask him why he was over here, trying to kill me and planting the black box in my house."

Dane stared at him.

"I'm just saying."

"I'm going to chalk that up to you going through a stressful time and being sleep deprived, and not that you actually think I don't know what to ask fellow officers of the law."

Liberty got up, gathered up the bowls and silverware and strode to the kitchen with her back straight. Great, she was embarrassed for him.

Tate stared back at Dane and said, "Really?"

"I could ask you the same thing." Dane didn't back down. What he did was glance at Liberty, doing the dishes and giving them space. "That woman is dead on her feet. She needs rest."

Tate nodded. "We both do."

"I can see as much." Dane paused. "You can use my trailer. It'll be safe. I'll go get the dogs, let them out for a while and then bring them back here."

Tate studied his friend and couldn't help thinking there was something Dane hadn't told them yet. Some reason Tate needed to remain under the radar. There had to be.

"What are you going to do about…?" Dane's voice trailed off and he motioned to Liberty with a flick of one finger.

Tate shrugged.

"Are you willing to let her get dragged down with you if this gets worse? Are you willing to put her at risk?"

"She's already at risk. She's a Secret Service agent. We're both trained to handle ourselves. Liberty needs to stay with me, because the only way we're going to figure this out is together."

"Because you need her with you? Liberty could go, meet up with her federal agent friends. She'd be fine. She's here because of *you*. So make sure you don't want her here because of you, too. Otherwise she gets the raw end of the deal."

"She broke it off with *me*." Dane knew that. They'd had that conversation many times.

"Yes, but you let her."

"Is that even supposed to make sense?" Tate hissed.

"If it doesn't, then maybe you aren't the man I thought you were."

Tate felt the sting of those words. They cut deep from a man he respected, a man he happily worked for even though he didn't especially need the money. His cost of living was low, but the work as a deputy sheriff paid for dog treats and put gas in his truck in the winter.

He said, "Maybe I'm just me, and I mess up."

"Maybe you messed *this* up."

Tate didn't disagree. It had to have been something big for Liberty to break off their engagement instead of talking to him so they could work it out.

Dane pointed at Liberty again. "Best thing that ever happened to you. Isn't that what you told me?"

"That was a long time ago." Probably two or three years now.

"Never met anyone like her. Never felt like this."

"Dane."

His friend didn't quit. "It's what you said."

"She told me it was done."

"Goes both ways, brother. You gotta fight for what you want."

Tate had seen Dane do as much with his wife. In fact, he did it every day because their marriage was long-distance.

"But what do I know?" Dane shrugged. "I'm just a hick-town sheriff."

Liberty called out from the kitchen, "Is it safe to come back over?"

The sheriff grinned. They'd obviously been talking about her, but she hadn't heard any of it. They'd kept their voices low, and Liberty had let them have their talk. Maybe he was convincing Tate to turn himself in to the Secret Service so they could clear this all up. That would certainly make her position a little easier.

Soon enough the Secret Service would want to know why she wasn't at Tate's house anymore, but running all over the county with their prime suspect. She wasn't looking forward to having that conversation with Locke.

"Come and sit down," Tate said. "Maybe now Dane will tell us the rest of it."

Liberty glanced at the sheriff but directed her question at Tate. "Did you tell him about the mine?"

Tate nodded, and the sheriff said, "I already called in to the feds about the explosion, and how the mine is big enough to house the kind of plane that went missing. They're going to head out to the site at first light."

"And there haven't been any updates, no ransom calls?"

Tate turned to her. "You think this was a kidnapping?"

Liberty said, "I don't know. We have the black box,

so that should tell us something—" of course, by "us" she meant the Secret Service "—and no one has found the wreckage. We would've heard more than that initial radio call if it had landed because there was an emergency. What explanations are left? Hijacking. An uneventful landing, maybe even miles from here so no one noticed." Liberty paused. "Like an abandoned ranch with an airstrip."

"Makes sense." Dane nodded. "There haven't been any updates from the feds in the last six hours, though the search is ongoing. They have the black box in their possession and they took the man from your house into custody."

"And the dead man near the mine?"

"It'll be processed by my guys and the information shared with the feds. That's how they want to play it."

Liberty nodded. "So they know someone is actively trying to implicate Tate in this."

The sheriff said, "Yes. The BOLO they have out for Tate has been updated. They don't just want a location—they want him apprehended for questioning." He paused, looked at them both in turn. "It's an upgrade from the first BOLO. They're taking a hard look at our man here." Dane pointed at Tate, who didn't even move.

Liberty would have been squirming in her chair if she were in his position. She couldn't believe Tate wasn't more worried about what might happen to him. He hardly seemed ruffled about any of this, even facing men who wanted to frame him. And kill him.

"You're in a sticky position," she said. "They know you work with Tate, and you're friends, right?"

Dane nodded.

"You're going to run into a conflict between that and

doing your job." Like she wasn't also in a conflict? But that wasn't her point.

"We already passed the conflict-of-interest stage."

Tate chimed in. "So what are you going to do, Dane?"

The sheriff looked at him. "I'm going to be a professional who fights for my friend's reputation. I'm not going to let them smear your name through whatever mud they want. And I won't let you go down for a crime you didn't commit. So if you need a character witness, I'm it."

"The Secret Service probably figures they know all they need to."

"And the blog doesn't help," Liberty said. "It makes you look like a raging hothead."

"I didn't write any blog."

"Of course you didn't," Dane said. "You're a technological dinosaur."

Liberty snorted, and Dane grinned at her. He said, "I've already reminded them. And if they look into it, I'm sure they'll figure out it's just another way to frame you for this."

"Which means it was planned. And it probably looks like it *was* me."

Liberty glanced at Tate. He was onto something. "Go on."

Tate said, "If they had enough foresight to start the blog months ago just to make it look like I'm angry and wanting to lash out, maybe by kidnapping three people, then they've been planning to do this for at least a year."

She thought about it for a moment. "So it wasn't just the fact that the opportunity presented itself. Unless that's part of it. It could be a convergence of events making it all possible now." There was a clock running for her to check in with the Secret Service. What if it was also true for the person behind the missing plane? "Either they were just ready, or something happened to make it now."

"But why Tate?" Dane asked.

Good question. "He came home—maybe that was the catalyst. There are probably a few who would have been good candidates. For some reason, they decided to pick him."

"A convergence of events?" Tate's expression held a touch of humor.

"Why is that funny?"

"Have you been reading snooty books again?"

"There's nothing wrong with the classics." Especially when they clearly expanded her vocabulary. "But that's not what we're talking about. We're discussing how to keep you *out of prison*."

"You're very cute when you're rallying to my defense."

Um…what? Liberty's mind blanked as she struggled to find words. Why was he being like this, and in front of Dane?

"Exactly." Tate glanced at the sheriff, a smile on his face. "Like I said. Cute."

Secret Service agents weren't cute. *Cute* was not part of the job description. And no one she worked with would have mistaken her for cute. Not the way she'd been the past year—closed off and professional. Liberty had pulled away from everyone, nursing her grief over Tate moving away. Finally admitting she'd done what she knew she had to.

Dane looked like he was about to burst out laughing. Tate figured that wasn't exactly uncalled for. He was acting weird, but he couldn't help it. What Dane said had stuck with him. All those conversations they'd had on the phone when Tate had been thinking about proposing to Liberty. Telling Dane all about how he felt about her, and how it was so different from what he'd expected. And even earlier, how Dane said he was in love with Liberty when Tate hadn't even realized it himself.

Tate watched her shake herself out of her flustered state. Even in the middle of all there was going on, Tate needed the lightness right now. Despite what she thought, he knew exactly the implications of what was happening. He could end up in prison.

His life was in danger, and so was Liberty's. If he let her go back to the Secret Service she could be leaving him with a target on her back. He didn't know for sure if she was in the Russians' crosshairs, but he wasn't willing to take the risk if she was.

The pleasure of watching her blush was short-lived. "We should head out." Tate got up. "You need sleep before you check in with the Secret Service."

"I really do." Liberty gave him a rueful smile. "I can hardly see straight I'm so tired."

"You should take my truck," Dane offered. "I'll tell the Secret Service you came here for help and I tried to bring you in for questioning, but you hit me over the head or something."

Tate wanted to laugh when there was nothing amusing about this situation. "I'm sorry we're putting you in this position. You could get in real trouble for helping us."

Dane shook his head. "I'm not sure what you're talking about. I found the flight recorder, and the intruder

I arrested at your house, when I went to look for you. I've called and called you, but haven't been able to get through. The truck in the river was reported and I logged it, single truck, no occupants. Probably stolen. And when I did see you, it was because you turned up at my house in the middle of the night, took a bunch of my groceries and stole my truck keys, along with most of my weapons. After all those times we hunted together, you know the code to my gun safe."

Dane lifted both hands, the picture of innocence. "I can take care of myself, Tate. Don't worry about me."

Tate nodded. There was plenty for them to be worried about, and he cared about Dane's future—mostly because if he didn't, then when his wife returned from her detail she would box Tate's ears for it. She was gone more than she was here, but it wouldn't be much longer before she was home for good. Three years tops, he figured. At least that was what Dane had told him. They had a plan to start a family after she retired from NCIS.

Dane would be a great father. The thought of it made him wonder what his and Liberty's children would have looked like had they gotten married. Liberty was the kind of woman who would excel as a mother. It was hard for everyone, and parenting had its ups and downs, but she faced challenges with courage. He knew she would be able to do it.

Dane tossed him the keys to his truck. "Groceries are on the back seat."

"You knew we'd come."

Dane shrugged. "I figured it would be good to be prepared."

Tate wanted to hug his friend but stuck his hand out for a shake instead. Dane clapped his hand in Tate's and then shook his head. He pulled Tate in and they slapped each other's backs.

"Why does that always look like it hurts?"

He turned to see Liberty watching, her head cocked to the side. Tate wanted to hug her, too. She looked so tired she was about to fall over. He wasn't much more awake than she was, but the coffee he'd had would get them to the camp trailer.

Dane's phone rang. "Yeah, Stella." He paused. "Seriously?... No. Thank you." He hung up. "That was my night dispatcher. One of the neighbors called in a tip. Someone matching your description came in my house."

"In the middle of the night."

"Don't worry. I know which old-man neighbor it was—he never sleeps." Dane gritted his teeth. "Watches way too much television. They must have gotten your picture out on the news last night. Anyway, Stella had to pass it on. The feds are on their way here. Now."

Tate moved to the door and glanced back, once again regretting the fact that he had drawn a good man into his own personal drama.

"Go out the back way. The truck is on the side of the house." Dane waved Liberty along with him. She hung back in the kitchen, though. Dane motioned to a duffel, the one he used for the gym. "There are clothes in there. Liberty is about my wife's size. They should do."

Tate nodded, blown away by his friend's generosity.

"Do you want me to tell them I didn't see Liberty, or that you coerced her into going with you?"

Tate wasn't sure he liked either answer. "Say what you want." He glanced at the kitchen. "Lib, let's go."

"You should probably hit me." Dane braced. "Make it look good."

"One sec." She rifled through a drawer. Over Dane's shoulder, Tate saw Liberty tuck something behind her back. She stepped up to the sheriff. "I want to say thank you. For everything."

"You're welcome, Liberty." He turned back to Tate and made a "come here" motion with his fingers.

Did he really expect Tate to hit him?

Liberty swung her hand up to the sheriff's neck. There was a short crackle, and Dane crumpled to the floor.

"What was that?"

Liberty held it up. "Stun gun. Saw it in the drawer earlier when I was looking for a dishcloth." She hustled with him outside, around the house to the truck. "I figure when he wakes up, his story will be all the more plausible."

Tate started up the truck and peeled out of the driveway, praying the Secret Service weren't waiting at the end of the street to arrest them both.

# SEVEN

Liberty gripped the handle on the truck door, her phone now dark in the cup holder. She'd switched it off so she couldn't be tracked by any agency looking for Tate. She wanted to reach for Tate's hand as he drove, but he was concentrating. No headlights. Tate made his way through the neighborhood by moonlight. The clock on the dash said 04:30. Her eyes burned with fatigue. Liberty rubbed them and focused on the road ahead.

Tate hadn't missed a step. "Exhausted?"

"Sure," she said. "But also kind of wired. Though I figure as soon as my head hits the pillow, I'll be out."

Tate swung the wheel to the right. One tire hit the curb, and he pulled to a sharp stop. "Get down."

Liberty ducked. Over the sound of the truck's engine, she heard a vehicle pass. Then a second and third. If this was the Secret Service it wasn't her team, not with that many vehicles. This must be the other feds investigating the plane's disappearance. FBI, or maybe even local Secret Service agents.

When the noise died down, Liberty lifted her head. Tate's upper body was twisted so he could look out the back window.

"FBI?"

"And Secret Service, I think." He paused. "Dane's story should hold, but we need to ditch the truck soon or they'll use it to find us."

"What about you? You know you could just go talk to them, right?"

"And get arrested?"

"You don't know that's their plan." Liberty settled into her seat and re-buckled her belt. "The plan was to come and *talk* to you. There's no warrant out for your arrest, because Dane or I would have known. So you tell the Secret Service about those men who tried to kill us, and how they planted the black box in your house. Then about the ones who tried to kidnap us."

It had been a *long* day.

"I need more time, Lib. I need evidence the Russians are framing me and how they're involved. We need to know who's calling the shots and where the plane is."

"We won't know if it was in the mine until they dig far enough to see."

"Which will take time."

Liberty sighed. "And I'm supposed to just put my career and my life on hold until you're sure it's the right time?"

Tate gripped the wheel but didn't look at her. "Bet that feels kind of unfair. Like when you gave my ring back with zero explanation as to why our relationship—the marriage we had been planning—all of a sudden wasn't working for you."

"Tate—"

"Don't bother. I don't even think I wanna hear it. At least not right now." He paused. "I'd worked through a lot of it, and tried to make peace with it. You showing back up here all of a sudden is *not* helping."

Liberty didn't say anything. Hot tears pricked her eyes for the millionth time today. Why had she thought coming here was such a good idea? Telling him she was seriously, truly sorry wasn't a horrible idea. Truth was, the feelings she'd had for him were still there. Still strong.

Too bad Tate didn't want to do anything except remind her how badly she'd hurt him.

"Sorry."

Tate didn't say anything. He just let her single word linger in the air between them.

For coming?

For breaking up with him?

Tate had been everything to her. The perfect partner in work and life, or so she'd thought. Then came the moment that had changed everything. The moment she had realized she couldn't be everything to him. If they'd stayed together he wouldn't get everything he wanted in life. And so she'd let him go so he could find what she had with him…with someone else. Any other choice would only have been selfish.

Tate pulled out onto the street. "Let's just get to Dane's camp trailer. We can sleep, and then in the morning, when we're both no longer fall-down tired, we can run through everything we know and see what's next."

First thing in the morning was less than three hours from now. She needed to send her team leader, Director Locke, a message before she went to sleep. Tate might not want to make contact, but Liberty intended to tell her superior everything—including how she'd lost her sidearm in the mine explosion. She'd already lost Tate, and if she lost her job as well then she really would have nothing left.

Liberty stayed silent for the remainder of the ride. Eventually whoever was behind all of this would realize Liberty and Tate were alive and show up again to try to kill them.

Liberty shivered. Tate turned up the heat and moved the vent so it blew in her direction. But her feeling cold had nothing to do with the temperature. Even in the middle of winter.

Tate pulled up at a stoplight. The road was empty except for a semitruck coming in the other direction. A container on the back made the thing look like some great, hulking beast bearing down on them.

Liberty smiled at the imagery only a day like today could produce, and watched the semitruck approach the light on the other side of the street. It didn't slow down. Their light must be green. But instead of heading on down its lane, the truck veered toward them.

Liberty's smile dropped.

Tate said, "What—"

The truck still didn't slow.

Tate hit the gas, and the engine revved as they shot from the white line, the light still red. The truck came toward them, gaining speed. It started to turn.

"Tate."

"I know. There's nowhere to—"

Liberty gasped. They were going faster every second, but the semi was, too. Tate had them almost to the curb and the row of parked cars.

The semi hit their back quarter panel, just past the driver's-side door. Liberty gripped the dash and held on for dear life. The momentum sent them into the cars. Metal scraped metal, and Liberty screamed. Tate roared, his knuckles white on the steering wheel.

Finally they cleared the back of the semitruck, and there was enough space for Tate to gun it between the car and the semi and get them away from the crazy truck driver.

Her breath came in gasps. "That wasn't just a coincidence, was it?"

Tate shook his head. "There's no way." He slammed his palm down on the steering wheel. "How did they know where we were and what vehicle we were driving? This is nuts!"

"Could Dane have—"

"There's *no way* the sheriff sold us out. He wouldn't do that. He's a friend."

"Okay," Liberty said, trying to placate him.

Tate shot her a dark look. Liberty said, "What?"

"Didn't happen to send any messages while we had a cell signal, did you?"

Her mouth dropped open. "You think that truck just tried to flatten us because of *me*?"

Tate just stared. "It's a logical assumption."

"And it can't be that it's yours?"

He shook his head. "My phone isn't even switched on. It isn't me."

Liberty bit down on her molars so hard it was a wonder she didn't crack anything. The man was completely infuriating, and she had half a mind to just demand he pull over so she could get out. Walk back to the hotel, wherever it was, through the snow still falling, and the freezing temperatures. "This is the worst day of my life."

Tate took a hard right. Liberty slammed against the door.

He said, "Sorry your visit has been such a bad experience."

* * *

Morning light streamed in the window and across Tate's face. He shifted on the couch of the camp trailer and stretched, even as he used those first few moments of wakefulness to thank God no one had found them here. They'd parked two miles away and left their cell phones turned off in the truck.

He lifted his watch from the table and sat up. Just past seven. If he slept any longer his schedule would be totally off, so he rubbed his eyes and got up. He glanced toward the bedroom area, four paces to the other side of the camp trailer. Liberty had slid the dividing door closed when she'd gone in there to sleep, but now it was halfway open.

Tate strode over and looked in. The blankets were rumpled, but their occupant was gone. He spun around, then strode to the door. Where on earth was Liberty? A flash of cold went through him. What if something had happened to her? He braced before he pulled the door open, wondering if gunmen were outside the trailer waiting to kill him. He grabbed the closest gun, checked it was ready and then flicked the tiny handle. He pushed the door open with his bare foot.

He'd forgotten shoes.

Liberty let out a squeal of surprise and looked up. In one hand was a drink tray holding two hot cups, and in the other was a white paper sack. "Tate. You're awake."

"And you were gone." He eyed the area around them, the wintry wind numbing his face while she entered, and then he shut the door. Liberty set the food down.

"You were asleep. And I was hungry." She sighed. "That was nowhere near enough sleep. But I woke up, and you were still sleeping. So I went out. I've been gone half an hour."

"Side trip to the truck?"

"I spoke to Locke, if that's what you want to know."

She'd gone to the truck? Tate couldn't believe she would do that without him. It was so dangerous. His stomach knotted. "And if there had been men waiting for you?" She would have been hurt, maybe even killed, and he would never have known.

She tore the paper bag open and grabbed a breakfast sandwich. "I am capable of being careful and keeping myself safe, thank you very much."

"I know you are." Tate knew there wasn't any answer to satisfy her. They would only get in an argument. The truth was, despite the fact that he knew she was a very capable agent, part of Tate went cold with fear at the idea of her being in danger. Liberty should be safe at all times, just for his peace of mind. Sure, it wasn't the reality of her life or the job she did. But tell that to Tate's heart.

He got a sandwich of his own and slumped down onto the couch. She'd been right about one thing—that wasn't nearly enough sleep. But they were going to have to suck it up because the longer they stayed here, the more danger they were in. Gunmen. Russians. Feds. It didn't matter who found them; it would be complicated no matter what.

Once there was some food in his stomach, Tate said, "Are you going to tell me if you learned anything?"

Liberty's mouth curled up on one side. She swiped her lips with a napkin and it disappeared. "There were a...few emails."

"Which means you had fifty."

"Fifteen voice mails, twentysomething texts and, yes, a whole lot of emails."

Tate winced. "Exactly how mad is Locke?"

Liberty scrunched up her nose in a move he absorbed like a starving man at a buffet. Apparently he'd missed that look. She said, "He wasn't exactly surprised I stuck with you."

"Oh, yeah?"

Liberty sighed. "I'd been at the truck all of a minute before he showed up."

Tate gasped, and a crumb of sandwich went down the wrong way. He coughed. "Locke *what*?"

"It's fine. He had the GPS on my phone activated. Apparently he's been tracking us every time the signal sent them a ping, and he was close by this morning when I turned my cell on." She sighed. "He's going to talk to Dane, get all that sorted out."

"He didn't try to convince you to bring me in?" Tate went to the window over the tiny sink and parted the blinds. "He's waiting outside right now, isn't he?"

"You think I'd turn you in?"

Tate shrugged. "It isn't so far a stretch from breaking up with me. I don't know what's going on in your head, Lib. And I need to be prepared."

"Sit down, Tate."

He leaned against the counter instead. "He could have followed you back here without your knowledge."

Liberty sighed. "Locke…cares what happens to you. He's here to convince the local Secret Service agents and the FBI agents who don't know you of the fact that you didn't do this. He's on your side, but you're so stubborn and determined to go it alone you're going to dig yourself into a corner Locke and I won't be able to get you out of."

"I'm not turning myself in."

Liberty gritted her teeth. He thought he heard a low noise from her throat, but couldn't be sure.

"I won't."

"Well, what are you going to do?"

"Find the source of all this." He sipped his coffee and thought through the plan as it came together in his head. "Find the person calling the shots."

"Easier said than done." She sighed. "And what are you going to do then? Beat it out of them? Maybe try a little coercion?" Liberty stared at him for a beat. "Is doing so going to help plead your case when the evidence stacked against you is so overwhelming?"

"Either you believe me and you're on my side, or you don't, Lib. You can't pick and choose." She'd stuck with him this far. If she left him and he had to do this alone… well, Tate wasn't so sure he'd be entirely okay with that.

She set her coffee down. "What's the plan?"

It took half an hour to get to the truck. Tate scanned the area for his old team as they approached the vehicle, but didn't see anyone.

"Locke is gone now."

But how far had he gone? The idea of the man waiting in the background, prepared to defend Tate, was baffling. Considering he hadn't exactly left the Secret Service in the best standing, he didn't figure he deserved loyalty of all things. Tate hadn't had anyone at his back for more than a year, and it had been a scary time, despite the fact that nothing necessarily bad had happened.

Now that Locke—and, yes, Liberty—occupied the spot, Tate felt safer than he had last night. In the heat of the moment it might not make much difference—if Locke was more than a second away and Tate's life was in the balance. But just the idea of them being prepared to fight on his side made him realize how much loyalty meant to him.

He glanced at Liberty and then started the engine. Maybe that was why her cutting him loose had hurt so much. It had been the ultimate move of disloyalty on her part.

Tate drove to the house Dane had mentioned the night before and pulled up a few doors down. "That house. The red one. It's the address the truck owned by our kidnappers is registered to." And the only thing Tate could think might yield any results.

"Our kidnappers?"

Tate nodded and pulled binoculars out of the bag. He seriously owed Dane. The man had thought of everything.

"You still remember snippets of information like that?"

It was just an address. "We broke up. Who I am hasn't changed, Lib." He studied the house—because otherwise he would get mad at her again—and then adjusted the focus so he could see inside the front window. Someone was asleep on the couch in the living room.

"Oh, no." Tate hadn't thought this could get worse, but apparently this day wasn't going to get any better. "Seriously?"

"What?" Liberty shifted on her seat. "What is it?"

Tate gritted his teeth, then handed her the binoculars. "My brother is in the house."

# EIGHT

"Why would your brother be in a place belonging to the Russians?" Liberty glanced from the house to Tate, then back to the house. It was run-down, even more than the other houses on this street. The front lawn was overgrown, and where some of the neighbors had empty driveways and mowed lawns, and others were just now leaving for work, the Russians' house had two beater vehicles in the driveway and a nineties sedan on the street out front.

"That is a real good question." He didn't sound happy, and why would he be? Braden was in there.

"Are you sure it's him?" Tate shot her a look, so she said, "It's a distance. How well can you see in there?"

"Well enough to know Braden is asleep on the couch."

"What do you want to do?" She wasn't exactly sure what his plan was, but she doubted it would involve sitting in the car and watching the house all day. Surveillance wasn't exactly Tate's strong suit. He much preferred action, and she didn't blame him.

Tate grabbed the door handle, but she waylaid him with a hand on his arm. "Tate…"

He looked at her.

Liberty hardly knew where to start, but decided to go with, "Be careful."

"I will."

"That's…not exactly what I mean." How was she supposed to put it? "I guess I mean it like, 'tread carefully.' Because what if your brother is there against his will?"

"I doubt it."

"But it's possible, right? Just like it's possible he isn't. He could be working with them." Something dawned on her. "Does he know computers?" Maybe Braden wasn't a technological dinosaur the way Tate was.

"Sure, I guess. Why?"

"I was just wondering if it was him who did the blog. He knows you better than anyone."

"I thought it was you who knew me better than anyone. How can Braden, when we hardly ever talk to each other?"

Liberty winced.

"We don't yet have plans to spend time together over Christmas, like most brothers do. Braden and I… It's complicated, okay? He blames me for a lot of things, like I'm at fault for everything wrong in his life. It's like he never grew out of that whiny kid stage where they knock over a priceless vase and then blame it on the dog."

Tate shrugged her hand off his arm. "I need to go over there and draw him out of the house. I need to look my brother in the eyes and ask him about this missing plane and these guys who keep showing up to take us out." He paused again. "Maybe it was even him who drove the semitruck right at us."

Liberty smoothed her hand on the leg of Dane's wife's pants. She'd thanked God the woman was a similar size, or she would be having a different set of problems right now. So far God had taken care of them. She could admit as much. They'd been in danger, and almost died several times, but He was protecting them. Watching over them. That wasn't in question.

If Braden really was part of this, there was no way God would allow him to be successful.

She hurt for Tate over the fact that he had to face the possibility of his brother not just disliking him but maybe also actively seeking to harm him. She didn't have any siblings, so she couldn't imagine what that kind of familial betrayal would be like, but she could see how it might hurt.

Liberty didn't pray for Tate about that, though. Because her hurt hadn't been healed. Not yet.

"You want me to tread carefully with a guy who might be trying to kill us?" Tate's eyebrows lifted. "Braden is a grown man who needs to take responsibility for his actions."

"If you go at him hard, he could shut down. Then we'll never get answers."

"Okay," he acquiesced. "I can see how you might be right. I can be gentle."

Liberty didn't want to react, but from his expression she figured she wasn't as good at hiding it as she wanted to be. She was exhausted, which never boded well for her ability to filter her thoughts and feelings from displaying themselves across her face.

"Okay," she said. "How do you want to do this?"

"You think I need your help?"

"Well, I'm not going to sit in the car."

"It's probably the safest place you can be."

It was her turn to shoot him a look, then she cracked her door. "I'll take the back. Make sure he doesn't get away if he decides to run. Or if there are others in the house. Call me if you need coverage for the front or someone to watch your back."

Liberty didn't wait for his response; she just got out and sneaked down the street to the house. The safety net of Locke knowing exactly where they were was a comfort. As was the fact that she heard Tate's door shut behind her, and then his footsteps. She wasn't alone anymore.

She crossed the grass and found the gate on the side of the house unlatched, then pushed it open carefully, praying it wouldn't squeak. And that none of the neighbors would notice two people sneaking around the house. Liberty hugged the siding past the overflowing trash cans and hoped no vicious dogs were hanging out in the backyard.

She stopped at the corner but saw only an overgrown lawn and no sign of animal occupants. Dogs would alert whoever was in the house to her presence, and she didn't want to take the time to calm them and fight off anyone else.

The patio was nothing but a slab of concrete with deep cracks and two ripped deck chairs. Liberty walked in a crouch to the window, then peeked inside. Two men—the same two who had taken them from the mine in their truck—faced a battered kitchen table, their backs to her. On the table was a laptop displaying a map of green terrain. One pointed to an area on the left side of the map, and from their body language it was clear whatever they were discussing was serious business.

Maybe even deadly.

His brother was alone, as far as Tate could see. He rapped on the window with his knuckles. Braden looked like he was still asleep, but at the slight noise he lifted his head and glanced toward where Tate stood outside. His eyes widened, an initial flash of surprise, which didn't spell anything good. Braden's gut reaction to seeing Tate was narrowed eyes and lips curled up in distaste. Like he didn't have time for this, even though he wasn't doing anything more pressing.

Tate motioned to the door, indicating to his brother that he should come out. Braden straightened out of the couch, his build very much like their dad's had been—long limbs, shoulders not nearly as wide as Tate's. It was hard to watch him move when he'd inherited their father's bearing.

Tate hadn't gotten much of anything, except his mother's ability to snap when she was mad. Her temper had been explosive, making her boys and husband band together in defense when that monster reared its head. Tate smiled at the memory of being fifteen, out in the garage with Braden and their father, lifting weights and waiting for Mom to cool off.

Braden opened the front door and lumbered out. "What do you want?"

It hurt to look at his face. So much of their father was in him, and yet Braden threw it away. Discarded all the good things he'd been given for the sake of solace found in substances that tore his body apart. Made his eyes red. Made his face worn and pale, looking older than he was.

"Crashed for the night with some Russians?" Tate asked.

"Wild party, what can I say? Sometimes you just fall asleep where you're at." Braden's attempt at humor was unconvincing.

"So you were partying with them. It wasn't just a ride home?"

Braden sniffed. "Why does this sound like an interrogation?"

"Maybe because two guys who live here kidnapped me and Liberty last night."

"Liberty's here?"

Tate ignored the comment. They'd only met once. "Those guys were likely going to kill us." He paused to make sure Braden's brain had caught up with what he was saying. "So I came here to find out who's behind a missing plane and the people on it, and who is trying to frame me for it all."

"Yeah, heard you were in some trouble."

"So you do know something."

"I know you're gonna want to watch your back." Despite his bravado, Braden frowned. "Didn't know Lib was involved."

He folded his arms. Braden didn't need to worry about Liberty. Tate would watch out for her. "Tell me what you know."

Braden leaned against the wall, a wry smile on his face. "Nobody tells me nothin'."

"You just said you heard I was in trouble," Tate said. "So where'd you hear it?"

"Around."

"How many people are in that house?"

"What's it to you?"

"Because they're trying to kill me. Or send me to prison." Tate's stomach knotted. "And Liberty is going to get caught in the cross fire." It was the only thing Braden seemed to care about.

The tactic seemed to work. Braden said, "I'm not getting involved. If you have a problem with the Russians, it's your deal."

"You won't even talk to them, find out who's calling the shots?" From the look on his face, Braden knew who was calling the shots. Tate pointed to the house. "You could find out why they're targeting me."

Braden didn't say anything. Which meant he probably knew exactly what was going on. Tate sighed. "Are *you* behind this? Because if you are, tell me where those missing people from the plane are."

Braden stayed silent.

"I'm not going to prison. I don't care if you do nothing to stop it. But I'm not going to let those people die."

"Like the way you let Mom and Dad die?"

Tate jerked his head back at the force of Braden's words. They were like a physical blow. "Mom and Dad's deaths had nothing to do with me. I wasn't there."

"I know. You were with me," Braden said. "I used to think you could do anything. School. Football. Girls. You were the man. Then Mom and Dad went away, and they never came back. You couldn't keep them here."

"It wasn't in my power to do that."

"Doesn't matter," Braden said. "I was a kid, and that's what it felt like. Sixteen years old, and you were my larger-than-life big brother who could solve any problem. Finish any fight. You could do it all. But you couldn't bring them back."

Tate squeezed the bridge of his nose. "I knew you were mad at me, but I didn't know this was why." He looked up. "Why didn't you tell me you felt this way? And why turn to drugs and the worst kinds of friends you could possibly find instead of talking to me?"

"My recreation habits are none of your business."

Okay, *that* was the brother Tate knew. Smart as a whip. Talk about being able to solve anything. The time Braden had fixed the toilet? Tate hadn't even known where to start.

"Besides," Braden said. "You left. Joined the army and found a life better than the one with me in it."

"I supported us. You were supposed to take the money and go to college."

Braden snorted.

"Instead you wasted it all on your *recreation habits*."

"My life is none of your business."

"It is now. You're hanging with people who want me dead or in federal prison. So which is it? Dead, or my reputation ruined and me incarcerated? Pinning a missing plane and three people gone squarely on my shoulders? Who would that benefit? Besides your ego, I mean."

Braden's lips thinned. "Wouldn't you like to know?"

"I'm pretty sure I already told you that's why I'm here."

Braden snorted out a burst of laughter. "I figure it serves you right, Mr. Super-Secret-Agent Tate Almers."

It wasn't the first time he'd realized his brother didn't just dislike him, but that he actually hated Tate. "Then

I guess you'll have to go with me to talk to the sheriff."
He reached for his brother, and Braden stepped back.

Tate followed him and caught hold of his arm.
"You're not going to warn them I know. You're going
to help me instead. Your brother." The two of them were
family, whether Braden wanted to recognize it or not.

Braden swung around. Tate saw his brother's fist
at the last second. He ducked his head to the side as it
whistled past his ear. Tate threw a punch into his brother's diaphragm.

Braden's breath whooshed out and he wheezed.

Tate braced. "We don't need to fight."

His brother didn't quit. He swung again. Tate ducked
and then pulled his brother's arm behind his back and
slammed Braden into the siding. "Enough. We're *not*
fighting, Bray." Their parents would be seriously disappointed with how the two of them had turned out.

Braden struggled against his hold. "I'm not telling
your best pal, the sheriff, anything."

"I'm going to get to the bottom of this with or without you. But I won't let you tip anyone off to the fact
that the Russians are behind this."

Braden grunted and renewed his struggle. Tate let go
with one hand and pulled out his phone to tell Liberty
what was happening. He'd just dialed the area code for
Washington, DC, when a gun fired.

From the back of the house.

"Sounds like Liberty might need help."

Braden was right. Answering gunfire sounded. Two
shots, then a third.

Tate was going to have to keep hold on his brother
while he helped her. He pulled him from the wall but
didn't see Braden's elbow until it hit his face. Tate stum-

bled back a step as pain reverberated through his head. His brother's footsteps fled away, and then the front door slammed.

Tate shook off the daze. He raced around the house and drew his gun out as he moved. Liberty turned the corner at the back, holding her left shoulder. Fear was raw on her face. "Go!"

Tate waited until she got to him, almost colliding with him.

"They're coming!"

She didn't slow. Tate glanced back as he raced after her. Two men rounded the corner. Tate found cover at the front corner of the house and fired two shots. They ducked down, and one hid behind a trash can.

The neighbors would call the police, and then surely the feds would come and investigate. Gunshots in a small town like this had to be part of the wider investigation, the search for Tate. What he wanted to know was who was out searching for the plane? The feds were completely distracted by all the evidence pointing at Tate.

He fired off two more shots, then raced after Liberty and caught up to her by the truck. Her face was pale. She pulled the door open with a wince. How badly was she hurt?

Tate turned the key and listened to it fire up. "You okay?"

"Through and through." That was all she said.

He gunned it out of the parking spot and spun the car around in a U-turn so he didn't have to drive past the house again. "Who were those guys?"

Liberty shook her head. She held her gun in her left hand, rested on her lap. That same shoulder was the injured one. Blood was visible between the fingers of her right hand, which gripped her left shoulder.

"That doesn't look good."

"Just get us out of here."

Tate glanced in his rearview mirror. "You'll have to hold on a little longer."

"Why?" She tried to turn to see behind them but stopped and groaned. Liberty closed her eyes and rested her head back.

"Because they're in the sedan, coming after us."

# NINE

Liberty bit her lips together and tried to fight the pull of the pain attempting to send her consciousness spiraling into black. It wouldn't hurt anymore, but it also wouldn't help Tate. He'd have to carry her from the car.

Maybe after they got away from these people behind them.

"It was the two guys from the truck."

"Behind us?" Tate's voice was tight. He was concentrating.

Liberty didn't open her eyes. Her stomach churned, and she could feel warm wetness under her fingers. The bullet had hit the fleshy part of her shoulder, right above her collarbone. She couldn't lift her arm now, and the spot where she rested the heel of her palm on her collarbone did not feel good at all. Maybe it was broken from the impact.

But the exit wound under her fingertips boded well. It hurt like nothing she had ever felt. Still, in the grand scheme of things, it had knocked her down but not out.

"They were looking at a computer in the kitchen." He needed to know this information in case she passed out.

"Well, right now they're racing after us."

"It was a map. They were pointing at it." She took a measured breath while the pain threatened to make her sick. "Planning something."

"You heard them?"

"No. It was the impression I got from what they were doing."

Tate tapped the steering wheel. "Hang on." He turned left. Liberty could hear traffic sounds around them.

She opened her eyes and found they were in town. It wasn't like rush hour in a city, but it was busy. "Isn't it dangerous to lead them through this many people?"

Tate glanced at her. "More people means they can't open fire or they draw too much attention. Plus, we might be able to get lost in this crowd."

"But we need to know what they were looking at on that computer," she said.

"They're chasing us, Lib. They shot you." His mouth was a thin line, his lips pressed together. "We're going to have a hard time turning things around so we can ask them questions. It hasn't worked for us so far."

"Did you talk to your brother?"

"It was hardly a conversation." Tate held the steering wheel like a race car driver. "Braden still hates me, but we knew as much. He's likely involved in this and doesn't care I'm going to go to prison, but that isn't a surprise either. Go figure. The link between the plane and the Russians? It's *me*."

"And Braden," Liberty said. "Maybe by Braden's design."

She'd met Tate's brother once and he'd seemed kind of…sad. He'd reminded her of Tate a whole lot, even despite his problems and the fact that he didn't see them as problems at all. Braden seemed content with what his life was, instead of taking Tate's tactic of always seeking to make his life better. Two converse ways of dealing with the tragic deaths of their parents. She wanted to do something for Braden but didn't know him well enough to push him to seek help.

Tate's life had become something different since he'd left the Secret Service. Some of the drive he'd lost was probably her fault. Still, he was fixing up his cabin and working as a deputy sheriff. He'd retained the push in him to make things better—just not himself.

Was it because he didn't think he was worth it?

She knew how he'd felt about her caring for him. He'd told her over and over that her loving him made him feel worthy of good things when he hadn't thought he deserved them. When she'd left, had Tate decided that seeking out love for himself wasn't worth it any longer?

Liberty's heart wanted to break all over again just thinking about it. That was precisely the opposite of what she'd tried to do. Only *because* he was worth so much—more than she could ever give him—she'd cut him loose from being tied to her so he could find more.

With someone else.

Liberty sucked back a sob, and Tate reached over to squeeze her knee. "Hang on. We'll be out of this in a minute. I have an idea." He paused. "Can you walk?"

She nodded. It would hurt to move, like it hurt to think right now—or to think past the pain, at least—but she could do it.

"Okay. One more block."

"Are they right behind us?"

"Two cars between. They're playing it cool, but they've been tailing us since we left the house. Probably waiting for a quieter stretch of road so they can run us off and shoot us."

A shiver moved through Liberty's body, one she wasn't sure was entirely about having been shot.

"There's a coffee shop up here. Side door in an alley between two buildings. If I can get the car in there, we can get in the kitchen on the side of the coffee shop. The place has a front and a back door—it stretches the length of the building—and they won't know which way we went out. There won't be time for them to split up and find out."

"Good." She didn't like the idea of being on the run again. That was, if they'd actually quit being on the run this whole time. Safety was an illusion at this point, and she had the painful shoulder to prove it.

Tate made a sharp turn between two buildings and pulled in just past a Dumpster. Liberty's fingers slipped on the door handle. Her head swam, and Tate appeared in front of her. "Up and at 'em."

Liberty gritted her teeth. Tate walked with his arm around her waist, his shoulder right up against her good one. Anyone who saw them would know immediately she was shot and needed help, but maybe that was a good thing.

They moved through the coffee shop's kitchen, which smelled like cinnamon. The air was thick and hot and made her gasp for the cold air of outside.

Tate led her down behind the counter and out onto the coffee shop floor. The line at the counter was at least fifteen people long. Kids, families. Safety vests and name tags. Search-and-rescue workers and volunteers. They had to be taking a break from searching for the plane. Or they were all fueling up for a hard day of walking through the backwoods to look for the missing people and the crash site.

"Liberty?"

She knew that voice.

Tate didn't slow. He weaved through the crowd and headed for the back door. Liberty glanced over her shoulder. "Alana."

"Are you…" She frowned, then drew her weapon. "Tate Almers!" Her voice rang out and the room went quiet. "Secret Service. You need to stop."

Tate's body stiffened and he turned. He put his front to her back and his arm around her waist.

He backed up farther. People around them spread to give them a wide berth. Tate looked at her and said, "Just let us leave, whoever you are."

She wore a badge on her belt. The woman was Polynesian-looking, and her beauty was understated.

"She's the rookie who replaced you," Liberty said over her good shoulder. "Now Alana's in love with Director Locke. The two of them are besotted with each other and planning a wedding for next summer."

Alana's eyes softened a tiny bit. There it was. Her weakness.

Tate said, "I don't care who you are. We're not going with you." Not when he knew his brother was intimately involved with this. That explained the why—Braden hated him. But it wasn't the whole of what was going on, and Tate needed to find out what the rest was.

"You have a gunshot wound?" This Alana person waited for one of them to answer her question, then said, "Liberty needs a hospital, whether you like it or not." She stepped as he did, keeping the gap between them the same. At what point would she swoop forward and try to grab Liberty? To *save* her from him, probably. As if.

"Liberty will be fine," Tate said. "If you want to help, it isn't going to be by taking me in. It's going to be by figuring out who's ordering the Russians around. And finding the plane."

"You're going to tell me where the plane is."

"Would if I could, *Alana*." Tate lifted his own gun and maintained his hold on Liberty. She'd told him Locke was on their side. So why was his fiancée trying to arrest Tate now? Cold permeated him. Liberty must have lied about their meeting.

Tate said, "I've never seen the plane, and I have no idea where it is or where those missing people are. You tell Locke I said so. Tell him I already have Russians on my back, and if I'm going to figure this out I don't need his people there, too."

"No, you just need one of them at your front."

Her words made him tighten his grip on Liberty. She'd been hurt, and if she stayed with him it was going to happen again. Maybe even killed.

As much as Tate cared about her well-being, he couldn't forget the fact that Liberty was a Secret Service agent first, and whatever she meant to him came second. Her loyalties would become clear soon enough. Maybe they already had. And maybe it would mean the difference between prison and freedom, but Tate wasn't sure he cared either way. This time with her was better than any of the long, lonely days of the last year.

"Let us go." Liberty's voice was soft. "Alana, let us leave."

"Can't do that. Tate is to be brought in for questioning. This isn't about you, Liberty. It's about those missing people."

Tate said, "Blaming it on me isn't going to solve anything. It's just a distraction from where your resources should be focused—on finding those people."

Alana didn't exactly disagree, judging from her face, but he knew the push of following orders. It was Liberty who said, "Tell Locke we know Tate's brother is involved with the Russians." She stepped back, forcing Tate to move with her.

A few more steps and his back hit the door. He prayed there weren't any Russian gunmen outside, ready to shoot them. Though if they did die, Alana would do her job to bring justice, and those men wouldn't get away with it.

"They're planning something else," Liberty said. Tate's back pushed the bar on the door and disengaged the latch. "Tell Locke I'll be in touch."

She wasn't contacting him again if Tate had anything to say about it.

Alana said, "Liberty…"

Locke strode out from a hallway. Saw Alana, saw them. His eyes widened even as he pulled his gun. Tate shoved himself and Liberty out the door and took off running. He couldn't judge if Locke would pursue them or not. Tate didn't know the man well enough, not anymore. He'd been sure Locke would throw every regulation there was at Tate for getting angry and nearly starting a fight with him. Instead, he'd turned around and offered Tate an early retirement deal. He'd been flabbergasted, to say the least. What kind of person did that?

But he had no idea whether the director would help him now or not.

"Over here." Tate pulled her around the corner and glanced back. Sure enough, a bus was headed toward them. Tate gave Liberty his coat to cover her wound and thanked God for perfect timing as they hopped on board. After riding the bus farther north than they needed to go, Tate and Liberty backtracked and then rode another bus three miles east. It was a risk, considering anyone on the bus could recognize them or see Liberty's wound and try to get her help, but he just kept praying.

Faith was all that had held him together this past year. If it hadn't been for God, he probably would have spiraled much like Braden. He'd tried to talk to his brother about the Lord, but Braden hadn't wanted to hear about it. His brother was stubborn, kind of like Tate. And though he'd continually asked God why Liberty had done what she had, he still didn't have an answer. He was still waiting.

And now she was here. Because God had sent her, so he could finally understand? Or was it so Liberty could gain something she needed? Perhaps it was so they could find these missing people. He didn't figure it was so he could go to prison. God didn't allow bad things into people's lives for no reason. He allowed them so people would cling all the more tightly to Him, to persevere and have a faith growing in strength all the time.

When they finally arrived back at the trailer, Tate unlocked the door and made sure he scanned the area for anything amiss. He held his gun ready and had Liberty open the door with her good hand. When he'd checked every spot someone could hide in, he said, "It's clear."

Liberty climbed the stairs like she was going to fall over. He led her to a chair and found the first-aid kit, then cleaned her up as best he could using Dane's admittedly extensive first-aid kit.

He didn't want to say it, but he had to. "Maybe you should have gone with that agent."

"You wanted me to leave you by yourself?"

Tate shrugged.

If Liberty had any strength, she'd have hit him. Seriously? The man had wanted to ditch her at every turn so far. He'd been trying to pass her off to other people again and again.

"Sorry I'm such a burden to you that you're still forced to try to find ways to get rid of me," she said. "Maybe you should have just left me on the bus. Or at the coffee shop. Or at Dane's house. Maybe you should have let those Russians kill me. Then I wouldn't be bothering you so much."

Tears rolled down her face, but she didn't make any move to swipe them away. He needed to know she hurt as much as he did, and she wasn't just talking about her shoulder.

Tate touched the sides of her face. Liberty couldn't handle it, so she shut her eyes. His thumbs wiped her tears away as she struggled for breath. "I'm only crying because my shoulder hurts."

"I'll get you some painkillers." Tate didn't let go of her. "Open your eyes, Lib."

When she did, he swam before her in the blur of her tears. "What?" He was probably going to tell her the real plan now, the one where he ditched her. She didn't want to hear it, so she said, "I came here to help you. I came here because I didn't believe you could do what they thought you'd done. But I haven't helped. Things are worse than they were."

"Not because of you."

"You probably would've been totally fine without me."

"Yeah, it's been working so well the past year."

Liberty sniffed. "What do you mean?"

"Probably about as well as your life has been working without me."

She frowned. "What does that mean? We should be out looking for the plane, and finding out what the Russians are up to."

Tate leaned closer to her. "Tell me your life is better without me, Liberty."

She opened her mouth but couldn't say anything. There was nothing to say that wouldn't be a lie.

"That's what I thought."

"Tate—"

He touched his mouth to hers, and all the feelings between them rushed back in one giant wave. Liberty's head spun. She lifted her hands to his shoulders just to prove to herself this was really happening.

Pain tore through her and she broke from the kiss, crying out.

"I'm sorry." He moved away.

Why was he sorry? It'd been the best kiss of her life.

But all Liberty could do was hold her now-bandaged shoulder and try not to cry like a baby. *Too late.*

Tate knelt in front of her as she sobbed. He handed her painkillers from Dane's first-aid kit and a plastic cup of water, which she managed to choke down while she fell apart.

"I should let you rest. I'll come back later with some food after you've had a nap."

Liberty shook her head, even as she leaned back in the chair. "Don't go." She wanted to cling to him, though she had no right to do so anymore.

"What is it?" His face was close again.

"It feels like you won't come back if you leave. Like I'll never see you again."

"Not going to happen, Lib." Tate touched her face again, this time with just one hand. "I'm right here. I've always been right here."

Liberty shook her head. "I won't be. I have to go, so you can have your family."

"Braden hates me. I don't have a family, Lib. I only have you."

"We have to keep working this case." Otherwise she was going to say something she would regret. She tried to push out of the chair, but he didn't let her get far.

"Stay. I'll be back soon."

"Tate—"

"You need to trust me, Lib. Trust I'll come back."

She heard the door shut, and things got fuzzy. Before long he was touching her face again.

Liberty blinked. "Did you find them?"

"I don't know what you mean, but I found something." He didn't look happy. Not even when he handed her a mug of coffee and sat to sip his own. "Drink up. We need to move. The longer we stay here, the likelier it is that we'll be found."

Liberty nodded. The clock over the oven blinked

noon, even though it was still morning. "How long were you gone?"

"Maybe half an hour. I went to Braden's apartment, and I'm glad I did." He held up what looked like a checkbook. "He has access to personal accounts belonging to Mountain Freedom Credit Union's bank manager."

"Check fraud?" The fog receded. She could feel the wound in her shoulder, but not as bad as it had been.

"I want to go ask the man and find out." Tate checked his watch. "It's Saturday, so the bank closes earlier today—in half an hour. I'll make us sandwiches, and we can catch him before he leaves for the day."

Liberty nodded and rested her eyes for another minute before drinking two more cups of coffee Tate made her from a jar of instant coffee and a kettle on the tiny gas stove. The sandwich wasn't her favorite but she didn't complain.

"Okay, I'm good." She started to get up.

Tate waved her back to sitting. "Give it five more minutes."

Liberty nodded. She remembered Tate's reaction to her being shot. Touching her face. That kiss. She'd drifted off thinking about it, thinking how it was the best kiss they'd ever shared, and it had taken breaking up and being apart for a year for her to have that.

*What is going on, God?*

This was supposed to be for the best. Maybe God was testing her resolve, forcing her to be certain she'd made the right decision in giving him up. Or perhaps Tate was temptation—which wasn't completely untrue, since the man made her mouth water even with the mountain man beard—and she needed to flee.

Liberty didn't know what the right answer was. She'd

been at odds with God for the last year, and it seemed weird to run back to Him now. All she knew was that in the heat of the moment she'd chosen Tate, not Alana and the Secret Service. Was this her answer?

Liberty didn't talk the entire drive to the credit union. She didn't even ask how he'd gotten Dane's truck back. How this trip would help find the plane, she didn't know, but she was willing to find out. When it was over, she was going to be the one to walk away. It was for the best.

"Want to wait here?"

Liberty shook her head and walked with Tate to the bank's front door. She wore a clean shirt that belonged to Dane's wife, which she'd been able to pull over her bandage and button up. Still, she didn't look good, and she wasn't fooling anyone. They were going to think Tate was mistreating her.

Inside, the bank was empty.

"Hello?" Tate called out. "Anyone here?"

Liberty turned in a circle. Lights on, front door unlocked. Someone should be behind the counter. Probably more than one person, actually.

"The sign is flipped to closed, which is weird."

She nodded but didn't look at him. Liberty walked to a row of offices and peered around a half wall.

"Hours on the door indicate they closed a while ago."

Liberty froze. "Uh, Tate?"

The nameplate said Gerald Turing, and she'd have been pleased to meet him even given the circumstances.

Too bad he was dead.

# TEN

Since no one started yelling at them for being in the bank after hours, Tate kept looking around. "What, Lib?"

He couldn't believe he'd actually kissed Liberty. Apparently he'd checked his brain at the door of the camp trailer when he'd gone inside. But she'd been hurt, and she was so valiantly braving her way through the pain. When he'd realized she was a little loopy from it, Tate had left her to rest.

If the Secret Service or FBI had found her there, she'd have been able to answer their questions. Or simply tell them he'd coerced her into going with him to the mine. He'd have had "kidnapping of a federal agent" added to the list of charges they wanted to slap him with. It wouldn't have added but a few years onto his sentence if they were successful.

If Tate couldn't prove their entire assumption about his involvement was wrong.

And now he was almost sure Braden was involved. He couldn't prove much past the smarm on his brother's face, or the look in his eye, but Tate wouldn't put it past him. Ever since Braden had tried out for football and not made the team Tate had been the star of in high school, things had gone downhill. Their parents' deaths had only been part of it; he knew as much from what his brother had said. Braden had always looked up to him, but somewhere along the line, wanting to be like his big brother had twisted into this vengeance.

Braden's apartment hadn't been anything but a sad reminder of the life of an addict. Despite the fact that Tate had managed to find a checkbook from the bank manager's personal account, there hadn't been much else. No family photos, or reminders of their parents. Nothing more than a few DVDs, grimy furniture and a kitchen that desperately needed cleaning.

Tate sighed and continued his sweep of the main area of the bank, then behind the counter where the tellers sat. No one was here.

"Tate?"

He almost didn't look at her, as he knew exactly what he'd see. Pale face, tired eyes. Lines around her mouth to indicate how much pain she was in. He probably shouldn't have brought her here, but he just hadn't been able to bear the idea of doing this alone. As much as Liberty had hurt him, it was clear those feelings hadn't died. Would they ever? Maybe the two of them were tied together.

Still, it didn't change the fact that their relationship hadn't worked. Liberty had broken it off because Tate just wasn't the kind of man she'd been able to see herself with long-term. An answer he'd be given by any woman, not just her. Tate wasn't "future" material, or he'd be married with a family by now. And their lives were even less compatible these days. They lived in different parts of the country, which meant it would be even harder to have a relationship.

If he was even looking for one.

"Tate." She sounded aggravated now.

He spun around, lifted his arms. "What?" Liberty's gun hung loose in her good hand. She could probably still shoot straight. She'd always been an excellent shot. But he'd been doing a lousy job of protecting her. "What is it?"

"The bank manager." She stood by the open office door in the corner. "I found him."

Tate strode to her. "I can talk to him. You wait in the truck—you look like you're dead on your feet, Lib."

She looked like she was going to be sick. "Dead?" She also looked like she was going to slap him.

"You know what I mean." He touched her shoulders, not worrying about whether the bank manager could hear them. He needed to say this. "I don't want you to get hurt." Although that didn't make sense because she *was* hurt. "It's more than that," he continued. "All this is my problem, and it's sweet you came here." Now he knew she'd done it because she cared about what happened to him enough to brave his ire over her actions. He lived every day like his life was in ruins. Like the aftermath of a great explosion, leaving devastation in its wake.

Tate moved his hand from her shoulder to her neck, feeling the warmth of her skin beneath his fingertips. He *needed* to feel it, because Liberty was real. Maybe the only real thing in his life.

Which was why he had to do this.

Liberty's gaze searched his, her brow furrowed.

"You should go back to the Secret Service." When she started to argue, he said, "I don't want you in the line of fire anymore. Not when I know Braden doesn't care at all about what happens to me. This is serious business, and you should make sure you're good to go home and get back to your job. Your life is important and so is your job." He took a breath. "Because I care about you too much to let you stay here with me."

He moved closer to touch his mouth to hers in one last goodbye. It would probably be a source of pain later, but Tate didn't care. He needed the memory of her sweetness to accompany all the anguish.

Liberty's breath touched his lips. "The bank manager is dead."

Tate halted, his mouth almost on hers. He looked over her shoulder into the office. The bank manager— at least, he assumed the suited man in the chair was him—had a distinct wound under his chin. His hand hung down by his side and a pistol lay on the carpet, as though it had fallen there.

"Oh." His brain struggled to switch from what he'd been thinking about—Liberty—to the dead man. He moved her aside and stepped into the tiny office.

"Don't touch anything."

Tate turned back, one eyebrow raised. He hadn't forgotten that much. Deputy sheriffs of small Montana counties didn't investigate suspicious deaths often, but he'd done the training.

"They can't pin this on you as well if you haven't left any evidence you were ever in the room."

She had a good point. Tate stepped back. "How about you go in while I call Dane?"

Relief washed over her face. As she moved past him, Liberty touched his elbow. "Thank you for what you said, and for caring about me." She was quiet for a second, and he gave her the space to think through the pain to figure out what she wanted to say. "I'm not leaving you. I've come this far, and I'm not a quitter."

She went into the bank manager's office while Tate stared at the back of her head. She *had* quit. She'd quit on them when she gave up their relationship…and for what? Certainly not anything better for either of them.

Tate's words rang in her ears as she moved toward the dead man. Liberty understood why he'd told her it was okay to go, but at every turn so far it had seemed like he wanted to get rid of her and then brought her anyway. She was getting sick of his back-and-forth. Or she would be if it wasn't for the fact that he now seemed to want to kiss her to accompany his goodbye. Liberty would have rather had kisses that meant they were staying together, but she had to face the truth—this was all she would get.

Gerald Turing, branch manager of Mountain Freedom Credit Union, had been killed at close range. A gunshot from farther away wouldn't have left a burn mark on the skin under his chin. Classic suicide, shooting oneself in the head. Liberty didn't want to assume it wasn't murder since that was always a possibility until it was ruled out. Still, at face value, suicide seemed the most likely cause of death.

The man was older. He wore a nice suit, a string tie and a huge belt buckle with an elk on it. He was clearly no stranger to mashed potatoes and pancakes. His mustache looked to have been gelled, and his cowboy boots had been shined.

"Yeah, Dane," Tate said into his phone.

Liberty glanced at the man who had once been her partner in everything. He frowned, his gaze found hers and he mouthed, *They're listening.* How he knew from less than a minute of conversation was interesting. Was the Secret Service going to trace the call? It had been less than a day, but Liberty had expected them to descend en masse at any point, and yet they hadn't. Tate was their prime suspect. Why hadn't he been caught and brought in for questioning yet?

Tate paced the credit union lobby and explained to Dane how they'd found the bank manager dead in his office.

They wouldn't need to trace the call now. Liberty continued her observation of the body, wondering exactly how many minutes she had until the feds and sheriff's department showed up here with their guns drawn.

Likely not long at all.

The computer screen was dark. Liberty used her sleeve to wiggle the mouse, and the display woke up. Gerald's email was open, a message on-screen in huge letters. It was written in a weird font that looked like a fourth-grade girl's handwriting.

*The deal goes down. There is no backing out.*

"Tate?"

He moved the phone from his mouth. "Dane said they cleared debris from the mine explosion." He paused, as though he couldn't believe what he was about to say. "They found the plane but no people inside. The feds think I knew where it was and blew it up to slow down their search. They still think I'm behind it, and that I know where those people are."

Liberty couldn't believe they refused to see things from another angle. "We just have to keep working this to prove you aren't." She pointed at the computer. "The bank manager, however, was completely involved."

Liberty told him what the email said. "Wait, there's

a reply." She scrolled down and read it aloud. "'I can't do this anymore. I can't be part of this.' That's all he sent back, and the email address is about as generic as you can get. The feds should look into it even though I doubt they'll get anything back."

Tate relayed the information to Dane while Liberty thought it through. Could Gerald and whoever he was corresponding with about this "deal" be referring to the plane's disappearance? If so, where were the people who had been traveling on it? There was no sign of the senator or the two White House staffers. And what about the pilot? No one had even mentioned him.

Tate was being set up, but was this all that was going on? The plane and possibly the kidnapping of three people could be a simple case of a demand for ransom money, or way more than that. Perhaps all this business with the Russians, and the bank manager's problems, were nothing but a smoke screen hiding what was really going on.

She wandered to the doorway, and pain tore through her shoulder. She wanted to sit down, but she could hardly do that when it would contaminate the crime scene.

Tate took her elbow. "Hey," he said. "Come over here." He tugged her into the center of the lobby.

Liberty concentrated on her steps as Tate led her to a waiting area chair, and she leaned her head back with a wince. "It looks like suicide, but I wouldn't be surprised if the investigators say it was murder."

Tate's dark gaze bore down on her.

"What?"

He shook his head, but the intensity of it didn't lessen. "If you're okay, we should leave. It won't be long before—"

Vehicle engines roared. Liberty looked out the glass front door where a stream of cars and SUVs pulled up outside the building. Red-and-blue lights flashed as men and women in bulletproof vests and waterproof jackets with ball caps with their agency lettered on the front jumped out, guns drawn.

Tate stepped toward her, covering her, but they didn't stop.

The feds poured through every door. A tall man with slick dark hair strode to the front as they were surrounded, at least a dozen guns trained on them.

Secret Service. FBI. State police. Even the DEA was here.

Liberty stood and moved close to Tate's back.

"Drop your guns!"

She hooked her lousy arm around his waist and rested it against his flat stomach. With her other hand, she held out her gun so the closest fed could take it. Tate hooked his arm under hers and took the weight off her injury. Liberty relaxed into him, thankful he was here and hopeful he could say the same about her. It just seemed right to move closer at a time like this, to close ranks, as it were, and stand together against what faced them. It was what she'd always wanted from their relationship, that mutual support.

The guy motioned to Tate. "And you." The Secret Service agent must be a local, because she'd never seen him before.

Where was Locke? They needed his support if they were going to get out of this without Tate getting life in federal prison.

Tate handed over his weapon. "Where's the sheriff?"

"Don't worry about your friend," the agent said. "Worry about what's going to happen to you."

An agent stepped forward and zip-tied Tate's hands. She winced when the weight transferred back to her shoulder. He glanced at her. "You need a sling for your arm."

All Liberty could think of was the last time they'd been tied up, and how easily Tate had gotten out of the same kind of bindings. He was making the choice to submit to them, and she respected him all the more for it. He could fight, though he wouldn't get far. He could refuse to help, but she knew he was garnering information that would help him.

When the agent grabbed her arm to tug her away from Tate, she cried out and clutched her shoulder with a hiss.

"Hey!" Tate moved toward her and guns were raised again.

The agent let go of Liberty, and she moved in front of Tate. "No one shoots him." She turned to Tate, her back to all those armed agents. "He didn't know I got shot."

"He hurt you."

She touched his bound hands with hers. "Sit down, Tate." Okay, so that wasn't what he'd thought she would say, given his reaction. He sat, but he didn't like it. A man like Tate, who was *all* man, wouldn't willingly take the lower seat when it was necessary to stand up for himself. But he did it because she asked.

Later, when there wasn't a crowd of people here, she would say what she had actually wanted to say to him.

"Good." She heard the agent step toward them. "I'm Agent Francis Bearn from the Bozeman office of the Secret Service. We found the plane. Now you need to tell us where the two of you have hidden those people."

Liberty spun around. Agent Bearn had his phone raised. On-screen were three people.

Scared and tied up, but very much alive.

# ELEVEN

Tate was getting sick of explaining himself over and over again, but Liberty was currently being assessed by an EMT so he wasn't going to start complaining. Concessions would be nonexistent until he convinced these feds he wasn't the person behind this missing plane.

Nevertheless, he couldn't help saying, "Maybe you should be out trying to find them, instead of here harassing a guy who has *nothing to do with it*."

The fed didn't react, but Tate's attention was across the waiting area so it was possible he'd missed it. Liberty winced, but he didn't think it was over what he'd said. The EMT looked like he was poking her shoulder. The man said, "Looks like you'll need a stitch or two, and likely some antibiotics. There's all kinds of germs in a gunshot wound."

Liberty nodded.

When the agent, Francis Bearn—what kind of name was that, anyway?—started to tap his foot, Tate looked up. Francis stood over him, likely to reinforce the fact that he was in charge and had full control over what happened to Tate next. Which he probably did, but he didn't need to make a big deal out of it like he was. Tate knew the drill.

"Whether or not you had anything to do with the missing people remains to be seen." Francis tapped the screen on his phone. "It's been thirty-six hours since the plane went missing, and right now cooperation is the name of the game."

"I don't need to see the picture again. I don't know where they're being held, but it looks like an empty room to me. Not sure that's going to help find them."

"That's not what I intend to show you."

Tate figured the man's displeasure was due to the fact that he hadn't been on a presidential detail in at least a decade. He was old enough he'd probably been a Secret Service agent for at least that long, if not longer, but Tate had never met him. Francis could've been here in Montana, and slipped through the cracks of promotion, never making it to Washington.

Tate would probably be mad if it had happened to him. Whether or not he'd channel the feeling into making a suspect in a missing persons case feel like the worst criminal in the world, well—he'd like to say he'd be professional enough not to make this personal, but he'd never been accused of taking a back seat.

Tate had been written up a few times, but for nothing more than infractions. It had happened in the army as well, so he'd figured it was just his personality. Some people didn't like those who inserted themselves into a situation when something didn't sit right with them. And in the old-boy's network of the Secret Service, it had happened a few times. Agents like Liberty and the rookie female he'd met in the coffee shop, Alana, didn't deserve to be treated like they weren't as good as all the male agents just because they were women. They didn't deserve to get called "Little Darlin'" and asked to fetch coffee for the men. They were agents, just like the rest.

Francis turned the phone toward Tate. "This is the first video we received."

"Video?" He'd thought it was just a picture.

The screen came to life, dark images and the muffled sounds of someone blowing into a microphone. The image panned to the first person: a suited man, the senator from Oklahoma.

He swallowed. "My name is Edward Frampton."

The camera panned farther out, to a woman in a white blouse and dark-colored skirt. Her hair was falling out of whatever she'd fastened it up with, and her face was streaked with dirt and tears. Her voice was shaky when she said, "My name is Bethany Piers."

The last person was a man, younger and thinner than the senator. The other White House staffer, along with Bethany. He lifted his chin. "My name is Anthony Wills."

The camera shifted, turned all the way around to a man in a ski mask. "And my name is Tate Almers."

Tate felt his eyes widen. He tried to place the voice, but it was a little distorted, so it was difficult.

Francis hit pause. "This is the third video, and the one where he makes his demands."

The Tate wannabe said, "Now that we're all acquainted, I'll lay out what I want. Two million dollars in nonsequential bills. No hidden GPS trackers either. And the release of Puerto Alvarez. I'll help you out— he's at Atwater. I'll text the address for the drop. You have twenty-four hours."

Francis paused the video and said, "That gives us

until six tonight. Only a few hours from now. And the length of time means he knows it'll take a while to get Alvarez here."

"That wasn't me." Tate looked at the wall clock. It wasn't even two in the afternoon, and they'd received this video message hours before Liberty had even shown up at his house. Was that really just yesterday? It felt like a week.

Liberty pushed away the EMT and strode over, her face pinched. "Of course it wasn't Tate in the video! Any fool could hear a difference in the voices. It actually kind of sounded like—"

Tate shot her a look, then shook his head. The distortion had been there, but it wasn't enough to cover it completely. He knew what Liberty was thinking. After all, his brother's hatred of him had been their biggest topic of conversation today. But Tate couldn't be certain.

And why would Braden be demanding the release of an inmate from a prison in California? Atwater was a high-security federal prison.

Liberty snapped her head around to where Francis stood watching their interplay. Tate was innocent. Francis needed to believe it, and Tate figured he needed to at least trust Liberty as a fellow agent.

"Since when have we been receiving ransom demands, anyway?" she said. "That's the first I've heard about it. This should have been mentioned on the news, maybe, don't you think?" She glanced around, looking for someone to agree with her. "Or I don't know, maybe *to the Secret Service.*"

"If you're referring to Director James Locke," Francis said, "he knows."

"He…" Liberty broke off, stuttering.

"The director has been fully briefed."

Tate wanted to ask Liberty to sit down before she popped a blood vessel getting all worked up, but he didn't think it would go down well.

She said, "I can't believe this. I would have been told."

"Lib." Tate needed her to calm down.

She pressed her lips into a thin line, then glanced at the ceiling like she was praying for assistance. How was her relationship with God? They'd gone to church together when they were engaged, but she hadn't mentioned Him since she got here.

Tate could use some quiet time with his Bible, but he hadn't stopped praying this whole time. It seemed like things were only getting worse—for the investigation at least. Things between him and Liberty were actually pretty good considering they'd kissed, and right now she was poised and ready to defend him.

Tate nearly smiled, but instead he said, "How was that video sent?"

"It was broadcast live on a social media account. We've looked into it, and it's an anonymous profile as far as we could tell. It was set up minutes before the first broadcast and is still open, which means they aren't worried it will get traced. Which likely means they've covered their tracks. But we are looking into it."

Francis folded his arms. "There have been two more videos so far. The first one got some attention, but we managed to squash it with a virus before it spread. And before the media turned this whole thing into a circus." He looked pointedly at Liberty. "The next two we kept from public view. In each video, the kidnapper claims to be you." He pointed at Tate. "And in one we see a wider view of him."

"And?" It had to be significant for Francis to bring it up.

"You're more muscled than him. He was skinny."

Liberty glanced at him, her eyes sad. "Braden."

Tate shrugged. "If you didn't think it was me, why have you been hunting me this whole time?"

Francis didn't answer. He just said, "Do you think your brother could do something like this?"

Tate shrugged, his attention drawn to the huddle of DEA agents in the corner. All three of them had pulled out their phones and were now typing furiously.

If he was running this investigation and the search for these people, he'd be chasing down Tate as his most solid source of leads as well. It made sense. "I wouldn't put it past Braden to do something like this. Or at least he might *want* to. It's the effort he'd have to put into the execution that I'm having trouble believing." He told Francis about the conversation at the house.

"So he is involved."

"Maybe the map on the computer wasn't something that's going to happen," Liberty said. "What if it already has happened? What if it was where they're keeping the people they kidnapped?" She turned to Francis. "Were you able to get a location from the video?"

"Each of the three were recorded in a new location. By the time we get to it, even minutes after the broadcast is over, they're already gone."

"So they find a place with Wi-Fi, log in and make the video, and then move on?" When Francis nodded, Liberty said, "That's clever. And completely frustrating."

Tate nodded. "Yes, it is."

"I'll put the word out, have your brother found and brought in."

He nodded to Francis this time, but didn't say anything. What was there to say? Braden had engineered this whole thing, or at least the fact that it was being blamed on Tate. What kind of brother was he when his own flesh and blood wanted to do this to him? He really hated Tate that much?

"And in the meantime," Tate said, "we do what? Wait for another broadcast, chase them down and find nothing?" Assuming the feds weren't actually planning to hand a federal prisoner over to this kidnapper.

"We're investigating, but we're also prepping to make the transaction," Francis said. "It's our best shot at catching this guy and making him tell us where the people are."

Tate sighed. "We need more."

The alternative would be devastating to the families of the missing people.

Liberty wanted to pace. Or throw something. Or yell at someone. Instead she stopped and shut her eyes for a second, taking a moment to pray. She was just lifting her head when Locke walked in, closely followed by Alana. The two were never far apart, even if to an outsider it would appear they had only a close working relationship. They had set the bar on having a professional attitude about their romance. Liberty felt a pang of…shame, maybe, when she thought about how she and Tate had been.

Sneaking kisses when no one was looking had been fun and all, but was hardly professional even if no one had caught them. Love made people act crazy, though.

Everyone said so. Still, if she could go back, she'd do it all differently.

But she would still do it all again. Because, as much as it hurt now, she'd needed him back then. She'd needed to feel…well, needed. Who didn't? Liberty couldn't even describe the feeling, knowing Tate loved her as much as he'd shown her he had.

"Lib?"

She glanced at Tate and shook her head. There was no reason to drag up the past, even if standing here made it feel like they could just slide right back into the place where they'd been so in love. The future had stretched out ahead of them, so far. So bright. Then with one diagnosis, the steel bars of a cell had slammed down over Liberty's life, and she'd realized she could never give Tate everything he wanted.

"Are you okay?" Alana's face was open. She'd probably never seen this version of Liberty. Since Tate's leaving she'd been closed off. Antisocial, and nursing her wounds. She'd pulled away from everyone.

Liberty didn't even know what to tell her. "Once we get this cleared up, I probably will be." She turned to Locke and said, "Want to tell me why you never mentioned videos when we talked?"

Locke shrugged. "I compartmentalized information in order to provide you with the best possible focus."

"Meaning you lied to me."

"Withholding information as your boss is not the same thing as lying, Agent Westmark." Locke wasn't going to apologize when he was convinced he'd done the right thing. Alana's brow held a tiny line, which Liberty figured meant she didn't completely agree, but Liberty wasn't going to mention it.

Her arm hurt enough that she'd like to just yell at all of them, when it wouldn't be completely warranted. Why did she do that when she was in pain? She should probably ask Tate, since it was what he'd done when she had broken up with him. However, that might not be a tactful question.

Liberty slumped into a chair and leaned back gently until her back touched the wall.

"You okay?" Tate's question was low and quiet, for her ears only.

She turned her head and found his face close. "The EMT gave me a shot, and it's supposed to kick in soon." She shut her eyes. "I feel like we've been one step behind this entire time. Everyone seems to have more information about this than we do."

Tate shifted beside her. "Yes, it does feel that way." He paused. "Makes me wonder what else they haven't told us."

"You're not Secret Service," Francis said, with no apology in his tone.

Locke moved to stand beside the local agent. "And Liberty was compromised."

Her eyes flew open, but Tate waylaid her with a hand on her arm. She said, "Gee, thanks, boss." Okay, so he was telling the truth. Still, did she want him saying so in front of Tate and everyone else? Not especially.

Locke said, "Your emotions are all tied up in this, and don't bother denying it. So we kept a close eye on you. The sheriff filled in the rest."

They'd been watching this whole time? That was probably why nobody had stormed into the camp trailer and taken Tate into custody. Tate had probably figured it was the fact that she'd made contact with her boss, but it was evidently also because the feds had been on their tails whenever they had a cell signal.

"So why make contact now?" Tate's question was one she wanted to ask as well.

"Apart from the dead man over there?" Francis lifted one eyebrow but didn't look to where investigators processed every inch of the office while the medical examiner peered at the body. "We're running out of time until the deadline, and we need you to make contact with your brother."

"You think I can find him?"

"You've done it already. There's no reason to assume you can't again."

Tate's jaw flexed. Liberty wanted to help, but what was she supposed to do? She wasn't going to figure this out alone. Only by all of them working as a team would they find those missing people. All of them, including Tate.

"So you don't think Tate is involved?" she asked them all. "You think Tate's name is clear, and he can help by finding his brother?"

"I still want proof beyond a doubt he's not part of this," Francis said. "So far it's just circumstantial, but I figure it won't be totally confirmed until this is over and we take it all apart. At least for now, I'm satisfied." He pinned Tate with a stare. "As long as you stay close."

"You're keeping me on a short leash?" Tate didn't sound pleased about it.

Francis nodded. Tate said, "And Dane? You know he's not part of this either, right?"

"The sheriff is facing no charges at this time, and I suspect not in the future either."

Liberty figured that was probably the best they were

going to get, considering Dane had technically become an accessory. Still, they weren't far past assuming Tate was guilty, which he wasn't. The whole thing was up in the air until they could prove for good who was actually behind the missing people.

She turned to Tate. "So we go find your brother?"

Tate shrugged. "I guess. We can backtrack, visit some of his haunts."

"We could go to his apartment together this time," Liberty said.

She knew Tate didn't miss her tone. He just chose to ignore it and said, "We can visit some of his friends as well."

"You'll want to start with the girlfriend," Francis said.

Tate's head jerked. "Braden has a girlfriend?"

Francis frowned. "Yes, the mother of your niece."

# TWELVE

"I cannot believe they didn't tell me about the videos."

Tate flicked on his blinker and glanced in the rearview at the government SUV behind them. No one had asked questions about the fact that they were still driving Dane's truck, which he'd told the feds they had stolen. That was the least of everyone's problems right now. Braden hadn't been at the house where Liberty got shot, and neither had the Russians. It had been entirely cleaned out.

Now they were headed to the address Francis had given them so the agent could listen to whatever conversation they might have with Braden's girlfriend. The one who was the mother of his child.

Tate could hardly wrap his head around it.

"Are you even listening to me?"

The feds had likely already activated the listening device, hoping they'd hear something incriminating. Everyone in the SUV behind them was probably busting up laughing at Liberty's "complaining wife" routine.

Tate glanced at her and kept driving. "Locke didn't think you were compromised because of your feelings. He knows you better than that, Lib."

"Does he?" She overexaggerated the question. "You don't know what he was thinking. Maybe I've gone off the deep end in the last year. Maybe I've been taking things too personally and he can't trust me to be a professional." She paused long enough to take in more air and start up again. "I've done nothing *but* be a professional this past year."

Part of Tate didn't want to know the answer to his next question, but also a part of him needed to know. "How have you been?"

Liberty's head flicked around in his direction, but he kept his eyes on the road instead of on her. She said, "How have I been?"

Tate shrugged.

"How do you think I've been?" she asked. "Lonely, Tate. I've been very, very lonely. But the frozen tundra of my personal life has nothing to do with my ability to do my job."

He wanted to explain how it was her fault, given he wouldn't have left if she hadn't broken their engagement. But was he going to mention it right now? No. "This might just be one of those things you've gotta let go, Lib. Locke made a decision and it's done. You don't like it, but there's nothing you can do. Can't go back in time and change the past."

He made a left turn and felt her hand touch his forearm. Her good hand, since she hugged the other arm to her body. The EMT had said she needed to see a doctor, get stitched up and get a prescription. And yet, she was here with him still.

He didn't know what it meant, and he also didn't know if he was okay with it. Tate wasn't a better option than delaying medical attention.

"Is that how you feel about what I did?"

Why were they even talking about this? He should be laying out the plan for how they were going to talk to his brother's girlfriend. The one who was the mother of his niece. At the very least, they should be talking about *that*. He hadn't had the first clue his brother had a child.

"Does it matter how I feel?" Tate shrugged his shoulder, but she kept hold of his arm. "It's done, right? Decision made. Thank you very much. Don't worry about how I'm gonna feel."

Liberty's hand slid from his arm then, and she swiped at her face. Great. Now he'd made her cry.

"Look, it doesn't matter." He didn't really know what else to say.

"It does matter." A sob hitched in her throat. He heard her try to hide it. "I'm sorry, Tate. I'm really sorry."

"We were together for two years, Lib, and engaged for six months. I thought I was going to spend the rest of my life with you, and then one day you just broke it off." He waited until he pulled up at a red light and then turned to her, uncaring whether or not anyone was listening. "Why, Lib? Why did you do it? And don't give me the same 'it's not going to work' reason. Because I don't believe it."

Liberty set her hand on her shoulder, over where she'd been hit by the bullet. Her body curved forward, her eyes squeezed and she jerked with each sob.

"Tell me why."

She shook her head without opening her eyes or looking at him. "I can't." Her voice was a whisper.

Tate stared at her.

Someone honked. The light was green. Tate pulled

away from the line and headed for the address Francis had given them.

What else was there to say? If Liberty wasn't going to tell him the real reason she'd broken their engagement, what was the point in pushing her?

While she collected herself, Tate found the house number. He pulled up a couple doors down and looked over at it. The whole street was low rent, and there were some trailers. A couple of them looked to have been there for years, added on over and over so now they resembled a hodgepodge of materials. Lawns were overgrown behind wire-mesh fences, where dogs roamed the front yards. A couple of Labradoodles barked at them.

"I'm going to talk to this woman. I want you to come in with me."

Liberty sniffed and smoothed back her hair. "Okay."

Her voice was small, like he'd kicked her cat. Which he would never do, even though it was seriously freaky to hang out in the same room as a hairless cat. He didn't particularly want to push her when she was hurt and upset, but the idea of facing his niece kind of terrified him. What if this was his only shot at a family, through his brother's child, and he messed it up the way he'd evidently messed up his relationship with Liberty? Tate didn't know if he'd be able to handle that on top of everything else, including the threat of criminal charges against him.

They walked down the sidewalk together, neither touching nor saying anything. Tate hated this tension. Sure, a huge part of him still had feelings for her. Probably even loved her. But he simply wasn't done grieving the loss of what they'd had.

And likely, neither was she.

Which meant this whole spending-time-together thing probably wasn't good for either of them.

Liberty stood to the side while Tate knocked on the door. She was exhausted after the crying jag in the car, which—added to the lack of sleep last night after her long day of traveling—made her feel like a wet rag. She probably looked about as good as one, too. Her eyes were hot and puffy, any makeup she'd been wearing long gone now.

Tate cocked his head in her direction. Ugh. If she'd known how it felt just having him train that gaze she'd loved on her, she never would've come. She didn't regret being here, but she hadn't prepared herself for how much it was going to *hurt*. Or the fact that he was going to ask questions.

Good thing she was never, ever going to tell him why she'd broken up with him.

He'd tell her she was wrong. He'd fight for them, and he'd probably win her over. Because that was Tate. Of course he would convince her staying together was the right thing. It was why she had to stand strong and fight the feeling that seemed to pull them together like magnets. If she gave in she would spend the rest of her life waiting for the moment he realized he'd stayed when he should have moved on.

No, thank you.

The door swung open. Natalie Stand was a slender woman who wore jeans and a tank top. She stood in the doorway, a chubby toddler on her hip. Despite having a heavy hand with the makeup brush, the woman was beautiful—Francis had been right about that. Her hair cascaded in loose curls that the baby had a handful of, strands of brown, gold and caramel. It was so pretty Liberty nearly gasped. Then she ran a hand down her own mousy blond hair, feeling even more disheveled than she had a minute ago.

The woman's penciled-on eyebrow shifted. "Can I help you?" There was a lilt of an accent, but Liberty couldn't place it.

Tate led the conversation, as they'd planned. "Natalie Stand?" When she nodded, he said, "I'm Deputy Sheriff Tate Almers, and this is Liberty Westmark. She's with the Secret Service."

The woman took a step back, whether involuntary or not. "Almers?"

Tate nodded. "Braden is my brother. He's actually why we're here."

The woman sighed. "You should come in." She led them to a living room peppered with baby toys, and Liberty spotted a couple of pacifiers. The kitchen was worn but clean, with the exception of a mug and a half-empty sippy cup on the counter. All normal stuff. There were books, magazines and DVDs on the unit by the TV, and a few pairs of shoes by the front door—some women's shoes, plus boots and sneakers, the kind a man would wear. A man with much bigger feet than Natalie.

She heard the toddler make some indecipherable noises then move off toward the TV. Tate had Natalie talking about how she and Braden had met, like this was a friendly chat. Liberty continued to study the room. The couches and coffee table. The ceiling.

A tiny hand touched the arm of the couch beside her.

Liberty stiffened.

Tate paused, midsentence. He might have looked at her. Probably frowned. Liberty didn't look at him.

The tiny girl rounded the couch and bumped into Liberty's knee.

She couldn't move.

Curly blond hair. The girl started and glanced up at Liberty, surprised she was on the couch. A war played across her face—smile at the new person, or cry because she had no idea who Liberty was and why she was there. Braden's nose—Tate had the same one—wrinkled on her face. The eyes were similar, set deep into her tiny face. She was beautiful, clearly Braden's daughter…and Tate's niece.

"Liberty?"

She started at his voice. The little girl took a breath and started to cry. Natalie swooped her up. "I'm sorry. She's usually such a people person."

Liberty tried to smile, but it felt false even to her. "That's okay," she choked out. "She's sweet." And Liberty was a liar. It hadn't been okay since she'd quit serving in the children's ministry at church. She hadn't even been able to look at a stroller since, and here God had asked her to face Tate's niece. It shouldn't feel like a slap in the face, but what was she supposed to think?

God had promised to give her the desires of her heart, hadn't he? But no. That wasn't her lot to enjoy in life. Liberty had nothing she wanted, and the lack of anything real she could call "hers" screamed at her every second of every day. But now wasn't the time to dissolve into a fit of crying over the unfairness of it all. They were supposed to be interviewing Natalie.

Liberty mustered up as much willpower as she could and straightened. She looked at Natalie without letting her gaze stray to the little girl, now sucking on a hank of her mom's hair. "Do you know of any dealings Braden may have had with locals of Russian descent?"

Natalie sat, and as she did so, Liberty realized it was a delay tactic. Settling herself and her daughter onto the couch took a moment, and she used it to compose herself and carefully craft her answer.

"Russians?" She blew out a breath, like she was thinking intently. "I don't know. He isn't here that much, and I don't know everyone he hangs out with."

"He doesn't live here?"

"No," Natalie said with a frown.

Tate had a *get it together* look on his face. "Ms. Stand already answered that question." He turned to the woman across from them. "Any idea where Braden might be now?"

Natalie shook her head.

"How about where he was last night?"

"Didn't you say he was with Russians?"

Liberty said, "Just that he was found at the house this morning."

"I have no idea where Braden sleeps on a regular basis, except for his apartment. He's here maybe every couple of weeks, give or take. Usually drops off money, mooches some dinner off me and once in a while hangs out with Tasha so I can go out with my friends." Natalie sighed. "It's not perfect, but it works for me. Tasha and I don't need that kind of dysfunction in our lives. It's too disrupting having to deal constantly with a toddler and a man who acts like one."

Liberty nodded. The one time she'd met Braden there had been glimpses of that, even when he was relatively sober. "How do you get ahold of him?"

Natalie shrugged. "I have his number."

Liberty glanced at Tate, who said, "Maybe you could give it to me."

Good, he hadn't already asked that question, so she didn't look like a total idiot. Again. Tate was probably going to ask her what had happened later. Questions she wouldn't want to answer almost as much as she hadn't wanted to answer questions about their breakup.

Natalie scrolled through her cell phone protected by a sparkly pink case, and then read off some numbers to Tate.

Liberty always assumed people knew more than they thought they did. At least, that had been her experience. So she said, "Think back to the last time he was here for a second. What time of day was it?"

Natalie didn't look impressed by the question. "Dinnertime, I guess. I was feeding Tasha cereal when he showed up."

"How long did he stay?"

"Long enough I had to make twice as much chicken as I'd planned."

"And he ate with you?"

Natalie nodded. Tate sat silently, letting Liberty ask the questions. Her next was, "What did you talk about?"

Natalie's eyes widened. "Actually we did have a conversation. Which was weird, because it's usually awkward since there isn't much to talk about. This time he stayed longer, and we talked about the old gym in Havertown that's closing. He used to be a member there, and he really liked it. He was bummed it was shutting down."

Liberty figured it was probably nothing, but on the off chance it could turn out to be something, she would accept it. She glanced at Tate. "Havertown?"

"Thirty miles, maybe. It's a smaller town." Tate was quiet for a moment. "Lots of places closing down because we have all the ski hills and vacation lodging, and their tourist trade isn't much to speak of."

That was probably why he wanted to sell his cabin. Make some money. Move on. The idea of it made her want to cry. She was never selling her condo. Liberty was going to die a spinster Secret Service agent, completely miserable even while being lauded for being strong and independent because she didn't need a man to take care of her.

Tate said, "Thank you for your time, Natalie."

Havertown might be nothing, but it was a potential lead at least. They stepped outside and started walking to the truck.

"I'm not even going to ask what that was with the kid," Tate said. "She did look like Braden, though."

Liberty nodded. She couldn't speak.

"And Natalie was lying."

"Maybe," Liberty managed to say.

They walked up to the Secret Service SUV, and the window on the passenger side rolled down.

"She was lying," Francis said, not looking any happier than Liberty felt.

Tate nodded. "I think she knows exactly where Braden is."

# THIRTEEN

Something was seriously going on with Liberty. As Francis talked, Tate tried to gauge what on earth it could be. She'd freaked out in Natalie's house, but Liberty liked kids and was good with people. Maybe it was him. Or he was just taking it too personally, and Liberty was just having a bad day—she'd been shot, after all—and she needed a nap.

*He* needed a nap, for that matter.

"...keep tabs on her. I'll have Intelligence dig deeper into her life as well. Find out if she has reason to hide your brother from us."

Tate realized he hadn't heard much of what Francis said. The agent in the passenger seat—Francis was driving, probably because he had to be in control all the time—smirked at Tate. He ignored Mr. Silent Opinion, and nodded to Francis.

"If she knows where her boyfriend is, we'll find out soon enough."

"And the search for the missing people?"

Francis said, "We're looking at a lot of possible places. We're stretched thin, but if there's something to be found then we're gonna find it."

A niggling thought edged into his brain. Tate wanted to grasp at it, figure out what was pinging on his radar. Something about the missing people. The videos? Their locations? It was a puzzle for him to solve, which on most days he'd have been happy to sit and mull over. Too bad that wasn't even an option right now. He'd have to make do with thinking about it while they ran down the leads they had.

Liberty said, "What about this abandoned gym in Havertown she mentioned?"

She looked so small, her face still paler than it should've been as she stood there with her arm hugging her body. The woman needed food and rest. Probably painkillers as well, though those were in the truck. Something to bring some pink to those cheeks and give her a bit of energy.

"Could be something. Could be nothing." Francis shrugged.

Tate said, "We'll check it out."

Liberty turned to him, her nose scrunched up. Tate stared her down. It was likely enough the abandoned gym would turn out to be nothing but a wild-goose chase, and Liberty would get a couple hours' reprieve from danger and stress. It sounded like the perfect assignment for them so the feds could concentrate on the most pertinent things and not waste time following dead ends.

They could get something to eat on the way, and Liberty could nap on the drive.

"Okay," Francis said. "We'll be on your tail the whole time, making sure everything's okay."

Which totally missed the point of reassigning resources to where they were best spent. Evidently Francis wasn't yet willing to let go of the idea that he could find whoever was involved by following Tate around. At least Locke and Alana were putting their focus where it would hopefully get real results.

Tate was willing to accept anything positive at this point. Those people were probably terrified they were going to be killed. "What about the ransom demand?"

Francis looked at his watch. "The US Attorney is taking care of the paperwork. He'll field it back to me when we're ready to move." He didn't look too worried about the looming deadline.

Tate did not share the man's lack of agitation. Still, he tapped the frame of the car window with his knuckles. "Then we'll be on our way."

Francis nodded, and Tate led Liberty to the sheriff's truck with one hand on the small of her back.

"Are you protecting me? You know I'm the Secret Service agent, right?"

Tate heard the amusement in her voice. "I guess old habits die hard."

Kind of like loving her and wanting to protect her. No one brought out those feelings in him but Liberty. If she just said the word, he would flip that protective switch back to on, and she would never have to worry about anything for the rest of their lives.

He glanced aside at her. Would she ever say the word and give him the signal that meant they were right back to the way they used to be? This time it would be new. They were different, they'd survived the last year apart and it had made them both stronger. The question was whether that strength could be part of their new relationship. He needed Liberty to give him some kind of sign, and then he could find out.

But, sign or not, until she told him the real reason she'd broken up with him, Tate had to wait. He had to know why she'd felt the need to cause both of them so much pain before he could open up his heart and let her in once more. Not to mention giving her the power to tear his heart out all over again.

Tate didn't like giving away any power, but that was what love was. Love meant giving up safety, security and any plans for the future, and putting them into someone else's hands. He'd been fully prepared to do that before. While Liberty, apparently, had not.

Tate hit the closest drive-through and got them both some fast food, and then watched for rogue semitrucks as he drove to the gym Natalie had mentioned. The Secret Service SUV followed from a distance, their surveillance equipment probably still active. If Francis was looking for Tate to slip up and expose his guilt, then the man was probably listening to everything. Including that conversation earlier, where Liberty had been crying.

She was asleep now, her tummy full of fatty foods she probably wouldn't have eaten if she had her wits about her. But the calories would do her good.

Tate pulled off the freeway and up to the light. He dug out his phone and tried the number Natalie had given him for Braden.

It rang and rang, and finally went to voice mail. It was a generic message, where the person hadn't taken the time to set up their own voice mail. He sighed and tossed the phone in his cup holder. It hit his soda cup and bounced down by his feet.

The light went green. Tate pushed the phone behind

his shoe just so it didn't slide under the pedal and cause him to crash the truck.

It was hard to believe his brother was involved in this. He'd always thought there was a kind of injustice to the fact that Braden hated him so badly. The kid had this tendency to take things too personally, and the adult he'd grown into wasn't much different. Still, it was a big leap from moody kid to a man intent on destroying the lives of three people and framing his brother for it. Taking down a plane was a huge undertaking.

There had to be someone else behind it. It couldn't be Braden alone.

Tate couldn't help thinking all this was serving to thoroughly distract the Secret Service. Even with some out searching for the plane, too many others—like Francis back there in his SUV—were entirely focused on Tate.

What if it was all a smoke screen?

Could there possibly be more to this than what they already knew? Tate didn't know what it might be, but he wanted to get to his brother and find out. Braden had to know. Or the Russians knew. If Tate could find their head boss, the one who called all the shots, he'd be one step closer to finding out.

One step closer to knowing why they were so intent on framing him as the prime suspect.

Liberty opened her eyes. The truck was stopped, and they were in a parking lot. Everything was still covered in snow, but she could live the dream—the one where it was eighty and she was drinking an iced soda with nothing to do but watch the sweat of condensation run down the outside of the glass.

In most of those dreams, Tate was right there beside her. He'd always looked good sporting a nice tan. She turned to him then, the subject of all the dreams she'd just been having. He was still in that giant coat, and in the credit union she'd noticed that his beard had hints of red coloring. She'd always loved his smile. When he was asleep, he never had that scowl on his face.

Liberty sighed.

"Feel better?"

"Actually, I do." She tried to stretch in the cab of the truck as much as she could without moving one arm. "Thank you for the food. And the nap time."

He nodded and Liberty took stock of the situation. None of her pressing problems had gone away. Eventually she'd have to see a doctor about her arm. It was manageable most of the time, but if she moved wrong, her shoulder screamed murder at her to quit it. However, she felt better. Not well enough she wanted to have another long conversation that ended in tears. Just well enough she was the first out of the car.

The building had been a full complex gym, with an Olympic-sized pool and everything. Now it just looked sad. The windows were busted, probably from kids with rocks or baseballs. The front doors were boarded up, and the sign that hung on the outside wall was missing a couple of letters. The rest of the letters were dusted with snow.

Tate rounded the hood of the truck.

"Hopefully it doesn't take too long to search this whole place," she said. He didn't seem to mind, though. His attention was on the SUV that had followed them from Natalie's house. Liberty looked over. No one got out.

"Guess we're on our own in there." Tate sighed.

"I'm sure we can handle it."

His lips twitched. "Sure, so long as the weight of snow on the roof hasn't compromised it. If it hasn't fallen in by now, it could collapse on top of us while we're inside."

"Wow. Such a happy thought."

They trudged across the snow-covered grass between the cars and the building. It was maybe ten feet at most. Liberty glanced back at the men in the SUV, just sitting there watching them do all the work. She knew she and Tate were on the cakewalk assignment, and she was fine with it. It was no secret she wasn't up to her normal operating level. In fact, she was far from it. She was going to need a vacation from her vacation when this trip was done. Not that this was either a vacation or an assignment—not with all that had happened. But it was almost Christmas, so that could be her *real* vacation.

She stumbled on something buried under the snow, and Tate caught her good arm.

"Okay?"

She nodded, too embarrassed to say anything. The part of her dream that wasn't set on the beach had been an extended Christmas montage where she and Tate drank eggnog, watched old movies like they'd done so many times and decorated a tree. They even walked the dogs in the snow, then returned home for hot chocolate. Food always featured prominently in her dreams, and it didn't matter if she was on a beach or in his beautiful Christmas cabin.

She couldn't believe he was selling it.

Liberty pushed aside those unhelpful dreams. It wouldn't do her any good to get more caught up in them than she had been. She surveyed the area instead, looking for any sign of life. It was midafternoon, so she'd figured kids might be running around the place getting up to trouble. Or maybe they were good at not getting caught.

None of the sidewalks around the place had been shoveled. She didn't even know where the sidewalks *were* underneath the snow, but it meant she could tell that no one had been here since the last snowfall. No footprints.

"You really like this weather?"

"Sure."

"Mostly I figure people are lying when they say that, because you can't possibly enjoy being this freezing." She glanced at him. "Can you?"

"I like it, Lib."

"Do you ski?" Aside from growing up here, there had to be a reason he liked winter enough to live in this part of Montana, where the snow was hip-height and her nose was numb. Did he like breathing in icicles and feeling like his legs were going to freeze solid?

"I ski a little." He studied her, like he was trying to figure her out. "You?"

"You know I don't." They'd never been skiing. They'd never even talked about it. She frowned at him. "And why would I do that in favor of lying on a beach, soaking up vitamin D and taking a nap?"

"Florida girl."

"Born and raised."

He grinned. "And now you're stuck in DC."

"I could move back if I wanted to. Or maybe I'll get stationed in Bora Bora next. That might be nice."

Tate frowned, then ran a hand through his hair. "Sure, I guess."

They circled the building with him leading the way. Liberty ignored whatever was going on in his head and pointed out a pertinent fact. "The door was at the front."

"I know. I'm looking to see if any of the entrances have been used at all, or recently."

Oh. Why hadn't she thought of that? "I think I'm losing my edge."

"I think you've been shot. That's enough to make anyone lose their edge."

"So you're not disagreeing with me."

Tate shot her a look. "You don't have to worry about not holding up your end of things."

"But what if I miss something, and—"

"Lib," he stopped her. "I've got you covered, okay?"

"You should have sent me with those EMTs."

"You could have sent yourself."

She pressed her lips together, then said, "Touché."

Tate chuckled. He stopped at what looked like a loading dock. "This has been used recently."

Sure enough, there were tire tracks. "Truck, looks like." Someone had visited this old, abandoned gym this morning.

"Let's find a door and check it out."

Tate used his shoulder to break the lock on the door to the side of the loading dock's garage-type door. He flipped on a flashlight and held it up, his gun hand braced on his fist holding the light. Liberty held her gun up, still tucking her left arm to her body. She'd be useless in a fight, but she could still shoot straight if she needed to.

The whole place was empty. It didn't take too long to walk through and then circle back to the loading entrance.

Tate studied the floor. "Looks like something might've been here." Sure enough, there were scratch marks. Like from pallets. "Whatever it was, it's gone now."

Liberty wandered to the door, its glass still intact and no board in place. She looked out at the other buildings. The part of the SUV she could see. Frozen trees. Rooftops.

A man settling a giant tube-shaped device onto his shoulder.

Aimed right at them.

"Tate." She said his name on a gasp.

"What is it?" He moved toward her, but she turned and shoved him back into the center of the building. Pain screamed through her arm but she ignored it.

"Run."

"What—"

"Rocket launcher!" she screamed. "Run!"

# FOURTEEN

The words penetrated Tate's brain, and his legs kicked into gear. He wanted to go back, to give himself reason to believe what his head didn't want to comprehend.

A rocket launcher in small-town Montana? Still, he ran like his life depended on it, because it likely did.

He would get hit if he went back. Liberty would get caught in it as well, or she would come back for him if he didn't move fast enough for her liking. The woman was a force to be reckoned with when she wasn't running on an injury and next to no sleep.

The explosion ripped through the building from his right, a wave of sound, then a feeling like an earthquake had split the ground. Smoke and fire rushed at them.

They reached a set of double doors and pushed through to the pool.

Tate grabbed Liberty, unable to take the time to be careful of her injury. He jumped off the edge of the empty pool into the air. The force of the explosion hit the big room. It hit them in midair, shoving Tate and Liberty toward the far end of the pool. He grabbed her as best he could and held her in front of him as he turned.

Tate's back slammed into hard tile. His head snapped back, and he blacked out amid an ocean of hot air.

He woke up sometime later. The face of his watch was cracked, the display blank where digital numbers should have told him what time it was. The room was lit by daylight, the tile of the pool black and littered with debris. Drywall dust danced in the air, and what had been the doors was now a giant hole in the wall. Twisted metal lay on sheets of broken drywall intermingled with snow. Cold air from outside now whipped through the room like it was a wind tunnel, rustling his hair.

He tried to move, but the pain in his head stalled any motion he might've been able to manage. Liberty's weight covered his torso and legs. Was she unconscious, as he had been? Tate managed to get his arm out from under him and winced at the muscles in his shoulder. He reached up and touched the hair on the back of his head. His fingertips came back wet with blood.

His phone.

Tate rummaged around for it, absently shifting Liberty. "Wake up, Lib." He didn't find his phone. Where was it?

The truck. He'd dropped it and kicked it behind his shoe, then had forgotten to bring it with him.

Tate bit down on his molars and searched Liberty's jacket pockets for her cell. When he found it and pulled it out, the screen was completely shattered. He pressed the button, but when it illuminated he couldn't even read what anything said.

He patted her arm and gently shook her. "Liberty." They were going to have to walk out of here. Provided he could put one foot in front of the other without falling over. He could hardly think through the pain. It felt like his head had been split open. There was probably a dent in the tile where he'd landed.

Liberty groaned, a long, low sound of intense pain. Tate shifted her off his legs so he could see her shoulder. Yep, she was bleeding as well.

Tate didn't want to wait, so he got his feet under him and lifted her as he rose to stand. While she blinked, Tate waited for the room to stop spinning. Then they started walking.

Where were Francis and his men? And firefighters? They needed an ambulance—now.

"Thank You, God, we aren't trapped," Tate said.

Liberty's mouth curled up. "Amen to that." She glanced around. "How are we gonna get out of here?"

Tate turned his body to look for an exit so he didn't have to turn his head.

Liberty gasped. "Tate!"

He looked back to see her whip off her coat. She winced but got her sweater off, and then put her coat back on. She balled it up. "Press this to the back of your head. I doubt you should be upright and moving around, but I don't think I can carry you out of here." She led him to the edge of the pool, and he climbed the steps. "As long as you're upright, I'm going to trust it so that we can get ourselves out of here."

Once he'd let go of the stair handle, Tate pressed the sweater to the back of his head. The touch whipped white shards across his vision like lightning. He almost blacked out, and then Liberty was under his arm with hers around his waist.

"This might be a problem." She worried her bottom lip. "But you need to keep that on there."

"Yes, ma'am."

Liberty made a tut sound with her mouth as she walked with him—slowly—toward a fire exit door at the far end of the pool area. "I did not miss that sarcasm."

Tate smiled. "I missed you."

Liberty leaned on the exit bar on the door. "Thank You, God, this whole place wasn't destroyed. Just the other end of the building." She hesitated a second. "Unless I push on this and the building comes down on us."

She glanced up at him. Tate couldn't seem to find the words to say. "Lib." He wanted to touch her cheek. Why did she look so worried?

"We can't wait. I have to risk it." She paused. "If we do get squished… I mean, we almost died already, but if we die now… I missed you. No matter what happens, I don't think that will ever change."

Tate loved hearing that, because he felt the same way. "Missed you, too, Lib." The words were kind of mumbled. When he leaned in to kiss her, the room started spinning.

"Whoa." She shifted under him. Tate's body moved without him intending it to. His shoulder hit the exit bar, and the door opened. They stumbled through, but Liberty got under his shoulder and lifted his body back upright like a professional.

Cold air whipped his face and clothes. It was entirely too light outside, so he shut his eyes. Snow crept into his boots as they walked.

"You're strong," he grunted. Which wasn't all he wanted to say, but it was all he could get out.

"Yeah, well." She groaned out the words. "It turns

out there's a lot of free time for strength training when you don't have a life or any friends."

"I'm your friend."

"Yes, Tate." There was a smile in her voice. "You are."

A police siren sounded close by. Tate groaned. "Too loud."

"It's Dane."

The sheriff said, "Sit down?"

"Yes, that's probably a good idea. He's really hurt, Dane. He's slurring his words." She lowered him into the snow and took the sweater. Did she need it? No, Liberty put it under his head. Then she yelled, "He needs an ambulance!"

Was he really that hurt? Tate tried to open his eyes, to get a look at her face, but nothing seemed to be working.

"It's on the way." Dane was quiet for a second, but then his footsteps got closer. "You don't look so good either, Liberty."

Worry permeated Tate's body like a cold frost, and he shivered, then reached for her hand. Was she okay?

"I'll go with him and get checked out myself when I know he's okay."

Dane didn't say anything for a while.

"Dane?"

"Yeah, Tate. I'm here."

Tate didn't open his eyes. Liberty said, "You're the only one here?"

"Help is on the way."

"What about the Secret Service? Their SUV was around that side, behind where we parked your truck."

Tate was glad she asked; he didn't seem to be able to make more than one or two words.

"There are two fire trucks over there that just got here," Dane said. "Not much left of my truck you guys were driving. The one parked behind it was flipped over. They're cutting the agents out now."

"What?" Tate snapped his eyes open. Too bright. He tried to sit up. Pain snapped through his skull like he'd been hit with a lightning rod. "They…"

Blackness rushed in from the edges of his vision and swallowed him whole.

"We need that ambulance!"

Dane touched her shoulder, but she shrugged him off. Tate's eyes had rolled back in his head, and then his whole body had gone limp. "He'll be okay, Liberty."

"You didn't see the back of his head." What if he needed surgery? What if his brain was bleeding?

Dane motioned to the vehicle as it pulled up. "There they are."

It took forever for them to climb out of their ambulance and race over. "He hit his head in the explosion." She didn't want to move away, but they needed room to get Tate on their backboard.

Dane helped her stand. "You okay?"

No, she wasn't okay. Her shoulder smarted more than she thought possible, but she pushed aside the pain to focus on what was happening.

"Update me," she said.

Dane didn't look convinced, but she saw the moment he decided to acquiesce. Liberty desperately needed to feel like she had a handle on this situation. It was so out of control.

"The fire department is cutting the agents out of their car. One is dead—"

"Francis?"

"Which one is he?"

"The driver."

"Then no," Dane said. "It was the passenger who was killed in the explosion. The driver and the two who were in the back seat are alive, but I don't know much more than that."

Liberty blew out a breath.

"They have some pretty bad injuries. All of them are unconscious. We'll have to see what the doctors say." Dane paused. "You're going with Tate, right?"

She glanced at the two EMTs. One said, "That's a nasty crack on the back of his head."

Liberty nodded, unable to say anything without dissolving into painful tears. She swallowed and looked at Dane. "Yes, I'm going with Tate. But you need to find Natalie Stand, because she told us to come here. And when we did?" Liberty swept her arm to encompass the building in its now disastrous state.

Dane nodded. "I'll pick her up."

Liberty fisted her hands by her sides. "I don't understand." The thoughts had barely coalesced in her mind, and she had no idea what they meant, but she needed to talk it through with *someone*. "Why shoot up this place? Isn't that a little obvious?" She paused. "They'll never get their money or the guy released from prison if the agents they're dealing with are in the hospital."

"So they were aiming for you and Tate, and the other Secret Service agents got caught in the cross fire?"

Liberty glanced around, trying to work it out. "Maybe. I mean, it's sloppy. They must not have known exactly who was in the SUV. And if Tate and I were the targets, why kill us? Doing that won't convince the Secret Service Tate was behind it. Not unless they're still trying to pin it on him, making it look like he's guilty even while he's helping solve this." That didn't explain things, though.

"The feds still don't know where those people are."

Liberty shook her head. "We have to find them."

Dane shot her a dark look. "I know that. I've been looking at the locations but nothing is jumping out at me as a possibility for where they might head next."

"We don't have an address for the ransom delivery?"

Dane shook his head. "If they keep to their timeline so far, there will be one more video before the ransom."

"And if they kill the first hostage during that live broadcast?"

"Let's pray they don't."

Could she do that? Could Liberty trust God with something so important when she'd spent the last year bemoaning the fact that He hadn't trusted her with something as important as having a future of her own? There was a mental block between her and letting God have full control of her life once again. As though she'd trusted Him with everything, and in return He hadn't done the same.

One of the EMTs called out, "Let's go."

She spun to watch the EMT lift Tate onto a backboard. His head had been secured, which made him look worse. A whimper worked its way up her throat. What if he died? He might not be in her life anymore, but if this injury killed him, she didn't know what she would do. She was already living only halfway, surviving but not thriving as she had when she'd been secure in their relationship and had God's goodness in her life. Now all she had was herself, and mostly it was just lonely.

"Go with them," Dane said.

He walked her to the ambulance and helped her in. Just before he shut the doors, he said to the EMT, "She needs to see a doctor as well."

The EMT shot her a look, like she'd disappointed him.

Liberty said, "That was the plan, okay?" She leaned her head back against the side of the ambulance and closed her eyes. The door shut, and the vehicle pulled out. For the first time in a long time, Liberty prayed. She asked for protection for both her and Tate, healing for him and help for those agents. Some of them would likely end up in intensive care for a while. Then she prayed the people behind all this would be caught.

While Tate got an MRI to make sure there was no bleeding in his brain, Liberty saw a doctor and got stitched up. The doctor wasn't too happy about the fact that she spent the whole time he was working on her on the phone with Locke. But the clock on the wall ticked closer and closer to the deadline for the release of the man from federal prison. A man they had learned was Venezuelan.

"You know we're not actually going to let him out, right?" Locke asked the question carefully.

Of course she knew that. She'd just never been in a hostage/ransom situation before. "You're not even going to consider the fact that three people might die if you don't?"

"They know the drill, and so do you." That didn't mean she had to like it. "We're looking everywhere for them. The locations picked were very specific. Wi-Fi they could hack, after hours. No people."

"It's Saturday. What location has Wi-Fi and is closed right now?"

"Aside from that credit union?" Locke said. "A handful of places. We're hitting each one, and we'll cross them all off before the deadline, so let's pray we find them."

"I will." Especially if it meant those people didn't lose their lives.

"How's Tate?"

"I'll know for sure when his test results come in. They said that the fact that he hasn't woken up yet doesn't necessarily mean anything."

Locke sighed audibly. "Okay."

"Find those people, Locke."

"Stay safe, Liberty."

She hung up, and the doctor shot her a pointed look but tied off the stitches. He could glare all he wanted, but she had work to do regardless of whether she'd been shot or not. He released her, and she sat in the waiting area.

Tate was wheeled to a room, and she sat with him. They'd bandaged his head, which made him look frail even though he was so big. He'd always been so strong. Protective.

Liberty brushed her hand over his cheek and sat by his elbow. "Wake up."

She didn't know what she would say to him if he did, but she just wanted to see the blue of his eyes. She wanted to see the way he looked at her, tell him she'd always loved him, even from the first moment they met. He wasn't like any other man she'd ever known. Some people might think that his independence was a problem because it caused him to butt heads with others, but she knew it was the thing that made him special. Strong enough to withstand everything he already had and still have the courage to go his own way, Tate had forged a path all his own.

Liberty wanted to soak up that strength. Maybe borrow it for a while so she could finally tell him why she'd broken up with him. She choked back a sob. Maybe one day he would even understand why she'd told him to move on without her, maybe even say he'd have done the same thing.

As Liberty watched the slow rise and fall of his chest, she couldn't help thinking how much she'd missed just being around him. The people trying to kill him had nearly succeeded. She'd nearly lost the man she loved.

What was she going to do about that, just sitting here staring at him? She couldn't have him. He would never accept her back, but she could help him to live more fully.

Tate's eyes started to flutter. A low moan issued from deep in his throat.

Liberty rushed out of the room before he saw her.

# FIFTEEN

"I'm afraid I'm going to have to advise you not to leave, sir."

Tate didn't look at the doctor. He was concentrating on putting his arms in the scrubs top they'd given him. "You said the test indicated everything was good."

"Doesn't mean there isn't a hole in the back of your head."

"Don't worry, Doc, I'll wait an hour before I go swimming." Maybe that wasn't intended for a head injury, but the doctor would get the idea he planned to be safe. Tate wanted to know where Liberty was. No one had answered their phones, and he'd thought for sure she would be here with him when he woke up.

Instead he'd been greeted by an empty room and the fog he figured was from whatever they'd given him to kill the pain in his head. *Thank You, God, for modern medicine.*

Finally he'd gotten through to Dane, who was coming to pick him up.

The doctor sighed. "I don't even know what to say to that."

"Whatever I need to sign, I'll sign." Tate shrugged

on his jacket, which was still damp, and sat on the edge of the bed. "But I gotta get out of here."

The doctor moved to the door. "I'll have an orderly bring a wheelchair. You are not walking out of here. No strenuous activity, and I'd advise you to curtail anything except for lying down as much as you possibly can. Any symptoms of disorientation, dizziness, blackouts or anything else at all and I want you back here, no complaints."

"Done."

Fifteen minutes later, Dane pulled up at the curb, Tate's dogs in the back seat. "That's my ride."

The orderly wheeled Tate out the door and up to the sheriff's vehicle, which was good because Tate didn't think he could have made it that far on his feet. Both dogs barked. The sound split through his head. "Quiet."

They stopped, and he glanced up at Dane, whose eyes widened. "Are you sure you're not supposed to be in there still?"

Tate ignored the question. "Where's Liberty?"

"She got stitches and a prescription."

He waited for more. "And?"

Dane sighed. "I dropped her off with Director Locke."

She'd gone back to work? Tate didn't want to accept the fact that she'd chosen work over him, but it was the truth. Was that what she'd done a year ago as well?

He'd always been a realist. They'd spent a lot of time together over the past couple of days, but evidently it hadn't been enough to convince Liberty she should trust him enough to share what she was still keeping secret. It was like she wanted to punish herself for something. To suffer—and make him suffer as well.

Dane helped him into the passenger seat. She wasn't

the only one suffering, but he didn't want to think about the fact that he'd cracked his head open. Liberty was hurt as well, and yet she insisted on continuing to hurt the two of them more by being in town and refusing to answer his question.

Tate rested his elbow at the bottom of the window, made a fist and leaned his head against it. She should never have come here if she wasn't going to actually talk to him. Really talk. She thought she was helping, but Liberty just didn't understand the fact that he couldn't handle small talk when there was so much more to say. Things that actually *meant* something. To both of them.

"Are you really okay?"

Tate looked at Dane out of the corner of his eye. "Just tell me where we're going."

"Last on the list of locations with Wi-Fi," Dane said. "In other news, Natalie Stand is gone. The daughter was with a neighbor when I knocked on doors seeing if anyone knew where she was. They all said she's private, but also that she frequently has male visitors, and only occasionally it's your brother."

"What is that supposed to mean?"

"It could be something other than what you're thinking. But the neighbors all said the same thing. Natalie has a varied social life, but she's a good mother. One of the neighbors said 'competent.'"

If she wasn't neglecting Tasha, at least it was something.

"There's more," Dane said. "One of the neighbors reported a late-night argument with a visitor. And get this—apparently they were yelling in Russian.

"Natalie Stand doesn't exist except for a driver's license and the birth record for Natasha Stand. She has a rental agreement, utilities. But nothing else. No birth certificate for Mom, or where she went to school. After the neighbor told me he heard Russian from one of her visitors I followed a hunch. Found a sealed juvenile record in Chicago for a Natalia Standovich. First driver's license photo she's a purple-haired sixteen-year-old, but it's her."

"So she came here to start over?" Tate said. "Maybe the Russians found her. Like her past caught up with her."

"Maybe." Dane didn't sound convinced. "The BOLO is out, and there's a deputy sitting on her street in case she comes back."

Tate wanted to nod but he was trying to avoid moving his head at all. "If she'd run, she would've taken Tasha." He couldn't believe he hadn't seen the signs that Natalie had been hiding her Russian heritage. She might have just moved on from the life, but it was also possible it hadn't severed all ties with her. Natalie—or Natalia rather—might be as involuntarily caught up in this as Tate was.

"Locke and his team are headed to the same place we are. The last place on the list they think those three people might be."

"They're probably on the road in a van."

The videos were made on brief stop-offs. Tate wasn't convinced they would find those people in time. Whoever was behind this wanted a Venezuelan released from jail and had a working relationship with the Russians. "If they keep them mobile it's harder to find them because they're constantly on the go. It's what I'd do."

"Then let's pray they aren't as smart as you."

Dane parked just down the street from the library.

The parking lot was full of vehicles, state police and government SUVs. The front door was open, and agents in vests were stationed by the door.

"They must have breached already."

He cracked his door and listened to the far-off cries of, "Clear!" Then finally the last call came. "Found them!"

Tate crossed the parking lot with Dane. The Secret Service agent on the door was a former colleague. The man lifted his chin but said nothing as Tate stepped inside.

At least fifteen agents filled the small-town library. On the cushioned chairs in the center sat the missing people: Edward Frampton, Bethany Piers and Anthony Wills. All three were tied up and gagged. The agents began to assist in untying them. Across the room Director Locke had a man facedown on the floor. His knee was planted in the middle of the man's back as he secured the guy.

Tate looked around for Liberty.

"I'm surprised you're out of the hospital. I heard you hit your head pretty hard." The female agent motioned to the bandage wrapped around his head.

"It's the latest fashion, you know?" When she cracked a smile, he asked, "Alana, right?"

"Alana Preston." They shook hands.

"You caught the guy holding these people?"

She nodded. "Not sure he's the head of the snake, as it were. But at least we're one step closer."

"Any idea where Liberty is, Alana?"

"Agent Westmark wasn't part of the breach due to her injuries. She waited outside by the vehicle."

"I didn't see her outside." He frowned, but it hurt his head. Tate turned and found Dane still behind him.

"You okay, buddy?"

"Where's Liberty?" He didn't like not knowing where she was. When this was done, she would leave with her team and take his heart with her. Still, she had to be safe and alive in order to live the life she wanted.

He strode to the door and scanned the outside.

Where was Liberty?

She planted her feet, but the man continued to drag her down the street.

Liberty had tried everything to get away. All because she'd been an idiot and actually *hidden* when she'd seen Tate and Dane show up. She was such a chicken she couldn't even face him. He was out of the hospital! She'd been torn between rushing over to help him, and what had been her final decision—crouching behind a car so he didn't see her.

That was where this guy had found her. Hoodie pulled so low over his head it cast his face into shadows, he'd hit her with a stun gun. Liberty moved at the last second, so the blast wasn't full force. She'd managed not to black out, but her legs crumpled and she'd hit the ground.

Then he felt around her. What on earth was he...? The man pulled out her gun and tossed it aside. So that's what he'd been doing. *Thank You, Jesus.* She tried not to think about what could've happened when he hauled her to her feet.

Liberty swayed, and he grabbed her. The wound in her shoulder pulled like the stitches were going to rip out. She tried to scream, but no sound came out of her mouth. The stun gun's effects made her brain fuzzy, but she could still think. She just couldn't do anything, or say anything. This man was going to take her away, and no one would know where she was.

She wanted to scream that she was being kidnapped and alert someone to what was happening. Tate was here. Why wasn't he saving her?

The man dragged her to his car, all the while muttering and cursing about how heavy she was. Excuse her for enjoying a doughnut sometimes. He didn't have to be mean about it.

Maybe Tate wasn't going to come. She'd have to get herself out of this.

Liberty gathered herself enough to finally be able to cry out. And she did. She screamed like her life depended on it—which she figured it likely did. She hadn't liked the feeling of not being able to speak at all, which added more volume and frustration to her fearful cry. The man slapped a hand over her mouth, muting the scream.

Liberty bit the hand.

He cried out and slapped her across the face. His grip on her never loosened, no matter how much she struggled to get away. Who was he?

"Let me go!" she yelled.

*Please, God. Let someone hear me.*

He lifted her off her feet and she flung her legs all over the place, trying to kick him. The man shifted her, then all of a sudden let go. Just dropped her. Liberty fell on her rump on the sidewalk. She cried out when pain shot up her spine.

Boots pounded the pavement, but she didn't have time to turn around. The man's body jerked, ready to run.

"Don't think about it, Braden."

Tate's brother?

Liberty sighed with relief that Tate was here. He'd heard her.

She shifted on the ground and found Tate and Dane both behind her, guns drawn. Tate was so good-looking. She tried to remember why it had been so important to leave him at the hospital, all alone, instead of staying and taking care of him.

Adrenaline bled from her muscles, and her shoulder sagged. Neither of them looked at her. "Hey, guys." She gave them a little wave. "Nice to see you."

Dane chuckled. "You okay down there, Liberty?" He asked the question as he stepped past her and cuffed Tate's brother.

Tate had a bandage around his head and looked as in need of a nap as she was.

She said, "Should you be out of the hospital?"

He held out one hand to her, his dark gaze on his brother. Liberty didn't pull on it too much and got to her feet using mostly her own steam. He ignored her question. "What just happened?"

"Well, I was—"

"Not you," Tate cut her off. "Braden."

Dane pulled him closer to Tate, and Liberty slipped around behind him. She was hiding from his brother, but she'd had a hard day. Liberty wanted to sit down. Instead she hugged Tate's waist from behind and leaned her forehead on the back of his coat. It was still damp. And cold. But the chill injected some life into her cloudy brain and woke her up a bit.

"Well?" Tate said. He shifted his arm so it held up her bad one, taking the weight off her wound.

Liberty didn't look around him at his brother. She just listened as Braden said, "Look… I don't know what I was doing."

"You were kidnapping her."

"I was helping!"

The sheriff made a scoffing noise. Tate's whole body stiffened. "Explain."

"They're trying to kill you guys. I had to get Liberty away from it, so I figured if I just stunned her and found a place to stick her until it blew over then she'd be good."

"She's a Secret Service agent, Braden, with a team to protect her. Not to mention me." Her heart swelled. Even if she didn't want to accept it, she had help. A family of people around her who were ready to close in if she needed them. She only had to ask.

"You're not up to it," Braden said. "You got blown up."

Tate shifted. "Who wants her dead?"

"You know who."

"You work for the Russians?"

"It's more complicated than that."

"Where is Natalia Standovich?"

Braden sucked in a breath. "How do you know about her?"

"I know a lot of things," Tate said. "Like the fact that you have a daughter."

"So?"

Tate repeated his brother's word. "So."

"What does it matter if I have a kid?"

Liberty swallowed. More people approached, which meant she needed to let go of Tate. She shifted away from his back, though she wanted more than anything to just live there. Maybe forever. Ugh. Why did he have to make her feel like this when no other man ever had? If he were anyone else, she could have walked away. Her reasoning would be the same, but it wouldn't hurt this much. The pain was tangible.

Tate shifted and clasped her right hand. "Not so fast," he whispered. "Not again."

Locke strode over. "What's going on?"

It was Dane who answered. "I'm taking Braden in. Attempted kidnapping."

Locke lifted one brow and glanced at her. Liberty nodded. The director said, "We'll follow you and bring the guy we have from the library. Are you set up to question two suspects separately?"

"Sure thing," Dane said. "Whatever you guys need."

"Did you find them?"

Locke glanced at her. "Yes. We rescued the missing three people, Agent Westmark. They're safe now."

Tate shook his head. "I still think it's a smoke screen for something else."

Beyond him, Liberty watched Braden smirk.

She said, "You know what it is."

Braden shrugged. "So what if I do?"

He'd just tried to kidnap her—even if he claimed it was to protect her—so she didn't particularly want to talk to him. But she needed to. Liberty put on her "agent" face, and said, "If you do, then you can tell us how to stop it. Tell us who you work for…or, better yet, help us bring down the whole operation."

Braden paled. "I don't…"

"That's not going to happen," Tate said. "We're not trusting him, Lib. He just tried to kidnap you. Braden doesn't come near you ever again, or he's going to have more serious problems than the load he has right now."

"What?" She pulled on his hand instead of setting it on her hip so he knew she meant business.

"No way, Lib. I'm not letting go."

"Braden can help us." Tate wasn't worried his brother would get hurt, was he? "He can be the bait in our trap to bring them down."

"There's no way my brother's being bait. He'll sell us all out and pocket the cash on the deal."

"It's our only option for—"

"The answer's no, Liberty."

Director Locke said, "Actually, it's a good idea." He looked proud of her, in a weird way. It wasn't a look she'd seen more than a handful of times. "Let's do it."

# SIXTEEN

"Don't doubt yourself now, Agent Westmark," Locke said. "Your instincts are right on."

Pride for Liberty, and how good she was at her job, swelled in Tate despite the fact that he didn't think this was a good idea at all. She looked nervous. Tate tugged on her hand so she'd move closer to him, so she could feel him beside her as she carried on the conversation with her boss.

Out of the corner of his eye, Tate saw Dane's attention was on him. The sheriff had better focus more on making sure Braden didn't get loose. He might have his hands cuffed behind his back, but Braden was wily. He could slip away.

Tate glanced at Dane and saw the man smile. Tate shook his head at whatever the sheriff was thinking. It became apparent when Dane motioned to Tate's hold on Liberty with a lift of his chin.

Tate shrugged one shoulder. Whatever pain obliterator he'd taken—painkiller was too benign for the warm numbness of what they had given him—had started to wear off. The throb at the back of his head was growing steadily more unavoidable. Kind of like a train bearing down on a car, stuck on the tracks.

No escape.

Too bad there was no time to worry about injury right now.

The conversation between Liberty and Director Locke ended, and the man walked off. Tate stepped closer to Braden. He felt Liberty flinch beside him but wasn't about to let her go. He'd done that when he'd been unconscious, and he'd woken up in the hospital to the world he'd lived in the past year. The one where she was absent, and he was completely, unavoidably alone.

There was no way he would allow that to happen again.

Braden looked everywhere but at Tate. Still, he faced down his brother. They needed information. "Was that you in those videos?"

Braden said nothing.

"He said he was me." Tate paused. "It was gonna be a different guy just now, but the one I saw looked like you." Liberty was the one who'd pointed it out, but he didn't want to draw attention to her right now. He wanted Braden's attention on him. Not on Liberty, scaring her more than she already was.

"Did you do all of the others, or just that one?" Braden still wouldn't look at him. "You're in this deep enough. You were with those prisoners at one point, which means you aren't going to be able to skirt out from under this one. Three strikes, isn't it? Means you're going away for a long time, Braden. You might as well tell me who has you involved in all this."

"And get killed in prison?" Braden's expression was incredulous. "No thanks."

"So instead you'll protect people who pull you into a threat on government personnel, like you don't know that's going to carry the maximum sentence?"

Braden's eyes were hard now. "Maybe it was my idea."

Tate tried to steel himself, but his body was just weak enough that he couldn't hold it together. "Why?" His voice was full of unshed tears.

"You're gonna cry for me now? Because I'm such a disappointment to big brother Tate, who never did anything wrong in his life."

That was what Braden thought? "Look—"

"No, you look," his brother said. "This ain't about you. Much as you want to think everything revolves around your so-much-better life."

"I'd have been fine if it didn't involve me, but I've been pulled into this at every point. They planted the flight recorder in my house, tried to kill me and Liberty—"

"I tried to stop it!"

"Because you cared so much that you needed to kidnap her?"

Braden let out a cry of frustration.

"I think you're in deep and you needed leverage. Cold feet?" Tate waited to see what reaction his brother would give him, but it didn't confirm or deny his suspicions. "Or you want to rise in the ranks so you were going to bargain your way up? Maybe secure a deal for Natalie, is that it?"

If his girlfriend was Russian, and she was perhaps on the run from her past, Braden could be involved in this as a way to secure her freedom. Oddly enough it would make Tate feel better, knowing his brother had done all this for noble reasons. At least then he would be able to understand it, instead of being completely perplexed over the fact that this man in front of him was actually his brother—his flesh-and-blood relative.

Otherwise Tate would spend the rest of his life wondering why.

But Braden gave him nothing. Not even when he was carted off to the sheriff's office to be detained.

Liberty drove the two of them in one of the Secret Service vehicles, since Tate refused to let her out of his sight. She didn't argue, but he didn't miss the look she shot him. The frown. He knew she was worried about his mental state with this head wound, but he was keeping it together. As long as the concussion didn't turn into anything more serious, he was more or less functional. He smiled to himself, then felt it leave his face. Didn't she want to stay? She'd left him at the hospital and was probably only not arguing now because he was hurt.

"Lib?"

She pulled up outside the sheriff's office and turned to him. "What?"

Her phone rang. "Hold that thought, I guess." She didn't look eager to know what he was going to say. She looked relieved.

Tate got out and waited by the hood for her to be done with her phone call, then walked inside with her. "Something important?"

She shook her head. "Doesn't matter. Are you okay?"

Tate shrugged, not feeling the need to share right now.

"Is that even the truth?"

"I'm not lying to you, Lib. The doctor gave me some things to watch out for. That's all."

She waited by the door, biting her lip.

"Come on, you guys," the desk guy said. "You're letting all the cold air in."

Tate let the door go and the man buzzed them in. Tate went straight to his desk. He sat but didn't rest his head on the back of the chair even though he wanted to. He just closed his eyes and rested his temple on his fist, his elbow on the arm of the chair.

Then someone was shaking his shoulder.

He looked up to find Liberty standing over him. She'd brushed her hair and secured it back in a ponytail. The sight of it made him smile. She was in work mode. He could handle professional Liberty, since she wasn't so hard to figure out.

"Dane and Locke are done questioning the man who held those people prisoner."

Tate nodded and stood. "How long was I out?"

"Half an hour, maybe."

He stretched. "How about you? Did you get some rest?" They both looked like they'd been through the wringer.

"We are a pair, aren't we?" She smiled. "Whoever is behind all this, we could just go scare them to death with how we look."

Tate gathered her into his arms and touched his lips to that beautiful smile of hers. "You never look bad. Even on a night like this. You're so beautiful, Liberty."

She melted into his arms, and he wasn't going to pass up the opportunity to kiss her some more. Regardless of what had happened between them, part of Tate would always belong to Liberty. And he realized then it was possible he would always love her.

Dane cleared his throat. "Uh, sorry to interrupt."

He didn't seem very sorry. Tate reluctantly turned to his friend. Dane grinned. "Time's wasting."

They followed him, despite the fact that what he'd been doing was decidedly *not* a waste of time.

Tate held Liberty's hand, ignoring the look Locke shot him. He knew how Locke felt, as the man had shared plainly his view of Tate and Liberty's relationship the day Tate quit the Secret Service. *You aren't good for her, Tate. I'm glad she broke it off, because she deserves better than a hothead like you.*

Except for the fact that it turned out it wasn't better. Not for either of them. There was a lot to resolve, but he wasn't letting Liberty go again.

Not ever.

*You're so beautiful.* Liberty hadn't been able to resist him. Not when she remembered every time he'd said that in the past. She'd call his name in the office to ask him if he wanted coffee, and he'd say, *Yeah, beautiful.* Like that was her name.

She'd loved it. And after the desert of the last year, Liberty had soaked it up like he was a fountain of fresh water. She just prayed it was going to last through what she would have to tell him. Even while she figured it was likely that he had a concussion and wasn't thinking straight.

She had to tread carefully and not lose the tiny part of what was left of her heart to him. That part she'd always kept for herself. Tate had most of it already, but she was in serious danger of just handing over the rest. Because if she had to cut off their relationship again, it would only hurt twice as badly.

"Alana checked out the phone the man had," Locke

said, all business. "It was used to make each video, and they were still stored in the phone's memory. We checked call history and text messages, but found nothing. It's clean aside from the videos, and it's unregistered." He paused. "The only thing of note is that the phone's browser was the home page for an email account. It was logged out, but we think that's how they're communicating with each other."

"Getting instructions from someone?" Liberty asked as she pushed aside everything that had just happened with Tate. They had to focus now, or this endless day of craziness would never be over. It was getting dark, and with the three hours of sleep she'd had the night before, Liberty was seriously flagging.

Locke nodded. "That's what we think. So Dane and I interviewed the man holding those people hostage, and I asked about the Venezuelan they want to be released. He claimed he had no idea who the guy was. He actually told me he'd only been with those people since earlier this afternoon."

"How can that be?"

Liberty nodded at Tate's question. She'd been about to ask the same one.

Dane answered, "I think they switched out, passed off the people they were holding and the phone to a different person every few hours. Maybe he only knew where *he* was supposed to take them and didn't know what instructions were given to the others."

"So they could've compartmentalized every part of this," Liberty said. "From the man at Tate's cabin with the flight recorder, to the ones who took us from the mine—the same ones I saw looking at the map. Then each one who was with the people they took."

She paused. "And how did they get the plane on the ground, anyway?"

Locke said, "Alana spoke with the senator and the two staffers. They said the pilot was in on it. He cut the radio and then landed in a field. The men who took them were evidently supposed to pay him, but they shot the guy instead before they towed the plane into the mine."

Tate tapped the table with his fingers, a move he did when he was thinking. "I guess it's possible if they were close to the mine and they had the right equipment. I can't believe no one noticed, though."

"They said it was very early Friday morning and the sun hadn't risen yet. Though if someone saw, they're likely dead." Locke's face was grim. "These people seem to be covering their tracks well through all of this."

"And trying to frame me."

Liberty glanced at Tate. "And involving Braden. Though, maybe it was his idea to make you a part of this."

"I'll ask him," Dane said. "He's next on my list for a conversation."

Tate nodded. "I still think it's weird they tried to kill me." He glanced at her. "Us. Multiple times. Framing me is one thing, but I didn't necessarily have to be dead."

"Maybe it was because I showed up?" She thought it through, and wasn't convinced, but it was a valid suggestion. "Or they simply figured you couldn't convince anyone it wasn't true if you were dead. A deal you made that went wrong?"

Tate made a face.

Liberty thought some more. "So they draw you in,

and all the Secret Service agents are so busy looking at one of their own—"

"Not anymore."

Liberty ignored his comment and said, "They wanted us looking the other way while they bargain for the release of the Venezuelan we have in prison. He could have nothing to do with this, just a name they used to ask us for something we couldn't get easily, like a van or money. Releasing someone from prison is more complicated."

"So again, they're trying to distract us?" Locke studied her like he was thinking through what she was saying. Liberty knew he respected her, but it was still nice to observe him taking her suggestions seriously.

She shrugged. "But if they really are just trying to distract us all from the search, trying to divide our focus so it takes us longer, it didn't work, did it? We found those people before the deadline, before they could make the next video."

"So we all go home," Tate said. "Job complete, everyone's headed home and the locals are tied up finishing out their investigation and dealing with the aftermath."

"You think they intended on it?" She stared at him, and he shrugged. She'd kind of figured he only kissed her because he'd hit his head and maybe he was reliving some old memories. But if he had the mental capacity to think all this through, maybe he'd been in his right mind.

He'd called her beautiful. And kissed her.

"What?"

Liberty shook her head. "Uh, nothing." She paused. "Do you think there could really be something *else* going on?"

Dane rubbed the stubble on his jaw. "The guy we arrested is clearly low level, so it isn't too far of a stretch to think he's being directed by someone else, given the email account. We need to find out who that person is."

Tate shook his head. "I'll bet Braden knows."

"That's why we should let him go," Liberty said. "He could lead us to them."

"That's a big stretch, Lib." He looked almost sad. "Braden isn't going to play alone. He'll warn them, and then whoever it is could go to ground and never surface again. Or Braden will just spin his wheels, and we'll be watching him for weeks."

Liberty sighed. "I could—"

"No."

Locke said, "Do you think you could convince him to help us, Liberty?"

She looked at Dane. "He's facing charges, right?" When Dane nodded, she said, "Can we offer him a deal? Immunity in exchange for information on who it is and whether there's a bigger plan in play?"

Dane said, "I can talk to the district attorney." He glanced at Locke, and then Tate. "It's worth asking the question. If Braden is worried about blowback, then maybe we can convince them to add witness protection to the deal."

She wanted Tate to be okay with the plan rather than just resigned to it. "It's a good idea."

Tate looked at her. "I'll be working on others, and hopefully something will yield a result."

It wasn't much, but she figured it was the best she'd get. As long as Braden cooperated, they might be able to get all the answers to their questions. Then Tate would see it had been a good idea.

The door flung open. Alana appeared in the doorway, flushed. "Braden got out of his cuffs. He beat up the agent who was watching him and escaped!"

They all stood up. Tate wobbled and set his hands on the table. She wanted to help him but held back so he didn't think she was babying him. Dane looked ready to jump across the table and catch him.

"Braden escaped?"

Locke talked over Alana. "Is Patrick okay?"

"He was just knocked out."

Relief flooded over Locke's face. "Good. We don't need any more injuries, and his getting hurt certainly wasn't part of the plan."

Liberty swung around. "What did you say?"

Tate's voice was hard when he asked, "You let my brother escape on purpose?"

Locke lifted both hands and shrugged. "Whoops."

# SEVENTEEN

"Are you kidding me?" Tate couldn't believe this. Locke had actually *planned* to let Braden go? "At least tell me you have a man on him, following him wherever he goes?"

"GPS tracking device," Locke said, with no remorse on his face for what he'd done. "Plus a man following at a distance. The tracker is just insurance in case we lose him."

Tate shook his head while Locke pulled out his laptop and logged in. He brought up a map, and after a second an orange dot popped up on-screen. "There he is," Locke said.

"No deal?"

Locke shrugged. "If Braden thinks he got away from us, then we get an honest response. We see his real motives, whether that's helping them succeed or bringing you down. Or both."

Tate figured he knew which it was. "We should head out and follow him." He didn't wait for agreement, or permission. He wasn't a Secret Service agent, so he didn't need Locke to tell him to go ahead.

Dane folded his arms. "I lent you guys my truck. You destroyed it."

Instead it was Locke who tossed Tate a set of keys.

Liberty held out her hand for the keys, and he dropped them in her palm. "Concussion plus driving equals no." The look in her eyes was soft.

"I could do it." Tate figured they needed to talk—or at least, he had some things to say—and he didn't need her team to hear them.

As they made their way to the vehicle, he said, "Thank you for driving." Truth was, he probably wasn't up to it.

She looked at him ruefully. "I didn't think you'd say that, of all things. But you're welcome." The smile was genuine, if tired at the edges. "You let me rest earlier. I figured I'd return the favor."

"I appreciate it." He took another pill and swallowed down half the bottle of water. "Seriously, I do." There was so much more to say, but he was exhausted.

Tate awoke when the car engine shut off. He pushed aside the edges of fogginess from sleep and looked across the street. "This the place?"

It was nothing but a closed-down old flooring store, still listed in the phone book last time he'd checked. Because, yes, he still used the phone book. How else was he supposed to find vendors for materials he needed? That and word of mouth were the internet of navigating a small town. Liberty wouldn't understand, so he didn't explain it. He doubted she could survive here.

Still, he asked, "What do you think of my town?"

"For vacation, or to live in?"

Tate shrugged, like there wasn't a world of difference between the two things.

"It's nice. I'd have to see it when it's not all covered under piles of snow, but there's a certain charm." She smiled. "And what's with the hospital? I wouldn't think there are enough people here to justify a whole hospital."

Tate said, "It serves three counties, but it was built because this movie star moved to a ranch just outside of town. He donated money to fund the entire construction and then some."

"Why?"

"Word is he has severe hemophilia. He wanted doctors and treatment—a whole surgical wing—close by in case there's an accident and he's bleeding internally."

"Wow, it must be serious."

"It can be."

"Do you know him?"

Tate laughed. "I've done some work for him. When he has friends visit and they need added security, he'll pull from local law enforcement. He's actually looking for a permanent security detail, but I'm still considering it. I'm not sure I want to do the work full-time. It's a lot of traveling."

"Oh." Something in her gaze looked a whole lot like a spark of hope. Because he might be getting a job? Tate must not be much of a catch if she was just excited he might be gainfully employed.

He pushed aside the disappointment and said, "So where's Braden?" It was dark outside now, and there wasn't much to see under the yellow glow of streetlamps. The truck smelled like cheeseburgers, and he realized why when she handed over a bag of greasy food.

"Inside the building. We can't get closer, so don't ask."

Tate shot her a look and took a bite.

"Dane told me, in no uncertain terms, not to let you get involved beyond staking out your brother. We have backup close by, and he said it was up to me to make sure he didn't lose his best deputy."

Tate felt his eyebrows lift. "He said that?"

Liberty nodded.

"Huh."

"I didn't doubt it for a second. You're extremely dedicated, no matter if you're remodeling a bathroom, protecting the president or bringing the law to a small Montana town. Maybe even if you're on protection detail for a movie star."

Tate laughed.

"Although I think the remodel might be a teensy bit of a waste of your abilities." She dropped her hand where she'd held her finger and thumb an inch apart, and took a sip of her gallon-sized drink. "The movie star job is a better fit, I think. But it's not my decision."

Everything in him stilled, and he worked not to show it. "I couldn't do the protection job on my own," he said very carefully. "I would need a team."

Liberty stared at him. "We're supposed to be watching the building." The words came out a whisper.

"Let me worry about Braden. If he slips out of this door and for some reason we don't see, GPS will tell us where he went." Why didn't she want to have this conversation? "There are plenty of people here watching Braden, right?"

Liberty swallowed. Nodded.

"You could work with me, Liberty."

"That's a huge stretch from being broken up, Tate."

He didn't smile, though a tiny part of him wanted to.

He knew this was irrational, but love was never clear-headed. "I know that. And despite the fact that the past couple of days have been crazy, it's clear to me things between us haven't changed much. Even though we haven't seen each other for a year, I know now I feel the same as I always did. That never went away." He paused. "Tell me you haven't thought the same."

"I can't tell you that." Liberty shook her head and looked out her window. "It would be a lie."

Tate said, "If you still care about me, and I still care about you, doesn't that leave us in a place where we should at least try to work things out?"

"By me quitting the Secret Service and moving across the country?"

That wasn't the part he wanted to talk about. Still, he said, "If you want me to move back to the East Coast, I would do it."

She turned back to him then, her eyes wide. "You would?"

"I've always known you were worth it, Lib. That was never in question." He sighed. "We had something good between us, something special, and I want to know why you threw it away. Why you threw *us* away."

His attention was half on the building's front door, watching to see when Braden came out, and half on Liberty and the conversation they were having. But he saw the tear that ran down her cheek.

She didn't move to swipe it away. She just stared at him as though he'd pulled the foundation out from under her world. And maybe he had. Maybe the thing that had come between them was so big, it had rocked her to her very core. He'd always thought it had to have been something huge. Liberty didn't make rash, emotional decisions. Despite her crying and then yelling at him that it was over, she'd stood her ground enough he knew she'd made up her mind, and there had been no changing it. That was what had made him so mad.

His head throbbed but he ignored it. This was probably the most important conversation he and Liberty were ever going to have. There was no way he would let an injury come between him and the answer he'd been wanting on for a year.

"Tell me why, Lib."

She sniffed but didn't move. Didn't say anything.

Her phone rang.

"Leave it."

She shifted and pulled it from her jacket pocket. "It's Locke." Liberty answered it, putting the call on speaker. "Yes, Locke?"

Tate gritted his teeth to keep from throwing the offending phone out the window.

"I just got a call from the hospital." Locke's voice was crackly through the phone. "Agent Bearn. Francis." The director cleared his throat. "He didn't make it through surgery. They tried to revive him, but there wasn't much they could do. His injuries were too extensive."

"Okay, thanks for letting us know." Liberty said the words deadpan, looking crushed while Tate's mind was a million miles away from this conversation. Was she going to claim she still couldn't tell him what had caused her to tear both of their lives apart?

"It's been a seriously long day." Locke sighed. "But I'll keep you posted if Braden moves."

Liberty hung up.

Tate said, "Tell me why, Lib."

\* \* \*

"I had a good reason." *God, I actually want to tell him.* So why couldn't she just come out and say it? That time in her life had been so painful, and she didn't relish the idea of reliving it. But Tate deserved to know.

"And as much as the reason still stands, I can see us together. Which is crazy," she said. "But you're right, since I got to Montana I see us as a team. It wasn't why I came here." She thought for a second. "I wanted to help you, but maybe I also wanted to see that you were in as much pain as I was… That blog." A sob worked its way up to her throat. "It was so horrible. Everything I thought you wanted to say to the Secret Service. To me."

"Lib."

"It was awful, Tate, and I thought it was you." She tried to collect herself. "Whether it turns out it was Braden or not, it hurt."

Tate reached over and slid his hand on the back of her neck. "I'm sorry for what he said."

"But you do think that. You think I wanted to hurt you, and that's why we broke up, or that you weren't worth me keeping you forever. He said so in the blog, and it's true. Isn't it?"

He didn't nod, but she knew.

"I wanted to be with you forever. And I wanted to give you *everything*. But that meant I had to let you go." She shook her head. "The number of times we talked about it. Working together somewhere, life after the Secret Service. Us. Kids." Her voice broke on that last word.

"We did say that, didn't we?" His tone was measured. So careful. There was so much tenderness in his voice, and there was no way she deserved it.

More tears escaped. Where Tate was, there would always be tears. At least that was how she felt. "I knew how much you wanted kids." She sucked in a breath. "And it wasn't even that something happened. Just a routine checkup. Oh, by the way, you have this medical condition. You'll probably never be able to have children. The chance of it happening is so minor you may as well consider it nil."

She couldn't stop. The words were flowing now, and if she broke off then she would never be able to finish. "I knew how much you wanted them—how much *we* wanted them. I would never be able to give you that, while someone else would."

Liberty looked at him then. His eyes flashed, wet with unshed tears. Movement out of the corner of her eye caught her attention. She looked over at the building. "Braden's leaving."

*Thank You, God, for something else to concentrate on.* He hadn't given her much, and it honestly felt like He'd taken more from her than He'd ever gifted, but God was still good.

Her struggles didn't change His inherent goodness or His grace in sending His Son for her. Why hadn't she remembered that? As she drove after Braden's car, Liberty realized she'd ignored Him for a year while she licked her wounds. She'd turned her back on God instead of letting Him minister to her and be what she'd desperately needed with Tate no longer in her life.

*I'm so sorry, Lord.* She should never have done that. It wasn't how love acted. And she did love God. She'd just put herself and her own hurt feelings above Him in her life.

A sense of peace flooded her.

*Thank You, God.* He was there with the riches of His grace, ready to extend comfort and hope even now. *Are Tate and I going to find our way back to each other again?* She desperately wanted to know if God's plan included that. After all, what had been the point of the last year? Liberty had grown stronger, forced to weather this all on her own. What if it was so she could go into a marriage with Tate on the firm foundation God had given her?

Maybe that had been His plan, even while she tried to figure her life out on her own.

"Liberty."

She glanced at the passenger seat where Tate wiped his eyes. He pulled up his sleeve and used the material to soak up the emotion. "I'm sorry, Tate."

She didn't want to admit that she should have told him, because she wasn't convinced it was true. If he'd never asked, she wouldn't have. And nothing had really changed. There was still this gulf of what they would never have between them.

Braden turned a corner that led to the center of town, and she followed him a few cars behind in the flow of traffic. If she had told Tate about her diagnosis a year ago, he'd probably have said it was no big deal. But the idea he might settle for something less than what he should have had hurt the most.

"I'm not sorry," he said as she drove. "Okay, maybe I'm sorry that I reacted the way I did to you breaking up with me."

She shook her head and took a left turn. "No, don't say that. I broke your heart, Tate. You were upset, and mad, and you had every right to be. I don't blame you and you shouldn't have to apologize."

"So where does that leave us? I can't say I don't want you to come here and work with me. That would be a lie."

And so they had journeyed full circle back to where they'd been a year ago. Liberty's heart wanted to break all over again, but there weren't any pieces left to shatter. She was going to have to tell him *again* that it wasn't going to work. She couldn't be who he needed her to be.

"Tate…" She hardly knew what to say.

The car in front braked, and Liberty did the same. If the GPS was right, then they were coming up on a spot where the road split into two right by a big chain store. On the other side of the street was the giant hospital.

They crawled to a stop in the line of traffic. She tried to peer around the car in front to see Braden, but it blocked her view. A car idled to her right, more cars behind both of them. The median in the middle was raised, blocking her in. She'd have to bump over it to get out of this spot and then drive down the center of the road.

There was nothing to do but talk.

"It really has been good to see you the past couple of days, despite the craziness and both of us getting hurt. I'm not going to regret coming here."

"But…"

She glanced at him. He was right; there was more. "But I still don't see how we could work together without falling in love more. At least, I couldn't. And it would only be even more painful than it was last time when you realize I can't give you everything you want."

"And if I tell you I don't need us to have kids, that I'll be happy with just you and me?"

She shook her head and kept her attention on the van that pulled up beside them on the other side of the raised median. "You say that now, Tate. But I don't want to be the biggest regret of your life."

"And if you already are?"

The pain cut through her like a knife. "I'm sorry." What else was she supposed to say?

"You can fix this, Lib. My biggest regret is how I walked away after you broke things off. But you're the only one who can choose happiness for us going forward."

Men jumped out of the van, guns drawn. She glanced at Tate, but her gaze fell on the window of his door—where more men jumped out of the vehicle stopped on his side.

The butt of a gun was tapped on her door. "Get out!"

# EIGHTEEN

"Do as they say." Tate's warning was met with a nod from Liberty. She didn't like it, but she would listen to him.

The man beside him cracked open Tate's door. "Let me see your weapon."

Tate pulled the gun he was carrying from the glove box. He handed it over with his other hand raised. There was no sense in fighting these guys. He and Liberty couldn't take four men—that he could see—without getting shot in the process. Not when they already had enough injuries between the two of them.

The man passed Tate's weapon to a guy behind him, and then tugged on Tate's arm. "Get out."

He moved slowly, which was fine because moving at all hurt. Sitting had been nice. The guy didn't need to think he was too agile. He wouldn't try as hard if he thought Tate couldn't fight back.

Tate cleared the door frame and stared the men down like an injured man who had no fight left. He wanted to look at the line of cars behind them. Surely someone was on their phone, calling 911. It was a risky move, taking them in public. And where was Locke? Surely he was in one of these vehicles, or had he been tailing Braden closer than Liberty and Tate? He could've been in front of them. Gone now.

*Help us, Lord.*

"You don't look so good, man." They walked him around the car to where Liberty stood beside a guy who was at least six foot two. He had his hand around her upper arm—her good arm, thankfully.

He looked for tattoos, thinking these guys might be more Russians, but couldn't see any. It didn't mean they weren't affiliated, though. Liberty looked scared out of her mind, making her appear almost helpless when he knew she was anything but. Likely most of the emotion was residual from the conversation they'd been having. He was only glad it served their cause.

*I'll never be able to have children.* And she'd given him up so he could have that family he'd always wanted—without her.

He'd barely seen the strength Liberty had inside her when they were together. He'd had no clue she was courageous enough to let him go. Would he have done the same thing? Tate would've liked to say yes, he'd have let her go to live her life, but maybe he was just too selfish, because Tate didn't think he could've ever let her go.

The barrel of a gun pressed into his spine. Tate started walking, his hands raised. "Wanna tell me where you're taking us?" He asked the question over his shoulder, half not even expecting a reply. They could have simply shot Liberty and Tate in their car, but instead got them out and were now transporting them elsewhere. Still, he was glad they were wanted alive, because he and Liberty still had plenty to talk about.

Tate and Liberty were shoved into the back of the

van, and silver tape was wrapped around their wrists.
Tate made sure he kept a gap between his wrists as they
were tied in front of him, and glanced over at Liberty
to see she had done the same.

The van set off, and they all jerked with the motion.

"I kind of thought you'd put up a fight." The one
who'd taken his gun studied Tate, almost like he was
disappointed. "But you didn't."

"Sorry I ruined your evening, but I don't plan on getting shot in the street."

The man glanced at Liberty. He touched her cheek.
"I can see why you keep this one around."

She turned her face away from the man's hand.

Tate said, "Don't touch her."

The gunman glanced at him. "I get paid to do what
I want."

"You're not taking orders?"

"I deliver. That's good enough." He shifted closer to
Liberty. "How about you, darlin'? What do you do?"

Tate said, "You have anything to say, you say it to me."

The man smirked. "That's cute, cupcake. But she's
cuter."

Tate looked out the front windshield but didn't know
which tree-lined road around town this was. Where
were they being taken? He worked at the tape, even
though he could break it faster with one swift motion,
easier than those zip ties the last guys had tied them up
with. That would be too noticeable right now, though.

These guys seemed to enjoy the rush of the capture.
Maybe they were hoping Tate and Liberty would try
to get away so they could hunt them down and catch
them again before they turned them over to whoever had
paid them. Maybe they did stuff like this for the rush.

When the van made the next turn, Tate's eyes widened. "We're going to my house?"

"We're going to the address they gave us," the gunman said. "What do I care whose house it is?"

Were the dogs here? Tate couldn't remember what Dane had said he'd do with Gem and Joey after he picked Tate up from the hospital, and they wound up taking Braden to the sheriff's office.

Probably he'd put them in the K-9 kennels. If they were here, though, they would be immensely helpful in taking down these guys. He didn't relish the idea that his dogs might get hurt, but they were trained in protection.

They pulled up on the snow-covered front drive, and the man closest to the door slid it open. Liberty shivered. Tate's Christmas lights had been turned off, but the porch light was on. The men held their weapons ready as Liberty and Tate were hauled from the van. They walked them to the barn.

"Inside."

Tate didn't argue, but he had weapons in the house if he could figure out a way to get to them. The barn had a few dog agility items and a bunch of indestructible toys Joey loved. The smell of dog hit him, and he felt the pang. He missed his buddies. They'd been his companions the last year, a gift from God to get him through the days of aching loneliness without Liberty in his life. *I know I've said it before, but thank You.* It was worth saying again now.

Tate was shoved to the far corner.

"Sit."

Liberty was told to sit as well, and she did so right beside him. Close enough her good shoulder touched his.

Tate's head pounded. Not just under the bandage, but also from the realization that Liberty hadn't given up on him because he wasn't worth keeping. He'd thought for so long it was only God who considered him worth anything. It was hard to let go of the belief that the woman he'd loved had thought him dispensable. He thought she'd given him up because he hadn't measured up, when the reality was otherwise. Liberty was the one who thought *she* wasn't worth it in their relationship.

Tate leaned over and kissed the top of her head. His heart broke that she'd thought being unable to get pregnant meant she wasn't worthy of his love and their marriage. They could be happy together. So happy. But she thought he deserved better.

And she couldn't have been farther from the truth.

One of the gunmen walked in the door. "They're fifteen minutes out."

The man who'd been talking to them earlier nodded. "Good." He turned to Liberty. "Means we have time for some fun."

Tate moved so he was covering her with his body. The man closed in and brought his gun down on Tate. He shifted at the last second so it glanced off his shoulder. The impact hit and he cried out. It felt like his shoulder had been shattered.

Liberty was hauled to her feet. "Let me go!"

The man dragged her across the room.

"Lib!" Tate called out, but it didn't help. He couldn't go to her. He could hardly see.

He heard her grunt, then cry out in pain. Then a thud. "Ow!" The man called her a foul name.

Tate climbed to his feet, swaying. He had to help her.

* * *

Liberty kicked out at the man, using the distraction of a fight to snap the tape on her hands. Her shoulder might be hurt, but there was nothing wrong with her legs. He grunted and fell to the floor while his buddies looked on, laughing.

"Guess you met your match," one of them said.

Tate was about to fall over, so she went back to him and they both sat down together. She wasn't going to stay anywhere near that awful guy again.

The men ribbed each other, apparently content to ignore her and Tate, which she thanked God for. They hadn't noticed she was free of her tape. She wanted to stay strong, which was way preferable to dissolving into scared tears.

She'd already cried enough today.

A car pulled up outside. Maybe more than one. Doors slammed, and she could hear the crunch on snow of people approaching. Tate was still beside her, ready for what was about to happen. Liberty wanted to hold his hand, but settled for her arm against his as she worked at the tape on his wrists. It was as close as she could get without sitting on his lap, which would have been very nice. She'd always loved having his arms around her.

Liberty didn't move, though, because neither of them could afford to get too close. Leaning on each other led straight to relying on each other, which led to trust…which ended with her never leaving because she couldn't imagine her life without him.

Exhaustion weighed down her body. At this point she would have paid money for a clean bed—maybe in a nice hotel room—and a solid fourteen hours of complete quiet. Maybe God could help with that—after He got them out of this.

The door opened and a bunch of men walked in. The tape on Tate's hands ripped all the way, and he lowered them to his lap so no one noticed.

A couple of the men who entered she recognized from when they'd kidnapped her and Tate at the mine. Braden was in the middle of the group, not looking happy. She felt Tate's reaction to seeing his brother with them. But maybe he wasn't here because he wanted to be. She still couldn't believe he would do this to a brother who loved him.

The lead guy said, "Where's the boss?"

The group of Russians and Braden parted, and a woman entered, wearing tight black jeans, a turtleneck sweater, four gold rings on her hands and a long unbuttoned coat with fur around the hood.

Liberty gaped. "Natalie."

Tate turned his head to her and said, "I think this is Natalia Standovich."

Liberty figured he was right. She didn't look like the woman with the small child they'd interviewed at home, who didn't know where her loser boyfriend was. This woman was the powerful head of a group of Russians who'd sent federal agents on a manhunt across four counties.

But why?

"Good," she said. "Everything is in place, then." More of an accent came through than she'd had before, completing the transformation of this woman from single mom back into Russian powerhouse.

Liberty tried to wrap her head around all of this. She hadn't thought Braden was any kind of mastermind, but neither could she imagine this woman calling the shots. Clearly Liberty had underestimated her.

"My part is done." The gunman Liberty had kicked started for the door.

Natalia nodded. "You'll be paid."

Each of the guys who had kidnapped her and Tate followed him out the door. Liberty was scared to think about what was going to happen next. *God, help us.* Where was Locke? Surely they'd seen what happened and would follow Braden's GPS to get here and find them.

"Why?" Tate's one-word question startled her.

Natalia shrugged. "As though I have time to explain all that to you. I'm a busy woman."

"I'm sure you are," he said. "But I want to know before I die. Why pin all this on me? Why draw teams of federal agents to this area? I know it's a smoke screen, but it seems risky to me. What is worth you doing all that?"

"You think I would bring them all exactly where I don't want to be seen?" She smiled. "You must not credit me with much intelligence, Mr. Almers. My plan is sound." Natalia lifted her wrist and looked at the face of a huge watch, much bigger than she needed. She noticed Tate's attention was still on her. "You like?"

Liberty gaped. Was she *flirting* with Tate?

Natalia sauntered over and crouched to show him the watch. "It belonged to my father," she said. "Now it's all I have left of him, since I got rid of the other evidence." Her smile was pure evil. She reached up and brushed hair off Tate's forehead.

Seriously?

Liberty didn't exactly want to get into a knockdown,

drag-out fight with this woman, but she clearly thought she could do whatever she wanted. Kind of like the gunman had, and Tate fought the idea every step of the way. His reaction was probably a lot like the feeling surging up in her right now.

Tate jerked his head away from her touch, and she laughed.

Liberty bit her lips together because the alternative was telling the woman to get her hands off him. "So, what now? You kill us and then do whatever it is you have planned?"

Natalia looked at Liberty as though she'd forgotten she was even there.

"We know the plane was just a distraction," Liberty said. "Still, it's kind of overkill, don't you think? A big splash, big headlines, big investigation. Search-and-rescue people. You probably got all the law enforcement personnel in the whole area in one spot looking for the plane."

"And yet you found it." She smiled, like she was proud of them.

"Not before you tried to frame Tate." Liberty's feelings were clear in her tone. "So what I want to know is what's such a big deal you needed a distraction of that magnitude just to get the cops to look the other way?"

Natalia's lips curled up. "Such a smart girl."

Maybe, but it wasn't Liberty who figured it out. It had been Tate. But she didn't explain that—she just wanted Natalia to tell them what it was.

Instead, Natalia stood. She stared down at them in silence for a cool minute.

Uh-oh. That wasn't good. Liberty figured she wasn't going to like whatever happened next.

Natalia pulled a gun from the back of her waistband and held it out. "Braden."

He stumbled, but caught himself as he walked over. His face paled, and his breathing was coming hard—white puffs in the cold barn. Natalia didn't even look at him.

"Braden, shoot them both."

# NINETEEN

Tate stared at his brother. Was Braden going to do it? Would he shoot Tate in his own barn? That might be the end to this. If Locke was going to get here—if the GPS on Braden was working and hadn't been discovered—then he would have been here already. That was how Tate knew the feds and the cops probably weren't coming. He and Liberty were going to have to figure out for themselves how to get out of this, because the alternative was getting killed.

Braden didn't take the gun. Instead, he grinned at Natalia and said, "Babe. You know I don't like blood."

"Yeah, I know." Natalia didn't look sympathetic or impressed by his humor. Her face was impassive, her tone completely neutral. "And I should also know I can't count on you to do anything useful."

"Seems like I did one thing, or you wouldn't have Tasha." That didn't get a reaction either, though Braden thought he was funny. He kept going. "So I guess I'm not completely useless after all." He folded his arms, a smug smile on his face.

Tate tried to figure out what on earth was driving his brother to play the situation this way. Braden wasn't going to achieve anything other than making Natalia mad—which was happening perfectly, considering the tips of her ears were now red.

She moved closer to Braden. "If you want your daughter to know her father past her second birthday—" her tone was low, lethal "—then you pull the trigger and make this problem disappear." She motioned toward Liberty and Tate with the gun. Liberty flinched and huddled against him.

Natalia said, "Because it seems to me like involving your brother, and now his Secret Service girlfriend, was *your* idea."

"It was good. You said you needed a distraction, so I gave you a federal manhunt."

"The downed plane and the missing people were the distraction. The videos, one better. Writing the blog and framing your brother did nothing but leave us in a corner, floundering to fix your mess. The fallout from your plan. While mine had none."

Braden swallowed.

"Since it's your mess, and we have yet to finish this job…" Natalia held up the gun. "Kill them now, and end this ridiculous attempt to improve your station."

He took the gun.

Tate's arm tightened around Liberty. There was no point pretending anymore that they weren't free of their tape. His brother was really going to do it. He was going to kill the two of them because this woman asked him to.

Tate bit the inside of his cheek so hard he tasted blood.

Outside, a car pulled up. Natalia huffed out a breath. "I thought we were going to be done with this before the Venezuelans got here."

That made Tate sit up. The ransom videos had asked for the release of a Venezuelan. He'd thought it could be a misdirect so the feds would be caught up in paperwork and not as many agents would be focused on finding the missing people. But if the Venezuelans were doing a deal with the Russians, Tate needed to find out what it was. He needed to know why they were here, in case it was the reason the pilot was bribed and those people taken hostage.

He'd been right. About his brother. About all this being a distraction. It wasn't a comfort, though, not when he needed more answers still.

Natalia sct her hands on her hips. "Finish them, Braden." She didn't try to lay on the charm like some women did to get their way. No, Natalia Standovich was 100 percent authority, even as she strode out of his barn.

Tate glanced at the shelves, the little cupboard underneath where he kept the radio. He didn't use it often. If he was on call, then the shortwave radio was how the sheriff's office contacted him, and he would stay in the house on those nights. Or use the handheld unit. But there was a radio in here, one he could use to get on the police band.

It was the only way they could get help.

No one stayed behind with Braden. His brother didn't look exactly happy as he stared down Tate. Still, his joking demeanor had disappeared.

"I guess this is the end." Tate's voice came out entirely more grave than he'd have liked.

"It's not like I want to do this." Braden pulled out a phone with his free hand.

"You might not be able to use that. There's no signal up here. The GPS we planted on you is probably not transmitting."

"Natalia found that when we were in town," Braden said. "Cuffed me across the face." He turned his head slightly to show the reddening bruise on his cheek. Braden pocketed his phone, silent for a second before he said, "I've lost my way, Tate."

"You think I don't know that?"

"I think you don't know much of anything about me."

"Druggie. Moocher." Okay, so these weren't compassionate words, or even helpful ones, but the man was about to kill him. Couldn't Tate say whatever he wanted instead of having to forgive right now? His brother didn't need grace or Tate's love, because he was going to carry out that woman's orders regardless.

"What is it, Braden?" Evidently Liberty saw something different.

Braden glanced at her. "I'm sorry I hurt you more than you already were."

"Thank you." Liberty said the words quietly. So quietly they were almost painful to listen to.

Braden frowned, then glanced at the barn door everyone had disappeared through. Looked at Tate. "I'm DEA."

"What?"

Liberty gasped.

Braden said, "I was given an undercover assignment." He blew out a breath. "Eighteen months ago now. Get close to the Russians, report back with intel. It was all going fine until Tasha. That was a onetime thing, not planned, not repeated. I slipped, got too close to Natalia. Now I have a daughter." He sighed. "Everything changed when she was born."

"So you've turned?"

Braden flinched. "I would never do that. But I can't bring down the Russians and keep my daughter safe when the person I'm trying to keep her safe from is her *mother.*"

"And you decided to make it so I was framed and imprisoned?"

"I needed you to see me. I needed you to help me get out of this, so I dragged you far enough into it that you couldn't ignore me." Braden ran a hand through his hair. "I knew it would be hard. It's not like you ever do anything wrong. Or need anyone's help. But I managed it."

Tate said, "Give me the gun."

"So you can kill me instead?"

"Just do it."

Braden handed it over reluctantly. Tate fired two shots into the ground. "That'll buy us a few more seconds, and save us from whoever she was going to send in to ask why you didn't do it yet."

"Maybe, but now she's going to send someone to get me because it's done."

Tate shifted and got up. "I'd better move fast, then." He opened the cupboard and turned the knob on the unit, keeping it low, and listened to the dispatcher talk about cows on the wrong side of a fence.

Tate butted in, explaining as fast as he could what was going on and requested all the backup he could get. He said he had DEA agent Braden Almers with him. He could hardly process the fact that his brother was a fed. It explained a lot, even while it contradicted everything Tate had ever believed.

"Copy that, Deputy. Help is on its way."

Tate breathed a sigh of relief and sat back on the floor. "We just have to stay alive until they get here."

Liberty shot him a look. "That's going to be easier said than done."

Liberty strode to the barn door, feeling every one of her aches and pains of the past two days. She opened it a tiny bit to peer out. She had no recourse if they tried anything, not when they had guns and she didn't. Liberty would likely be dead in seconds. Still, she wasn't going to sit around and wait for help while trying not to die.

Tate hissed something, probably for her to get away from the door, but she waved him off. Outside the Russians stood around a shiny Cadillac SUV. A dark-haired man in a cream suit talked to Natalia.

Liberty tried to listen, but all she could hear was the swirl of winter wind whistling in her ears. She couldn't hear anything they were saying, but the conversation didn't look happy.

She turned back to Braden. The DEA agent. Liberty certainly hadn't seen that one coming. A man who'd lost his way and ended up tied up with the wrong people's business? That she could see. The fact that he'd started down that road with the best of intentions was both honorable and the saddest story she'd ever heard.

She needed to know what he knew.

"What made you join a federal agency?"

Braden looked over at her. He knew what she was doing, and it wasn't just a friendly chat between two people who would've been related except for a medical diagnosis.

Tate had sat down again, not looking well at all. This

day had been harder on him than anyone, especially given the fact that she'd actually told him why she'd broken up with him. Hopefully now he'd see she was right. And yet, he looked at her with so much promise. Liberty couldn't even think about them—the *them* that might be an *us*—right now.

Braden sighed and sat on an upturned barrel. "Tate had just finished with the army, and he was joining the Secret Service. I was floating around doing odd jobs. Mostly transport. One day I do this delivery, and the guy opens a crate before I leave. It's all AK-47s. The place suddenly swarms with cops and I spend two days answering questions. It turned out I'd been hired to transport them by the DEA, if you'll believe it. They needed some no-name who wasn't connected to bring down this weapons dealer.

"They paid me for the job and about a month later called me again. Asked if I was up for another job. Over the next year it got pretty regular. Take this over here. Do a pick-up for this guy, but let us look at it before you drop it off, because we want to know what he's selling." Braden's gaze had gone dark, as though he had seen things he wished he hadn't.

"There's no record anywhere of me working for the DEA," he continued. "You won't find it, no matter how deep you look. They keep me undercover almost constantly, but the work I do is good. It saves people's lives." He shot Tate a look. "Guess my cover is blown now, though."

"No one is questioning the good you've done, Braden." She needed to say it, because he looked like he needed her to say it. "I'm very proud of you." Liberty shot his brother a look. "And so is Tate, I think."

"Yeah, I am, Bray."

His gaze flicked to his brother, a sheen of tears in his eyes. "But I lost my way, Tate." He looked like a remorseful little boy. "And I don't know if I can get back."

"You have to." Tate stood. "Because you need to go out there and act like we're dead."

Braden cleared his throat. He nodded.

Tate got up and pulled his brother into a hug. "I'm proud of you." He paused. "Tasha is beautiful."

Braden's face twisted, and tears ran down his cheeks. Liberty wasn't going to say it out loud, but that visible emotion would make his story about having killed them more believable. It might even buy them time to wait for rescue.

"Go now, okay?"

Braden nodded, and his gaze locked with his brother's for a long moment. Then he walked out the door.

Tate tilted his head, motioning her over to him. Liberty didn't have the strength to argue. He held out his arms and she walked into them on an exhale. His chest was warm under his sweater, and she slid her arms around his back underneath his coat. Tate leaned down and kissed her head.

"Thank you for being here. I don't think I could've done that without you."

She smiled against his sweater. "You're very welcome."

"I can't believe he's DEA. I didn't even think of it. I just assumed he was a loser."

"That's what he needed you to believe, Tate. Because otherwise you'd have asked too many questions."

Tate's arms tightened for a second, making her hiss at the pain in her shoulder. "Sorry."

"We'll be out of here soon."

"You need a doctor."

She looked up, one eyebrow raised. "So do you, honey."

Tate was quiet for a moment, and then said, "You haven't called me that in a long time."

"I know."

She wanted to tell him she would stay. She wanted to, so badly, but he was the one who needed to be okay with the fact that they would never have children. If he wasn't, Liberty didn't know how she would ever get over him. It would take more than another year for her to grieve seeing him again, knowing all the feelings between them were still there.

"Liberty." He shifted and took hold of her cheeks in the soft way he had with her and no one else.

She nodded beneath his touch. "I know."

The door swung open and hit the wall of the barn.

They both turned around to find Natalia standing there, gun raised.

"I see," she said. And then glanced back over her shoulder. "Kill him."

Tate lunged forward. "No!"

Natalia squared her aim, and Liberty saw it coming. Tate was right in the line of fire.

Natalia fired, but Liberty was already moving. She grabbed Tate and twisted him, swinging him to the side in midair.

The bullet hit her side, almost to her back.

They hit the ground.

Tate rolled, but Liberty couldn't move. She couldn't breathe.

"Police, freeze!"

"Drop the gun! I said, drop it!"

"Hands up."

"Federal agents!"

Liberty blinked and looked up at the ceiling, cobwebs in the corners. Her chest hitched with every breath as her body fought against the pain of movement.

Tate's face came into view. "Liberty." Tears rolled down his cheeks. "Why did you do that?"

She fought for breath, but it hurt. It hurt *so* badly.

"No, no. Just hold on, okay? We'll get you out of here."

"Tate!" Braden was alive?

"Somebody help!" Tate's roar made her flinch. He saw it and touched her cheeks. "Everything is okay, just hold on."

Liberty didn't think everything was okay. But all she could say was, "Missed you."

And then everything went black.

# TWENTY

Tate sat in the chair, ate in the chair and slept in the chair until she woke up. The only break he'd taken was for the doctor to check him out. He'd jarred his head in the fall and then blubbered like a baby in front of basically everyone he knew until the ambulance doors closed.

Then it had been all about work until he could get to the hospital.

He'd almost collapsed when he walked through the door, but Dane had been there to catch him. Tate's name had been cleared, and Dane had given back his badge. It was more of a symbolic move than anything else, but he'd been given back his position again and the respect that came with it.

Now all he needed was for Liberty to wake up.

Tate couldn't believe she'd taken a bullet for him. He was the one who was supposed to have been protecting her, and there she went throwing herself in harm's way to protect him. And it could have killed her. So easily.

He looked at her, lying in that bed. Pale face. Wires. Tubes. The steady beep of her heart on the monitor.

He didn't know whether to throttle her for what she'd done, or just be extremely grateful.

If she let him, Tate intended on spending the rest of his life showing her how grateful he was. They'd proven they were miserable apart. And they'd proven they were a great team together.

Liberty had broken up with him *because* she loved him so much.

And because she loved him that much, Tate was never going to let her go.

Liberty swam to the surface of consciousness. Her body was numb, and not in a way she liked. Breath hissed from her mouth, and she heard someone say, "Uh-oh."

Liberty blinked, and Tate's face swam into view.

"You're mad."

Her thoughts coalesced like puzzle pieces, but she couldn't see the image yet.

"You're going to drive the nurses crazy, aren't you?" That smile. She'd always loved his smile. "Don't worry. I'll make sure everything is good. You just worry about getting better."

He leaned down and kissed her forehead, and Liberty slipped back into sleep.

Tate watched her eyes flutter, and then open. She'd woken up several times, but hadn't spoken yet. Unless he counted the meds-induced babbling that made no sense. Although it had been interesting when she talked about how cute he was.

He smiled to himself as she came to, wondering if this would be the time he'd be able to tell her everything that had happened since she'd been shot.

"Hey." Her eyes shut for a couple of seconds, then opened again.

"Hey." Tate settled on the side of the bed. "How are you feeling?"

"Weird."

He nodded. "They moved you from ICU to a regular room. You're out of the woods, but it cost you your spleen."

"I never liked that thing anyway."

Tate smiled. "I love you. I'm glad you're back."

"So am I."

He meant more than she probably knew. Not just the fact that she was awake, but that she was back in his life as well.

But he didn't talk about that now. He gave her a drink of water, and the nurse got the doctor. They checked her out. Progression would be slow, but it would be evident. She wasn't supposed to move a lot, or get stressed out. Just rest.

Tate nodded. "I'll make sure she does."

Liberty shot him a look, which he ignored. When the doctor left, she looked at him. He ignored that as well. "Want to hear what has happened?"

She scrunched up her nose, but he could see in her eyes that she wanted to talk about something else.

Tate started in anyway. "Braden explained what the Russians and the Venezuelans had been into. A big deal, monumentally big, actually. The Russians had been hired to safely get a container full of guns and drugs across the border. There was money and diamonds. But it gets worse. When we seized it, in conjunction with the DEA and state police, we found four girls and a boy in there as well. Hidden behind all the stuff." His voice hitched. "Just kids." That had been the hardest part, even given the victory of being able to rescue those missing children and start the process of returning them to their homes.

He went on, "The truck was leaving the country, bound for a plane just over the Canadian border, where the Venezuelans were going to transport all that stuff back home. The ransom demand for their man to be released from prison was supposed to be part of it, and when the feds rounded up everyone at my house, they were seriously mad that hadn't happened. Of course, Natalia didn't care, she just lawyered up and started naming names to get a lighter sentence."

He shook his head. "I'm not sure it's going to happen, when she orchestrated the hijacking of a plane transporting federal employees."

Liberty said, "Wow."

He nodded. "It was a victory for sure, and we have everyone involved. It's going to take the Secret Service, DEA and state police some time to unpack it all, but it's over."

She bit her lip. "What about Braden?"

"Natalia threatened to kill him," Tate said. "He's talking to the US Attorney about a deal to get him and Tasha into witness protection."

"But you'll never see them again."

Tate took her hand and threaded his fingers through hers. "But they'll be safe."

"Tate."

He looked up. "Kids or no kids, I'm not going to let you walk out of my life."

"I can't walk, Tate. I'm in a hospital bed."

He didn't smile. "You know what I mean. We're a great team, and we never stopped loving each other."

"I love you, Tate. That's never changed."

"I'm going to be here until the day they let you go, and then I'm going to take you back to DC. We'll make this work, Lib. Because I can't bear thinking about the alternative. It'll be worse than this past year." He paused. "I love you so much. I want us to be together, and I'll do whatever I have to to make that happen."

"And if I was to resign from the Secret Service and join your private protection team?"

"You want to take the job?"

"I want to be where you are. And you love it here."

He nodded. "I do. But I want to be where you are as well."

"Good." She tugged on his hand with her good one until he leaned down and she lifted her chin. Tate kissed her gently, but for a long time.

"Good." He smiled. "And I had Alana get something for me while you were out." Tate stuck his fingers in his jeans pocket and pulled out the now-warm metal, which had been in his dresser drawer. He held up the engagement ring he'd given her the first time.

"Marry me, Lib. Again."

"Again?" Her lips twitched.

He laughed. "You know what I mean."

"Yes," she said. "I'll marry you *every* time."

"Whatever happens, whatever the future holds," he said, "I don't want to face it without you."

\* \* \* \* \*

*A detective discovers the hacker he's tracking is the woman he fell for years ago, but she insists she's being framed. Can he clear her name and save the family he never knew existed?*

*Read on for a sneak preview of*
Christmas Witness Conspiracy *by Maggie K. Black, available October 2020 from Love Inspired Suspense.*

Thick snow squalls blew down the Toronto shoreline of Lake Ontario, turning the city's annual winter wonderland into a haze of sparkling lights. The cold hadn't done much to quell the tourists, though, Detective Liam Bearsmith thought as he methodically trailed his hooded target around the skating rink and through the crowd. Hopefully, the combination of the darkness, heavy flakes and general merriment would keep the jacket-clad criminal he was after from even realizing he was being followed.

The "Sparrow" was a hacker. Just a tiny fish in the criminal pond, but a newly reborn and highly dangerous cyberterrorist group had just placed a pretty hefty bounty on the Sparrow's capture in the hopes it would lead them to a master decipher key that could break any code. If Liam didn't bring in the Sparrow now, terrorists could turn that code breaker into a weapon and the Sparrow could be dead, or worse, by Christmas.

The lone figure hurried up a metal footbridge festooned in white lights. A gust of wind caught the hood of the Sparrow's jacket, tossing it back. Long dark hair flew loose around the Sparrow's slender shoulders.

Liam's world froze as déjà vu flooded his senses. His target was a woman.

What's more, Liam was sure he'd seen her somewhere before.

Liam's strategy had been to capture the Sparrow, question her and use the intel gleaned to locate the criminals he was chasing. His brain freezing at the mere sight of her hadn't exactly been part of the plan. The Sparrow reached up, grabbed her hood and yanked it back down again firmly, but not before Liam caught a glimpse of a delicate jaw that was determinedly set, and how thick flakes clung to her long lashes. For a moment Liam just stood there, his hand on the railing as his mind filled with the name and face of a young woman he'd known and loved a very long time ago.

Kelly Marshall.

*Don't miss*
Christmas Witness Conspiracy *by Maggie K. Black,*
*available wherever Love Inspired Suspense books*
*and ebooks are sold.*

LoveInspired.com

# *Love Harlequin romance?*

## DISCOVER.

Be the first to find out about promotions,
news and exclusive content!

**f** Facebook.com/HarlequinBooks

**y** Twitter.com/HarlequinBooks

**◉** Instagram.com/HarlequinBooks

**⑂** Pinterest.com/HarlequinBooks

ReaderService.com

## EXPLORE.

Sign up for the Harlequin e-newsletter and
download a free book from any series at
**TryHarlequin.com**

## CONNECT.

Join our Harlequin community to
share your thoughts and connect
with other romance readers!
**Facebook.com/groups/HarlequinConnection**

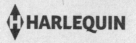